Eve Makis was born in Nottingham to Greek Cypriot parents, who emigrated to England in the 1960s. After graduating from Leicester University she studied journalism and moved to London to work as a reporter for Middlesex County Press. In 1994 she left London for Cyprus, where she worked as a writer, radio presenter and as a freelance reporter for the London *Evening Standard*. She returned to England with her Cypriot husband in 2001. They now live in Nottingham with their daughter. *The Mother-in-Law* is her second novel, her first, *Eat, Drink and Be Married*, was voted the Young Booksellers International Book of the Year 2005 and is also published by Black Swan.

Praise for *Eat, Drink and Be Married*:

'A clever balance between heartwarming comic moments and events with dark undertones is what I found most intriguing . . . Her observations are consistently sharp and keep you engaged to the uplifting conclusion. An easy-to-digest and highly enjoyable read' *Daily Express*

'A novel of irrepressible good humour and, like the Greek Cypriot recipes that are peppered throughout, is a real treat to savour' *Nottingham Evening Post*

'Heartwarming, funny, tragic and uplifting . . . the story has a feelgood factor to equal *My Big Fat Greek Wedding*' Narinder Dhami

'A funny and warm-hearted account of cross-cultural experience' *Waitrose Food Illustrated*

'This exploration of the Greek Cypriot community in the 1980s is a delight. Charming' *The Bookseller*

D1136169

Also by Eve Makis

EAT, DRINK AND BE MARRIED

and published by Black Swan

THE MOTHER-IN-LAW

Eve Makis

BLACK SWAN

THE MOTHER-IN-LAW
A BLACK SWAN BOOK : 0552773247
9780552773249

First publication in Great Britain

PRINTING HISTORY
Black Swan edition published 2006

1 3 5 7 9 10 8 6 4 2

Set in 11/13pt Melior by
Falcon Oast Graphic Art Ltd.

Black Swan Books are published by Transworld Publishers,
61–63 Uxbridge Road, London W5 5SA,
a division of The Random House Group Ltd,
in Australia by Random House Australia (Pty) Ltd,
20 Alfred Street, Milsons Point, Sydney, NSW 2061, Australia,
in New Zealand by Random House New Zealand Ltd,
18 Poland Road, Glenfield, Auckland 10, New Zealand
and in South Africa by Random House (Pty) Ltd,
Isle of Houghton, Corner of Boundary Road & Carse O'Gowrie,
Houghton 2198, South Africa.

Printed and bound in Great Britain by
Cox & Wyman Ltd, Reading, Berkshire.

Papers used by Transworld Publishers are natural, recyclable
products made from wood grown in sustainable forests. The
manufacturing processes conform to the environmental
regulations of the country of origin.

For Maria Makis

Electra

It looms above the window of my workroom like an ocean liner. A ship sailing through murky waters in the dead of night. Hot air oozes from a pipe, condenses and floats past an external light. The darkness blankets white pebbledash, dull aluminium window frames and a vandalised buzzer. A dark-haired woman leans out of a second-floor window to smoke, risking life and limb for her fix of nicotine. I reach out for my cigarette packet and light up in solidarity. The windows of the weathered apartment block opposite connect me to other people, albeit strangers. I watch them with interest, stealing glimpses of their lives.

I glance across at Adam, sitting contentedly in his armchair, leafing through a music magazine, his long legs stretched out in front of him. My husband likes the comfort of routine and does not hanker after change. His feet are firmly rooted, whereas mine are itchy and hover above solid ground. I wonder how he would feel about starting a new life elsewhere, somewhere warm and hospitable. I am falling out of love with this city, jam-packed tube rides, traffic queues and anonymity. I grew up in a seaside town where everyone knew everyone and lived in each other's pockets. Our third-floor apartment buzzed with activity. Neighbours drifted in and out. Drank coffee, mint tea and rosewater cordial on a veranda overlooking a busy street, rife with sounds of life. Excitable women news-mongering on the narrow pavement below. Workmen digging up the craggy road with pneumatic drills, taking forever to repair a pothole. Saucepans clattering, taps running, knives speed-chopping in kitchens across the street. Teenagers practising wheelies on mopeds whirring like giant mosquitoes. The near-obsolete tinkle of a bicycle bell.

'I'm going to bed,' Adam says, pushing up on the armrests, the magazine sliding off his lap onto the floor.

I glance despairingly at my watch. 'But it's only ten-thirty. The night is still young.'

'I must be getting old. I can hardly keep my eyes open.'

'Don't go to bed. We need to talk.'

'About what?'

I puff tensely on the cigarette. 'Don't play dumb, Adam. You know perfectly well about what.'

'Let's talk tomorrow. Right now, I need my beauty sleep.'

Tomorrow may be too late. I need a decision tonight.

'When tomorrow? Before you go to work? When you get back? After supper? When would be a convenient time? Do I need to book an appointment to talk to you?' A forced smile belies my frustration. I don't want to appear desperate, to be accused of pressuring him.

'First thing in the morning, I promise. Now, why don't you come to bed?'

'I can't. I'm expecting Miroulla. She fancied some company. I invited her over.'

'Then you won't be on your own and I can go to bed without feeling guilty. Goodnight, my darling, enjoy your evening.' He plants a warm kiss on my lips before leaving the room.

My husband goes to bed with the chickens and wakes up with the crow of the cock. His digital alarm clock shrieks like a siren at 6 a.m., and up he gets in a flash to shower and dress. Early to bed, early to rise is not the norm where I come from. My compatriots are up at dawn, enjoy an afternoon siesta, and sleep when tiredness knocks them down like skittles. Night-time should be savoured slowly, like a rich dessert, not willed away as if it were an inconvenience. When darkness falls I mooch around the house, indulge my sweet tooth, work until I drop or stretch out on the sofa channel hopping, falling asleep unawares, carrying myself to bed when and if I wake up.

I stub out the cigarette in the glass ashtray on my workbench and begin polishing a silver brooch with a soft cloth. Rubbing away the dull patina to liberate pure, untarnished, wonderfully shiny metal. Inside a ring of silver are loops and tightly wound swirls of filigree, radiating from a dome of variegated blue and turquoise enamel. I handmade the brooch as a birthday present for my mother-in-law, an olive branch, one more attempt to win her affections, a futile sortie in a lost battle.

Our ancient king-size creaks in the next room as Adam adjusts his position in the bed. The small television on mute keeps me company, bubbling away in a corner of the room like molten lava. My mind flits from the work at hand, to unfinished projects, to my friend Lydia and her son Alvaro, to my sister Martha and her devil of a husband. My brother-in-law Sotiris is a die-hard gambler with a weakness for East European pole dancers. Every so often Sotiris forgets he has a wife and four children and plays out his fantasies in disreputable pubs that sell women together with their alcoholic beverages. He imagines, while young women press up against him and stroke his fleshy knee, that he is desirable, a young Marlon Brando. That a woman half his age, with the body of a goddess, can see past the watermelon gut.

The toilet flushes. Adam pokes his head round the door. 'Come to bed. It's late. I don't think Miroulla's coming. You look tired.' He shakes his head, the early bird clucking like a mother hen.

I stand up and salute.

He takes off his slipper, waves it in the air, and chases me to the bedroom.

We fall into bed and snuggle up. Tickling one another, laughing, tussling beneath the sheets, our arms and legs knitted together. He pulls off my T-shirt, kisses my ear, gently works his way down my neck and across my shoulder, making my skin goose-pimple. And then the doorbell rings and Adam flops down beside me, cursing his luck and my fondness for late night company.

The kitchen table is strewn with sweet nibbles. With Miroulla's home-made biscuits, small squares of *paklava* and peanuts in a burnt-sugar coating. We sip Greek coffee, speak in our mother tongue and reach out intermittently for sugary snacks. I chew on an almond-filled pastry, closing my eyes in anticipation of the taste, enjoying a moment of concentrated pleasure, licking my syrupy fingers clean. Greek coffee and *paklava* coming a close second to sex.

'So what else is new?' Miroulla asks.

'I've finished Margaret's brooch.'

'Why did you bother making it at all? That woman has never shown you any love.'

'I don't expect everyone to love me, *thea*.'

Miroulla scrunches up her soft, plump face. 'Margaret isn't everyone. She's your mother-in-law. What the hell is wrong with that woman? You're a treasure, Electra. Pure gold. If you were married to my son, if God had blessed me with a child, I would be doing forty somersaults. I would have to lose sixty kilos first, mind you.' Miroulla laughs. Her fleshy shoulders shake. She has no qualms about laughing at her own jokes. Miroulla is a pseudo-aunt. A distant relative whom. I call '*thea*' or 'aunty' as a mark of respect.

'Adam has never let his mother get between us.'

Miroulla's mouth shrivels derisively like a slug doused with salt. 'Don't speak too hastily, my love. It's early days in your marriage. Do you think your mother was happy when you took home an Englishman? The poor woman cried herself to sleep for many weeks, accepting your decision.'

'I gave her no choice in the matter. I've never let anyone tell me what to do, how to live my life.'

Miroulla sips her coffee noisily, a cinnamon-coloured moustache forming on her upper lip. She licks it away and looks at me knowingly, her eyebrows riding up, her small head leaning to one side above a robust neck. 'Why isn't your husband so forthright with his own mother?'

'Adam has to be more careful.'

'Pah! Why is that? Is Margaret made of cut glass?' Miroulla leans back in her chair, resting her hands on an abdominal pouch large enough to house marsupial triplets.

All I can say in my husband's defence is: 'There are reasons why Margaret must be treated with care. She's had a difficult life. She's suffered.'

'She's not the only one. And that doesn't give her the right to be mean to you. What have you ever done to her!'

Adam has a formal, respectful, deceitful relationship with his mother. One with crippled lines of communication. In Margaret's presence his comments are guarded, his laughter measured, his emotions controlled. 'I have never been able to talk to my mother,' he says, refusing to admit that things have got far worse since he met me. If daughters-in-law were food and could be ordered in a restaurant, Margaret would have chosen a simple salad with a light dressing. What she got instead was a rather more piquant version with black olives, capers, feta cheese and thick virgin olive oil. Margaret finds the Electra Salad unpalatable. This bitter truth hurts me more than I care to admit.

When she first met Adam my own mother said: 'What do you see in him, child? He's so pale. So fair. So thin. Is he sick?' My reply was, *'Skase, Mana.'* 'Shut up, Mother.' I put her in her place before her tongue sprouted wings. I laid down the ground rules early on and warned her against interfering, saying there was only room for two in a marriage. Mama has adhered to my rules, knowing better than to transgress.

What did I see in him? What did I see in a bunch of long limbs as flimsy as saplings? In the concertina of bones he calls a chest? I never liked thin men until I met Adam and looked beyond the chassis. I liked my men triangular on top, ribs covered with a generous layer of muscle. I liked them dark and healthy-looking, preferably astride a Harley. I have sampled my fair share of sun-kissed brawn and generally found it to be vacuous. I come from a seaside town in Cyprus where one can overdose on the body beautiful. Where gym culture, founded by our ancient ancestors, is alive and well, a breeding ground for narcissistic men who fall in love every morning when they look into the mirror. Take a short stroll along the beachside promenade and you will see a fair few beefcakes whose stride is impeded by too much inner thigh. Who sit with their legs wide open, airing their gonads. Who pretend to be dark and brooding when in actual fact they have nothing to say. Who will never realise that the brain is a muscle too and needs flexing on occasion.

What did I see in him? Standing us side by side would not give you the answer. You might even say we look ill suited. Adam is tall and slim. '*Anamisi*', I call him, my 'one-and-a-half' man. I was denied my fair share of height and allotted curves too generously. Other differences? My husband is health-conscious and eats like a sparrow. I could eat my husband and the sparrow and still have room for dessert. Adam engages his brain before speaking. Me – I say the first silly thing that pops into my head. Where I am excessive, Adam is restrained, an equation that in my opinion results in a healthy balance.

'And how's your poor sister?' Miroulla asks.

'Her husband's still a donkey. Cousin Kikis, delivering eggs to a customer early one morning, saw him leaving a dingy hotel with a gaudy red-head on his arm.'

Miroulla tuts. 'Kikis, the egg-and-gossip-monger? I expect he spread the news far and wide.'

'Everyone knows the truth except for my sister.'

'Cyprus is a small place. Infidelity and a taste for prostitutes can't be kept quiet for long.' Miroulla polishes her teeth with the tip of her tongue.

'Martha prefers to believe that her husband is out all night earning the family crust.'

'That man is filth. The only crust he generates is the one he leaves on musty bed sheets.'

'My sister actually feels sorry for her husband. She thinks he's working himself to death.'

'If only! Marriage is like a game of Russian roulette.

Some are lucky enough to draw blanks. Others – blam! They shoot themselves in the head. You are one of the lucky ones, Electra. You married a decent man who adores you.'

My workroom is a metallurgist's heaven, kitted out with implements for refining, grinding and melting. Once a small second bedroom, of little practical use, it is now equipped with soldering iron, burnishing machine and an array of hand-held tools, resembling medieval instruments of torture. Lock me in my workroom for a week with a chunk of metal, preferably gold, and I will re-work it into raindrop earrings or an intricate cross. In this small domestic space where I make my living, I have recreated the workroom above Papa's shop. Every day after school I would climb a spiral staircase with no handrail to watch him work, marvelling at his dexterity. With a magnifying glass lodged in his right eye, he would pick up minuscule pieces of metal with pincers, position them on tiny joints and melt them in place with a soldering iron. He would cut wafer-thin lengths of gold into tiny pieces, mix them with acid and melt them in a Greek coffee cup over a bunsen flame. When the cooling gold took on the texture of milk skin he would pour it into an old pickle jar fitted with electrodes and filled with a pungent mix of water and *cianuro* powder. In this noxious-smelling solution he suspended his low-grade metals and, as if by magic, plated them with 24-carat gold.

'Don't touch that. Don't touch this,' Mama warned, 'the workshop is no place for a girl.' Tradition ruled that my brother Minos follow in Papa's professional footsteps. Well, TRAD-I-SHON, pronounced with such solemnity as it was in *Fiddler on the Roof*, could go to hell. Minos gave up his evenings to study with Papa reluctantly, his efforts were half-hearted, his workmanship laughable. His earrings had all the delicacy of doorknobs. Asked to design a simple pendant, he would sketch a Medjool date. He lacked patience, imagination and a steady hand. At heart my brother was a white-collar man, who liked to wear a suit and keep his hands clean. He opted for a regimented life, the nine till early-afternoon hours of a bank teller. Against my mother's wishes I became Papa's young apprentice. At first I was only allowed to watch, and to hurry downstairs whenever the shop doorbell rang to serve customers. I darted down the rickety stairwell at full speed to secure a sale. 'Kyria Mantovani, you look like a princess in that necklace,' I lied, honing the valuable skill of blah-blah required to sell. Mrs Mantovani, her hair gathered up on top of her head, looked like an artichoke gone to seed. 'My daughter could sell ice in the north pole,' Papa would say, with pride. 'Electra will never go hungry.'

I swept floors. Polished machinery. Gathered up the gold dust and fragments scattered on the workbenches. Papa melted down, purified and re-used these precious scraps. While my sister Martha learned to stuff marrows, I was busy stretching out pencil-sized pieces of solid gold into 20-millimetre strands, reducing the metal in size by feeding it through a series of bronze cylinders, each fractionally smaller in diameter than the one before. Like Papa, I grew three of the nails on my right hand until they were an inch long, using them to hold down lengths of filigree and work them into loops and tight coils. I learned the dying craft of *triferenion* – Cypriot filigree – and produced work beyond the capability of any machine.

I have inherited Papa's work ethic, his restlessness of soul. Papa sketches designs over breakfast. Talks shop over dinner. Digests his evening meal and heads back to the workshop, leaving his wife to watch her daily diet of soaps. 'Why don't you stay and keep me company?' Mama complains, knowing he is as difficult to pin down as a fly; as incapable of keeping still as Maritsou, the town's most conspicuous compulsive obsessive. Maritsou spends her days sweeping the streets around her house, filling black bin liners with rubbish. Praising God that litter breeds and gives her empty life a purpose. 'The only difference between your father and Maritsou,' Mama says, 'is that she has been certified.' Like Papa, I try to squeeze every last constructive minute out of my day, to keep some part of me in motion, be it my feet, my hands or my mouth. Adam is quite happy to get home from work and laze around.

'I once asked Mama why she named me after a woman who conspired in the murder of her own mother.'

'What was her reply?' Adam spoons Bran Flakes into his mouth, making me feel guilty for my choice of breakfast: a plump almond croissant, topped with nut flakes and dusted with icing sugar.

'She asked what in God's name I was talking about. Said she named me after a woman who gave birth to nine children, worked in the fields from morning to night picking crops, and lived to the ripe old age of ninety-six.'

'Your great-grandmother?' He sips stinky green tea.

'According to family folklore, I'm her mirror image.'

'She was beautiful too, then?' He winks at me and I am charmed by his flattery.

'She was a small thickset woman with no front teeth and skin as wrinkled as a walnut, actually. I can only hope that with the blight of Great-grandmother's looks comes the blessing of fertility and a long life.' I thrust my right palm under his nose. 'Look at the length of my lifeline. You won't be getting rid of me for a while.'

'I couldn't live without you, Electra.'

I turn my hand to the side and point to two faint lines at the base of my little finger. 'Look here. This is the number of children I was meant to have.'

'I was wondering where this conversation was leading.' He puts down his spoon, his appetite ruined. 'You know I'm not ready for children. Not just yet.'

'Anyone would think you were Peter Pan the way you talk, blessed with the gift of eternal youth. Wake up, Adam. You're no spring chicken. Forty is no longer looming on the horizon, my love, but knocking on the front door.'

'I'm just not ready.'

His response depresses me.

'That's too bad.'

'Why?'

I can't tell him why. I skirt around the issue instead

and try to force his hand. 'Because my biological clock is ticking away and soon we'll be counting your spermatozoa on the fingers of one hand.'

He smiles and leans back in his chair. 'Don't panic. Men are still fertile into old age. I heard about a man who fathered a child in his nineties.'

'Bully for him. He may well have sown his seed and secured his bloodline but did he live long enough to see his child grow up? Could he kick a football round the park without dislocating a hip?'

I take a deep breath and count to ten, struggling to suppress my hostility towards Adam. I have waited patiently, hopefully, angrily, for his change of heart, popping my daily pill. Risking thrombosis, a stroke and cervical cancer to inhibit conception. Squandering time and my childbearing years. Stewing in resentment, drooling at every baby I passed in the street, wanting more than anything in the world to be a mother. And then, as if through hoping I had made it happen, I missed a period.

Last night, after Miroulla left, I locked myself in the bathroom and opened the pregnancy kit I had bought earlier that day from the chemist. I pulled out the instruction sheet and read it, my stomach bobbing like a buoy below my ribcage. While Adam slept I followed the instructions to the letter, closed my eyes and waited two excruciating minutes.

'You've littered the road to parenthood with unnecessary obstacles. Our finances must be watertight before we start a family. We must buy a house with a garden in a quiet street. You must be promoted and my jewellery business must start making a healthy profit.

When will you be ready, Adam? On the thirty-second of the month, as we say back home?'

'Just give me time . . . please.'

'Time is not on our side. I don't want to end up like Miroulla with only a dog, not a child to call my own. I need a baby I can swaddle like stuffing in a vine leaf.'

And it seems that soon I will have one. Because what did I see when I opened my eyes last night? Something I hoped for but did not expect – a faint blue line. I carried out a second test and realised with elation that the pill is not full proof, that I had defied the odds. I could hardly contain my excitement, my elation. I wanted to shout my news from the rooftops, to poke my head out of the window and stop passers-by with shouts of, 'Hey there! I'm pregnant!' I wanted to shake Adam awake, to crack open a bottle of Champagne, to phone my mother in Cyprus and hear her cries of joy. I phoned Lydia instead with the news and cried quiet tears of desperation and happiness, alone in the bathroom. And then I went to bed and contemplated how and when to tell my husband. I want Adam to come round to the idea of fatherhood before telling him I'm pregnant, not to just go along with it for my sake. If I break the news and see disappointment in his eyes, I will be tempted to crush his nose with my fist. 'O, kindly, benevolent, munificent God,' I will pray each night before I go to bed, 'please save my husband from a bloody nose.'

I walk across to the open window and light a cigarette. Adam, critical of my bad habit, screws up his face.

'Don't worry,' I tell him. 'It's my last.'

'Really?'

'Yes, really.'

'Good,' he says, failing to ask why.

Mama was an unusual choice of bride for the son of a wealthy jeweller with forty *donums* of land to his name. The only riches she brought to the union were humility and a good reputation. Grandmother was keen for her son to marry a simple village girl with no pretensions, raised to tend house and husband. A girl who would always be grateful to her in-laws for bettering her. 'Choose virtue over beauty, son,' Grandmother counselled, 'a beautiful woman is more trouble than she is worth.' Mama was picked, still green, from her mother's simple mud-brick cottage and set to ripen three hundred kilometres away. Her in-laws built her a palatial house with Corinthian columns and a sweeping marble veranda. When war broke out and the palace was lost, and home became a Red Cross tent, Grandmother's crude hypothesis was proven right. The village girl did not sit beating her chest, lamenting her fate. She put her hands to better use. A girl who came from next-to-nothing could get by on very little. She knew how to bake her own bread. How to skin a rabbit and pluck a chicken. How to spend a paltry sum and produce enough food to fill the stomachs of four hungry children who sat with mouths gaping like newly hatched sparrows.

Mama was married in a sleepy Paphos village where she was born and grew up. An olive-strewn backwater, set among the gentle foothills of the Troodos mountain range. Baggy-trousered men, with white moustaches tweaked upwards at the ends, took ringside seats in the village coffee houses to watch the priest lead the bride and her kin across the paved village square and up the flagstone steps that led to the small stone church of Agios Andreas. Later that day at the wedding feast they sucked soft, aromatic lamb off the bone and licked their greasy fingers clean. They toasted the newlyweds with swigs of Keo brandy and sweet red wine. They laughed until their stomachs hurt at the satirical chant of the village bard who warned the groom he faced castration by his father-in-law if he mistreated the bride. My parents danced without touching, hands on hips, mother's gaze lowered humbly like a geisha's. They touched for the very first time between the starchy sheets of their marital bed, which by morning bore the evidence of Mama's innocence.

Twenty-five years earlier, my maternal grandmother Elpida – or Hope as she was aptly named – had walked across the same village square and mounted the same weathered steps to stand before the altar with a man she barely knew. The wedding festivities lasted three days and nights. Elpida was treated like the Queen of Sheba for seventy-two hours, pampered and fussed over, then promptly forgotten as attention turned to the next transient queen.

Her betrothal was negotiated at a formal meeting between the parents. A generous dowry was secured by her in-laws and sealed with a handshake. 'I was worth no more than a four-poster bed and half a dozen chickens,' Elpida used to grumble, shaking her head.

Everyone in the village was invited to the wedding. 'May the couple's path be strewn with roses,' they had said, graciously accepting the invitation. 'My path was strewn with your grandfather's whisky bottles,' Elpida complained, scrunching up her Cabbage Patch face.

On day one of the festivities, women gathered to stuff the wedding mattress, to scatter it with silver coins, to carry the lumbering thing overhead in a celebratory dance. To honour the venerated mattress on which the sixteen-year-old bride would later reject her husband's advances and lie crying, traumatised by the harrowing sight of Papou's genitalia. The women rolled a baby back and forth across the mattress, wishing the couple a fertile union and preferably a boy. To take the family name and propagate it. To become a miniature version of his *papou* and follow in his father's footsteps. 'I prayed for a girl,' Elpida said. 'There is no greater wealth than a daughter to look after you in old age. But I had boy after boy after boy before God granted me my wish.'

On the morning of the wedding the groom was lathered and shaved by his father, in the presence of male friends and relatives. 'You are headed for the gallows, my friend,' the best man goaded as the violinist played an upbeat tune. Papou dry swallowed, unable to react with a razor blade held so close to his throat. Later, when the priest uttered the words 'to love and obey', Papou stamped on the bride's large foot, as his best man had instructed, to let his new wife know who was boss.

If looks could kill my grandfather would have dropped dead right then and there. The look Elpida gave him was withering. Foot stamping or no foot stamping, the game was lost. Elpida was large and outspoken and went on to rule the roost. My grandparents were cohabitees as well-matched as cat and dog, Persian and pit bull. My grandmother raised four boys and a girl. Gossiped over the back yard fence. Cooked and cleaned. Refused her husband his conjugal rights on religious holidays, as any good Christian woman should. No sex for forty days over Easter; no unclean thoughts on those interminable saints' days that swallowed up half of the rest of the year. Papou shaved men's stubble for a living and drank the night away in the local *cafene*. He spent little time at home, complaining that his wife was a *faousa*, a nag, the 'plague'. He died in his forties of cirrhosis, his liver scarred by alcohol and blackened (his mother Andrianou liked to say) by Elpida's incessant nagging. 'That woman drove my poor son to an early grave,' Andrianou proclaimed loudly at the funeral. Afterwards Elpida left Paphos to live with her only daughter in the Karpas peninsula. She refused to lodge with any one of her four sons, saying it was a grave mistake for any mother to share a roof with her daughter-in-law.

Electra

'. . . *Happy Birthday, dear Margaret, Happy Birthday to you!'*

Adam and I stand on her front step, arm in arm, singing our greeting to Margaret. She looks me up and down, finding fault. I am reminded of the day we first met. The day she was polite and hospitable but could not conceal her profound disappointment. I have worked in sales and know how to read a person's face. Margaret disapproved of her son's choice. I could see it in her eyes, in the set of her lips. In the way she couldn't bear to touch me, as if by touching she might commit herself to accept faulty merchandise.

Margaret's grey hair is short, well-cut and tucked behind earlobes garnished with tasteful single-pearl earrings. She has a pleasant face blemished only by the sourness of her expression. By the vexed slant of her eyebrows and her disapproving, downturned mouth. By the rigid set of potentially appealing features and the angry furrows that run from her nostrils to the corners of her mouth. Someone should have said to young Margaret: 'Beware, my girl, of pulling that face, the wind might change.' I constantly fight the cultural impulse to take her in my arms and plant a kiss on each of her powdery cheeks. My mother-in-law's personal space is impenetrable.

We walk along the plastic liner running the length of the hallway. The liner protects Margaret's carpet from wear and tear from the footsteps of two lodgers who live on the third floor. I follow Adam into a magnolia-painted living room where framed watercolour prints of flowers and buildings and seascapes hang. The curtains and sofa and cushions are awash with peonies and sweet peas and roses.

'Aunty Electra!' Adam's nieces run up to me with outstretched arms, shrieking their welcome. I kneel down and clasp them in my arms, burying my nose in their fine, blonde, fresh-smelling hair. Amy and Elizabeth have sweet, oval faces and delicate features like their mother Caroline. Both are dressed in floral pinafores, their fringes held back with jewelled Alice bands.

Caroline gets up. Kisses me. 'They couldn't wait to see you, Electra.'

I open my shoulder bag, pull out two brightly coloured packages and hand them to the girls. 'They only love me because I bring presents.'

Caroline gently squeezes my arm. 'Thank you, Electra. You too, Adam.'

'The presents are all Electra's doing. I can't take any credit for them,' he replies, moving across the room to shake his brother's hand. My husband stoops apologetically, hands in his pockets. His elder brother

John, several inches shorter, stands with an air of natural authority. My brother-in-law is clean-shaven and dressed in designer casuals. He is a handsome version of his mother, with boyish features and a hard-won smile.

'Can we open our presents, Mummy?' Elizabeth asks.

'Yes, open them.'

The children tear off the paper, exposing two plastic dolls, one on roller skates, the other wearing skis. Amy hugs the roller-skater to her chest. 'This is just what I wanted but Mummy wouldn't let me buy it.'

'That's because you two already have more than enough dolls,' Margaret says irritably, belittling the gesture, stating a truism, angry that I have stolen the limelight. I have been cursed with the ability to read her face like a book, to interpret her double-edged comments and telepathically pick up on her feelings. She thinks I have an unhealthy influence over the children. That I have charmed them like the Pied Piper, bought their love with gaudy gifts and wooed them with my infantile humour.

'You can never have too many dolls, can you, girls?' Adam says, winking at me.

I am painfully aware that my voice is louder than those around me, that my whole aura is noisy and offensive to Margaret. I am the bull, Margaret and her family the china. I say 'her family' because here I am permanently the outsider, the square peg. 'Could you move aside and let me take a picture of my family?' she'd said on my wedding day, outside the church, too quietly for her younger son to hear. Meekly I moved aside, stepped out of the frame, while Margaret immortalised a wedding day minus the bride. Yes, I felt rejected. But the snub did not come as a total surprise. I had Margaret sussed by then. I knew she was a cold fish who thought her son too good for me.

John hasn't yet looked me in the eye, to acknowledge my presence. 'Hello, I'm over here,' I want to call out with a wave. I suspect Margaret has poisoned him against me by voicing her suspicion that I married Adam to secure a share of the family fortune. A fortune in bricks and mortar, owned by a woman who thinks she will live for ever. Who saves her china and covers her furniture and hoards her treasures like a magpie, in case they fall into the wrong hands. Who can, for all I care, be buried with all her worldly goods like an ancient Egyptian princess.

I had the chance to wed a bigger fish than Adam once. When I was eighteen a Cypriot cheese-making tycoon asked me to marry him. If I had consented I would now be sitting beside my own swimming pool, drinking spritzers, not living in a run-down flat in Acton. I would be swathed from head to toe in Gucci and Versace, lunching with similarly clad ladies. A Filipino maid or two would be cleaning my house and raising my children while I would be busily filing, waxing and exfoliating. Networking with the island's elite. Driving up and down a café-lined High Street in my metallic coupé. 'There goes the cheese-maker's wife,' people would say, eyeing me with envy. My face would secure me the best seats in the house, a restaurant table by the window, the reverence of club doormen. Big cheese! Well, I would rather live on bread and cheese than marry a man for his money, lie in silk sheets with my spiritual mismatch. I married my husband for love, and would marry him again a thousand times over.

Margaret tugs at the ribbon tied around the present and pulls off the metallic paper. 'Thank you, John. Thank you, Caroline. They're beautiful.' She holds up a packet of lace handkerchiefs, her eyes watering. 'They look very expensive. You really shouldn't go wasting your money on me.'

'Perhaps you should use one to wipe your eyes, Mum,' Adam says.

'Oh, no. They're far too nice to use.'

Margaret picks up my modestly wrapped packet, containing the handmade brooch. She pulls off the string, tears at the brown paper and levers open the box. I watch expectantly, nervously, wanting her to love it and me, surprised at the hope for a miracle that still lurks within me. The blueness of the enamel is the same shade as Margaret's eyes. The design is based on a nineteenth-century piece I saw in the Cyprus Ethnographic Museum. Margaret looks at the brooch and smiles but her eyes are devoid of feeling.

'Thank you. It's very nice,' she says, closing the box and putting it down on the coffee table, feeling no need to take the brooch in her hand and study its intricate design, rewarding all my efforts with a niggardly crumb a hungry bird would turn up his beak at.

'Who wants a cup of tea?' she asks.

'That brooch is more than nice, Mum. It's bloody marvellous.' Adam does his best to make amends but the damage has been done, the damning adjective uttered.

'Is it one of your own designs, dear?'

'Electra designed it for you. She's been working on it for weeks. Why don't you try it on?' Adam's tone is indignant. A subtlety lost on his mother.

'I will . . . later. I don't want to thread a pin through my silk shirt.'

Adam glares at her.

'Can I have a look?' Caroline reaches for the box, overcompensating with her gushing praise for Margaret's apathy, lifting the spirits my mother-in-law confined to the doldrums. 'Electra, this is incredible. I love it! You're so clever. Girls, come and look at this.' Her two little women fuss over the trinket, calling it a 'precious jewel'. Elizabeth tries it on and struts proudly around the coffee table.

John wags a finger at his daughter. 'Elizabeth, put it away. It's not a toy.'

Caroline unpins the brooch from her daughter's lapel and puts it back in the box, sending the girls out into the hallway to play. I force a smile and offer to make tea, feeling deeply upset and unappreciated. Adam follows me into the kitchen.

'I'm sorry about Mum.' He wraps me in his arms. 'She's *so* unappreciative.'

'Your mother's not too good at expressing her feelings.'

'She was moved to tears by a packet of stupid

hankies,' he says, echoing my own thoughts. 'I wish you'd never gone to all the trouble of making something for her.'

'It was no trouble.'

'I'm really pissed off. I wish we could leave right now.'

'Don't be silly. It's your mother's birthday. Go back to the living room and spend some time with your family.' I send him away, preferring to lick my wounds alone.

Darjeeling. Assam. Ceylon. Earl Grey. Margaret's tea cupboard is well stocked. I find a packet of camomile and put it to my nose. Its soothing smell reminds me of my grandmother Elpida and the kitchen home in which she boiled up camomile to make remedies for boils, conjunctivitis, insomnia and morning sickness. When her husband died Elpida moved across the island to live with her daughter. She insisted on living in the *blistario*, the concrete outbuilding housing my mother's everyday kitchen, refusing to share our living space and interfere in family life. An extension was built on to the *blistario* to create a bedroom, toilet and shower room, the water heated at Grandmother's request by a wood-burning stove. Elpida ate her meals separately and rarely entered the main house.

She was God-fearing in the literal sense, the product of a puritanical mother who filled her daughter's head with oppressive stories about heaven and hell, for whom there was no division between folklore and religious doctrine. 'Stop swinging your legs or else your parents will die,' she warned her daughter. 'A woman must never set foot inside a church when menstruating,' she instructed. 'You hear that dog howling? It's a bad omen, my girl. Someone close will be taken from us.'

Elpida's peculiar take on life became part of our everyday reality. We accepted her odd rituals, shrugging our shoulders when she rushed into the yard, crossing herself, clutching the blue stone that hung from her neck and protected her against the evil eye. The sight of a priest early in the morning was a bad omen that filled Elpida with dread. She avoided contact with our neighbour, the widow Agathou, because it was widely believed that this poor, maligned woman could curse a person by simply looking into their eyes. If she happened to cross Agathou in the street, Elpida would hurry home to light her incense burner and expunge the curse in a cloud of smoke. According to Elpida the devil played an active role in her daily life, hiding her belongings, turning fresh milk sour, making her trip up in the street. She was quick to cover her mouth with her left hand when she yawned in case he entered through the gaping void and took possession.

Bread was sacred to Elpida, both its baking and its eating. She would cup a hand beneath her chin to catch falling crumbs. If a morsel happened to drop, she would pick it up, kiss it and ask for Christ's forgiveness. If Mama was baking bread and Elpida suspected she was on her period, she forbade her daughter from preparing the yeast, saying impure hands rendered it ineffective. When she cut her nails Elpida flung the trimmings over her shoulder. Not, as I had thought for many years, to blind the devil but for a far more convoluted reason. When she appeared before God and had to present all her bodily parts and He demanded her nail clippings, she could excuse herself by saying she had thrown them over her shoulder and did not know their whereabouts.

Poor Elpida's life was circumscribed by superstition and old wives' tales. If she heard a buzzing in her right ear she took this as a sign that she was being praised. If her left ear buzzed, she believed herself to be the subject of criticism. If both ears buzzed simultaneously, she wished good fortune on her well-wishers and cursed her enemies. When she developed tinnitus, Elpida lived with the paranoid delusion that she was the hottest topic of conversation locally.

Her delusions took a turn for the worse when she dreamed the Virgin Mary paid her a visit in the *blistario* and warned her that a tragedy would soon befall the village. The following day Elpida found a greasy footprint on the step leading into her home, proof in her mind not of a mere social call but an actual holy visitation. She sought a second opinion from her church-going friends who carried out a thorough investigation of the evidence. There were no greasy footprints before or beyond the steps and no oil spillages in the vicinity. They concluded that a superhuman being capable of levitation must have made the solitary impression. The local priest, called in to adjudicate, could neither confirm nor refute Elpida's claim. He blessed the step, said 'maybe' a miracle had occurred, and advised Elpida to preserve the footstep under a pane of glass. 'Maybe' was enough to convince the highly suggestible and set the village gossip mills in motion. 'Maybe' led to a double-page spread in the island's leading newspaper, featuring a photograph of Elpida, a blurred picture of a concrete step, and numerous quotes from local people. 'Two hundred villagers have so far visited the site of the miracle' it reported.

The newspaper article triggered a stampede to Elpida's door. Believers came in their droves, mostly women, bearing *tamata* or offerings for the Virgin of lanterns, candles and icons. The *blistario* came to resemble a holy grotto with Elpida sitting as roundly as Father Christmas inside. Visitors knelt to kiss the glass before entering singly to hear her story and touch the hand of the woman blessed by a miracle. They came, they touched, they cried communally, they feared the Virgin's ominous prediction. Elpida basked in the attention, thrilled by the magic that had touched her mundane life. News spread to the Diaspora. A party arrived from England, another from Australia, to meet Elpida and explore a village suddenly deluged with miracles. A neighbour claimed to have bottled crimson raindrops. 'The clouds above the village are raining down blood!' she declared. Children and adults chased shadows, depictions of the Virgin Mary which appeared momentarily on walls and trees and buildings. Pilgrims flocked to the village, to the delight of the local confectioner, the tobacconist and Andricos the kebab-maker. Business had never been better.

My siblings and I watched from the sidelines. Strangers touched us, stroked our hair and offered us sweets. We were the next best thing to a tête-à-tête with Elpida. We neither believed, nor disbelieved, we simply watched events unfold with detachment, enjoying the carnival atmosphere in our back yard. Papa was scathing of the 'silly women' taken in by Grandmother's fanciful ideas. He kept his distance, spending his evenings in the local coffee house in the company of like-minded men who thought their wives and the village had gone mad.

Elpida's gloomy prophecy was realised a month later when Turkish troops invaded the northern tip of the island and began moving southwards. 'Our village will never be invaded,' Papa declared at first, believing the crisis would be resolved in a matter of days. At Mama's insistence he eventually locked up his shop, filled the tank of his green Morris Minor and loaded his children into the car. We took only the bare essentials, believing we would be back within a matter of days. Our bare legs stuck to the sweltering leather seats as we sat waiting for Elpida and her luggage to join us. She refused to leave, claiming the Virgin had come to her in a second dream, telling her to stay put. Her mind was made up and we had no choice but to leave her behind. A week later our village was invaded and Elpida barricaded herself inside the *blistario*, living on the food she had stockpiled, largely ignored by the contingent of Turkish troops billeted around her. When food ran out and Elpida's will to live did not, she ventured outdoors, holding up a white handkerchief, begging mercy from her captors.

A Turkish soldier drove her to the outskirts of the village and released her into the charge of the UN.

Several days later when she was reunited with her daughter in a refugee camp, Elpida had good news to report. She claimed to have buried Mama's valuables and the stock from Papa's shop, inside an empty olive-oil can, beneath the lemon tree in the back yard. Papa dismissed the claim immediately, saying it was lunacy to believe the allegations of a delusional woman. The island was subsequently partitioned and for three decades we were denied access to our village. Whenever times were hard in the post-war years, Papa teased his wife with the words: 'Don't worry, Eleni, our fortune is safe and sound, buried beneath the shade of a lemon tree.'

Elpida died forty days before travel restrictions on the island were lifted and free access was granted to occupied lands. Mama, still dressed in mourning black, journeyed back to her old home, Elpida upper-most in her thoughts. What if my mother wasn't crazy after all? she thought. What if a tin below ground contains my children's inheritance? Hope swelled as she travelled along familiar roads, passed olives with gnarled and pitted trunks and silver-grey cypress trees holding their pointy heads aloft, like dignitaries amid hoi-polloi. Long-dormant hope ruptured its confines as she drove into her village and sampled her first taste of Anatolia. Every street and place name had been changed to Turkish, the church was a mosque, red crescent flags flapped in the breeze and a square-jawed bust of Kemal Atatürk sat on a plinth in the village square. It felt like a place trying too hard to reinvent itself, crudely negating its former existence. She kept 'what if' to herself as her husband pulled up outside the whitewashed house in which she had once been mistress. She was overcome with emotion, bombarded by memories, as she stepped over the threshold of her old home and walked from room to room with its new occupant, a Turkish Cypriot woman, who expressed her hope that the house would one day be returned to its rightful owners.

The house was now a shabbier version of the one she had left, the *blistario* an empty shell, the once-fertile yard a scrap of dry land with no tree of any description left standing. No blossom-covered orange, no sprawling fig or mighty carob, no prickly pear tree or yellow-studded lemon. Mama felt foolish and dismayed. Her husband had been right after all.

Adam

I seethe quietly on the sofa beside Caroline, bitterly disappointed with Mum. For an apparently sophisticated woman she has a very limited vocabulary. 'Nice' you call a boy, a suit, a slice of pizza – not a handmade brooch. Mum could have shown a bit more gratitude. Electra's disappointment was palpable. It seeped across the room like volcanic slurry and set me on fire. Now cups and saucers clatter in the kitchen. My generous wife is always first to offer Mum help, flying in the face of rejection. In Mum's eyes Electra can do nothing right, whereas Caroline is exemplary, an angel, a perfect match for my brother. I am not my brother and never will be. A tofu wife, like pretty-pretty Caroline, would bore me senseless.

John talks about his design business, about his move to larger premises and the predicted doubling of his turnover in the coming year. My brother loves to bandy figures. To slip casually into any conversation the exorbitant sum he paid for his golf clubs, his handmade suits and fuel-injection car. While John talks about the importance of networking, of wining and dining his clients in Michelin-star restaurants, my forefinger wriggles like a worm inside the pocket of my bargain-basement trousers and nestles in the hole puncturing the lining. The disparity in our finances only causes me discomfort when I see Mum looking so impressed.

'How's life on the local rag?' John asks.

'Same as ever. Still earning a pittance. Still driving a rust heap.' I am happy to play the role of impoverished younger brother. John and I are chalk and cheese. One a prince, the other a pauper. One the product of Mum's will, the other of Dad's philosophy. John was educated privately at Mum's insistence while I was sent to the local state school where Dad believed I would receive the most rounded education. For all his airs and graces John drew the short straw, not me. He was sent away to board against his will and grew up before his time. He has shouldered the burden of Mum's expectations ever since.

'Why don't you apply for a job on one of the nationals? They're always looking for good subs. Maybe I could find you something through one of my media contacts.'

'No, thanks. I have no intention of working shifts or commuting into central London. I'm quite happy where I am, thank you. I like finishing work at a decent hour and going home to my wife.'

Mum shakes her head. 'You are exactly like your father.'

I have no qualms about being thought of as un-ambitious. 'I would retire tomorrow if I had the chance.'

'I think Adam has a very healthy attitude to life,' Caroline says nervously.

John smirks. 'That's very charitable, darling, but not very realistic. Life costs. Private schooling costs. Designer shoes cost. Need I go on?'

'I just mean . . .'

'You mean to offer my laid-back brother moral support. Well, enjoy the easy life now, Adam, while you still can. When children come along, you'll be forced to work all the hours that God sends.'

Electra gallops into the room with Amy perched on her shoulders, clutching two strands of her wiry hair and flicking them like reins.

Caroline gets up and reaches for her daughter. 'Electra, put her down. You'll hurt your back.'

'Leave her. She's as light as a leaf.'

'You mean, feather,' Mum says haughtily, always first to point out Electra's linguistic errors.

'In Greek they say leaf, Mum, and if you ask me it sounds better alliterated.'

Electra turns on her heel and canters out of the room, ducking under the doorway, Amy laughing. I watch the easy way my wife relates to the girls and my heart sinks. I married Electra under false pretences, withholding the truth, burying it away in my sub-conscious, thinking it would never raise its ugly head. How can I tell my wife, knowing how desperately she wants to be a mother, that we can never have children of our own?

Electra

I thought cucumber sandwiches were a myth until I married Adam and met his mother. Now a plateful of fictional food lies unappetisingly before me. We munch on bread that looks and tastes like polystyrene ceiling tiles, spread with pastes that smell like cat food. Margaret has opted for tuna paste instead of flakes, for orange-coloured processed cheese instead of the real thing. Her sandwiches are neat white crustless squares, decorated with sprigs of parsley.

The children are subjected to a barrage of dos and don'ts. Don't talk. Don't slouch. Don't reach out across the table. Amy looks so miserable I am gripped by the overwhelming desire to cheer her up. I grab a couple of black grapes from the bunch in the centre of the table, lodge them in my eyes and pull a silly face. Amy smiles but knows better than to laugh. Following my lead, she slots two carrot-stick fangs into her mouth, making her sister giggle and expel chewed sandwich into her hand. John glares at Amy and tells her to stop playing with her food.

'If you've both finished you might as well leave the table,' Caroline says, anxious to avoid confrontation.

The conversation is as oppressive as the dining room with its dark wood panelling, heavy curtains and gilt chandelier. I itch to leave, to do something ridiculous, to hear Adam's laughter. When I am expected to be good, I have a tendency to play the fool. I dry swallow white bread and tangerine cheese while contemplating ways to liven up these proceedings. More fun would be had standing vigil over a corpse.

'I haven't told you Electra's news,' Adam says, sensing my mood. 'She's just set up her own website. Electra's designs are now on-line.'

'Well done,' John says in a tone one might use to address a labrador returning a frisbee.

'Thanks.'

John has never shown any interest in my business. He considers it a hobby not a serious moneymaking proposition. John's business has had time to mature while mine is still a young bird acquiring its flight feathers. I would love to pick John's business brain and ask his advice, if only he were less chauvinistic. If he took more interest in what his wife had to say instead of casually disregarding her comments and finishing off her sentences. If he praised Caroline for more than just her mothering and domestic skills. John is pleasant to the eye, his comments carefully guarded. Softly and cleverly he has crippled the confidence of his spouse.

'So, you're still tinkering with trinkets, are you?' he says, making my blood boil instantly.

'Trinkets!' Adam says, turning red in the face.

'You're so bloody patronising, John. Electra makes gold and silver jewellery. One-off pieces that take months to finish. Like the brooch she made for Mum, which you didn't even bother to look at?'

'Jewellery, bangles, trinkets. It all means the same thing, doesn't it?'

'Yeah. Like local rag means newspaper.'

'Exactly.' Adam's admirable attempt to defend me makes no impression on his thick-skinned brother. 'I think you're being a little over-sensitive. I didn't mean to offend you.'

'Adam's always getting the wrong end of the stick,' Margaret says to her ally and partner in crime. 'He always takes everything I say the wrong way.'

John turns to his mother. 'Well, I hope you won't misunderstand what I am about to suggest. There's something important we need to talk about and since we're all sitting round a table this seems like the perfect opportunity.'

'What is it?'

'This house is far too big for one person to live in, and too expensive for you to maintain. You need to think about selling up and buying something smaller.'

Adam shakes his head incredulously. 'Surely this discussion can wait? Do we have to have it today of all days?'

'No, it can't wait. This house is falling down around Mother's ears and no one seems to be noticing. There are problems with the guttering, the boiler, the electrics, the roof. The place needs a substantial amount of money spending on it, money that Mother hasn't got.'

'Let's both chip in and get the work done,' Adam says.

John smiles slyly. 'Do you have a spare fifty grand lying around? We need to face facts. Mother's not getting any younger. There will come a time when she won't be able to go up and down two flights of stairs.'

'Why don't we cross that bridge when we come to it?'

'Don't talk about me as if I'm not here.' But Margaret's voice lacks its usual acerbic edge.

John reaches out for her hand, instantly disarming her. 'You know I have your best interests at heart. Someone,' he says pointedly, 'has to plan for your future. There are things every family needs to discuss. Unpleasant things. Things no one wants to think about. For example, have you made your Will yet?'

'For Christ's sake, John. It's Mum's birthday.'

'Do you want the taxman to pocket our rightful inheritance?'

'Personally, I don't care. Perhaps that's why I drive a rust heap and you drive a beamer.'

John, the sensible brother, has killed off and buried Margaret on her birthday; sold off and divided up her estate.

'Isn't all this a little premature?' she asks weakly, her customary fight sapped.

John looks into her eyes and I watch her melt, regress, reverse roles with her son, become a child counselled by its parent. 'No one knows what the future holds. What lies around the corner. Father was a prime example of that. What if, heaven forbid, something happens to you before you've had a chance to tie up all the loose ends?'

44

'You're right, John. I do need to start thinking about the future?' Margaret has been swayed by the power of this son who can do no wrong, who has always proved his good sense. 'Just tell me what I have to do.'

'Nothing. I've done it all for you. I've had some papers drawn up by my solicitor and all you need to do is sign them. They're in the car. They give Adam and me the right to handle your affairs if ever you become incapacitated.'

'While I'm still fit and healthy, I want to go on living in my house,' Margaret says, mustering her last vestige of free will.

'Of course. There's no question of you being turned out of your own home against your will. Let me fetch the papers and we'll get the formalities over and done with.'

John gets up and goes out to the car, leaving in his wake an awkward silence and an embarrassed-looking wife. Margaret looks dejected, one foot planted irrevocably in the grave. Adam glances across at me, his eyes signalling disapproval and helplessness. John came here to clinch a deal and will leave with a contract signed and sealed. Today should have been a day to celebrate Margaret's life, not to focus on her death.

I wash. Caroline dries. We chitchat. Talk about her new kitchen and the weather, avoiding the heart of our lives. Caroline seems distracted. Unsettled. I feel instinctively that a dark shadow mars this woman's apparently sunny existence.

'Are you OK?' I ask.

'I'm fine,' she answers, looking surprised that I should pick up on her non-verbal messages.

'Fine' is such a non-committal word. Does Caroline feel adequately well or very satisfactory? 'Fine' is a fair description of her marriage. A comfortable, aesthetically pleasing match. John and Caroline have everything in common but nothing to talk about. No sparks, no cheeky banter, no stolen glances, no hints of volatility, flow between them. My friend Lydia's untraditional family with all its difficulties and unexpected rewards is more appealing by far than John and Caroline's sanitised life.

'You must be pleased that John is doing so well.' I mention her husband's name and watch for signs of discomfiture. Caroline strangles the dishcloth and rubs frenziedly at the inside of the sink.

'Yes. Of course. But he works too hard. Sometimes he stays at the office and works through the night.'

'That must be difficult.'

'It is. I hardly see him at all. But I suppose that's the price he has to pay for success.'

'You both pay the price.'

'Oh, I'm at home with the girls all day, I've got it easy. Or so John keeps telling me.' She smiles to indicate that this is merely a statement, not a criticism. I have never known Caroline to utter a bad word about her husband.

'You're raising two young children single-handedly.'

'And poor John works day and night.'

'So do you.'

I wonder if Caroline is deluding herself like my sister. If she is shying away from some unpalatable truth. Caroline is sweet, kind and ultra-feminine with a soft, slightly reedy voice. She is the sort of woman who liquefies when her husband buys her flowers or a box of chocolates, who loves pseudo-romantic gestures, a woman woefully lacking in cynicism. I have no time for stereotypical love tokens. Roses, diamonds, soft toys, eating out on Valentine's Day in dire risk of being handed a cellophane-wrapped carnation produced from a bucket. When birthdays or anniversaries loom Adam walks on eggshells, knowing I am difficult to please.

'When do you and Adam plan to start a family?' Caroline asks.

'Uh . . .' I try to keep the good news to myself but it shoots from my mouth like reflux. 'Actually, I'm pregnant.'

A wave of mixed emotions washes over me then. Happiness, embarrassment, an irrational fear that uttering the words might tempt fate. The same kind of fear that prevented my sister from buying clothes or deciding on names for her children until they were safely deposited in her arms.

'How fantastic! I'm so happy for you both. The girls will finally have a cousin.'

I swear Caroline to secrecy and glance at the children playing quietly in a corner of the kitchen. Their natural exuberance is curbed at every juncture by parental edicts not to shout, not to run, not to scream. I was a different breed of child. Wild and unruly, a girl who climbed trees and chased boys through the village square until late in the evening. I played beneath a ceiling of unremitting blue. Ate fruit picked off roadside bushes. Fished from a rocky outcrop with a home-made rod alongside my brothers. I was not wary of strangers and had no fear of abduction. My only fear was of the fictional *koulas*, the bogeyman, who my grandmother warned came out when it rained to prey on children. I was not driven in an armoured pod from one activity to the other and back home to stagnate in front of the television. I was allowed to get dirty, to exhaust my natural energies, to interact with the natural environment. I had a wonderful childhood full of adventure.

The war took my home but it did not break my spirit. I was too young to mourn the loss of a fortune, too full of life and curiosity to sit and brood. I never thought of myself as a victim – life was simply a current I followed. I had a new town to explore, new friends to make. My parents were so busy rebuilding that they allowed their children to roam like feral cats. For five years I shared a mattress with my sister at the foot of our parents' bed. We lay on our backs, watching small lizards scuttle across the ceiling, their transparent stomachs full of mosquitoes. My eldest brother Minos shared the second bedroom with his fiancée Eleni. Thomas, who was eleven, catnapped in the hallway on a row of cushions. Elpida slept on the sofa, in her billowing nightdress, beneath the wooden blades of a ceiling fan, circulating hot air. Relatives wandered in and out. Papa's sisters, their children, my paternal grandparents. Mama fed everyone without complaint, frying eggplants, soaking haricot beans to make *fasolia*, stuffing courgettes with rice and minced meat. No one ever left Mama's table without praising the culinary expertise of a cook whose cupboards may have been half-empty but whose cup was always half-full.

Lydia

Lydia lay on her back, drifting in and out of sleep. Savouring the precious half-hour of nothingness that preceded frantic activity. Her body felt light and buoyant, as if encased in a warm mist of water droplets. She was not in bed, wrapped in a pure white duvet, but floating on a powdery cushion of cumulonimbus. She heard Alvaro enter the room and pad softly around the bed on bare feet. She did not have the energy to open her eyes, to summon her voice and tell her son to go and put his slippers on. He stepped onto the cloud, a brown cherub in red underpants, a celestial Mowgli, his feet sinking further into white softness with every step. Lydia heard a faint: 'Hiya, hiya, hiya'. The sound did not tally with her waking dream. Silence, birdcall, the rush of air would have been more fitting, not 'Hiya', accompanied by the bang of a small foot on laminated floor. The cherub was practising his karate moves, slicing through the cloud with his hand, moving closer to the bed, missing his imaginary target and chopping, not cloud but his mother's windpipe.

Lydia shot up in excruciating pain, clutching her neck.

'Sorry, Mum! Sorry, I didn't mean to hit you. I was aiming for the pillow.'

Lydia coughed violently, trying not to bring up her supper of chicken soup. Suddenly Alvaro clasped his small hand tightly over her mouth, obstructing her breathing. As she straddled the woozy state between consciousness and asphyxiation, Lydia realised that her son was not trying to smother her but simply following maternal instructions: 'Cover your mouth when you cough . . . cover your mouth when you cough'. She pushed his hand away and gulped oxygen, flopping backwards onto the pillow, breathing hard until the need to retch subsided, covering her neck lest another karate chop went astray. Alvaro brought his face close to his mother's flushed one, his missing bottom teeth making him look slightly satanic.

'Mum, I love . . .' he looked dreamily into the eyes of a mother waiting for the word 'you' '. . . fried eggs,' he finished. 'Can I have some, Mum? Now, Mum. Please.'

He threw off the duvet. Cold air displaced warm, rushing through the fibres of Lydia's T-shirt, pinching her bare legs.

Lydia licked her finger and rubbed at the red stain soiling the lap of her skirt. Rehydrated tomato juice spread further through the olive-green fibres. Traffic lights turned from amber to green. She stopped rubbing and turned her attention to the road. Miasmic and chock-a-block. A mottled sky seeped unrelenting drizzle that dulled the vibrancy of freshly unfurled foliage. Winter was reluctant to relinquish its hold. It grumbled and bellyached like a child unwilling to take turns.

It was too late now to drive back home and change. The elongated stain would smile wryly up at her for the rest of the day, reminding Lydia to lie a napkin in her lap next time she ate *Pa amb Tomaquet*. Tomato bread was her first finger food, her after-school snack, her evening meal when she felt too lazy to cook. Last night, the tomato she'd rubbed onto thick bread had spurted pulp into her lap. In the morning, running late, she had sloppily pulled on yesterday's skirt.

Alvaro pulled down the passenger-side visor and looked up at his reflection in the mirror. He pulled a jar of hair gel out of his school bag and unscrewed the lid. Small fingers scooped out a clod of opaque slime. They ran it through his thick, black hair and tugged his fringe upwards into a shiny quiff before wiping themselves clean on the car seat. Lydia swallowed down a chastisement before it shot like a bullet from her mouth, wounding its intended victim and causing an unnecessary rumpus first thing in the morning.

She rooted through her handbag for a tissue. Steering with her right, rooting with her left. Pushing aside house keys, a dog-eared notepad, lipstick squashed inside its lid, the leg of a plastic toy, chewed gum wrapped inside a supermarket receipt. The traffic slithered forward, overtaken by ambling pedestrians. Lydia eased out a tissue and handed it to her son, asking him to wipe the seat. He rubbed so hard at the gel that the tissue disintegrated into white flecks, further littering the car and defeating the object. Alvaro flung the intact portion of tissue over his shoulder, like an indolent Roman emperor discarding a chicken bone.

'Sorry, Mum,' he said, instantly negating his crime. The tissue joined sweet wrappers, crisp crumbs and lolly sticks. A week's worth of Alvaro's rubbish. For the sake of her blood pressure, Lydia had begun to turn a blind eye.

The car crawled to a halt at red lights. Lydia inspected her son's head. Nuggets of gel twinkled in the blackness of his hair. She reached out to adjust Alvaro's pliable fringe and smooth out the gel. He pulled his head away, out of reach, and told her to 'get off'.

'Elvis always let his mum fix his hair in the morning,' Lydia said, feeling it reasonable to assume that Gladys Presley, doting mother that she was, had run a comb through young Elvis's hair every morning. Lydia constantly used her son's Elvis fixation to her own advantage, inventing a rock 'n' roll icon who loved doing homework, always tidied his bedroom, ate up his greens, cut his toenails without making a fuss and never argued with his mother.

Alvaro straightened in his seat. His interest had been sparked by Lydia's white lie. He allowed his mother the liberty of fiddling with his sacred quiff.

'Did she always do his hair?' he asked.

'Always.'

'What happened when she died?'

'By then he had learned to do it himself.' Lydia's answer was feasible.

'Are you going to die?' Alvaro's curiosity lunged laterally.

'Not for a while.'

'In how long?'

'When I'm much older. I hope.' Lydia touched her tender neck, thinking how close she had come to choking just hours earlier.

'Is Grandma going to die soon? She's really old.'

'She's not that old.'

'If Grandma dies and you die, who's going to look after me?' Alvaro's tone was matter-of-fact.

'Uhm.' The question unsettled Lydia. She was a single mother and an only child. 'Adam and Electra will look after you. They're your godparents. Your second mum and dad.'

'Oh, good.' Alvaro sounded pleased. 'Can't I live with them before you die?'

'No, you can't.' Lydia felt unappreciated, and feared that her son yearned to be part of a nuclear family.

'How do you get to heaven when you die?'

Lydia's head started pounding at the temples. She wished Alvaro would not force her to think so early in the morning. He rarely allowed her the luxury of wading into full consciousness from the shallows, but threw her in at the deep end.

'You kind of float.' Lydia turned on the radio to distract his attention. He turned it off.

'I want to see a dead body floating into the sky.' His tone was demanding, petulant, as if he was asking for the newest electronic toy, as seen on TV.

'It's not the actual body that goes to heaven but what's inside.'

'What, like the heart and brains?'

A grisly vision of body parts headed skyward, like a

gory Chagall, flashed before Lydia's eyes. 'No. It's something called a soul.'

How could she tell her son that after death a body simply decomposed? She wanted him to believe in the comforting fairytales his grandmother told him. About heaven and an omnipresent God. Lydia's mother Consuelo was determined to save her grandson's soul from joining her daughter's in purgatory for the sin of agnosticism. Lydia let her mother read to Alvaro from the Bible, seeing no harm in any story, whether religious or pagan, which excited her son's imagination. He relished equally the drama in David and Goliath and *The Sword and the Stone*. He acted out both tales in the days that followed their narration. Firing dried chickpeas at his grandmother with the aid of an elastic band, plunging a bread knife into a crusty granary loaf.

Consuelo's uncensored account of Christ's passion had made a spectacular impression on him. After that he refused to go to Easter Mass, believing he was expected to witness a live crucifixion, crying out: 'I don't want Jesus to die!' Finally reassured by his grandmother that Christ's trials and tribulations took place a 'very long time ago' he'd finally agreed to go to church. On returning home he stripped down to his underpants, drew lipstick dots on the backs of his hands and the tops of his feet, and wandered round the house with a bamboo-stick cross draped across his shoulder. Consuelo watched her grandson's antics raptly, as if viewing a hallowed vision of St Francis.

* * *

Alvaro walked ahead of his mother along the school driveway, dragging his new backpack over soggy tarmac. An older boy ran past him, patting his head and shouting: 'All right, Elvis?' to which Alvaro responded with a moody pout and a regal wave. Lydia wondered if anyone had noticed her son's shoes. Worn as usual on the wrong feet. A physical manifestation of Alvaro's peculiar thought patterns. Her son believed that outward-pointing shoes made his small feet look bigger, exaggerated his bandy Elvis swagger and turned his boyish steps into a manly strut. Lydia feared that he was in too great a hurry to grow up, to become man of the house and protect his womenfolk. He had never been a timid boy welded to his mother's side. He was confident, gregarious, the joker in the pack. Alvaro's most-hated reprimand was 'naughty boy'. Lydia tried to avoid this admonition, though it was a fitting one for a boy who was wilful, obstinate and exasperating. 'Naughty boy' shattered the image he had of himself and reduced him in stature. Consuelo insisted on littering her censure with this phrase, in making it a self-fulfilling prophecy. Lydia steered clear of an insult that only served to antagonise and belittle her touchy son.

Alvaro's collars were turned up. His white shirt was open at the nape. Given the opportunity, a plastic medallion would be swinging from his neck. Alvaro had an un-childlike sense of style, inspired by his iconic hero. He liked shirts with wide collars, smart trousers with a crease down the leg, and shiny waist-coats (courtesy of Consuelo). With his hair slicked back, eyeliner sideburns and rolled-up paper dangling cigarette-style from the corner of his mouth, he looked like an Italian waiter, an extra from *Bugsy Malone*, an aspiring Galliano. To force Alvaro into clothes not to his liking was a battle. To catch him, hold him down, prise his kicking legs into a pair of unwanted trousers, was a feat in itself. The aftermath was tears, a barrage of insults, a painful thump from one of his thrashing arms. Suffering bemused looks from fellow shoppers in the supermarket was preferable to curbing Alvaro's style statements and provoking his rage. Lydia had stopped apologising for the strange little man who swaggered beside her.

Instead she allowed her son the comfort of his quirks and rituals. She had learned, through bitter experience, that forcing her square child into a round hole would only lead to upset. If she shouted, he screamed. If she smacked, he lashed out. If all that came out of her mouth was a litany of dos and don'ts, he stopped listening. It had taken seven challenging years for Lydia to understand her son and devise strategies to handle him. She was firm when necessary. Let things go that need not be pushed. Lydia feared what Alvaro might have become in less careful hands. He was a boy who liked routine, order and consistency. Who had to be fed, on time, a supper exactly to his liking. His toys, once carefully lined up, had to stay where they were. He reacted like a bull to a red rag when thwarted with the word 'no'. Sometimes it could be substituted, to avoid confrontation, with 'perhaps', 'we'll see', 'maybe later', 'not at the moment'. Other times, such as when Alvaro insisted on playing with a steak knife, 'no' had to mean 'no', regardless of the consequences. All Lydia's efforts were confounded by Consuelo, the doting grandmother who badly needed a crash course in child psychology. Who gave her grandson a steak knife if his heart desired it. Who shouted for no good reason, and stayed mute when there was every cause to reprimand. Who did more harm than good by always, eventually, yielding to Alvaro's demands. A grandmother's role is to spoil, she insisted, a parent's to discipline.

Alvaro took a crab-shaped spinning toy out of his pocket and ran up to Jack, his new friend, a boy with mousy hair and a sallow complexion who looked more like Lydia than her own son. Alvaro had a round cherubic face and honey-coloured skin that darkened to a burnt sugar colour in the summer. The two boys stooped to watch the crab revolve at high speed. They kicked it as it spun full tilt against the school fire door and watched it rebound. A real crustacean would be lying shattered, legs akimbo, by now. Lifeless as the frogs that Alvaro found in the back garden and squeezed a little too hard, that sank like stones to the bottom of his makeshift ponds.

Alvaro picked up the plastic crab and handed it to his friend.

'You can have it,' he said.

Jack slipped it into his pocket. Lydia sensed her son's need to connect with his own sex, to redress the balance of a home life where femaleness prevailed. She had once believed that nurture was the predominant force in a child's life and made every effort to buy her son gender-unspecific toys. Glove puppets, kaleidoscopes, musical instruments, chunky wooden toys painted in bright, primary colours. She'd refused to buy guns and swords, determined to raise a peace-loving boy who would one day make the perfect husband. Lydia had failed in her endeavour, or else Nature had triumphed. The harder she tried to suppress Alvaro's atavistic instincts, the more soil he chewed, the more stones he sucked on, the more swords he made out of sticks, the more worms he pulled apart, the more karate kicks he practised on his grandmother. Sometimes Lydia wished she were hermaphrodite and could fathom the needs of his sex. Alvaro had to learn to survive in the world as it was. He had to graze his knees and bloody his nose, learn to throw and deflect a punch, pledge allegiance to a foot-ball team and kick his ball through a neighbour's window.

Lydia spotted Kane in the distance. Arms out-stretched, weaving through the throng of children, his dark hair stubble-short. His mother Anita walked past, pushing her baby daughter in a buggy, her broad hips swaying beneath her *salwar kameez*. She smiled. Fleshy cheeks rose like leavened dough, prettying her face. Lydia smiled back, wondering why her son no longer played with Kane, his best friend through nursery, reception and year one. Anita stopped at her usual spot, at the foot of the grassy bank, and adjusted her headscarf. Kane circled his mother and baby sister three times before swooping down to land beside Jack and Alvaro. He was ignored. He took flight once more to follow the boys to the top of the grassy bank where Alvaro began gyrating his pelvis and playing air guitar. He attracted a small crowd of children, some looking amused, others puzzled. As Kane inched his way towards Alvaro, Jack turned and thumped him hard in the chest, knocking him off his feet. He sprang up quickly, looking embarrassed and upset, and ran back to his mother. No one else had noticed the offence. Not Anita who was rearranging the blanket around her baby. Not Jack's mother who was chatting nearby. Not even Alvaro who was too busy entertaining the crowd. Only Lydia saw and charged up the grassy bank towards the boys, just as the whistle blew and the children descended like an avalanche.

Adam

I feel safe with Electra beside me in the bed. Her body radiates warmth and a sweet cinnamony smell. My wife guards my psychological well-being, exercises the gamut of my emotional repertoire and saves me from myself. My life would be lacklustre without her. Electra is extraordinary. A hand-wrought creature with all its charm and imperfections. Life with her is always interesting, a challenge, a cultural education. We live in a repression-free zone, where feelings are aired without fear of offending and no subject is taboo. Where one can shout when the need arises and grudges have a short shelf life. Electra has freed me from my childhood bonds and prised me slowly out of my shell, exposing my soft underbelly. For five years I have been an open book with a crucial page ripped out of my narrative.

Electra rolls onto her back like a cat, stretches out her arms and yawns. I watch her, thinking how beautiful she looks, how peaceful, how I could never betray her. A feline caterwaul punctuates the early-morning silence. High heels clacking on concrete grow louder before fading into nothing. The hum of a car engine crescendos, clashes into gear, then splutters its way into the distance. Far-off laughter echoes, an auditory imprint as lasting as the flicker of a shooting star. I focus on the extraneous in an effort to stave off the dark thoughts that linger on the periphery of my consciousness, that draw me like a vision in the corner of my eye or the dizzying lure of a cliff edge. Sleep was once my solace, a sigh of relief at the end of the day. Lately, worrying preoccupations have begun hijacking my peace of mind when I lay my head on a pillow. I used to read until my eyelids dropped, until I sank seamlessly into sleep. Now sleeping is an effort and fiction offers no escape.

When I was a student I knew a young man who went to sleep and never woke up. Climbing into bed at the end of the day is no definite guarantee that one will get up in the morning. There were no signs, not a hint that his heart would stop during the night. An unfinished essay lay fanned out on his desk, beside it a half-eaten chocolate bar. Cigarettes poked from the fullish packet on his bedside table. His long shoes formed a V-shape, the tip of the chevron pointing towards the dead youth. A vivid description of the room was painted by the friend who had found him. It spread like wildfire, sending shock waves through the halls of residence that reached me with a dull thud. I was not moved to tears as others were but accepted the aberration with detachment. After all, the chances of dying in one's sleep are statistically negligible.

Now, nineteen years on, that youth who slipped

from sleep into death has begun to haunt me. The shock did not rebound off my thick skin, as I had thought, but penetrated it and lay in wait. It is not death itself that I'm afraid of, but the manner in which I might meet my end. Dad slipped away little by little over several years, regressing from adult to incapable child. From kind, articulate man to fractious stranger.

Electra grinds her back teeth and turns her back to me. I run my hand up and down her arm, marvelling at the softness of her skin, the golden colour of her neck and the crazy, corkscrew curls that fan out over the pillow. I love Electra's untamed looks. She has long dark hair and eyes like a striated cross-section of nutmeg. Her face would not look amiss amid the Fayum portraits, those ancient faces depicted on mummy cases discovered in the Greek cemeteries of Roman Egypt. Like the noble faces of her ancestors, hers can look sweet, wistful, and profoundly melancholic.

Not everyone can see what I love in her. Mum will never understand. How could she when she barely knows the man who lies beyond the surface of her son? I am no stranger to her disapproval. Maternal censure has marked every juncture of my life. I left home to live on a kibbutz for a while. I studied sociology and dropped out after my degree to travel the world. I married a woman who does not fit the bill socially and speaks with the wrong kind of accent. Mum has never openly expressed her bigotry. She thinks her mocking remarks, made behind Electra's back, entirely acceptable, as is the constant drip-drip of criticism offered up as well-meaning advice with the addendum 'I am only trying to help'. Mum should not try to outwit me. Words are my vocation. Nuances my livelihood. I play with words, I shuffle them like cards in a pack, I turn phrases arse about face.

Electra is the only woman who has ever made me laugh from the heart. I laugh with her and at her – but never cruelly. Her sense of humour is typical of the culture from which she hails. It is slapstick, black, Chaplinesque. It exalts the idiosyncratic, the far-fetched and the utterly ridiculous. Electra laughed until her stomach hurt when Mr Bean bowed abruptly and head-butted the Queen. Modelling herself on her comic hero, she has danced the tango with a parsnip and moon-walked for dinner guests. She has perfected the gobble of a turkey, and can make a cigarette vanish from her hand and reappear behind her ear.

Now Electra turns on her side and backs into me, moaning contentedly. I draw her towards me and kiss the base of her neck, working my way up to her ear-lobe. Pulling my wife closer to me, feeling our bodies mould like Plasticine. Sinking into the spongy bed and beyond, aroused by the softness of my wife's skin, the curve of her buttocks, the small of her back.

Electra's body stiffens and she opens her eyes. 'The telephone's ringing, Adam.'

'Ignore it.'

The ringing stops, then starts again, reality intruding a second time, spoiling the moment. Electra gets up wearily and goes out into the hallway while I close my eyes, feeling hot and unsatisfied. Minutes later she rushes back into the room.

'Adam, get up, quickly! Your mother's had a fall. She's in hospital. Come on, get dressed. Let's go.'

* * *

We take the stairs. Three flights. Unnerved by tight spaces, Electra refuses to use the lift. We walk hand-in-hand along a tunnel segmented by swing doors. One whiff of hospital and the past floods my consciousness. Holding Dad's hand, our disparity in height, walking for what seemed like miles, the resonating click of Mum's heels. Peering into wards at the sick, an alien race that bore no relation to me. Feeling frightened and exhilarated. Sitting outside a consulting room, staring into space, unaware of the bombshell that would imminently strike and derail my life.

'The smell of this place makes me feel sick,' I say, trying not to breathe too deeply, concerned about the airborne germs that surround us.

'Me too.'

'Ever since Dad fell ill I've hated hospitals.'

'You must have gone through hell.'

'It was a horrible time. Especially for Mum. She found it really difficult looking after him, and to be honest, they weren't the happiest of couples before he got sick. Mum thinks life dealt her a bum card and I suppose it did. That's why I try to be patient with her, understanding, to excuse her moods. I know what she's been through and I wouldn't wish her experience on anyone.

'I've been thinking about Dad a lot recently – about his illness, about my own health and how incredibly lucky I've been. How many men get to my age without losing a tooth or breaking a bone? Without spending a single night in hospital? I'm expecting my luck to run out quite soon.'

Electra looks up at me and slows her stride. 'I thought I was the hypochondriac, not you. You've got nothing to worry about, Adam. You look after yourself. You eat properly. There's not an ounce of fat on you. You were born with the gift of good health.'

My wife couldn't be more wrong. I may look healthy on the outside but something voracious could be nestled at my core, eating me away from inside.

My neck muscles tighten as I walk along the corridor, through a set of double doors and into the orthopaedic ward where Mum is lying in bed, arms folded across her chest, looking pale and older than her years. Her right leg is plastered to the thigh and raised in a sling-like contraption. Her eyes are shut, her expression pained. In the neighbouring bed lies an emaciated woman with a deathly complexion and a dry mass of white hair, connected by tubes to a bag of blood. A large woman, in a pale blue hospital gown and floral slippers, inches her way forward on a Zimmer frame. Grunting as she moves, her breathing laboured. Electra tightens her grip on my hand as we stand beside Mum's bed, debating whether or not to wake her. I reach out and gently stroke her cold fingers.

'Adam. Thank goodness you're here,' she says opening her eyes.

'How are you feeling? What happened?'

'I don't know exactly. I feel so confused and dis-orientated . . . I remember opening the front door and stepping outside. I remember my leg twisting and feeling the bone snap. I don't know whether I tripped on the front step or blacked out. Thank goodness my lodger found me on his way out and phoned for an ambulance or else I might still be lying there.' She tries to move and winces. 'The doctor says I have a fractured femur. My leg will be in plaster for two to three months. I really don't know how I'm going to cope.'

'Don't worry, you'll manage. Three months isn't such a long time.'

'And what if I didn't trip? What if I passed out? What if I'm losing my mind too, Adam?'

'You're not losing your mind.'

'I can't bear the thought of spending a single night in here, surrounded by all these old women. That one . . .' she points to her neighbour '. . . spent the whole night mumbling and screaming. I didn't get a wink of sleep. She's ninety-eight and just had a hip replacement. You really have to wonder why they bothered!'

The white-haired woman starts to groan and turns her head to look through me with opaque eyes. 'Nurse,. I need the toilet,' she whimpers. 'Nurse, I need the toilet. I need the toilet. Please help me.' She stretches out a scrawny arm and claws the air with her fingers.

A nurse arrives, carrying a bedpan, and closes the curtain around the old woman's bed.

'There's no way I'm using a bedpan,' Mum complains, as the smell of faeces breaches the curtain and permeates the ward, turning my stomach.

'How will you get to the toilet at home up a flight of stairs, Margaret?' Electra asks. 'When you come out of hospital, you'll have to stay with us.'

'I don't want to be a burden . . .'

'You won't. We insist. Don't we, Adam?'

I stare at my wife in numb disbelief. It's hard to imagine a worse scenario – Electra and my mother under one small roof. A healthy version of Mum would be bad enough to live with, a sick one will be impossible.

'Don't we, Adam?' Electra repeats, when my response is slow to come.

'Yes, of course. You must stay with us.'

My thoughts instantly turn to John and Caroline and their picture-book cottage by a stream, the ideal place for Mum to recuperate. 'Does John know you're in hospital?'

'No, I only gave the hospital your number. There's no need to bother your brother.'

'He needs to be told, Mum. I'll go right away and ring him.'

I make my way to the ward exit and back along the glazed tunnel, pushing open a succession of swing doors. Moving aside to make way for trolleys carrying post-operative patients. John will save me, I tell myself, and make up for all the duties he has reneged on over the years. Where was he when Mum's boiler burst and flooded the kitchen? When she thought she heard intruders in the dead of night? When Dad took a turn for the worse? John was living his own life, being a busy man, thinking of number one. It is time for him to inconvenience himself for a change. Time for the good daughter-in-law to be put under Mum's searching spotlight. I dial John's mobile number and wait for him to answer.

'Adam! How are you?'

I hear music in the background and female laughter. 'Mum's had a fall. She's broken her leg. I'm calling you from the hospital.'

'What! How did it happen?'

'She fell down the front step.'

'I'm not surprised. I've been complaining about that step for ages. It was an accident waiting to happen. Someone should have got it fixed.'

His accusatory tone suggests I am the 'someone' responsible for Mum's broken leg. 'Why didn't you sort it out, if you knew it was so dangerous?'

'Adam, I live a long way away.'

'When are you coming to see her?'

'I won't be able to come for a while. I'm away on business at the moment.'

'But Mum needs you.'

'I really can't come, Adam. I'm in the thick of things at the moment.' A woman calls out my brother's name, in an overly friendly tone, arousing my suspicions that John's trip is not strictly for business purposes.

'What's going to happen when she leaves hospital? She can't go back home.'

'Of course not. That place is a death trap.'

'She'll have to stay with you. You've got more space than we have and Caroline's at home all day.'

'Impossible, Adam. It's not convenient for Mother to stay with us at the moment.' His tone is cold, business-like. The woman in the background calls out his name again.

'Who's calling to you, John?'

'My secretary. I told you, I'm on a business trip. Mum will have to stay with you until we can sort out an alternative arrangement. I have to go now. I'll call you later.'

With that he switches off his phone, ending our conversation without even a goodbye. I imagine him turning back to the woman and apologising for his rudeness, taking up where he left off. 'Mother's a trouper,' he'll tell himself, as he has told himself so many times before. 'Mother's a trouper,' he said, when Dad was taken from us. I head back to the ward, disappointed and angry, struggling to accept my interim fate.

I enter a ward in chaos. Mum's white-haired neighbour rocks in her bed, calling out: 'I want to go home. I can't go home. I haven't got any money. I can't go home. No, I haven't got any money. Take me home. I want to go home.'

Electra stands beside the woman's bed, stroking her hand. There is blood all over the white sheets, on the woman's face, a thick brown pool of it under Mum's bed. Nurses rush into the ward and mop it up with thick wads of tissue.

'The silly old woman pulled out her drip,' Mum says, exasperated. 'How am I expected to get better in a place like this?'

Electra

Cousin Vicki's tale is unremarkable yet it haunts me. I have lived it a thousand times in waking dreams. Imagine waking up late on a fine summer's day. The birds are singing. The cicadas humming. You walk out onto the veranda of your fourth-floor apartment and feel the sun gently fingering your face. Your vista is the sea. An expanse of smooth, ultramarine stretching into the far distance, forming a horizon with the azure sky. Living high up, you feel like an eagle. The view is breathtaking. You wish you could stretch out your arms and fly like a gull over the red-tiled rooftops and far, far out to sea. Voices filter upward from the vegetable market below. The ice-cream man passes on his bike, ringing his bell, calling out *'Triantafilo, triantafilo'*. The thought of his rose-flavoured sorbet makes your mouth water. Someone shouts out your name. 'Vicki! Vicki!' You look down and see a friend. 'See you tonight,' she calls, waving then disappearing into the narrow mouth of a side street. You are sixteen and in love with life.

Without warning nature is silenced. The sounds from below grow muffled. The distant buzzing of a wasp slowly crescendos, becomes the deafening whirr of a bomber plane that flies so close you can see the pilot in his cockpit. A piercing scream from below jolts you as fiercely as an electric shock, uprooting your bare feet. You run, still in your nightdress, out of the flat and down a flight of stairs. An elderly neighbour with arthritic hips eases her way down the stairwell, slowing your escape. And then a bomb drops with deafening resonance, somewhere close by, leaving a crater where once a row of houses stood. The old woman screams and collapses. You want to jump over her body and run for your life but human compassion overrides your fear. You help her back on to her feet and take her arm, leading her slowly down the stairs. Disturbing thoughts dart like flies through your mind. Are your parents safe? Where is your brother? Has the crater swallowed him up? Your own life becomes unimportant. The safety of others is everything.

To condense a long and common story, you escape on foot, leave behind a town on fire, spend the next eighteen months in a tent waiting to go home. You never do. The place where you were born and grew up, once a thriving coastal town packed with tourists, home to a population of 37,000, becomes a ghost town. Pigeons nest in the eaves of five-star hotels. Herring gulls and lizards monopolise the wide expanses of sandy beach. You can skirt the periphery of your town by car and view it through a telescope but it is strictly out of bounds. You are left with nothing but the nightdress you were wearing when you fled. Gone are your belongings, your community, the roof over your head. You exchange one identity for another. One that is inferior. You are now and forever a refugee. Whether you live in a box or acquire a house as big as a palace, the branding is indelible.

I heard many stories like Vicki's after the invasion. Testimonies of people ousted from their homes, working through their traumas, voicing their problems in the hope of feeling better. These stories sounded to my six-year-old ears like macabre fairytales. They kept me awake at night. I did not see ghouls, monsters and dragons in my sleep. I saw and heard bombs, apartment blocks collapsing, dead bodies lying like rotten fruit in gutters. When I watched the bombing of Baghdad those nightmare visions came back to me. My tears and fury were empathetic. I had tasted similar horrors and knew all too well the aftermath of bombing raids and senseless carnage. Lives derailed, changed beyond recognition. Pain that never heals but festers like a septic wound.

We left our village before the bombing started, thanks to Elpida's visions or fertile imagination, call her gloomy prediction what you will. We escaped the napalm bombs with our limbs and our family intact. We felt lucky, blessed. We had each other and our green Morris Minor. We had an indomitable mother whose true colours shone in the face of adversity. Though food was in short supply, we never went hungry. Mama would wait until we had all finished eating before satisfying her own hunger on leftovers. 'It fills me up, just watching you eat,' she used to say.

She queued early to secure the best Red Cross hand-me-downs for her family. She mended holes and polished shoes, making sure we were always well turned out. Mama slipped without resistance from her comfortable middle-class vantage to the bottom of the class structure. She took whatever state welfare was offered and saw no shame in cleaning other people's homes for extra pennies. 'Your mother is a saint,' Papa often says, 'without her I would be nothing.'

Martha has inherited mother's selflessness. Unfortunately, she has fallen into the hands of a man who exploits it. An unappreciative man who expects to be treated like a king. I blame my sister's poor choice of husband on the war. On the erosion of our social standing as a family. Before the invasion Martha was a catch. The daughter of a wealthy goldsmith, town mayor, esteemed owner of a thriving business and forty *donums* of land. A man who planned to build his daughter the best house in the village when she got married. After the invasion Martha became the daughter of a penniless refugee with nothing material to offer a prospective groom. When Sotiris proposed my sister hastily accepted, grateful that any man would be willing to take her on without a dowry. Sotiris has never let her forget his generosity.

'Martha, *café*,' he commands when he wants a coffee, and off my sister goes to fill an *imbrinki* with water. 'Martha, *bino*,' he says when hungry, hoisting his legs up onto a pouffe while Martha springs into action like a wind-up toy, peeling potatoes and frying pork chops. How often I have wanted to grab that heavy frying pan from out of her hand and serve my brother-in-law a fatal blow. His hollow skull would crack as easily as an egg and out of it would roll a brain the size of a chickpea.

Martha's experience did not endear the institution of marriage to me. No man, I vowed, would ever make me feel like a marketable commodity, my value determined by my dowry or the size of my father's bank account. I left Cyprus to study in England, turning my back on dowries and small minds and tradition, welcoming the anonymity one enjoys in a bustling city. I served in a bar at night and studied during the day. I worked my way through a degree and a series of postgraduate courses in business management and jewellery design.

I met Adam in the bar where I worked and wowed him with my magic tricks and cocktail-making skills. He began walking me home from work. We talked and laughed and sang silly songs all the way to my front door. For months he kissed me gingerly on the cheek and walked away while I wondered when he planned to make his move. I fancied Adam. We had fun together. I looked into his eyes and knew instinctively what kind of man he was. His love of a rusty old Rover was wonderfully endearing. He embodied everything I respected. He was humble, self-deprecating, incredibly kind, a gentleman. He prized character above all else and treated me as his equal. This was a man I could safely lose my heart to, I told myself, a man I could be happy with. Unfortunately, Adam came with strings. He came with a mother who judged me from day one on my financial status. Who heard I worked behind a bar to make ends meet and dismissed me out of hand. I fell in love then plunged head first into the trap I had tried so hard to avoid.

When a person loses everything their attitude to money can go somewhat awry. At one extreme are those who become avaricious or miserly. Who rebuild their fortune, penny by penny. These people live like paupers on the interest of their savings. They are jealous of others. They ride mopeds to protect their cars from wear and tear. They would rather pull out their own teeth than pay dental fees. At the other, facing the misers and shaking their heads in disbelief, are those who care little for money and even less for status symbols. This group are risk-takers, battlers, they want desperately to win but are not afraid to lose in the process. When they have money they spend it, waste it, give it away. When it is in short supply they live by their wits. They know money can cause untold strife but never buys true happiness.

I stare wistfully out of the window, feeling like a caged animal. The dark-haired woman two floors up rests her elbows on the window ledge and her chin in her hands. Perhaps, like me, she is restless and longs to be somewhere warm and sunny. The seedy world beyond my window looks uninviting at this time of night. Last week a woman was attacked and left for dead in an alley two streets away. Adam has too close a link with such grim realities. Scary headlines stick to him at work, like fluff on a black jacket, and rub off on me when he gets home. 'Jogger Attacked On Common' . . . 'Gun Terror At Filling Station' . . . 'Gang Killing On High Street'.

'You've really stuck to your guns this time. Well done.' Adam sits in an armchair, watching me suck on a rolled-up bus ticket. 'How long now without a cigarette?'

'A few weeks,' I mumble. My system hungers for nicotine but the health of the growing baby overrides my craving. 'I've missed smoking. It calms me down, helps me to relax.'

'I'm very proud of you. I never thought you'd do it. Welcome to the abstinence club.'

I spit out the damp roll of paper. 'I will never be like you, Adam. A member of the clean-living, calorie-counting, buttock-clenching fraternity, an advocate of moderation and smelly tea.'

'I wasn't always the anal man you see before you, Electra. Surely you remember? I used to be quite . . . hip . . . cool . . . sought-after. I lived dangerously.'

'I remember you propping up the bar every night.'

'That's only because you worked behind it.'

'You drank like a fish.'

'God, I miss those days. And I especially miss having hair.'

'You still have hair!'

He rubs the top of his head. 'It feels more like a blanket of moss these days.'

'I'll still love you when you're bald and skeletal.'

'And I will love you when you're plump and round and as pitted as an orange.'

'Thank you, my love.'

'Ditto.' He blows me a kiss.

I sip decaffeinated coffee, black and sweet, irritated by the thought that it won't perk me up. 'I'm feeling really homesick at the moment. I miss the family. The other night, while you were sleeping, I kept thinking about them, worrying that Papa would have another heart attack and I would never see him again. My heart started racing. I couldn't breathe. I thought I was going to die.'

'You had a panic attack.'

'My parents are not getting any younger. I need to see them more than once or twice a year.'

'Then book a ticket to Cyprus. Go and see them.'

'How can I? Have you forgotten your mother's coming to stay in a few days.'

'Thanks for reminding me! Come on, let's go out for a walk, to take your mind off things.'

'No. It's too cold and dark.'

I used to love being out at night when I lived in Cyprus. Sunset on the island brings a welcome change of tempo. The population wakes up from its siesta and engages in eating, drinking and *gamaki* – flirtation. In my hometown I walked without fear, along poorly lit streets, from my parents' flat to the bars and cafés and palm trees lining the promenade. Breathing in the scent of salty air, striding to the rhythmic hum of cicadas. Cursing the mothers of the men who crawled the kerb in souped up cars, to gawp. Feeling no intimidation from the would-be gigolos, the *gamakia*, who walked behind me (and every other woman) seeking attention with calls of 'psst, psst' as if I were a cat.

I pull a tissue out of my sleeve and blow my nose. 'I can feel a cold coming on. I'm all bunged up and my head's ringing like a church bell.'

'You'll be fine.'

'That's what they said to my godfather and now he's six feet under. A common cold, his doctor said. The poor man had influenza.'

'Why don't you come to bed?' Adam gets up, heads for the door.

'I will. As soon as I've finished my coffee.'

Loneliness enters the room when Adam leaves. I stare across at the shabby apartment block. A neighbour paces before a lighted first-floor window. His hair is shoulder length, wavy, mostly grey. His eyes shadowed and intense. He holds a mug in one hand and a ream of white papers in the other, drinking and reading while the world around us sleeps. He sees me staring and raises his mug in salute before disappearing into the room beyond. I have had my eye on this man for a while, spied on his movements and seen nothing untoward. Wondered whether he would make a suitable date for a friend who has given up on love. A friend who turns heads when she walks down the street and wouldn't know a sexual advance if it bit her on the nose. Lydia has turned her pretty face to the wall and given up on men.

The regular hum of Adam's gentle snore, as faint as the flutter of a dragonfly, has not yet begun. Rattling, rasping, hissing like an angry cat, frothing at the mouth like a spittlebug, are my bedtime specialities. I am a disruptive bed partner. Laughing, babbling, lashing out in bed, I lead a second life in my sleep. All my frustrations and fears come to the fore. In my dreams I am always battling or running, escaping from some evil force. I am a restless soul, hailing from a troubled race, from an island blighted by war, occupation, and more recently a stock market crash. We all bought shares during the short-lived boom, without anticipating the bust. We spent our savings, pensions, borrowed money, re-mortgaged our properties. Grocers, fishermen and garbage collectors, even 'lame Maria' as we say in Cyprus, bought shares. We talked of nothing but capital gains and dividends, exchanged far-fetched stories of paupers who became millionaires. If we happened to make a million, it was not enough – oh, no – we wanted two, three, a billion at least. We ridiculed those too cowardly to invest and believed in the fallacy that money could be made easily.

On our half-island where casinos are banned and gambling is in the blood, dabbling in the stock market became as common as purchasing a scratch card. Our menfolk met with their stockbrokers every morning to smoke cigars and drink Greek coffee. To buy, buy, buy and sell, sell, sell. Cigar sales rocketed as shares began their downward spiral. The banks encouraged us to buy by making borrowing easier and announcing optimistic market forecasts. They washed their hands of responsibility and turned to litigation when the free-for-all turned into a freefall. When shares plummeted and fortunes were lost. The 'cowards' had the last laugh.

Those in the know, the 'big market players', pocketed their gains early on. The grocer, the fisherman and the garbage collector watched their savings dwindle. As did Papa, who was advised by a friendly stockbroker to buy shares in an insurance company. 'Do it for your grandchildren, *koumbare*,' he said, 'you will set them up for life.' Against his better judgement and without his wife's knowledge, Papa invested the few savings he had in fool's gold. Nine months later his shares were worth half their original value. 'Don't sell your shares. The experts say the downturn is temporary,' he was advised. The experts were wrong. 'Eh, that's life *koumbare*, some you win, some you lose,' the broker said, making a quick exit from my father's life in his Porsche cabriolet.

Papa was well acquainted with financial ruin and should have known better. In 1974 the war took his home, his land and his livelihood. He had been young enough and strong enough back then to recoup his losses. A quarter of a century later, back at square one with no hope of making headway, Papa sank into depression. The thought of driving his car off a cliff edge into the sea offered some relief from the guilt that gnawed at his insides. At least then his family would benefit from his life insurance policy. On a warm spring morning, as the sun coaxed wild tulips and myrtle blossom into life, Papa felt a crushing pain in his chest, radiating through his arm and neck. He collapsed on the front step of his shop and was bundled into the back of a passing builder's truck, for a bumpy drive to hospital. He regained consciousness in a hospital bed with his wife and four children standing over him. He closed his eyes when he saw us and said he wished he had died. We asked him why. '*Yiati, Papa?*' 'I have lost our savings. Everything your mama and I worked to create has gone,' he replied. Mama shook her head deridingly and said: 'Open your eyes, you silly man, and look around you. These children are our creation. Now hurry up and get better, there is work to be done.'

Adam

The bedroom is dark, illuminated by a band of light at the foot of the door and the glaring pink digits of the alarm clock. I toss and turn before cocooning myself inside the quilt to count sheep. Some leap effortlessly over the fence in my mind's eye, others stumble and trip. A heavy-set sheep makes its way to the fence, holding up the queue. A scuffle ensues when a lamb pushes its way to the front, and the mental image that should relax me descends into chaos. I abandon sheep-counting and give free rein to my thoughts. I think about Mum and her broken leg, about Electra and her desperate need to have a child, about Dad and the awful secret I have kept from my wife.

I force myself out of bed and go in search of Electra, hoping she will relax me. I find her in the kitchen, standing beside a kettle blowing steam. She looks surprised to see me.

'Can't you sleep?'

I shake my head.

'Is something wrong?'

'My head's spinning. I keep thinking about Dad and what happened to him.'

Electra pours boiling water into a mug, drops in a herbal teabag and hands me the drink.

'I thought I was over that trauma. I thought I'd managed to put it all behind me.'

'Has something happened to make you feel so anxious?'

'I'll be forty soon. Dad wasn't much older than me when he started getting sick. What if the same thing were to happen to me?'

'There's no reason why it should. Your father had Alzheimer's. He was unlucky.'

'I know that but . . . I just feel . . . confused.'

'You have nothing to be confused about. Everything in our lives is as it should be. We're healthy. We're both working. We have a roof over our heads. We love one another. What more do you want?'

'Nothing. I want everything to stay just as it is.'

'It will,' she says, spooning decaffeinated coffee into a mug.

'I'm impressed, Electra.'

'By what?'

'First you give up nicotine and then caffeine. What's going on?'

She throws me a hostile glance. 'I'm taking more care of myself, Adam, that's all.'

'Why did you look at me like that? What's wrong? What did I say?'

'Nothing.' She shakes her head and turns away.

* * *

Electra is splayed on the sofa, the television summarising bad news from the day before. I switch it off and cover my wife with the sofa throw. She is difficult to wake once sleep finally conquers her, like a rhino laid low by a tranquilliser dart.

Sleeping when and where the mood takes her is one of Electra's many bad habits. When we first met I tried to retune my body clock to her erratic sleeping patterns. Staying up until the early hours of the morning, drinking coffee, fighting sleep. Listening with anticipation to the earliest birds begin their call, a precursor to sunrise. Watching the sky's gradual shift from black to charcoal, through several shades of blue. Waiting for the grey veil to lift and give way to vivid colour. I felt wide-eyed at sunrise but lethargy dogged me the rest of the day. Late nights and early mornings soon took their toll. Deprived of sleep, my mood swung from animated to languorous. One day I fell asleep at my desk, chin pressing down on my computer keyboard. Three pages of YYYYY later, I was woken up by a tap on the shoulder and the disgruntled face of my editor. 'Y, Y, Y indeed are you falling asleep at work?' he said. 'This is a newsroom, not a snooze-room. Liven up or I'll be looking for another sub.'

It would be kinder to let her sleep but I need to wake her. To say goodbye before I go to work. To leave without planting a kiss on Electra's lips would leave me feeling bereft and set my day off course. I am a creature of habit and cherish such small comforts. Worryingly, my behaviour is becoming increasingly ritualistic.

'Electra . . . Electra.'

She waves her hand in the air as if shooing away a fly.

I nudge her awake. She stretches out indolently and looks up at me with eyes as dark as Kalamata olives.

'Oh, Adam. I didn't sleep a wink last night.' This is Electra's daily mantra. An untrue statement she has come to believe.

'You've been snoring for ages. I could hear you from the kitchen.'

'I think your ears were ringing, my love.'

'And you were shouting in your sleep. "*Pastichi, pastichi.*" What's *pastichi*?'

'It's a Greek macaroon. Given to guests at a wedding. I went to bed on an empty stomach last night. It's no wonder I was talking about food in my sleep.'

'You polished off half a roast chicken last night.'

'That bird was the size of a pigeon and I was up 'til four o'clock this morning working it off. I may well have been snoring this morning but, I can assure you, I was not relaxing. I had a very bad dream. I spent the whole night being chased.'

'By what? A Greek macaroon?'

'Ha, ha. Very funny. No, your greedy wife was not dreaming about macaroons. She was being chased by a hooded man, riding a camel. I was running through a desert. Sweat was dripping from my body. My bare feet were sinking into burning sand. I needed water but all I could see for miles around were sand dunes, golden-brown like sugar syrup. This hooded man . . .'

Electra's account of her nightmare washes over me. I focus on her gestures and her effervescence. On the childlike widening of her eyes; on a mouth that pouts and grimaces; on gesticulating hands that emphasise the drama of her desert escapade. Electra's dreams are long, convoluted and recalled in great detail. Her Technicolor epics feature wars and famines, car chases, lavish balls, death and disaster. She refuses to admit that her nightmares stem from the movies she falls asleep watching.

'Is this going to take long? I have to get to work.'

'Wait! The best bit is still to come. I dropped through a hole in the sand and found myself in the sea, struggling to keep my head above water. I started sinking like a stone, water rushing in through my mouth and nose. Just when I thought I was going to drown a dolphin appeared out of nowhere and carried me back up to the surface. I wonder what it all means?'

'It means you have an overactive imagination and should stop watching late-night movies. Or else you should give up jewellery design and write a film script.'

I head for the door.

'*Adamos mou.*' 'My Adam' she calls me, in that sweet voice that is always a precursor to an unreasonable request. 'You haven't forgotten, my love, that you are looking after our godson tomorrow? I'm going shopping with Lydia.'

'Do I have to?'

'Yes.'

'How long for?'

'No more than a couple of hours.'

'But I've never looked after Alvaro on my own before.'

'Then it's time you did.' Sweetness gives way to irritation. Electra is not a woman given to begging.

'But . . .'

'No buts! In our culture a godfather is one step down

from a real father. And as Alvaro's real father is not around, you have a greater responsibility.' She points to the clock on the bedside table. 'Any more talking and you're going to be late for work.'

He arrives clad in a white tasselled costume and out-landish sunglasses, *Elvis Presley Unseen Archives* carried under his arm. Electra quickly bundles Lydia out of the door, denying me the chance to ask: 'What do I do with him?' 'When are you coming back?' 'Does he need feeding?' He stands in the hallway looking up at me, his eyes partially obscured behind dark lenses, waiting for me to use my adult initiative.

'How about a DVD?' I take the easy option.

'OK, Adam.'

I select the longest running animated film I can find and insert it into the player. He sits on the sofa, takes off his glasses and waits. I press play and head for the door.

'I'll be in the kitchen if you need me.'

I sit at the kitchen table, drinking green tea. Flicking through a music magazine, listening to Radio Three, not unhappy after all to be boy-sitting, humming along to 'Gymnopédie No. 1'. Twenty minutes pass without incident. I get up and make my way to the loo on tiptoe, anxious not to draw attention to myself. The moment I start relieving myself I hear a scream and see Alvaro standing beside me, looking shocked.

'What? What's wrong?'

'Ugh, Adam! Your willy nest is hairy.'

I bundle my genitalia back into my underpants, cursing myself for having left the door unlocked.

'Alvaro, please let me pee in private.'

His gaze remains firmly fixed on my crotch.

'Why is your willy nest hairy?'

'All men have hair down there.' I put my hands in my pockets, feeling awkward. He mimics my stance, putting his hands in the pockets of his jumpsuit.

'Did Elvis have a hairy willy nest?'

'Yes. And you will have one day. Now, please leave. I'm really desperate.'

'So am I. Undo my suit, please.'

Gingerly, I tug at the Velcro strip running the length of his back and watch the polyester suit slide to the floor. He pulls down his red underpants, arches his back and splashes urine all over the seat as if marking his territory. I look away, feeling uncomfortable, wondering what Alvaro is likely to say to his mother when she returns. I head back to the kitchen and my magazine, trying to forget about the tightness in my abdomen. Alvaro walks into the kitchen and stands beside me.

'Why don't you go and watch the film?'

'It's boring. I've seen it before.'

'Do you want to draw?'

'Boring. I want to play.'

'Play what?' I ask, dreading his reply, unwilling to exert myself on a Saturday morning.

'Aliens. I'll be an alien invading earth and you have to try and shoot me dead, with this gun.' He grabs a banana from the fruit bowl and hands it to me.

'I don't like guns.'

'I love them. You be the alien then. I'll shoot you dead.'

'What do I have to do?'

'Run away and try to hide. I'll chase you.'

I hand back the banana and get up, running in slow motion towards the kitchen door. He stabs me in the buttock with his gun.

'You have to run faster than that.'

I run through the hall, in and around the living room, dodging banana bullets, getting poked and jabbed, Alvaro threatening to blow me to smithereens. I jump behind the sofa, crawl on all fours into the bedroom and lock myself in the wardrobe. Alvaro bangs on the door, demanding I come out and surrender. I open the door and walk out with my arms held high, hoping capitulation will draw this game to an end.

'Alien invader, you will die,' he screams, head butting me in the stomach, sending me toppling backwards into the open wardrobe, standing over my crumpled body, hands on hips.

'I win,' he says. 'What shall we do now?'

'Something less strenuous?'

'Can we make a guitar?'

I untangle myself and stand up. 'I've never made a guitar before.'

'It's easy. Granny makes them all the time.'

'What do you need to make a guitar?'

'Cardboard and silver foil.'

'We don't have either of those materials in the house. Sorry. We'll have to do something else.' I have no artistic flair, no drawing ability, no desire to turn a cereal box into a Stratocaster. The boy doesn't listen, but wanders off into the kitchen opening cupboards and drawers.

'Alvaro, there isn't time to make a guitar. Your mother will be here soon.'

'What's this?' He holds up a Cornflakes box.

'That's full of Cornflakes. We can't use that.'

'The Cornflakes are in a bag. You can take them out. Granny does.'

He pulls out the waxed bag and hands it to me before continuing his search for silver foil, sending me off to find sticky tape, glue, string and felt-tip pens. When all the materials have been gathered we sit side by side at the kitchen table, constructing a silver guitar. While Alvaro cuts out and colours in a plectrum, I am told to attach strings to the instrument. When I hand him the finished guitar, he gives me a contemptuous look and hands it straight back.

'That's no good,' he says.

'Why not?'

'It only has five strings.'

'There's no more string in the house. Perhaps we could cut one in half.'

'That would look stupid.'

My patience wears thin. 'Alvaro! I'm sure your mother doesn't like you using words like that.' It is time to assert my authority, to put my foot down, to show this boy who is boss. 'There's no more string. You'll have to make do with five strings on your guitar.'

The boy grabs the guitar and flings it on the floor. 'It's a stupid guitar. I hate it.'

'Alvaro, you're being very naughty.'

'And you're being an idiot.'

He rushes out of the kitchen, kicking the door frame, slamming the door, locking himself in the bathroom, volubly declaring his hatred of the guitar. I am out of my depth. Angry with him. Afraid he might do himself harm with my disposable razor. A blood-curdling vision of Alvaro slashing himself flashes through my mind.

'Alvaro, come out!'

'Go away. Leave me alone.'

'Come out now . . . or else.'

'Or else what?'

'I'll break down the door and drag you out of there.'

He perceives my warning as a physical threat and starts screaming.

'Adam's gonna kill me! Adam's gonna kill me! Where's my mum? I want my mum.'

I breathe deeply, trying to calm myself, my fears about the razor intensifying, vowing never to boy oit ever again. I look down at my feet, wondering what to do and where I might find string? The answer is staring me in the face.

'I've found some string, Alvaro. Come out, please. I'm sorry I shouted.'

I untie my shoelace, pull it through the eyeholes and push it under the door. He stops screaming. I hear the hesitant pad of his footsteps moving closer to the door.

'I need a shoulder strap as well.'

'I have another piece of string, exactly the same length. Now come out. Please.'

I untie my other shoe and pull out the lace. Alvaro opens the door, looking tearful. He follows me into the kitchen, my feet slipping out of my shoes, and together we finish the guitar.

'This is the best guitar ever,' he says, hanging it from his shoulders.

'Shall we listen to some Elvis?'

'Yeah. Cool,' he says, offering me his palm to slap.

In the living room the boy turns to page thirty-two of *Unseen Archives* and copies the Elvis pose, arms outstretched, legs open, head to one side. I switch off the film and put on an Elvis CD. Alvaro requests 'Hound Dog' and is jolted into life, as if by an electric current, when the music starts. His singing voice is flat and unmelodic but his moves are remarkable, a joy to watch, the boy is a born entertainer. He bears a startling resemblance to Elvis in his prime. The music takes me back to the attic room where I listened to father's LPs, where my love of music began, where I danced alone to 'All Shook Up' and 'Blue Suede Shoes' and 'King Creole', where I pored over record sleeves, absorbed by the glamorous image of the good-looking man with slicked-back hair and sideburns. He captivated me thirty years ago as he captivates the boy today, with his talent and his looks and his animal magnetism, Elvis is the man every boy wants to be. Time passes unnoticed. The boy dances. I watch and remember my own childhood.

Electra comes bounding into the living room, clicking her fingers and swinging her hips as the boy sings 'Blue Suede Shoes'. She grabs me by the hands, pulls me off the sofa and we dance together. Lydia reaches for Alvaro and the four of us twirl and bop and kick out our legs, before exchanging partners. I twirl the boy round and around, enjoying the sound of his infectious laughter. When the music ends he weaves dizzily across the room and collapses on the floor beside Electra.

'So, was my son well-behaved, Adam?' Lydia asks.

'He was no trouble at all.'

'I was bad,' the boy says. 'I called Adam an idiot.'

Lydia blushes. 'Alvaro! How could you? Adam, I'm really sorry.'

Electra pulls the boy towards her and kisses the top of his head. 'Why did you do that?'

'Don't ask why, Electra,' Lydia protests. 'He shouldn't have said it under any circumstances.'

'But, Mum, Adam made a guitar with five strings.'

Lydia shakes her head. 'Say sorry to Adam.'

The boy crawls on all fours towards me and puts his arms around my neck. 'Sorry, Adam.'

His small body is ductile and yielding. He looks at me with doleful brown eyes, his face so close to mine I can feel his warm breath on my cheek. I squeeze him in my arms and tell him not to worry.

Electra

Bubbles fizzle on the surface of the *avgolemoni* soup. I take the pan off the heat to stop the egg from curdling and spoon out a ladleful to sip. The creamy egg and lemon soup is a panacea, a cure for physical ailments, broken hearts and fractured bones. I swallow a mouthful of plump, short-grained rice and am reminded of a far-off place where life was carefree and pleasures simple. Of a kitchen outhouse that oozed mouth-watering food smells. Of a grandmother who visited her chicken coop early in the morning to select the biggest bird for her pot. Who wrung its neck without flinching, as easily as you might snap the end off a string bean. Whose decapitated ingredient sometimes made a final hopeless dash for freedom, circling the back yard at breakneck speed, before its last unceremonious slump to the ground. When Elpida made *avgolemoni* she boiled her chicken until the flesh slid off the bones. She added rice instinctively to the chicken broth and squeezed in lemon juice through her fingers, using her hand as a sieve. My soup, though a poor relation, is a sensory connection with the past, a continuation of tradition, a comforting reminder of a woman whose culinary legacy lives on.

I throw away the eggshells and wipe down the worktop with a wet cloth. Adam's key turns in the lock, startling me. He has arrived with his mother earlier than expected. I was planning to change out of my tracksuit into something more mother-in-law friendly. My morning was spent dusting and polishing, my Ecocloth whirling over surfaces like a dervish. Hopefully Margaret will overlook my failure to dress for the occasion of her extended visit. I stifle the urge to dash across the hallway and lock myself in the bathroom, entering as pupa, emerging as moth.

Adam walks into the house backwards, hauling a wheelchair up the front step. Once inside, he twists the chair round and wheels Margaret down the hallway to our flat. I hold the door open for him. My mother-in-law looks small and childlike in the bulky hospital chair, her slim shoulders slumped. I am surprised by the tender feelings I have for this woman who has never shown me any tenderness, by my readiness to wipe the slate clean. Familiarity has bred in me irrepressible feelings of affection for Margaret. Allowances must be made for her quirks and shortcomings. She has suffered more than most. She spent years caring for a sick husband and was widowed in her prime.

'Hello, dear.' Her greeting is borne on a heavy exhalation.

'Margaret, welcome to your new home.'

She tries to lift herself out of the wheelchair,

pushing down on the armrests. 'I want to get out of this thing.'

'Just a minute, Mum. I'll fetch your crutches.'

Adam hurries out of the door, returning a few minutes later with the crutches and a bulky suitcase. He lifts Margaret out of the chair and props her up.

'Where shall I put Mum's suitcase?'

'In our bedroom.'

'I could do with a lie down,' Margaret says, 'this plaster is impossibly heavy.'

She inches her way towards the bedroom, hopping on her good foot, her plastered leg dangling.

'Adam, can you help me, please?' Margaret's needy tone spurs him into action. He carries his mother's suitcase into the bedroom, helps her lie down, lifts her legs up on to the mattress and takes off her shoe. A look of discomfort distorts Margaret's features. 'I'll never be able to sleep on this bed. It's far too soft.'

'I'll put a wooden board underneath the mattress, if you like.'

'Where will you two be sleeping?'

'On the sofa bed in the living room.'

'Why don't I sleep on the sofa bed?'

'Because it's very lumpy and uncomfortable, and Electra thought you would be more comfortable in our bedroom.'

'I can't imagine feeling comfortable anywhere with this thing on my leg.'

'A bowl of soup might cheer you up,' I say, hoping the *avgolemoni* will lighten Margaret's mood.

'I hardly ate a thing in hospital. The food was horrendous.'

96

'You sit up, Mum, and I'll fetch you a bowl of Electra's lovely soup.'

Adam leaves the room. I unpack Margaret's suitcase, storing her underwear and nightdresses in the chest of drawers beside the bed, hanging her shirts and skirts in the wardrobe.

'I wrote Adam a list of all the things I wanted from the house. I hope he found everything.' Margaret rears up to a sitting position. 'I have a present for you, dear. It's in that black plastic bag you're holding.'

Margaret's unexpected gift is a pleasant surprise. Is it a sign that she is ready to bury her hatchet? A long-awaited white flag? My optimism is short-lived. Inside the bag is a large navy blue cardigan with a white-embroidered collar and gold buttons.

'It's lovely,' slips disingenuously from my mouth. 'Thank you.'

'Try it on. Let's see if it fits.'

If my own mother had presented me with such offensive knitwear I would have handed it back and questioned the state of her sanity. Now I pull the cardigan on over my tracksuit top.

'It's very elegant, dear. Very flattering.'

I feel as elegant as a Kurdish refugee and anxious to store the offending item in the back of my wardrobe, never to be seen again. I pull it slowly off my shoulders, not wanting to appear ungrateful.

'Why don't you keep it on, dear? Show it to Adam.'

'Yes, I will.'

Margaret lies back down on the bed, staring up at the ceiling. 'It's a beautiful cardigan. I bought it for myself just before I broke my leg. But it's far too big

97

for me and I won't be able to take it back while this thing is on my leg. You might as well have it. You probably need it more than I do.'

So her gift is not a conciliatory gesture but an attempt to undermine me, a comment on my size. Where once Margaret's snide comments rebounded like raindrops off an armadillo's back, now they puncture and hurt. I curse the tears that prick the corners of my eyes, the reproductive hormones that have made me hypersensitive to criticism. Pull yourself together, Electra, I tell myself, as I leave the bedroom and head for the kitchen.

Adam looks me up and down, his brow furrowing. 'What an earth have you got on, Electra! It looks like something Mum would wear.'

'It's a present from your mother.'

'Then be grateful she doesn't buy you presents very often. Take it off, Electra. Give it back to her. You look like lamb dressed as mutton.'

'I don't want to hurt her feelings. I'll take it off later.'

He puts his arm around my shoulder and looks into my eyes. 'I'm sorry about all of this.'

'All of what?'

'Lumbering you with Mum.'

'Don't say it like that. We'll be fine.'

'I hope you're right, Electra. But I have a terrible feeling in my bones . . .'

'Do you like the soup, Mum?' Adam smiles hopefully, knowing Margaret has never been fond of my cooking.

'It's very tasty.'

Hallelujah! First a gift and then a compliment.

'How did you make it, dear?'

'I boiled up a chicken to make a broth, then added rice, lemon juice and eggs.'

'Did you take the skin off the chicken before boiling it?' Margaret asks.

'No. The soup tastes better if you leave the skin on.'

'And how many eggs did you use?'

'Six.'

'Six!' Margaret puckers up her lips in disgust. She stops eating and hands Adam the bowl. 'I can't eat that soup. It's riddled with cholesterol.'

Her phraseology is more suited to a thing damaged by insect larvae or invaded by fungus than a bowl of chicken soup. In my hypersensitive, progesterone-riddled state Margaret's rejection of my *avgolemoni* is infuriating, a slight against my grandmother's memory.

'I don't think you need worry about cholesterol, Mum. You need to think about building up your strength.'

'Cholesterol is a killer, Adam.'

He glares at his mother and shakes his head. 'The soup's delicious. If you're not going to eat it, then I will.'

A candle flickers on the mantelpiece. Adam sips from a glass of red wine. I lie on the sofa bed beside him, wondering how and when to tell him about the baby. The sash window rattles. A cool breeze seeps through the warped frames, stroking my bare legs, lightly fingering my arms, pleasantly chilling my cheeks.

Adam puts down his glass and pulls the quilt right

up to his chin. 'It's freezing in here. We need to get those windows insulated and bleed the radiators.'

'Do you know, my grandmother used to live in a mud-brick house heated by an ox.'

'How do you mean?'

'Her house was half-stable. She grew up in a stone cottage with no electricity, divided into two by bales of hay. In winter she and her family slept on one side of the house, and a donkey, a goat and an ox slept on the other.'

For Elpida, living with livestock was as natural as cohabiting with a dog or a cat; more natural in many ways since the relationship was symbiotic. In return for food and shelter the goat provided milk, the donkey transport, and the venerated ox pulled the plough. On cold winter nights the animals were the only source of heat, raising the temperature and keeping the family warm. The presence of the ox, its bulk, its strength, its blessed breath, was a comfort to Elpida as she slept beside her siblings on a row of wooden boards. Its smell was no more offensive than the aroma of wet earth on a rainy night or the sweet scent of wild thyme burning in the grate.

'How would your mother feel, knowing her in-laws were born in a stable?'

'My grandmother raised six children in a two-bedroomed cottage. Dad's origins were pretty humble.'

'Is your grandmother still alive?'

'I doubt it. I don't know, to be honest. Mum fell out with Dad's family years ago and we lost contact.'

'Aren't you curious to know if your grandmother's still alive?'

'Yes, I am. I've thought about her a lot over the years. We were very close once. She was a wonderful woman, very kind and loving. I should have tried to make contact years ago. Now . . . it's probably too late.' Adam flicks up a corner of the quilt. 'Come in and warm me up.'

I slip beneath the covers and run my hand along an expanse of tartan.

'Take your pyjamas off.'

'With Mum in the next room?'

'Can she see through walls? Are you planning to abstain from sex for the next three months?'

'No. But I'll just go and check she's asleep first.' Adam swings his legs out of bed and gets up. 'I won't be a minute.'

'I may have changed my mind by the time you get back.'

He hurries out of the room and returns a minute later reassured that Margaret is fast asleep. He pulls off his pyjamas and lies down beside me. I stroke his smooth chest and take off my T-shirt to feel his soft skin against mine. He pulls me close and kisses me with his wine-flavoured mouth. Anxieties about my changing shape melt away. I bite into his neck as if he wore a sweet semolina cake. Nibble ear lobes like candied cherries. Run my hand down his rib cage and sink my nails into his back. He climbs on top of me and, overcome with desire, I claw his buttocks.

All of a sudden, he pushes me to one side and sits up, looking around wide-eyed. 'What's that banging noise?'

'The pounding of my heart. Lie down. Don't stop.'

'No, someone's banging. Maybe it's Mum. Perhaps she can hear us.'

'We haven't made any noise yet.'

'No, but the bed springs have.'

'Let's do it on the floor then. Right now. I'm on fire, Adam.'

A dull and rhythmic thudding reverberates around the room.

'It's definitely coming from Mum's room. I think she's banging on the wall.' Adam jumps out of bed and puts on his pyjamas. 'I'll be back in a jiffy.'

I lie on the bed listening to a murmur of voices from the bedroom. To the hurried pitter-patter of Adam's feet along the wooden floor. To the boiling of a kettle and the making of tea, to the clink of a china cup and saucer being carried along the hallway. My carnal hunger subsides and my eyelids grow heavy.

'Electra . . . Electra!' Adam gently nudges me awake. 'I'm sorry to wake you but Mum needs the toilet. Do you mind taking her?'

'No. Of course not.'

'And I'll clear a space on the floor by the time you get back, OK?'

'Don't bother. After taking your mother to the toilet I can't imagine feeling very sexy. And she might hear us and start banging the wall again.'

'You're right,' he says, disappointingly, giving up too easily.

Lydia

The day had dragged by lazily. Selling a king-sized bed and a wardrobe had earned Lydia commission which would pay for Alvaro's new school shoes. She had been sucked into furniture sales like lunar matter into a black hole. Sucked in and held fast, hoping a wormhole would materialise and lead her to another universe. She had recently been promoted to lighting manager. An accolade that brought with it the unenviable duties of constantly changing spent bulbs and replenishing stocks. Knowing the difference between task, accent and general. Lydia perambulated the first floor of a department store stocked with bedroom, living-room and bathroom furnishings, with a dispiriting maze of consumer durables.

She was a veritable Cinderella, standing at the counter, waiting for something magical to happen, for life to take on a brighter hue, waiting for that eureka moment when her mission on earth became crystal clear. She had already met her prince but a kiss had turned him into a frog and he had hopped away, never to be seen again. Lydia longed for a life change, to leave her job and live on some idyllic Mediterranean island where Alvaro could run about in his red underpants terrorising lizards and she could spend the day in a kaftan, strumming away on the guitar she would learn to play. These waking dreams were always marred by Consuelo's guest appearance. While Lydia stood on a marble veranda and watched a burning sun set over a panoramic expanse of beach, Consuelo would appear, clad in her chequered apron, brandishing a spatula. 'Lythia,' she would shout, 'you seen the remo contrrrol?'

Consuelo's voice jolted her back to a reality where there were bills to pay and a son to support and a job to go to. The black hole had become a comforting burrow, the better of two ills. Better certainty than uncertainty. She had once thrown caution to the wind and followed her heart, only to have it kicked and trampled like an inflated bladder in a primitive game of football.

Lydia turned her key in the lock and pushed open the front door. Thick salmon-coloured shag pile, flock wallpaper and a darkwood dado ran the length of her mother's narrow hallway. The dusky hall, with its light-absorbing hues, was no reflection of the rest of the house. Inconsistency and overstatement characterised Consuelo's abode. Her bedroom was bright yellow, her bedding all the colours of the rainbow. The dining room, furnished in red, grey and black, was a celebration of 1980s bad taste. Stencilled pigs, cows and chickens leaped and cavorted on the kitchen walls. The house was a testament to Consuelo's passion for DIY and her insistence that her husband (a painter and decorator by profession) bring his work home.

'*Que Cabron. El Bastardo. Hijo De Puta!*' A barrage of Spanish curses, terminating in 'son of a bitch', welcomed Lydia home. She found Consuelo in the living room arguing with the credits of the South American soap opera *Esmeralda*, shouting over the upbeat strains of Spanish guitar, standing amid a sea of marble, melamine and gilt.

'Mum, what's wrong?'

Consuelo brandished the remote as if it were a gun and angrily shot the television shut.

'*El bastardo!* He leff his wife and hiss chile.'

'Who?'

Consuelo shook her head and puckered her lips. 'Tha good for nathin' playboy Juan-Carlos.'

'Don't get so emotional. It's not real-life, Mum.'

'No!'

In Consuelo's mind the storyline of her favourite South American soap opera, accessed via satellite, was a glitzier rewrite of her own daughter's experience.

'Tha poor Maria, stragglin to raise her chile all alon. *El bastardo!*'

Alvaro pushed open the living-room door.

'Mum, watch your language.'

'Hiss only a chile. He dasen anderstan.'

Alvaro walked into the room wearing brand-new football strip, complete with shin pads, a red sweatband and silver football boots. A gold medallion hung from his neck, suggesting Elvis was never far from his thoughts.

'Hi, son. Did Granny take you shopping again?'

'He tol me all the boys at school they gorra football kit. I say, "Alvaro, if all the boys they gorra kit then you gonna have a kit." My grandson hiss no a second-class cirrizon.'

'Alvaro, you've never been interested in football.'

His interest in any sport had always been short-lived.

'I am now. I support Manchester United,' he said, turning round to display V. Nistelrooy emblazoned on his back.

'Why Manchester United? Why not a team closer to home?'

'Because Jack supports them and they wear red.'

Pillar-box red was Alvaro's favourite colour.

'Mum,' he said, 'can we go and play football in the park?'

'Do we have to? I'm exhausted.'

'Please.'

Alvaro flashed his big brown eyes and Lydia could not refuse him.

'I'll go and change.'

Her heart sank like a silicone implant thrown into sinking sand. The thought of playing football in the park, in full public view, filled her with a creeping sense of dread. Lydia was slight of build and abhorred strenuous physical activity. She ran under duress, rarely exercised and had never sat through a match or game of any kind. To aid her son's healthy development, however, she had been forced to tackle a disparate variety of sports from ice-skating to go-kart racing. Becoming a human punch bag when Alvaro developed a fleeting interest in boxing. A kick bag when Karate Kid inspired him to try his hand at martial arts.

Lydia changed into an androgynous green tracksuit, in an attempt to blend in with park vegetation, while Alvaro played football in the hallway with his grandmother. Consuelo was exceptionally agile for a woman in her late-sixties. She stopped the ball with her small foot and kicked it forcefully to her grandson. She jumped to catch a volley and headed it back to Alvaro, long strands of white hair escaping her tight bun and writhing like grass snakes. 'I could have been a gymnast,' Consuelo often lamented, 'if my parents had encouraged me. If they had had the means to support my talent.' On the mantelpiece was a picture of the young Consuelo, standing on her hands, her pigtails hanging limply down like rope. She was determined to encourage and support any interest her grandson developed, spiritually and financially, to live through him the dream she was denied. Hence the purchase of football strip, a tennis racquet before that, and a body board for when or if Alvaro decided to hit the surf.

He followed his mother out of the house, waving goodbye to Consuelo who stood at the window, looking troubled and anxious. Lydia felt her mother's pity follow her out of the door and along the stone path like liquid mercury, lapping at her heels, propelling its vapour into the car. Consuelo thought a woman was only half a person without a man, that Alvaro was only quasi-boy without a father. When her husband died Consuelo had wanted to follow him into the grave, to give up on life. It was not until Lydia lost her own husband, in less tragic circumstances, that her mother decided she had no choice but to live, for the sake of her grandson. Consuelo had enjoyed a long and happy marriage with her first love, a quiet, henpecked, beloved man. She'd celebrated her Ruby Wedding Anniversary a week before her husband died of a stroke.

Lydia knelt in goal, her tracksuit top and an empty drinks can makeshift posts. Alvaro flattened a clod of earth with his foot and put down the ball. He took ten steps back, ran forward and kicked the ball wide.

'Bad luck. Try again.'

'The goal's too small,' he said with a moody pout, commanding his mother to move the tin can and make the goalmouth bigger. He dropped the heavy leather ball a metre in front of the goal and kicked it hard. It rebounded off Lydia's shoulder.

'Save!' she cried, attempting a cartwheel, managing half a handstand that failed to impress her son. Alvaro angrily folded his arms across his chest.

'That doesn't count. I was just practising.'

'Move the ball back further next time. You were too close. That hurt.' Lydia rubbed her shoulder.

'Van Nistelrooy to take the next penalty,' Alvaro said, commentator-style, before setting down his ball, taking a few steps back and sprinting in an arc to kick. Lydia dived to her left, dropping onto moist earth like a sack of potatoes, inadvertently deflecting the ball with the same, ill-fated shoulder. Alvaro marched off to kick a tree.

'I don't want to play!' he shouted.

'Come on. I'm sure you'll get it in next time. That was a lucky save.'

Reassured that no skill was involved in the saving of his goal, Alvaro decided to play on. Lydia let his goals whiz past her head and roll in an inch from her feet. She complained about her own ineptitude while Alvaro boasted of victory. He seemed far more interested in the drama and bravado of the game than in honing his skill. He fell down a lot, clutching his shin. Circled the goal pulling his football shirt over his head. He cupped his hands over his mouth to emulate the roar of the crowd and announced, after scoring a succession of easy goals, that girls were 'crap at football'. Lydia had had enough.

'Alvaro, don't use that kind of language. And who told you girls can't play football?'

'Jack said.'

'Girls do and can play football.'

A tinny rendition of the *Magic Roundabout* theme tune captured Alvaro's attention. He spotted an ice-cream van pulling up in a side road opposite the park and dashed towards it, through the small clump of trees that offered seclusion, past a young couple stretched out on the ground and two little girls in flower-print dresses making daisy chains, miniature clones of the curly-haired woman who lay beside them on the grass with her eyes closed. Lydia wondered how any mother could look so restful in a public place, close to a road, with two small children by her side. Alvaro had never allowed her the luxury of resting in his presence. If she were to close her eyes for any length of time he might decide to root through a bin, mark a tree with his scent or befriend a vagrant and leave for a life in the circus. He had repeatedly threatened to pack his bags and attempt a pilgrimage to Graceland. A middle-aged man hurled a frisbee over Alvaro's head that was caught in the jaws of a leaping Labrador.

'Alvaro, wait!' Lydia called out, chasing after him, wondering when and if he intended to stop at the kerb. Seeing a bus and her son on the same trajectory, running with her heart lodged in her throat, calling out to deaf ears.

'Alvaro, stop . . . stop!'

Alvaro ran faster. Lydia was too slow to catch him up. A vision of her son being thrown into the air and cracking his head on concrete flashed before her eyes. A vision that had her kneeling at his side, cupping his head in her hands, wailing inconsolably. The bus and Alvaro were only seconds away from collision as Lydia screamed again: 'STOP!' Alvaro stopped dead at the kerb and bent down to tie his shoelace. Panic over. The shakes and leaden legs its aftermath.

Lydia stopped running and noticed that she had become the object of general bemusement. The couple rose up on their elbows to gawp at her. The man stopped throwing his frisbee to stare. Even the dog, its head cocked to one side, wore a mystified expression, wondering why the muddy woman, dressed like an elf, had been screaming herself silly. Lydia reached her son. He took hold of her hand and looked up with anger-melting, chocolate-button eyes.

'Are you all right, Mum? You look really sweaty.'

'Did . . . you . . . hear me . . . shouting?' Shortness

of breath scuppered Lydia's effort to sound furious.

'I stopped at the kerb, like you always tell me to.'

They crossed the road sedately. Alvaro ordered a ninety-nine.

'Sorry, son. I'm out of flakes,' the ice-cream man said cheerfully, without realising the seriousness of his offence. Lydia watched her son's face drop and sensed his bitter disappointment. In Alvaro's mind a ninety-nine without a flake was as bogus as apple pie without the apple, a hotdog without the sausage.

'I want a flake,' he declared, his eyes filling up.

'Why don't you have something else?'

'I don't want anything else. I want a ninety-nine,' Alvaro shouted.

A queue of children jangled their coins in the queue behind them. Alvaro's refusal to listen to reason began to chafe.

'Alvaro, I can't make a flake appear out of nowhere. Please have something else.'

'I want a flake.'

'There are no flakes.' Anger simmered below the surface of Lydia's seemingly calm demeanour.

'I want a ninety-nine!' he cried petulantly, kicking the side of the ice-cream van.

Lydia fought the urge to grab him by the arms and shake him, to force an apology out of him. In his heightened emotional state Alvaro was unlikely to co-operate. The ice-cream man leaned out of the hatch to inspect his van for damage before glaring at Alvaro and asking: 'Do you want an ice cream or not?'

'I want a flake, you horrible man!' Alvaro screamed.

If there were time and space, if a queue were not

being held up, if the ice-cream man looked friendlier, if Lydia were not so angry and embarrassed and muddy, she might have bent down to talk to her son. Engaged with him on his own level in true textbook fashion. She might have tried to calm him down and reason with him. Instead, she grabbed Alvaro round the waist and carried him under her right arm, kicking and screaming, across the road and through the middle of the park, critical eyes boring into her from every direction. The young couple sat up, horrified by the sight of a monster child grabbing at his mother's hair. The serene mother gazed at her own flower-clad girls with pride, glad she had not been cursed with a child made of slugs and snails. Lydia trampled her tracksuit top, bundled her son into the back of the car and strapped him in, tugging her fringe out of his grip. She sat in the driver's seat, too shaky and agitated to drive, wanting to scream, waiting for her son to stop flailing and shouting abuse, to stop saying he hated her. The sharp point of a plastic toy hit the back of her head, making her eyes water, dissolving her anger into self-pity. She stooped over the steering wheel, covering her face, refusing to cry, to be beaten into submission by her own child.

Slowly but surely the tantrum subsided. Alvaro's limbs grew limp. The emotional whirlwind ran its course, leaving both parties confused, bruised and drained. Lydia glanced at her son through the rear-view mirror, wiping his bloodshot eyes, struggling to regain his composure. His tantrums had become more frequent of late, sparked by the most innocuous of triggers.

'Mum, why does my dad hate me?' he said after a long silence.

The lid of his feelings had to be blown off, not prised.

'He doesn't hate you, Alvaro. How could he, when he doesn't know you?' Lydia's voice was sharp, hostile. Her son had hurt her, physically and spiritually. She needed time to recuperate.

'He left because he hated me.'

'Whatever gave you that idea?'

'Jack said so.'

'Jack's wrong.'

'Jack plays football with his dad. No one plays football with their mum or their gran.'

'Has Jack said anything else?'

Alvaro shook his head, but his eyes contradicted this denial. Lydia asked the question again, to draw all the poison out of his system. If he held back now there would be more tears later, more pent-up anger to release, another clump of fringe pulled out of Lydia's head.

'He says people from hot countries can't play football.'

Lydia smiled at the ridiculousness of such a comment.

'Mum! Don't laugh.'

'I'm not laughing. I'm smiling.'

This silly comment had, for whatever reason, deeply affected Alvaro.

'Has Jack ever heard of Rivaldo and Ronaldo? Brazil's pretty hot. Jack talks nonsense. I don't think you should spend so much time with him.'

113

'But he's my best buddy.'

'Why don't you play with Kane instead? Like you used to.'

Alvaro shrugged and unclipped his seatbelt. He climbed into his mother's lap and nestled his head in the crook of her shoulder.

'Sorry, Mum,' he said, starting to cry, causing tears to well up in her eyes too, 'I'm sorry I was so bad. I love you, Mum.'

Lydia squeezed Alvaro tightly in her arms, knowing his apology was heartfelt.

'It's OK, son. It's OK.'

Lydia's head hurt, her eyes ached. She felt tearful and wretched but could not push her son away, not even for a second. If she did, who or what would he turn to for comfort? She believed it was better to forgive too quickly than to let Alvaro suffer or leave him to the far from tender mercies of friends like Jack.

Adam

I snuggle up to Electra's warm back in an effort to get back to sleep. My head will not oblige me with a Sunday morning lie-in. Thoughts too horrible to articulate jostle for space inside my skull, colliding like a swarm of bees trapped in the hollow of a tree. Only physical activity of some sort or a blast of music through headphones will temporarily drown them out. Pink digits metamorphose against a background of black. 6.01. 6.02. My head refuses to acknowledge the day assigned to rest. 6.03. There was a time, in the distant past, when nothing got under my skin. When alcohol-induced oblivion carried me through the weekend, without a thought for the morning after. Before I reverted in my late-thirties to the anal, self-disciplined child I once was. Now I drink in moderation, eat sensibly, sleep at a reasonable hour and get up far too early.

I feel healthier in body since moderation became a way of life but my head is a chamber of horrors, teeming with fears and uncomfortable preoccupations. I feel an unwelcome change fermenting inside me, a transmutation from armour-plated insect to sentient man. Events that have no real bearing on my life have begun to impinge on my inner world. I can no longer shake off stories of injustice with an indifferent shrug. I am still incensed by the gung-ho regime, and its partners in crime, that devastated a country's infra-structure with a shower of cluster bombs, which blew off children's limbs and generously offered to replace them with plastic.

I chose to watch the bombing of Baghdad and its aftermath on the Greek channel ERT, clutching my wife's hand as if the world were coming to an end. We watched mighty buildings reduced to biscuit crumbs, saw families, not collateral damage, lying dead in the rubble. ERT is refreshingly uncensored, unsanitised, unhindered by the watershed and English teatime sensibilities. It does not hold back for the sake of 'good taste'. Those visions have left an indelible imprint on my substrata as enduring as fossilised excrement. They have unhinged me in some way, filled me with rage, made me more susceptible to tears. 'Men don't cry,' Mum used to say whenever my bottom lip quivered. 'Men don't cry' echoed in my head when I watched Dad, huddled in a corner, crying like a baby. Tears marked the start of his decline and may be indicative of mine. I have my dad's brow, his chin, his hair colour, a good proportion of his genetic makeup. I may well have inherited the genes that left the grey cortex of his brain incurably tangled.

Electra manoeuvres herself backwards, into the crook of my curved body, fitting as snugly as a baseball inside a leather glove. I nestle my face in a nest of curly hair, wanting to forget. I breathe in the smell of sweet perfume, caramelised onions and smouldering iron. Electra takes my hand and slips it beneath her T-shirt, backing further into me. I run my hand along the contours of her body, dipping into the valley of her waist, across her sand dune hip, down her gently sloping thigh and back again. She feels soft and slimy to the touch, as if lathered with a viscose lotion. I wonder what kind of cream my wife applied to her body before going to bed? I lift up the covers and see that her arm, her thigh, her knickers, my fingers, are smeared with a brown, unsavoury-looking substance.

I get up and nudge her awake. 'Electra . . . Electra!'

She pulls the quilt tighter around her and yawns.

'Why are you up? I thought we were going to play.' She makes a grab for my pyjama bottoms.

'Keep your hands to yourself – you're covered in shit.'

'What are you talking about?'

I pull back the covers. 'Look.'

Electra glances down at her body, looking momentarily confused. She runs her finger along the sludge and licks it.

'What the hell are you doing?'

'This isn't shit, my love. It's chocolate. Black, Belgian and too good to waste.'

'Why are you covered in chocolate?'

'I brought a chocolate bar to bed with me. I must have fallen asleep before I had a chance to finish it. Why don't you climb back into bed and help me eat it?'

This is not the first time I have shared a bed with my wife and her late-night snacks. I have woken to find Electra clutching half-eaten chocolate digestives, sharing her pillow with a Creme egg, sleeping face to face with a marshmallow.

'I need a shower.'

My early-morning ardour has been dampened.

'Some men like their partners covered in chocolate.'

'You don't look very appetising from where I'm standing.'

Electra pulls off her T-shirt. 'Does this look more appetising?'

I slip back into bed to be enveloped by my wife's sweet-smelling arms.

Electra

Margaret has been shut up in the bedroom all morning. Knocking on the wall intermittently with her crutch to request tea, breakfast on a tray, visits to the toilet. Chicken roasts in the oven. Pork cubes soaked in red wine and fried with coriander simmer on the hob. Fruit salad cools in the fridge. Cinnamon-infused syrup soaks into filo pastry parcels filled with crushed almonds. White lilies, Margaret's favourite, sit in a glass vase on the coffee table. The music magazine pile has been straightened into a perfect cube. The flat has been vacuumed, dusted, cleared as much as possible of Adam's junk and clutter. My husband is both a hoarder and innately messy.

The table is set in readiness for our guests. I sit at my workbench inspecting a teardrop earring, shaped from a single strand of gold filigree. If Papa were here he would hold the earring up to natural light, rotate it in dextrous fingers and say, 'Bravo, Electra.' Papa holds me in high esteem and says everything I touch turns to gold. This comment does not stem merely from the fact that I shape gold for a living. Papa would never consciously seek to belittle me with a witticism. He believes that I was born lucky. That whether I work with gold or not, gold will be the outcome of my endeavours. I was the first and last of his children to win a scholarship to study in England, to live in the metropolis, to follow in his footsteps. He applauds my business acumen, thinks I am secure financially and knows I have married a good man.

His confidence in me was won early on. Aged seven, I was out walking with my grandmother Elpida when a pomegranate fell from a roadside tree onto her head. The rind split but grandmother's scalp fortunately remained intact. She cursed the fruit, called it a damned nuisance and kicked it with her sandalled foot into the road. What a shame, I thought, that the king of fruit with its pointy crown should be crushed at any second beneath the wheels of a double-cabin truck. I picked it up and put it in my pocket, staining the pocket of my white summer dress burgundy. 'That fruit is cursed. Throw it away at once. It has already tried to kill me,' Elpida said, throwing it in the bin.

Later that day, I fished it out of the rubbish and hid it in a shoebox at the back of my wardrobe. In homage to the fruit that slowly began to rot and smell rancid, I modelled a replica from a lump of clay and showed it to Papa. He was so taken by the detail that he made a mould and cast a dozen copies in cadmium. He silver-plated the cheap metal in his glass jar, polished the dull silver on his burnishing wheel and displayed the metallic fruit in his shop window. A week later he had sold all twelve and set about making more in his small workroom above the shop.

My pomegranates became a popular wedding gift, boosting the shop's income and Papa's kudos in the jewellery-making community. 'The world has gone mad,' Mama said, 'why would anybody choose to buy a pomegranate over a cross, a heart, a St George, an image of the Virgin?' 'The fruit is an ancient symbol of fertility, woman,' Papa told a wife who remained resolutely unimpressed. Mama grew up in a rural village where local produce was considered a practical necessity, not a thing of beauty in its own right. Villagers were too busy eating, drying or crushing their pomegranates, figs, olives and dates to eulogise them. A pomegranate is run-of-the-mill when it grows in the back yard. In summer the ripe fruit bursts and drops seeds, staining the ground below it and attracting long-bodied hornets with dangly legs and a painful sting in their abdomens.

Adam's key turns in the front-door lock. 'I'm back,' he calls, returning from the off-licence. Rejuvenated by his arrival, Margaret comes out of the bedroom and makes her way on crutches to the front door, ahead of me.

'Hello, darling,' she says. 'What took you so long?'

I have begun to feel somewhat excluded from their tender domestic exchanges.

'The traffic was terrible.'

Adam takes off his jacket but does not stoop to kiss me as he normally would, his routine hampered by the presence of his mother. 'Mmm. It smells nice in here.'

'Have you been frying something, dear?' Margaret sniffs the air.

'Yes. But I didn't use any oil.' I resort to a white lie to ward off a discussion on the evils of saturated fat.

Dressed in a woollen twin set Margaret looks prim and elegant, like a third-generation china doll. She looks surprisingly uncrumpled for a woman who has spent the morning lying in bed. Adam hangs his jacket on the rack beside the door, fitted before my time, beyond the reach of a vertically challenged mortal. I turn the latch on the front door and a spider the size of a two-pence piece darts across my hand. A feeling of revulsion overwhelms me. My stomach lurches.

'Arghhhh!' The scream that leaves my mouth is ear-piercing. '*Banayia mou. Voitha me!*' 'Holy Virgin, help me,' I screech, rubbing my hand manically, trying to erase the lingering sensation left by scurrying legs.

'What? What's wrong?' Adam drops his keys and rushes to my aid.

'A spider touched me. It's there. Look . . . in the corner. Get rid of it.' I grab an umbrella from the rack to arm myself and stand on tiptoe, whimpering.

'You're not scared of that little thing?' Adam's calm demeanour is infuriating.

'No. I'm having hysterics for the fun of it.'

Adam disappears into the living room and returns with a rolled up magazine. He plants his feet as far away from the spider as possible and uses the magazine to shepherd the arachnid out of the front door. It gets to the step before doubling back and heading straight for my feet. I leap out of its path and scream.

'What the hell are you doing? What kind of man are you?'

'One that doesn't like killing spiders.'

'Kill it! Kill it!'

'I thought I'd put it outside.'

'Why? So it can come back indoors and torture me? So it can multiply and fill the house with baby spiders? Are you mad?'

'Touch this,' Adam says, pointing the rolled-up magazine at me.

'What for?'

'Take the first step to overcoming your fear. Touch something that has touched the spider.'

'I don't need therapy. Just kill the fucker!'

'Electra, it's only a spider. It can't do you any harm.'

'Oh, give me that.' I grab the rolled-up magazine and end the spider's life with a powerful wallop, splattering the glossy cover with yellow innards, throwing the murder weapon violently onto the floor.

'I wanted to read that,' Adam says.

It is only when the threat has subsided and my heart rate slowed that I notice Margaret's stony expression.

'Oh, Margaret. Please excuse my language. I lose control when I see a spider.'

Her shrug suggests hysteria is no excuse for bad language.

Squeezed into the porch behind a pane of frosted glass are two incompatible forms that have the makings of a comic double act. A dog stands between them, barking, pressing his black nose against the glass.

'Electra *mou*,' Miroulla calls out, her voice more piercing than any doorbell.

'You didn't tell me they were coming,' Margaret

says, sounding perturbed. Her rudeness angers me.

'You knew we had guests, Mum. We thought you might appreciate some company.'

'You know I don't like dogs, Adam.'

'We'll keep Baby locked in the workroom. Don't worry. He won't go anywhere near you.'

I open the door feeling angry, anxious to make my aunt and uncle feel welcome. Miroulla squeezes me against her fleshy body and presses her soft face against mine. My surrogate mother has upturned bowling-pin legs that end in plump feet. Her black, backcombed hair has been lacquered to withstand a gale-force wind. Gold drips from Miroulla's neck, her wrists, her fingers, her earlobes. She doesn't believe in saving her jewellery, in locking it away for posterity.

Uncle Nikoli is as dinky as a bookend, his skin the texture of crumpled linen. Swept-back hair, the colour of cigarette ash, accentuates his high distinguished-looking forehead. A weathered tweed jacket and reading glasses, perched midway down his aquiline nose, give him the look of a retired university professor. Nikoli, engaged in a lifelong love affair with Greek poetry, has been a factory foreman all his life. He came to England in his twenties to get an education but worked instead to accrue a dowry for each of his three younger sisters. A dutiful act that robbed him of a formal education but failed to quench his love of learning and lyrical verse. Nikoli is a gentleman, his intellect untainted by arrogance. He kisses my cheeks and hands me a heavy saucepan.

The couple's cherished chihuahua Baby shuffles in. Cocooned inside a furry grey jacket, he looks like a puffball on legs. He looks up at Adam and starts yapping.

'Hello, Baby,' Adam says, failing to sound friendly to a dog whose yap is unquestionably hostile.

'She's warnin you to look after her Electra,' Miroulla says, with the usual jumble of pronouns, laughing and throwing her arms around my husband's waist. He squeezes her in his arms, failing to notice his mother's sour expression.

Baby latches on to Adam's trouser leg and starts tugging.

'Why does Baby hate me so much?' he says, trying to yank his trouser leg free.

Nikoli grins. 'You're the biggest thing in the room. He's cutting you down to size, showing you he's not scared of you.'

'I don't think he could do me much harm.'

'You be saprise. Our posman he nelly lose a finga when he pud his hand through the letta box,' Miroulla says, kissing Adam on both cheeks. 'Is a good job he's only pud his finga through the letta box. You know whar I mean?' Miroulla, the doyenne of innuendo, cackles unashamedly. My aunt has lived in North London since the 1960s but has yet to master the English language fully.

She turns to my mother-in-law. 'Mar-ga-ret. How are you?'

'As well as can be expected, in the circumstances.'

'Nikoli, take Baby into the workroom. You know Mar-ga-ret she don' like dogs,' Miroulla says.

'Do you need anything?' Adam calls after him. 'A tray of any sort?'

'Don warry, Adam. My Baby she's toilet train,' Miroulla replies, following me into the kitchen.

'How are you, my love?' Miroulla asks, reverting to our mother tongue.

'I'm fine.'

'How are things with your mother-in-law?'

'Not bad.'

Miroulla smiles wryly. 'She didn't look too pleased to see us. As if I care. I didn't come to see her anyway. I came to see you and Adam. That woman is as cold as an ice cube. How did she manage to raise a lovely, warm boy like him?'

'I think Adam takes after his father. By all accounts he was a wonderful man.'

'Why did he marry a witch like Margaret? Perhaps she put a spell on him.'

'I bet she was really pretty when she was young.'

'Now, she's a dried-up old prune with a sour face and droopy jowls. A woman needs a warm heart and a bit of meat on her bones to satisfy a man.' Miroulla pinches my cheeks. 'I see you're filling out, my girl. Is this a sign of good news? Do you have something to tell me?'

'No. And stop fishing.'

'When do you intend to start a family, Electra? When it's too late? You don't want to end up like me, my girl.'

'There's nothing wrong with you. You're happy. You have Uncle Nikoli.'

'That man is my life. I'm lucky to have found him.'

People often question why a sagacious man like

126

Nikoli is married to such an apparently unsophisticated woman. People are generally blinded by appearances. Miroulla pampers and spoils Nikoli and is happy to assume the role of intellectual underdog. She fusses over her husband and satisfies his every culinary whim. Nikoli is naturally so sedate he is in danger of falling into a coma. He needs a woman like Miroulla to inject some vitality into his life. The couple met through a marriage broker specialising in difficult cases. Miroulla was on the shelf and gathering dust. Nikoli, trapped like Alice in her fictional Wonderland, lacked the social skills required to engage a woman in conversation and win her heart. Miroulla and Nikoli submitted pictures to the marriage broker and leafed through the misfits album, looking for a partner. Miroulla ruled out the prospect of the accountant with the cauliflower floret ears, the teacher with the lazy eye, the restaurateur with the abundant belly and the ice-rink head. Her heart skipped a beat when she laid eyes on the smiling face of little Nikoli. A month after meeting, the couple set a date for their wedding. Though her childbearing years were then a distant memory Miroulla yearned for a baby. Nikoli bought his wife a dog and my aunt became the devoted mother of a long-haired chihuahua.

Nikoli swirls Five Kings in a bulbous brandy glass. Beside him on the sofa Margaret sips tea. Charmed by his eloquence, she listens to him extol the virtues of Elytis, one of Greece's most celebrated poets. 'A master of free verse ... winner of Nobel Prize for literature . . .' he says to an enchanted Margaret who leans ever-so-slightly towards him and touches his arm. The green-eyed monster rears its ugly head, casting a shadow over Miroulla's angry brow.

'I have a casin called Marios,' she interjects, crossing one plump leg across the other, 'he's no so clever. He's bin in England for thirty years and still he don speak no English. When his ferst daughta she was born the nurse she say, "Mr Nicolaides, your daughta she's eight pound." My casin he took a ten-pound note from his pocket, gave it to the nurse and told her to keep the change.'

Miroulla cackles though she has told this story many times. Margaret stares at her blankly, trying to fathom the meaning of her broken English.

'My casin he's so stupid, for twenty years he thought the local Chinese restauran it was an ice-cream shop.'

'Why, *thea*?'

'Because pag-oda in Greek it means ice creams and the restauran is called Pagoda . . .You can't blame poor Marios,' Miroulla continues. 'My casin he's god bad *geneologia*. How you say tha in English, Electra?'

'Genealogy.'

'Ah, same as the Greek?'

'From the Greek,' Nikoli says.

'My casin's mam and dad they were ferst casins. He cam from a small village where relatives they marry relatives. You know, like the English *aristocratia*. How you say that, Nikoli my lav?'

'Aristocracy.'

'Is the same word again? Anyway, tha village is full

128

of stupid people. Mar-ga-ret, you god any crazy relatives?'

My aunt has unwittingly said the wrong thing. I have not shared the fine detail of Margaret's life with my family.

'Not that I can think of,' she replies icily.

'Your family is all intelligence?'

'Well, my family is very small.'

'Don say tha, Mar-ga-ret. We all one big family now.' Miroulla's comment is not as generous as it might at first appear. A smirk lurks at the corners of my aunt's thin lips. Margaret glances at me with that all-too-familiar look of resentment in her eyes. I am responsible for polluting her family with crazy cousins and mad aunts.

Baby starts yapping and scratching at the workroom door. Nikoli gets up to check on the dog.

'He's kep us awake all night last night,' Miroulla says. 'I think my poor Baby she's gorra terribol tammy ache.'

'Have you tried Calpol, *thea*?'

'Very fanny, Electra. Bat I'm no as stupid as my casin Mario.'

'Miroulla, get your bag. We have to leave,' Nikoli calls from the bedroom.

Miroulla pushes down on the armrests to lift her heavy body up from the seat, before charging out of the room. 'Electra, Adam,' she calls, 'Baby she's been sick.'

Adam follows me out of the lounge. We poke our heads round the workroom door and catch a whiff of something acrid, nasty. Nikoli cradles Baby like an infant in his arms, kissing his snout, whispering words of comfort into his fluffy brown ear. Miroulla is down on padded knees wiping up a pool of yellow dog vomit with a tissue. Baby has chosen to empty the contents of his canine stomach, not on the expanse of bare floorboards, but on a small rectangle of sea grass.

Miroulla looks up. 'I'm sorry, darli, bat we can't stay to eat.'

Adam

Mum gathers a chunk of apple onto her spoon. She tips the spoon to drain the juice before chewing the fruit with all the enthusiasm of a woman eating ground glass. I am used to sitting opposite a woman who enjoys her food, who closes her eyes in anticipation of the taste and eats with her fingers. Mealtimes have become a chore since Mum came to stay, a monotonous procedure necessary for survival. The telephone rings. Electra wipes her mouth and rushes off to answer it. An oppressive silence fills the jangley space she occupied. Left alone with Mum I feel nervous and tongue-tied. I wonder if she realises the effect she has on me. Mum puts down her spoon and crosses her arms across her chest, assuming the position that always precedes unwelcome advice.

'Do you really think it's a good idea to take out a bank loan at the moment?' she asks in her testing-the-water tone of voice.

'You don't need to worry about our financial affairs, Mum.'

'But I do, Adam. I'm your mother.'

'And I'm nearly forty years old! Electra needs to invest some money in her business. It will only be a small loan.'

'Why should you shoulder the burden of a loan that has nothing to do with you?' Her petulant tone is intensely irritating.

'Electra and I are a couple, Mum. We do things together.'

'You do know interest rates are going up?'

'I have no choice but to know. I have the misfortune of editing the business pages every Tuesday.'

'Then why put your head in the lion's mouth?'

'Because I have faith in my wife.'

'And what if her business fails?'

'Then at least she's tried.' I spit out the words, struggling to maintain my composure.

She looks at me with a wounded expression. 'You don't need to be so hostile, Adam.' I see a stubborn, tight-set face. A frail, ageing body and a leg in plaster. My irritation slowly gives way, as always, to concern for her feelings and a desire to keep the peace.

'Are you enjoying the fruit salad?'

'Not really.'

Even fruit, it appears, is contentious. 'Why not?'

'It's too sweet.' Mum lowers her voice and hands me her dessert plate. 'Pour mine in the bin quickly, before she comes back. And, please – don't tell her I threw it away. You don't have to tell your wife everything, you know.' Mum thinks we have as great a right to share secrets as clandestine lovers. 'You really should watch your sugar intake, Adam, and your diet in general.

That pork dish your wife made was terribly fatty. Did you see the layer of oil floating on top?'

'She made it for her uncle.'

'And ate most of it herself.' Mum chuckles to alleviate the sting in her comment before glancing at the door. 'Can't her uncle help her out with a loan?'

'No, he can't.'

'Why not? His wife was covered head to foot in gold.'

'He and his wife live on a pension. And anyway, Electra wouldn't dream of asking them for money.'

'What about her parents?'

'They don't have the means.'

'No, I suppose not. Didn't her father lose all his money on the stock market? Perhaps you'll get a share of the family fortune buried underneath the lemon tree.' Mum smirks. Her joke as usual is laced with sarcasm.

I start to clear the table, feeling annoyed, trying to focus my attention on Electra's voice and a high-pitched monologue in Greek, a language I am gradually absorbing. I use identifiable words, like a compass, to navigate my way through a sea of vernacular. Sotiris . . . Holy Virgin . . . sister . . . wanker . . . float from the hall-way into my consciousness.

'Why are you clearing the table? She may want some more dessert.'

'She' has a name. Her name is Electra. I have grown tired of Mum's refusal to afford my wife this courtesy.

'Who is she talking to?'

'Her mother, I think.'

'Are they arguing?'

Electra's tone can sound aggressive to the untrained ear. 'No. They're just talking.'

I have grown accustomed to the excitable way my wife talks to her family. A noisy exchange punctuated by loud exclamations might only be a discussion on the price of artichokes. When I first met Electra's family I found the noise they made dizzying. Chit-chat sounded like a catfight. I'd imagined an encounter with a Greek version of my own family. What I found instead when I stepped through the door of Electra's family home was a lateral Greek universe, where the rules of engagement were otherworldly. The small flat was packed with aunts, uncles, cousins, siblings, innumerable children. Black-clad grandmothers with friendly, wrinkled faces. All had come to inspect me and announce their verdict on Electra's fiancé. Thrust into the midst of these short people, I felt like Gandalf among the Elves of Middle Earth. I was kissed, pummelled, patted and stroked. The children circled me like sharks, closing in on their kill. Electra soon grew tired of acting as interpreter and set me adrift amid a sea of gesticulating hands, forcing me to sink or swim. The air was thick with food smells, unrelenting rounds of tea and coffee were served, female bodies were in perpetual motion.

Electra's father sat at the head of the dinner table. A chair was pulled out next to him and I was led towards it. Guests sat on wooden, plastic and metal chairs, gathered from bedrooms, the kitchen, the balcony. Electra's mother and aunts carried a procession of platters out of the kitchen, into the dining room, over-loading the table. I had never seen such a wide variety of food served in one sitting. The eating-fest commenced, a lattice of arms reaching out across the table to help themselves. Clinging to my English sensibilities, I sat and waited, smiling inanely, feeling uncomfortable. My plate was quickly filled without my being asked.

I ate fried potatoes and fatty red meat, delicious dishes topped with béchamel and vegetables swimming in olive oil. I munched until I felt like an overstuffed courgette, of which I ate four. '*Pastos*' and '*Englezos*' were the first two Greek words I learned. 'Thin' and 'Englishman' were used as liberally as salt that day. After dinner the kitchen became a battleground with women beating a path to the sink, fighting to do the washing up. When I offered to help, arms shot up in horror and I was forcibly removed from the kitchen and instructed by Electra to interact with the men. I drank brandy, smoked a cigar and nibbled pistachios, though my stomach protested, while the women made coffee and dished out dessert.

The novelty of my arrival quickly wore off. Efforts to speak to me in broken English slowly petered out. Within the space of an evening, my initiation was complete. The black-clad women seemed to forget I was English and began speaking to me in Greek. The children sidled up beside me on the sofa, looking up at me with their big, dark eyes, calling me Uncle Adam – *Theo Adamos*. I sipped sweet wine and felt happily intoxicated, soaking in the scene around me. Absorbing the customs, protocol and mannerisms of another culture. A culture I felt privileged to be experiencing from within.

'Why is she shouting?' Mum asks as Electra's loud babble floods the kitchen.

'She's not shouting. She's just speaking in a loud voice.'

Mum rolls her eyes, wearing thin my patience. If there were cracks in my marriage, her remarks would serve to widen them and distance me from my wife. I wish Electra would hurry back to the kitchen and lighten the gloomy atmosphere with her animated chatter.

'Adam, it's high time you changed this kitchen. It's a disgrace.' The focus of Mum's attention switches from Electra to the room. 'The worktops are warped. The cupboard veneers have come away. That cooker is falling to bits. If you had fitted a quality kitchen ten years ago, like I told you, it would have lasted you a lifetime.'

'Changing the kitchen is not a priority at the moment.'

'Your brother has just had a new kitchen fitted. Bespoke. Solid wood. The marble worktop was imported from Italy.'

'Good for John.'

'If you and your wife were both earning a regular salary you would have more money to spend on yourselves and this flat. It's looking very rundown.'

I feel as rundown as the flat, browbeaten, tired of fighting my corner. I am ready to blow yet I hold back, anxious to preserve the shaky balance between mother and son.

Electra

Mama's call was well-timed. Could she sense my desperation? Did she know her daughter was feeling like a caged animal? That she was shovelling fruit salad into her mouth as if there were no tomorrow, to stop herself from saying something inappropriate. In Margaret's company I become a caricature of myself, confirming her worst fears that her son married a crazy Greek woman. Mama's singsong voice was an antidote to Margaret's dispiriting drone. I was happy to hear her voice but saddened by her news about my sister, Martha.

Apparently she found a telephone number in her husband's trouser pocket, scrawled on a scrap of paper in what looked like red lipstick. Shaking with fear, she dialled this number, hoping her worst fears would not be realised. A woman with a thick East European accent answered the telephone and wasted no time in telling Martha that Sotiris was her lover. My sister packed her bags and moved in with our parents, full of fighting talk, saying she would not be made a fool of again. Sotiris turned up on the doorstep, crying, begging

137

forgiveness, saying he had learned his lesson. Once again Martha chose to believe him, blaming the vile girls in hot pants for luring her husband away, for sinking their manicured claws into other women's property, for offering sex on a plate. This seedy scenario is becoming all too familiar back home, where middle-aged men like my brother-in-law are spicing up their mundane lives in the arms of young women imported from impoverished countries, employed to dance, expected to do a little extra.

I remember the Martha-that-was with a heavy heart. The breathtakingly pretty girl with long limbs and golden hair. My sister was once crowned Orange Queen for her beauty, at Famagusta's annual Orange Festival. She sat on a gilt throne, dressed like a muse, crowned by a wreath of myrtle, leading a procession of floats decorated with Jaffas and Valencias. Not even her wedding day lived up to the pomp and pageantry of being crowned Orange Queen. Martha married young and has aged prematurely. Her eyes are sunken, her hair brittle and split, she walks on calloused feet. When a woman lets herself go, who can blame her husband for looking elsewhere? some might say. In fact, Martha's looks survived the rigours of childbirth, of weaning, a decade of sleepless nights, financial hardship. She even accepted without much ado her husband's fondness for cards, believing every man should be permitted one vice. But one was not enough for Sotiris, whose philandering has broken Martha's heart, sapped her of fight and whittled away her self-respect. Though her spirit lies in tatters, she is desperate to sustain the myth of a happy family life.

Only divorce, Mama says, can save the daughter who is sinking. Only Martha can make this decision and must not be coerced, she insists. Mama is careful not to judge, not to name call, not to denounce her son-in-law in front of his children. Papa has held back the anger raging inside him, not wanting to make the situation worse. But it seems there is no cure for Martha's rotten marriage. Without delay she must remove Sotiris from her life like a troublesome tooth. The thought of a pending extraction is always worse than the act itself.

I hurry back to the kitchen, my head teeming with troubled thoughts. I put on a brave face and suppress all evidence of raw emotion in the presence of my new mother, the one whose heart is a block of ice.

'Is everything all right?' Adam asks.

'Not really.'

'What's wrong?' Margaret asks, hungry for gossip. 'Problems at home?'

'My sister's having a hard time with her husband. She's on the brink of divorce.'

Margaret shakes her head knowingly. 'I knew that man couldn't be trusted when I met him at your wedding. There was something very distasteful about him. A shifty look in his eyes. I'm very good at reading people, you know. I have very good intuition.'

I look at Adam and a smile curves his lips. Perhaps he too is remembering how animatedly Margaret talked to Sotiris at the wedding, how she was charmed by his compliments and full of praise for him after the event. Margaret's opinions on people, coloured by her prejudices, couldn't be more wrong.

'Does anyone want a hot drink?' Adam asks, opening the fridge, reaching for a litre of milk.

Margaret turns to her son and I know what she is poised to say before she has even opened her mouth to speak. 'I hope you don't mind me saying, Adam, but your fridge is unlikely to be energy-efficient when it is packed so full of food.'

A Greek saying springs to mind. *The world around us burns and your wife puts on her makeup.* While I deal with emotional distress, Margaret fixates on the contents of the fridge. Then another saying from my youth worms its way into my consciousness. *Speak to your son if you want your daughter-in-law to hear.*

'For Christ's sake, Mum. Electra did our weekly shop today. That's why the fridge is so full.'

'Do the two of you get through so much food in a week?'

'There are three mouths to feed now.'

'You've always been such a small eater, Adam.'

I smile in spite of myself, tickled by the implication that I am as voracious as a locust, and I turn to my mother-in-law. 'We need a bigger fridge. There's not enough space inside that old thing.'

'Fridges are very expensive and you two have other priorities at the moment. I would suggest you look after the one you have.'

Adam storms out of the kitchen, his cheeks bright red.

'What's wrong with him?' Margaret asks, looking baffled.

I follow him out, wondering how much more of her nastiness I can take. When I first met Adam his fridge contained a wedge of mouldy cheese, half a can of beans and a fungal tomato. I disinfected the yellowing shelves and packed the small fridge with food. Far from approving of the change, Margaret equated our well-stocked fridge with greed, waste and needless extravagance. Now she is clearly under the impression that all Adam's hard-earned cash is ending up in my stomach, that I am literally eating my husband out of house and home. Well, I am happy to forgo clothes, cosmetics and annual holidays but I will not skimp on food. My mother's fridge is never empty, a wealth of snacks cram its roomy shelves. Peeled prickly pears, glistening in a bowl. *Mahalbi* – jellied cornflour dessert – floating in rosewater cordial. *Halloumi* made with goat's milk, the perfect accompaniment to watermelon. *Glyko tou athashou*, a sweet white almond preserve, gathered on a spoon and nibbled or licked like a lollipop.

'Why don't you leave the peel on, dear? It's full of vitamins,' Margaret says, standing over me, leaning forward on her crutches. I smile and stop peeling, roughly chopping the carrot instead with the peel intact.

Margaret picks up a baby courgette. 'Why don't you buy the larger courgettes, dear?'

'The smaller ones are sweeter.'

'And twice the price.'

'I don't really look at prices when I'm shopping.'

'You should.'

'You're right.' What alternative is there but to agree? A childish altercation? 'No, I shouldn't.' 'Yes, you

141

should.' Over courgettes? I quickly chop the remaining vegetables. She turns to leave. I close the kitchen door behind her and breathe a sigh of relief. No sooner have I turned on the gas, added oil to my pan and begun sweating out the onions than I hear the ominous thump of Margaret's crutches, a sound I have come to dread. She stares at me through frosted glass, waiting for the door to open.

'Why on earth are you frying those onions?' she asks, glaring. 'The vegetables in a soup don't need to be fried.'

'I'm sweating out the flavour.'

'You're destroying the vitamins,' she says, berating me for the crime of vegetable homicide. I take the pan off the heat and pour the opaque onions into the bin. Under her watchful eye, I chop a second onion. 'Just put all the vegetables in the pan together and pour in some boiling water,' she says, intent on getting her own way, leaving the kitchen safe in the knowledge that I have made her soup, not mine.

My week has been marked by such submission, by the compliant nodding of my head, by a smile belying my frustration. I have been subjected to an unending trickle of advice, as if I were five not thirty-five. Don't overfill the washing machine. Why don't you wash the sweaters by hand? Why put the sheets in the dryer when you could hang them outside to dry? 'Margaret,' I have wanted to say but stopped myself, 'I have been washing my own clothes since I was fifteen. You have your way and I have mine.' Post-It notes have begun appearing beside plug sockets with the message 'Switch off when not in use' and a row of exclamation marks.

I reach for my mobile phone and dial Lydia's number desperate to offload, launching headlong into my tirade.

'Objects have begun moving telekinetically.'

'Electra, what are you talking about?'

'I go in search of a banana and find the fruit bowl has moved. I stand in the shower and reach for the shampoo bottle. Puff! It has vanished. Where do I find it? In the bathroom cabinet. The armchair has moved from one side of the living room to the other.'

'Your mother-in-law has been moving things around?'

'A fair conclusion, Lydia, but no! Adam asked her the other day why she had moved the armchair and she said, "How can I move a heavy chair, son, when I can barely walk?" Hence my conclusion – telekinesis.'

'Just turn a blind eye, Electra. She won't be there forever.'

'Neither will I if things carry on the way they are. I don't know how much more I can take. I've seen her when she thinks no one's looking rummaging through drawers in the bedroom, the living room, the kitchen.'

'What do you think she's looking for?'

'Evidence. Against me. But she won't find it. The drawers are full of Adam's junk. As soon as she leaves I'm determined to sell this place and move on to neutral territory where I can stamp my mark. "When does my son intend to buy himself a new kitchen?" Margaret says. "When will my son get round to changing his curtains?" *His* curtains. *His* kitchen. Who am I exactly? The lodger? Home help?'

'Don't work yourself up, Electra. You don't want to get over-excited in your condition.'

'"Can you straighten the sheets, dear? Can you pass me my bag dear? Can I have another cup of tea – not so milky this time?" It's not what she says that annoys me but the way she says it. Sometimes she barks at me, Lydia. When she asks for her bag, she wants it *now*. When she calls out for tea, she wanted it yesterday. Be patient, Electra, I tell myself – the woman is in pain, frustrated, at your mercy. Be kind. Generous. Serve with a smile.'

'I think we need to meet for a coffee. It sounds like you're going crazy in there.'

'I'm pretty wound up, I have to admit, and I can't even have a good argument with my husband to let off steam. Shouting is no longer allowed in this flat. Adam and I conduct our arguments in a whisper. "Keep your voice down, Electra," he says, "Mother might overhear." "Don't tell me to keep my voice down," I scream. "What's the matter with you, Electra?" he asks. "Why are you being like this?"'

'Why don't you tell him what the problem is?'

'What am I supposed to say? "Your mother's driving me crazy. Your mother rifles through our belongings like a spy. She's an irritable and demanding house-guest." I don't want to turn Adam against his mother. What should I say, Lydia, to a man who has buried his head in the sand? Should I say in a whisper, behind a closed door, fearing Margaret might overhear . . . "Hey, bozo, I'm pregnant"?'

'You should have told him about the baby ages ago.'

'I can't tell him at the moment. He's not himself. To be honest, I'm quite worried about him.'

'You should be worrying about yourself.'

'But Adam's changed. He's uptight and tetchy. He's not sleeping well. I think he's keeping something from me.'

'Why don't you ask him?'

'There are so many things I want to talk to him about but there is never a right time.'

'I've never known you and Adam to keep things from each other.'

I pick up the salt canister. 'We're not the Adam and Electra you knew.'

'Don't say that. You're the only happily married couple I know. The only couple I believe in.'

Margaret pushes open the kitchen door and walks in.

'I have to go, Lydia. I'll call you later.'

Margaret looks at the salt as if it were rat poison. 'Don't add too much salt. It's a killer, you know. Once you get accustomed to the taste of food without salt, you'll realise you don't need to use it at all.'

I feel myself boiling up inside but follow her instructions nonetheless. I like salt. I come from the land of salty foods, of *halloumi* and feta and olives in brine. Salt may be a killer but so is stress. And my stress levels are currently sky high. Any more pearls of culinary wisdom and I will keel over in an untidy heap. Would my demise elicit Margaret's sympathy? Not likely. She would stand over me, shaking her head and pursing her lips, asking herself how any woman could collapse with such lack of grace.

'The soup is lovely, dear.' Margaret pays herself an undeserved compliment. The soup has the consistency of dishwater and tastes of cabbage. What does it need? The Electra touch. A sprinkle of salt, a dash of olive oil, some lightly fried pancetta, a handful of croutons. I used to eat lunch at my desk. Now, I am forced to sit in the kitchen with Margaret, struggling to make polite conversation.

'Have some more, dear. It's good for you.'

'I'm too full, Margaret.' I pat a stomach craving food with a modicum of flavour.

'If you eat properly now, you won't be hungry later.'

'I don't have much of an appetite today.'

'I hope you don't mind me saying, dear, but you seem to have put a little weight on lately. You should watch your calorie intake. You don't want to end up like your aunt.'

I flush with anger and battle hatred. My opponent strikes below the belt. Her words jolt me like a foetal kick in the abdomen. Oblivious to the offence she has caused, Margaret witters on about the benefits of healthy eating while I seethe. '... weight gain is a slippery slope. Once you put on weight it is very difficult to lose it. Body shape is genetically pre-determined, of course. Adam has his father's body shape. That boy is lucky. He will never put on weight.'

'He's far too thin, if you ask me.'

'The way you cook, dear, it's a wonder he's not twice the size.'

The gloves come off. My sparring partner no longer pulls her punches but condemns me to my face. And of what exactly am I guilty? Using quality ingredients? Adding olive oil and lemon to my boiled potatoes? Sautéing my vegetables? Bad wife. Evil wife. Burn her at the stake for the sin of abusing her husband with flavoursome meals. Yet again I must defer to her age and position. But this is one concession too many, more than I can stomach. Her comment is as tasteless as her soup. I need to leave the house before I say something I may live to regret. Margaret is cruel and spiteful and I will not play her games.

'I have to go out, Margaret.' I get up and leave the kitchen while she is still eating, ignoring the disgruntled expression on her face.

'Where are you going?' she calls after me.

'To buy some milk.'

'But we already have milk.'

'We might need some more. My fat aunt is coming to visit this evening.'

The wind rises and swoops. It flips up my hair and throws it over my face as I march angrily down the street. Experiencing for the first time in my life the surge of relief one feels when escaping the aura of an overbearing parent. I never felt the need to escape from my own parents. I could always be myself in their company, never needed to lie. Now it seems I am paying my dues for the privilege of having exceptional parents.

Papa nurtured his children according to a healthy philosophy, one that should be a mandatory part of socialisation. As a rule his generation spawned lofty patriarchs. Papa was the exception. He never smacked, never judged, never belittled his children. Whenever I was naughty and the neighbours shouted, 'Give her a whack, Petrakis,' Papa would shake his head and look

147

at me with a wounded expression, crippling me with his gentleness. My father shaped his children with kindness, not aggression. 'You are too soft, Petrakis,' the neighbours would say reproachfully, slapping their own children about without a second thought, losing their respect, whereas Papa secured mine for ever. Children are like elephants, they never forget. In my eyes Papa is a divine being, up on a pedestal with the best of them, on a par with all the legendary men who achieved greatness through pacifism. I have had my fill of pettiness and disrespect. When will it end? How long does Margaret intend to punish me for the sin of being me?

I notice a grey squirrel lying in the road ahead, blood oozing from its mouth. Its tail flutters upwards, waving like a hand. I run into the road, wondering if the animal can be saved, only to discover that the wind is playing tricks with my mind, lifting up the feather-light tail. There are worse things in life than a difficult mother-in-law, I tell myself, staring down at the dead squirrel. We all have our cross to bear and mine is Margaret. The honk of a car horn shatters my moment of reflection. I look up, see a Subaru hurtling towards me and run without looking, back onto the pavement, knocking into an unsuspecting pedestrian, sending him ricocheting against a high stone wall. Down he goes like a skittle, onto his back, splayed as unceremoniously as the squirrel but less bloody and thankfully still breathing. Broken glasses lie skewed across his face. His nose is badly scratched and caked with grit.

'My God! I'm so sorry.'

He moves slowly on leaden limbs, straightening his glasses and trying to stand. I know this man from somewhere. I struggle to put a name to the grazed face. I juggle alternatives in my mind, realising with alarm that I have grievously assaulted my neighbour, the insomniac.

'Are you all right? Can you hear me?'

'My ears are the only part of my body still intact.'

Humour in the face of adversity is a very endearing quality. As the poor man slowly lifts himself off the ground I begin to size him up, to ask myself if he would make a suitable partner for my friend. He has a kind, though somewhat disfigured, face and a sexy Scottish accent.

'We're neighbours. Don't you recognise me? Can you see through those glasses?'

He peers at me through cracked lenses, squinting. 'Oh, yes. You're the woman who never goes to bed.'

I like this man. 'Let me help you up.' I hold out my hand. He thinks twice about taking it. 'You must come to my place. I will clean you up. On second thoughts, perhaps that isn't such a good idea. My mother-in-law is staying with us at the moment. She might not take kindly to my bringing a strange man home. Even a wounded one. I tell you what, let's go to your place.'

'I'm fine. Don't worry, I'll sort myself out. Nice to meet you . . . I think.'

He takes a faltering step away from me, his ankle twisting as he walks. I grab his arm and feel the curve of a healthy bicep. 'I won't take no for an answer. You may need hospital treatment for that ankle. And your nose . . . it doesn't look too good.'

'That's God-given.'

'You know what I mean. You don't want that wound getting infected.'

'I'll be fine. And I certainly don't need hospital treatment.'

'That's what my cousin Kikis said when he stepped on a nail. Until his jaw locked and he started convulsing. They took him to hospital on a stretcher. That nail was nearly the end of him.'

'You'd be a great scrum half,' my neighbour says, grimacing as I gently dab the side of his face with antiseptic lotion.

'Not in my condition.'

'You have a condition?'

'I'm nearly three months pregnant.' How easy it feels to tell a stranger. How impossible to share this news with my husband.

'Maybe you should be the one sitting down?'

'No, I'm fine.'

I fire questions at him. Are you married? Do you have children? What's your name? What do you do? He answers. Divorced. Yes, two. Sean. Songwriter. I have a fleeting vision of Lydia and my neighbour sitting cross-legged on the floor strumming away on their guitars and Alvaro dancing between them in his Elvis costume. I offer to make coffee while Sean Sellotapes his glasses together. I switch on the kettle and explore the kitchen, opening cupboards and pulling out drawers, looking for signs of dysfunction. The kitchen is clean but not anally so. The fridge contains rocket leaves, a jar of pesto, sun-dried tomatoes and other indicators of a culinary imagination. There is no tat. No clutter. No pictures of pert female bottoms stuck to the fridge door. There are no feminine touches which might suggest a regular girlfriend. No flowers on the windowsill. No ice cream in the freezer. No washing up gloves.

Over coffee I continue my interrogation. Are you single? Do you like children? How old are you?

'Either you're a very nosy person, fed up with your husband, or else you have a single friend,' he says, smelling the rat.

'I am both nosy and have a single friend, with a wonderful son.'

'Yes, I am single. Yes, I like children. I have a son and daughter of my own. I see them twice a week and it breaks my heart to say goodbye. And, finally, I turned thirty-eight last week.'

'Perfect! You're young enough for my friend but too old to play the field.'

'A man is never too old to play the field.'

'I've never seen anyone up here with you.'

'I don't parade my conquests in front of the window.'

'When did you last have a girlfriend?'

'Isn't it time you went home?'

'As soon as we make our arrangements I will leave you in peace.'

Margaret

The skin around my anklebone prickles and pulsates. I poke a knitting needle down the side of the plaster and wiggle it about before lying flat on the bed, succumbing to lethargy, trying to focus on something other than my desperation to scratch. Every day my sense of frustration intensifies. I feel as helpless as a newborn baby. For two months now I have been deprived of my independence, my home, my friends, my weekly games of bridge.

I have missed my own house. It stands in its original condition amid a row of butchered Edwardian villas. Dissected, reconfigured, clumsily converted into rabbit hutches for high-density living. Damp basements and weathered attics have been turned into luxury flats. Cupboards under the stairs, suitable only for storage, have become separate studies. Space on my road comes at a premium. Sadly, many of my former neighbours have sold their homes to developers. The pariahs are probably waiting at this moment for my joints to seize up, with lump hammers and plaster boards at the ready. As long as there is breath in my lungs, no one will get their hands on my property. And when my breath runs out, I will come back to haunt the four floors of young professionals occupying the ruin of my house.

Adam's bed is too soft, his sofa too spongy, his style of living not at all to my liking. My son and his wife live in disorderly fashion and overlook the finer points of cleanliness. A dusty thread hangs from the cornice. A gentle breeze swings it back and forth like a jungle vine. This room is not conducive to restful sleep. It needs a fresh coat of paint and new curtains, its shabbiness a reflection of my son's deteriorating state. Adam is not the boy he used to be. He has let himself go. Frayed at the edges like an unstitched hem. The change in him may not be noticeable to others, in the same way that a torn pocket is hidden from view, but no alteration escapes a mother's keen eye. No one knows a son better than the woman who raised him. Not the humble observer, nor the fair-weather friend, not even a wife.

Only a woman can keep a household and a husband in order. In this household where roles are not clearly defined, confusion reigns. This household is not run but chased after. There is no set washing-day. Clothes are ironed on the hop. Meals are eaten at irregular hours. Dirty cups are left in the sink overnight. Magazines and newspapers litter the lounge floor. My son and his wife are wastrels. High-voltage lights are left on overnight. The central heating blazes when it needn't be on. Food that could be saved in a Tupperware container and eaten the next day is frivolously thrown away. Anyone who has lived through a war knows such wastefulness is a sin. Adam might just as well be throwing his money into the rubbish bin. The cupboards are full to bursting with sugary snacks that feed my daughter-in-law's seemingly insatiable appetite. Adam's wife is gaining weight at a phenomenal rate. If she's not careful she will blow up like a balloon and end up like her aunt. I knew the second I laid eyes on that girl that she was predestined to grow fat. Adam's choice of wife has always been an enigma to me. She is attractive in an exotic sort of way but no match for my son. Adam has always been stubborn and journeyed against the grain. I can only assume that his marriage was an act of defiance. I will never understand why.

A sparrow on the window ledge puffs out its tiny chest and exhales a trill. A creeper, climbing the wall outside, pokes its tendril through the partially open window. I feel as lifeless as a dead branch hanging inert, one that will never sprout new growth but only drop to the ground and decay. I long to feel an energising breeze against my skin. To walk against the wind and feel my leg muscles working again. A sharp twinge in my left knee takes my breath away, a reminder of the osteo-arthritis turning my bones to crumbs. What does the future hold for me? Only physical decline. Hydrocortisone injections have forestalled the need for a plastic knee. Analgesics provide relief from the drudgery of throbbing pain. Healthy living has kept me mobile. I swim, walk and eat sensibly. I refuse to end up in a wheelchair at the mercy of others.

The telephone starts ringing. I grab the crutches from beside the bed, force myself to stand and make my way into the hallway. A woman on the other end of the line asks for Mrs Reynolds. 'Speaking,' I say, absentmindedly. The call is from the hospital and I assume it has something to do with my leg. The woman tells me that the date of my pre-natal scan has been rescheduled and gives me a new date and time, saying the hospital will post a reminder card. I put down the receiver and realise with dismay that my son's wife is pregnant. I sit on the hallway chair feeling depressed, wondering why I wasn't told, worrying about my son's future. A child will trap Adam in a marriage he is bound to grow out of. A child will tie us to that woman for ever.

A chemical smell, reminiscent of a car battery, wafts into the hallway from the workroom. I get up, intending to close the door, but decide instead to step inside a space I am never invited into. A block of bright sunlight illuminates a room thick with flickering motes, an unhealthy mix of dust and metal particles. A letter on the desk catches my attention. 'Certified Bailiffs and Enforcement Agents' is scored in red ink across the top. I pick up the letter and read. 'We hold a warrant against you for monies owed to H.M. Customs and Excise. You have incurred a cost of £12.50 for the issue of this warrant and the total now required is £2416.65. Recovery action will be withheld for six days from date of postage of this letter.' The letter is dated 9 July. What does this mean? That in three days the bailiffs will turn up and take my son's belongings? 'Failure to pay as instructed will result in distress being levied on your goods,' is the final threatening sentence, one that chills and infuriates me. I sift through the letters, one by one, my anger rising as I discover the full extent of the problem. There are several unpaid invoices and a quarterly telephone bill that amounts to more than I pay in a year. Calls to Cyprus run the length of the itemised section. Beneath the bills is a copy of a bank transfer. Money has been sent from a UK bank account in Electra's name to a Cypriot account in her sister's name.

I turn from the desk to the window, wondering how to talk to my son without being accused of interfering. Standing before me, caught in the frame of the opposing window, is the architect of my son's potential ruin. Adam's wife has her back to me. She is drinking from a mug and talking to a man wearing glasses. She throws back her head and I can almost hear the shrill pitch of her characteristic cackle. Is this an innocent encounter? Coffee with a friend? I am prepared to give her the benefit of the doubt until I see her reach out and touch the man's shoulder, then his face. The evidence is sickening and conclusive. Electra is not only squandering my son's money on her family, she is having an affair right under his very nose. I move away from the window filled with rage and indignation, wondering if this stranger might even be the father of her child? How do I cure Adam of love blindness and make him see his wife for what she really is? My son has been bewitched by an unscrupulous woman, hell-bent on destroying him.

Lydia

Lydia had spent the day on autopilot. Talking about lampshades, thinking about Alvaro and his worsening behaviour. Her son was a conundrum to her. As soon as she thought she'd worked him out, he quickly reconfigured. This time Alvaro had done a U-turn, reverted to being a troublesome toddler. He was more demanding of late, angrier. Refused to be swayed by reason. He was slipping out of Lydia's grasp like a wet fish. She had to tighten her hold, usurp Granny's control and strengthen the connection between mother and son. Consuelo said her grandson's fractiousness was nothing more than a phase, one of many such on the road to manhood. Lydia was not convinced. She believed Jack to be a negative influence on Alvaro's life.

Lydia had taken the afternoon off work to pick her son up from school, to disarm him with a treat, to take him to his favourite fast-food restaurant for a portion of synthetic food and a self-assembly toy. She hated the place with a vengeance, its smell made her nauseous. It was a poisonous Tardis that offered inducements no child could refuse. Lydia limited their visits but feared that always saying no would only serve to make cardboard chicken and toothpick chips as seductive as forbidden fruit. She would engage her son in conversation amid a plethora of smooth plastic and glib slogans, inside a place where aggressive marketing was dressed in child-friendly colours. While he munched she would fret about the empty calories passing through his oesophagus and along his digestive tract.

Alvaro would eat with the zeal of a starving child before piecing together his toy. He would attach limbs to torso, beak to head, wheels to chassis, instinctively. He was adept at fiddly construction, skilled at model-making, dextrously pulled to bits and reassembled alarm clocks and radios. The tinier the innards, the more taxing the rebuild, the greater the pleasure for Alvaro. He revelled in the construction of abstract forms. Consuelo's garden was a minefield of modern sculpture and miniature totems made from rocks, stones, plastic cartons, twigs, leaves, feathers, snail shells, string and cutlery. Alvaro's creations, lovingly constructed, resembled ruins ready to topple. Lydia was forced to mow the grass around her son's three-dimensional jigsaws. When the wind and rain wrecked his handiwork he set about reconstructing exact replicas.

Alvaro's models and drawings had always differed from the flat, anthropomorphic designs produced by his peers. He held his pencil like a paintbrush and filled his paper with sketchy, fluid lines that made little sense until the drawing was complete. He started with an ear, sketched whiskers, drew a crooked limb, scribbled a scruffy mane . . . the end result a lion in motion. He drew the same lion again and again, until it was perfected. Then he moved on to clowns, always coloured red and blue, with stripy braces and crooked flowers growing out of black top hats.

Children dribbled out of the school entrance, clutching coats, bags and letters, jumpers tied around their waists. A tiny girl with plaited hair took hold of her mother's hand and obediently walked away, not tugging or running off ahead, her shoes un-scuffed, her shirt tucked neatly into her skirt. Lydia marvelled at the compliancy, the delicacy, the otherworldliness of small girls. Bigger ones, she suspected, were ruled not by their parents but their hormones. She wondered what impact an absentee father had on a girl. Did she crave the tenderness only a father could supposedly give? Did she feel cheated of a knee to sit on, a thick neck to throw her arms around, a stubbly cheek on which to practise her kisses? At least Alvaro would go out into the world with some knowledge of the opposite sex. He had stroked Lydia's bare leg, seen her naked in the shower, sniffed and tasted her hair, put his hand up her skirt for a sneaky feel of her thigh.

She felt a tap on the shoulder and turned to see Jack's mother. 'Hello. Are you Al's mum? I've been meaning to talk to you for a while but you always rush off so quickly in the morning.'

'Hi. Nice to meet you. I'm Lydia.'

Jack's mother was tall and slim and wore a thick layer of makeup. 'I'm Michelle. My friends call me Miche.'

Lydia doubted this woman would ever be a friend of hers. She planned to discourage Alvaro's friendship with Jack. It seemed to be doing him more harm than good.

'I don't normally see you after school.' Michelle scratched her cheek with a long synthetic nail. 'Who's the woman who picks your son up? Al's nanny?'

'No. My mother, Consuelo.'

'Are you Spanish?' Michelle's pencil eyebrows rode up half an inch. She looked impressed.

'Mum's Spanish. Dad was English.'

'I love Spain. I go there every year to get my fill of sun, sea and sangria.' The cliché made Lydia cringe inside. Michelle gazed up at the grey sky with a look of incredulity. 'Why on earth do you live here when you come from Spain?'

'I was born here. England's my home.'

Kane's mother walked past, her son and a buggy in tow. She smiled warmly at Lydia, steering her pram through the school gate, the backs of her open-toed sandals clacking against the tough soles of her bare feet. Anita radiated contentment. She appeared to have no aspirations beyond raising her children and cooking elaborate meals for her husband. Consuelo said she was great company. Quiet, unassuming, Anita had a laugh as piercing as a pneumatic drill, that erupted from the pit of her stomach and spread like contagion. When Kane and Alvaro were friends Consuelo often visited Anita's home after school to nibble on sweetmeats and samosas, to watch her hostess roll out chapatti dough and cook it over a naked flame.

Michelle drew her face closer to Lydia's and motioned towards Anita. 'I think those are what you might call childbearing hips.'

Lydia smiled involuntarily, feeling disloyal, instantly ruling out the prospect of ever connecting with Michelle. Jack's mean spirit was not a genetic blip. Lydia felt irritated suddenly by Michelle's patent leather boots and skinny eyebrows, her tight designer jeans and the dark streaks in her blonde, poker-straight hair. She was a Costa-del clone, a woman with perfect teeth and a fake tan, all affectation and pretence, as substantial as cardboard chicken and toothpick chips. Electra would eat her for breakfast. She would chew her up, spit out her bones and complain about her lack of meat. Michelle was not Lydia's style of woman.

Alvaro ran up to his mother, dumping his bag at her feet. His face was flushed, his white shirt grimy, his shoes caked in mud. A tidier-looking Jack handed his belongings to Michelle. 'Can Jack come to our house?' Alvaro put his hands together as if in prayer.

'Of course. Perhaps one day next week?'

'No, today. Please, Mum. Please, Mum. Please.'

'It might not be convenient.'

'I don't mind if you don't mind,' Michelle said, dashing the hopes Lydia had of spending quality time with her son.

The boys ran through the hall, across the kitchen, past Consuelo sitting at the table and out into the garden. Consuelo rooted through a pile of papers, the telephone receiver wedged between shoulder and ear.

'Hi, Mum.'

'Shh! Don speak.'

Lydia made two mugs of coffee and sat in the chair opposite her mother, watching her scribble digits on a notepad with a green felt-tip pen. Consuelo put down the receiver and picked up her mug with a self-satisfied grin.

'This time I've definitely wone.'

'Won what, Mum?'

'A holiday for two in Paris.'

Consuelo handed her daughter a green, official-looking letter, a Guaranteed Prize Authorisation Form. According to this letter Consuelo Gomez had been allocated a top prize and all she had to do to claim it was telephone the prize line and jot down a six-digit number.

'How long have you been on the phone, Mum?'

'Ten . . . fifteen minutes.'

'Look here, did you read this? It says calls cost one pound fifty a minute. You've just spent around twenty pounds for nothing.'

Consuelo snatched the letter back. 'I've spend twenty pound for a holiday in Paris.'

'I'll believe it when I see it.'

'You look.' She turned the paper over. 'Ol these people they wone. Why I'm no gonna win? Brian from Glue-chester, hiss won. Consuelo from Acton, she's gonna win too. You wai an see.'

'Give me that.' On the back of the letter Brian from Gloucester held up a cheque for £25,000.

Consuelo never failed to reply to letters promising her prizes and cash sums. She read these letters with steely concentration, believing the hype, convinced

162

that one day she too would be a jackpot winner. She had 'won' several foreign holidays, steeped in restrictive and prohibitive conditions. Tickets for one with ridiculously high supplements for a second traveller. Trips to unspecified hotels, on inconvenient dates, that came with the risk of sharing a bedroom with a stranger. By the time Consuelo had deliberated over whether or not she should go, her travel vouchers had invariably expired.

'If I don win that, maybe I'm gonna win this?'

Conuelo held up a scratch card with a £50 million top prize. With eyes wide and adrenaline coursing through her veins she scraped off the metallic coating with a coin, praying for three in a row. 'Sheet! Is not my locky day,' she said, examining the card.

If she did not feel her husband's omnipresence, his spirit lurking in every corner of the house, Consuelo might have indulged her fondness for gambling in the nearest casino, standing rigidly at a blackjack table, holding her breath, praying for an ace and a ten. Her husband had disapproved of gambling and kept Consuelo on the straight and narrow. When Harry was alive she'd satisfied her gaming spirit by collecting supermarket points and tokens, by keeping her eyes open for offers and cut-price deals. A couple of pence off her washing powder, two pots of yoghurt for the price of one, a free dishcloth with every purchase. Consuelo was neither miserly nor money-minded. She thought nothing of splurging her pension on toys and clothes for Alvaro. Her passion was fuelled by a desire to milk the system, to use her ingenuity to get something for nothing.

'What would you do with fifty million pounds?'

'Give it to you and my grandsone. Wass an al woman gonna do with fifty millions? I'm no gonna live long enough to spent it. Anyway, when are you gonna tek me to the bingo?'

Lydia had foolishly agreed to take her mother to a bingo hall, to sit in a neon-filled room full of casino rejects. 'Soon. I promise.'

Harry's death had robbed Consuelo of a chauffeur and a bosom buddy, a husband keen to satisfy his wife's every whim. Lydia felt herself to be a poor substitute. Consuelo and her husband had been inseparable. Watching television side by side on the sofa, snoring concurrently in the sunroom. While Harry peeled potatoes, Consuelo floured squid. While he vacuumed the house, she polished and dusted. Once a week the couple set out on an excursion to the nearest deli to stock up on Chorizo sausage, dried pulses, fresh herbs and firm crusty bread. At first light on Sunday morning they paid a visit to DIY heaven, a 20,000-square-foot hangar housing stippling brushes, paints for marbling, and ginger-coloured glazes used for turning yellow Formica into grainy oak.

Consuelo's over-painted, over-experimental, clutter-infested house had nurtured Lydia's love of minimalism. Her own bedroom was a stark white sparsely furnished square, a peaceful zone where she could sit and think, the only place she was afforded privacy. Consuelo said her daughter's room was reminiscent of the sanatorium in which she had briefly worked. Lydia had forbidden Consuelo from entering her room, to clean, to rummage through drawers, to vacuum under the bed. Lydia needed a burrow, devoid of her mother's touch, a place where she could be herself and indulge in private interests. Where she could hum a tune into a Dictaphone and scribble lyrics in a notepad; where she could smoke the occasional cigarette and use the battery-operated device that made her feel like a fully functional woman.

Lydia only bought herself a vibrator after much deliberation and soul-searching; after Electra literally took her by the arm, pulled her into a sex shop and ordered the appliance for beginners. The woman behind the counter handed Lydia a box containing what looked like a children's toy. She was reluctant to use it at first, thinking it would sully her in some way, that its use smacked of desperation. Feeling particularly brave one night, she'd raided Alvaro's laser gun for batteries and embarked on a voyage of self-discovery. Like an old virgin who finally relinquishes her chastity, Lydia wished she had taken the plunge sooner and not wasted so much time deliberating.

At first she felt a little foolish, her sense of loneliness exacerbated, but slowly, slowly, with practice and patience and growing self-awareness, the vibrator had become the highlight of her day. It eased tension, put a smile on her face, helped Lydia sleep and gave her a feeling of well-being. Its only shortcoming was that it interfered with the reception of Consuelo's satellite channel. Lydia discovered this one night when her mother started hammering on her door, complaining that the television was hissing, that a clinch between

Crystalle and Juan-Pedro had been rudely interrupted. Lydia switched off the device, followed her mother into the living room and found the picture quality to be perfectly crisp. She returned to her bedroom and continued where she had left off. 'Is hissin again,' her mother called out. Lydia returned to the living room. 'Is all right now,' Consuelo said. After a series of similar exchanges Lydia deduced the root of the problem and remained in suspended animation until the end of Consuelo's late-night soaps.

Lydia was in a sexual buffer zone, not ready to commit, unwilling to crush her morale with unsatisfying one-night stands. The burrowing mammal was her only option for the time being. It could not give her love, or the satisfaction of bodily contact, but it elicited intense, novel and hugely pleasurable sensations. Lydia's only fear was that no man would ever be able to live up to its reliability and unerring performance.

She got up. 'I'd better start making tea for the boys.'

'You relax, Lythia. You've been workin all day. I'm gonna do it.'

Consuelo was up and apron-clad before her daughter had a chance to protest. Cooking for her grandson was an expression of love, a mandatory activity built into her daily timetable. While eating lunch Consuelo planned her grandson's evening meal. While he ate his supper she devised his breakfast menu. What troubled her was Alvaro's refusal to sample anything Spanish. He turned his nose up at Chorizo, requested oven chips not *Truita de Patata*, and rejected paella on the basis of its colour while eating bland, boiled Mr Bens. He sniffed sarsuela and grimaced, balked at the sight of anchovies, aubergines, chickpeas, lentils and olives. Consuelo's attempts at breaking him in gently by adding crushed garlic to his mashed potato, or boiling up his baked beans with a bay leaf, had consistently failed. Alvaro always sniffed his food before putting it into his mouth. If the smell was not to his liking he pushed his plate away and refused to eat.

The smell of grilled sausages filtered into Lydia's bedroom. She lit a cigarette and sat beside her open window watching the boys play football in the garden. Holding her cigarette below the window frame, stooping to inhale, letting the smoke trickle out of her mouth, anxious to keep her bad habit a secret from her son. An unexpected knock at her bedroom door caught her mid-drag and made her cough.

'Lythia, can I com in?'

Lydia flicked her cigarette out of the window, mindful that Alvaro's back was turned. She sprayed the bedroom with perfume and opened the door.

Consuelo walked in and sniffed the air. 'What you wanna eat tonight?'

'Anything, Mum. You know I'm not fussy.'

'Wass tha horribol smell?'

'It's new perfume.' She held up the bottle.

'Is smell very bad.' Consuelo shrugged and headed for the door. 'You've always had a fonny taste in perfume, Lythia.'

Lydia reached for the telephone beside her bed and

dialled Electra's mobile number. She had stopped calling the flat in case Margaret answered and she was forced to make conversation with a woman she found thoroughly unpleasant.

Electra sounded pleased to hear her friend's voice but spoke in a whisper saying Margaret was lurking close by. She talked about her growing sense of frustration, her morning sickness and then asked after Consuelo.

'Mum's fine. I'm not. She nearly caught me with a cigarette.'

'Aren't we too old to be having this conversation?'

'In Mum's mind I will always be the moody adolescent who spends hours locked away in a bedroom that smells of charred perfume.'

'You're a grown woman with a child.'

'But I haven't moved on, have I? I still live with my mother and smoke in secret, scribble lyrics in a notepad and hum tunes into a Dictaphone.'

'You're very musical. You should send some of your songs to a music publisher.'

'Don't be ridiculous. I have no intention of taking my hobby beyond the bedroom door. Exposing my inner world to strangers. What chance does a thirty-four-year-old single mother, with no musical experience, have of breaking into the music industry? I'll leave pop stardom to Alvaro.'

'What's my godson up to anyway? Can I talk to him?'

'He's out in the garden trying to play football with his friend.'

Lydia watched the boys from her bedroom window,

kicking a ball into a narrow improvised goal. Her son had two left feet. His ball never travelled in a straight line but vertically over and round imaginary posts, always wide of the target. Alvaro did not appear disheartened, taking laps of honour around the garden, stuffing grass triumphantly down his shorts. Jack was a different ilk of boy. Athletic, precise, ultra-competitive, less theatrical, punching his small fist in the air when he scored. He was a cheetah, stalking the ball, honing his concentration, sprinting to shoot. Alvaro was a lion cub, bumbling playfully, kicking with uncoordinated feet.

After heading his ball into goal, Jack kicked down one of Alvaro's totems, then a second. Lydia was shocked by her son's sudden disregard for the structures he'd lovingly constructed, by the way he carried on playing as if nothing had happened.

'Hey! That boy's wrecking Alvaro's garden sculptures. He's kicking them to pieces.'

'Then tell him to stop.'

'No, I won't. Alvaro has to learn to fight his own battles. I can't always be with him.'

'I never knew he liked football?'

'I think he feels obliged to like it because his best friend likes it. He's joined the after-school soccer club. Mum takes him once a week and stands on the sidelines, cursing the English weather.'

'Com in, boys. Your tea is ready.' Piercing vibrational waves emanated from Consuelo's larynx and travelled out of the kitchen window, across the garden, over the low wooden fence and through the door of the neighbour's greenhouse. Lydia watched in amusement as her neighbour jumped out of his skin and dropped his secateurs.

'I have to go, Electra. They're just about to eat.'

The boys' washed hands still bore traces of mud. Alvaro's fingernails, thrust into moist earth, were rimmed with dirt. He shovelled forkfuls of sausage and mash into his mouth and swallowed the food down in chunks. Lydia hovered in the kitchen while Consuelo folded towels in the laundry room.

'What's for pudding?' Alvaro asked

'Ice cream. Do you like ice cream, Jack?'

'Yeah,' he said, looking up and spotting a knobbly brown sausage hanging from a hook. 'Ugh! What's that? It looks disgusting.'

'That's Grandma's sausage,' Alvaro replied.

'Thas e real sausage,' Consuelo said, walking back into the kitchen. 'Is no lie that Engleesh robbish your eatin. Is call *E Slachichon*. My daughter hees buy tha for me from the Portobello Market. You wanna try som, Jack?'

Jack shook his head.

'In Catalunia we have many types of sausage. They made with wine and garlic and herbs. Som they made with bread soaked in pig's blod, others they soft like pâté . . .' Consuelo extolled the virtues of the Spanish sausage while spooning soft-scoop vanilla ice cream into dessert plates.

Michelle scanned Consuelo's schizophrenic living room. 'Nice place,' she said, looking amused. Her eyelashes, thickly dredged with mascara, reminded Lydia of hairy black butterfly larva.

'This is Mum's house not mine.' Lydia felt the usual compulsion to disassociate herself from the décor.

'Where do you live?'

'Here, with Mum.'

'You and your husband live with your mother?'

'Alvaro and I live with Mum. I'm not with my husband.'

'Oh, I'm sorry to hear that.' Michelle blushed, seemingly ill at ease with Lydia's marital status. Lydia wondered why? Did Michelle think having a spouse was always, under any circumstances, superior to not having one?

'What's there to be sorry about?'

'It can't be easy, bringing up a child on your own.'

'It's easier than bringing up a child with the wrong man. I'm very lucky, I have Mum to help me.'

'You need to find yourself a nice bloke.'

Was it mandatory to travel through life with a Siamese twin? Lydia was happy travelling light, without complications. The prospect of introducing a man to her son filled her with dread. If she saw disinterest in the eyes of the man, she would send him packing. If she glimpsed disappointment in the eyes of her son, she would crumble.

'You sound like my mother.'

'I'm Lythia's motha.' Consuelo walked into the room, smelling of fried fish, extending a small, flour-dusted hand.

'¡Hola, Consuelo! ¿Como esta?'

Consuelo's face lit up. She pulled Michelle down to eye level by the shoulders and kissed her on both cheeks before replying at high speed in her mother tongue.

'*Muy bien, gracias. Y usted ¿como esta?*'

'Sorry, I didn't understand a word you said. I've only just got the hang of "hello" and "how are you?"'

'How you know to speak Spanish?'

'I spend a fortnight every year in the Costas.'

'Why you not try Catalunia? We have the best cuisine in Spain, you know.'

'I can't get the kids to eat anything Spanish.'

'My grandsone hees the same. Blody kids!'

'Hiss a very nice lethy. Very goo-lookin an tall,' Consuelo announced when Michelle had left with her son.

'Everyone's tall compared to you, Mum.'

Consuelo had always looked up both physically and metaphorically to women who resembled the well-groomed protagonists of her soap operas. She did not preen herself beyond combing her grey hair and moisturising her olive skin, but admired women whose faces were as thickly caked as a paint palette. Lydia knew her mother would never be able to see the beauty in simplicity and understatement. Her house was a jumbled testament to her aesthetic leanings.

Lydia went in search of her son, hoping to monopolise him for the remainder of the evening. She found him in the back garden, reconstructing his totems, in the rain. Positioning stones, realigning sticks, standing back to examine his structures from a distance.

'Tell tha boy to com inside,' Consuelo called from the kitchen window.

'Let him finish, Mum.'

172

It had grown cold. Alvaro needed a bath. To call him inside before he had finished would only serve to make him anxious and spark an argument, though. Lydia put her coat on and braved the rain to search the muddy ground for missing pieces. Collecting them in a bucket, handing them to her son.

'Mum,' he said, when he had finally finished, 'can Adam take me to football practice next week?'

'No, Alvaro. You'll have to go with Granny.'

'Please, Mum. Can I call him now and ask?'

'No. Adam's still at work when you have football practice.'

'He can finish work early. He's my godfather, isn't he? I'm going to call him.'

Alvaro rushed into the house, trailing mud through the kitchen on his way to the telephone. He dialled Electra's number. Lydia heard the high-pitched lilt of her friend's voice, imagined her enthusiastic response to Alvaro's request and knew that Adam's fate was sealed.

Adam

My wedding day. A hotel function room in Cyprus. Patterned carpet. Rubber plants. An abundance of kitsch. Seating for nine hundred. The pianist plays 'Endless Love' on a nasty little keyboard, accompanying impassioned vocals in a thick Greek accent.

Prompted by my mother-in-law, I lead a reluctant Electra onto the dance floor. Guests clap frenziedly. Electra leans her head on my ribcage and drags me in staccato fashion across the laminated floor. I may not be the greatest dancer but I am a music lover and any rendition of this song would have made my skin crawl. I sweat profusely beneath the snug-fitting pinstripe, which makes me look like a monochrome stick of rock. It is late-spring. Thirty degrees Celsius outside. Air-conditioned within. Piping hot inside my jacket. I try to focus on forward-back, forward-back, forward-forward-back. The bride's heel pierces my big toe. The pain is excruciating. I flinch momentarily but carry on stoically as the song draws to a welcome end.

This is the beginning, not the end, of my humiliation. Tradition dictates that the groom and his two left feet, accustomed to English rhythms, must dance to the strains of violin and bouzouki while guests pin money on his jacket. I am forced to smile appreciatively and thank Aunt Miroulla when she sticks her pin not in cloth but in flesh. I drink half a crate of Keo beer, knowing the worst is still to come, that I am expected to dance with my father-in-law and a succession of best men I barely know. My head is spinning when I take centre-stage once more, arms outstretched, clutching one end of a white hanky, my dance partner holding onto the other.

At first my moves are jerky and uncoordinated as I struggle to remember the steps Electra taught me in the days leading up to our wedding. I am a fish out of water, an ungainly white boy trying to swing it with the natives. Slowly, slowly, bolstered by Keo, I start to get the hang of it. There is nothing to it really, I think. Just keep a tight grip on the hanky, strut like a cock on heat, and slap a heel or two. Not content with getting the hang of it, I crouch down and kick my ungainly legs like a Cossack, mimicking the moves of my best men. I am proud of myself, impressed by my natural flair. An over-ambitious kick topples me. I fall flat on my back and stay there, like a beetle unable to right itself. Far from disgracing myself, I appear to have pleased the crowd, which applauds and wolf whistles. Electra, who finds the spectacle hilarious, is doubled over with laughter.

A best man pulls me onto my feet and I continue unabated, twirling and twisting like a madman, clapping my hands, wanting the music to go on for ever. All too soon, it is time for the maids-of-honour to dance with the bride. I leave the dance floor with the air of a Roman combatant exiting an arena, blowing my lovely bride a kiss, feeling like the luckiest man alive. I join a group of men. They light up a cigar and hand it to me. I put it to my lips, squint like a big-shot Mafioso and draw the smoke into my mouth. It tastes good. I labour under the illusion that I am hardier, more Alpha-male than I'd thought, until I wake up in the morning, limbs leaden, voice hoarse, my tonsils the size of ping-pong balls.

Electra

The setting is fit for the cover of *Country Life*. A glass
jug filled with Pimm's and lemonade sits on a wooden
table beneath a striped awning. A long-limbed woman
with fine blonde hair sits at the table with one leg
crossed over the other, sipping from a tall glass. Beside
her is a slim grandmother, legs covered with a tartan
blanket, looking out on to a cottage-style garden.
Rosemary, lavender and sage grow among perennials
in semi-circular beds lined with gravel. A galvanised
watering can and stone sundial are strategically
positioned among the herbs, bushes and miniature
fruit trees. Wisteria in flower scrambles over a wooden
pergola. Two girls, blown off a Laura Ashley poster,
run up and down the S-shaped lawn, laughing, chased
by their smiling uncle. A handsome man wearing a
rugby shirt turns steaks on a spanking-new barbecue,
a wine glass held in one hand, metal tongs in the other.
The only thing marring this summer image of
domestic bliss is a short woman with wiry hair and
ballooning breasts who feels fat and self-conscious

in the tight-fitting top she has chosen to wear.

Some pictures speak a thousand words. Others conceal the truth. And the truth behind this summer image of perfection is that the meat is burning and rain clouds are gathering and John is shouting at the children to stop pulling leaves off the Japanese maple. And my mother-in-law is waxing lyrical about the house and the garden and the pre-washed, pre-cut salad that came with a pre-prepared dressing, making me feel thoroughly unappreciated, the runt of this litter. And Adam is gulping down wine and growing redder by the minute, in an effort to calm the nerves his mother frayed on the journey to John's house by sitting in the front passenger seat and telling him how to drive. 'You can drive back,' he whispered in my ear when we arrived. 'I'm getting drunk.'

One of John's steaks bursts into flames. He skewers it with the fork and lifts it up, waiting for the burning coals to die down. I could teach him a thing or two about barbecuing but I doubt he would appreciate my advice.

I sip from a glass half-filled with white wine and think nostalgically of family barbecues back home – on the beach at sunset, overhead a string of lights powered by a generator. The cooking meat flavoured with oregano and lemon juice and served with salad, pitta bread and louganiga – spicy sausages. 'I should have fetched some *louganiga*. They're wonderful on the barbecue,' I say, my tastebuds awakened by this mental image and the smell of charcoal smoke lacing the air.

'What are *loug . . . arn . . .ig . . .* I won't even attempt to say it,' Caroline says, smiling. 'I wish I could speak two languages with such fluency.'

'I still have my accent. I don't expect I will ever lose it. In fact, I hope I never do.' I look across at Margaret, my comment aimed at this woman who likes to correct my pronunciation, who looks at me as if I'm stupid when my o's come out as a's and I roll my r's a little too roundly. '*Louganiga* are beef and garlic sausages.'

'Where do you buy such delicacies, Electra?'

Adam sits beside me, panting a little from over-exertion.

'I don't buy them. Every time I go to Cyprus my mother sends me home with a bag full of food. I put most of it in the freezer and eat it when I'm feeling a little homesick, which is quite often these days.'

'I've noticed you eating rather a lot,' Margaret says, her friendly tone suggesting her comment is benign, a simple observation.

'I'm not surprised she's eating more,' Caroline says. 'After all, she is . . .'

'. . . a comfort eater, that's what I am, and I'm not ashamed to admit it.' I cut Caroline off mid-sentence, my glance warning her not to continue. She looks confused but thankfully gets the message.

Adam picks up his glass and gulps down wine. 'Do you remember the time your grandmother put a bag of cannabis seeds in my suitcase without telling me?'

Margaret looks at him aghast. 'Cannabis seeds?'

'Don't worry, Margaret, you can't get high on them.'

'Unless you plant them in a warm spot and wait a few months.' Adam's tongue, loosened by alcohol, bypasses his brain.

Margaret frowns. 'I don't think smuggling drugs into the country is something to joke about.'

'I don't think you get locked up for the possession of seeds.' My knowledge of Britain's drugs laws fails to impress.

'Whyever did your grandmother do such a thing?'

'The seeds were for Aunt Miroulla.'

'She's a dark horse,' Adam says, flashing the cheeky smile I have missed.

'She uses the seeds to flavour her Easter pastries, her *flaounes*.'

Adam, oblivious to the scowl on his mother's face, leans towards Caroline. 'Doesn't my wife look beautiful today?'

'Adam, you're drunk,' his mother says, screwing up her face.

'Electra's positively blooming,' Caroline says. 'And she's lucky to have a husband who pays her such lovely compliments.'

'John,' Adam calls out, 'why don't you pay your wife a compliment?'

'She cooks a great Dover sole,' he replies, heading for the table with a loaded platter, laying it in the centre of the table. 'I hope you all like your steaks well done?'

'The steaks look marvellous, darling,' Margaret says, a sentiment echoed by Caroline, both women trying to please their emperor.

Adam screws up his face. 'Steaks! They look more like lumps of coal. I'll stick to the salad, thanks.'

Five frazzled steaks and three bottles of wine later, John raises his glass to make a toast. 'Let's drink to Mother who's handling this broken leg business with real stoicism.'

'I'd like to propose a toast to my wife, too,' Adam says, 'for looking after Mum so well.'

John clinks glasses with his brother. 'To Mother and Electra.' He flashes his wife a drunken smile and leans back in his chair. 'What's for pudding, darling?'

'I've made some . . .' Caroline is interrupted by a piercing scream from the far end of the garden.

Elizabeth comes running up to the table, red-faced and upset. 'Mummy, Amy poked me with a stick,' she screams, her eyes streaming.

Amy hurries towards her sister. 'No, I didn't, you liar.'

'Yes, you did.'

'It was an accident, Mummy. I swear.' Amy stares at her sister defiantly.

'No, it wasn't. You're the one who's lying.'

'Calm down, girls, please. We have guests.' Caroline stands. 'Let's go inside and sort this out.'

Elizabeth stamps her foot. 'But she's lying, Mummy.'

'No, I'm not.'

'Yes, you are.'

'STOP IT! Both of you,' John shouts, startling us all with the ferocity of his tone. I watch the girls' faces drain of colour as their father springs up from his seat, with a demonic look on his face, his eyes bleary and bloodshot. He grabs Amy by the arm, pulls her towards him and slaps the backs of her bare legs. 'I've warned you before about lying.'

'Daddy, stop it! She didn't mean it. It was an accident,' Elizabeth cries, pulling at her father's arm.

'Then *you* must have been lying.' John releases Amy and grabs Elizabeth, smacking her legs also, making her small body shunt forward. Her cheeks flush with anger and humiliation. She glances reproachfully at her mother before bursting into tears.

'John. Please.' Caroline covers her mouth, her own eyes watering.

'Go to your rooms, both of you.'

The girls run inside howling. Charred meat and chive dip send pungent fumes from my churning stomach into my mouth. John's sudden switch from jaunty host to ogre is a shocking spectacle, his treatment of the girls unjustified. His drink-induced temper a worrying portent. Caroline takes a step forward.

'And you sit down. Leave them,' her husband commands. 'They both have some serious thinking to do.'

'I was going to fetch the trifle,' Caroline says weakly, walking away.

Adam glares at his brother. 'Don't you think that was a bit harsh?'

'Children need to know who's boss. You can't let them run around like savages.'

Margaret nods. 'I fully agree with you, son.'

'You could hardly describe your girls as savages.'

'Just wait until you have children of your own before you pass judgement. Those two could test the patience of a saint.'

'My father never hit me once and I got up to more than my fair share of mischief,' I say indignantly, sickened by John's short fuse, wondering how a brute like him would have raised a demanding boy like Alvaro.

Adam glances at his watch saying it's time we went home and the sky growls as if voicing its disapproval of our host. Heavy rain pelts the awning and gushes from the rim like a waterfall, darkening the grey stone patio slabs, splattering our legs, breaking up our happy gathering.

Mama's happy, tearful call came the evening of 21 April 2003. I was sitting at my workbench, sketching a new design. Channelling my nocturnal energies into work, feeling more than a little sorry for myself. Wishing there was more to my life than work and sleep, wondering when, if ever, spring would decide to make an appearance, thinking fondly of home. The telephone rang. I answered it and Mama gobbled like a turkey down the line. 'Denktash has opened the borders, we can go home!' I went cold, needing time to digest this news. 'Did you hear me, Electra?' Mama said, wanting me to share the joy she would later discover was unfounded.

After thirty years of enforced division, the Turkish Cypriot authorities decided to lift travel restrictions on the island. Greek Cypriots were permitted to visit the north every day from 7 a.m. to midnight. Likewise, Turkish Cypriots were allowed to cross the border southwards. Several days after the announcement my parents joined a ten-hour queue at the checkpoint in Nicosia to embark on the journey they had dreamed about for three decades. They were keen to go as soon as they could, fearing the border might close as arbitrarily as it had opened. It was a hot day. The mood was upbeat. Half a dozen people fainted in the queue, toppled by the heat and the intensity of their emotions.

For many refugees, my parents included, the journey was unsettling. The realities they encountered shattered the hallowed images of the past they held dear. Some found their houses lovingly cared for by Turkish Cypriots who welcomed them with open arms. Others found crumbling ruins, stripped and looted, occupied by a succession of careless house sitters. My aunt returned to a house that was freshly whitewashed, its shutters painted a cheery Mediterranean blue. She knocked on the door sheepishly, her stomach in knots. Her knock was answered by a tanned and healthy-looking German expat in shorts and flip-flops who shooed her off the front step as if she were a rabid dog. 'Go away,' he said, 'this is my house now. I bought it. You have no right to it anymore.' And then he closed the door in her face, before my uncle had a chance to reach up and grab him by the throat. Aunty led her husband away. The last thing she wanted was trouble in a place that suddenly felt foreign and threatening. She realised on her tearful journey south that she had lost her home twice over in one lifetime and wished to God she had never gone back.

In the space of three weeks 350,000 Greek Cypriots crossed over to the north. In coaches, cars and on foot. Streaming northwards en masse as they had once been forced to stream southwards. Many believing free movement to be a step in the right direction, a positive shift towards a mutually acceptable solution to the Cyprus problem. Papa calls it a cynical ploy by the north's leader Denktash to silence Turkish Cypriot demands for a settlement and boost the north's ailing economy with an injection of cash. 'We Greeks are unscrupulous donkeys,' he said. 'We have spent millions of pounds in the north. Buying bargain goods. Staying in cut-price hotels. Gambling in Turkish Cypriot casinos. Eating cheap meals in the fish restaurants of Kyrenia. Putting our stomachs before their principles.' What free movement has proved is that Greek and Turkish Cypriots can co-exist, that they can overcome the enmity created by politicians. Though emotionally charged, the daily pilgrimages to ancestral homes have been largely trouble-free. What free movement has exacerbated is the island's most burning issue: who owns what?

Mama was very disappointed by what she saw across the border. 'They've sold our properties to buyers from abroad. They've built holiday villas on our land. The Turkish Cypriot developers call it "exchange land", compensation for the land they lost in the south. Perhaps they should call it by its real name – something for nothing. Villas in the north are dirt cheap. Foreigners snap them up and don't bother asking questions. They don't ask for title deeds, they don't care who rightfully owns the land they sit sunning themselves on.'

'They won't get away with it.' I reassured her. 'We still have legal rights to our property and our land. We can claim compensation through the European courts. Those who buy illegally face consequences. You can't enter a hornet's nest and not expect to be stung.'

The north has become a haven for British criminals, who languish in the sun safe in the knowledge that they cannot be extradited to the UK. They live in veritable palaces and see no ethical problem in building entire holiday villages on refugee land. Let the natives fight it out, they tell themselves, filling their coffers. What do we care? They put up signs saying 'Let Us Build Your Dreams' and wait for the gullible, unprincipled and stupid to come flocking.

My nieces and nephews have no memory of a time before partition. Before territorial lines were erected to divide two ethnic groups. Barbed wire, armed soldiers, blue and white lookout posts, hillsides scored with hammer and sickle, are part of their natural landscape. These children belong to a generation with no first-hand knowledge of those 'on the other side'. Nurtured in a post-war era, they have a more acute sense of 'them' and 'us'. I remember a time when we were all just one – compatriots. I remember, as if she left my life yesterday, a Turkish Cypriot girl called Oya. She had big brown eyes, long lashes like a young calf's and a thick, olive-smelling plait reaching down to her waist. She wore a brightly coloured headscarf fringed with sequins. I remember Oya as a small, slim girl with a cheeky grin and new teeth sprouting gappily from the ridges of her pink gums.

We were friends. Neighbours. Kindred souls. Largely unaware of the animosities fermenting around us. Unlike other girls, we did not like playing housewives or shelling broad beans for our mothers. We liked to hitch up our skirts and explore the countryside. We climbed trees, walked along fallen trunks with our arms outstretched, collected spiders and beetles and stored them in matchboxes. We picked bright red corn poppies in spring to put in our hair. Our hideout was a hollow trunk, wide and bulbous, large enough to house two small, crouching girls with a love of conversation. In that thick trunk, sheltered from the powder keg of reality, we pored over Oya's prized atlas. It made the world look so small and accessible. On it Cyprus was a pinhead. England no bigger than a child's fingernail. Oya wanted to travel, to see the places her well-read grandfather had only experienced in books. The Hanging Gardens of Babylon, the Pyramids at Giza, the Taj Mahal, Granada's Alhambra.

In a village where sameness prevailed, Oya's cultural differences made her interesting. At funerals her brethren wore bright clothes. Long, loose-sleeved garments in red, yellow and blue. The women wore tightly wrapped headscarves that made them look like Red Cross nurses. Our funerals were monochromatic affairs. We followed the hearse from church to cemetery like a procession of blackbirds. Other differences were less obvious. Our meals were variations on a theme. Oya's family ate spinach-like *molohies*, cooked in a rich tomato sauce. We ate *moloshes*, a form of nettle, boiled or fried with egg. Oya's mother made cornflour *muhallebi* with milk and pistachio nuts. My mother's *muhallebi* was nut-free and flavoured with blossom water. Oya's father drank *raki*, a clear, aniseed-flavoured grape spirit, which turned cloudy when mixed with water. Papa sipped the equally potent grape-derivative *zivania* with his *meze*. We drank the same thick coffee, spoke the same language, indulged in identical syrupy desserts.

We were equally good hosts and innately hospitable.

Back then we enjoyed the best of both worlds. When Oya's family celebrated the Muslim festival of *Bayrami*, breaking their month-long fast, her mother always delivered loaves of freshly baked bread to our home. When we celebrated Easter, Mama repaid the gesture with a tray of cheese-and-raisin-filled *flaounes*. When Oya's brother was circumcised and spent the day in a *jellaba* crying, I was invited to join the party in my friend's back yard. When the village celebrated a Christian festival, Oya's family put on their Sunday best and joined the festivities, the *banayiri*. Stalls with striped awnings lined the cobbled streets outside the church, selling dried fruit, nuts, seasonal vegetables, household implements and freshly fried *logmathes*. Oya and I gave our pennies to the *kazandi* to play a rudimentary game of tombola, hoping to win a plastic game or a soft toy.

They were magical, innocent days, teeming with simple pleasures. In the weeks leading up to the invasion everything changed. I was not allowed to visit Oya's house. Fraternising with a Turkish Cypriot was considered dangerous. The friendly and familiar suddenly became threatening. There was neither time nor inclination for goodbyes when we drove away from our village. We thought we would be back within a matter of days. Back to the status quo we had left behind.

In the ensuing months, away from home, cut off from everything I knew, I yearned for Oya. I nagged my parents for news of my friend. I asked my brother if I could send her a letter. 'Any letter must go via Turkey,' he said, 'it must travel hundreds of kilometres to reach a village just across the border. Forget Oya. She is our enemy now.' I was devastated. How could this be? Oya was the kindest person I had ever met. I never mentioned her name again. I could not bear to hear her slandered. What I failed to realise back then was that my seventeen-year-old brother, a gentle boy whose stomach churned every time Yiayia slaughtered a chicken, had no option but to hate. He was an army recruit, soon to be stationed on the green line, being taught to kill or be killed. And how could he kill without hating?

Adam

I trudge across a viscose field towards the pitch, a freezing wind whipping me with cold lashes. Penetrating the fibres of my duffel coat, jumper, T-shirt, vest and long johns, through the layers designed to pad me out and provide insulation. Alvaro walks beside me, wearing football strip and a rainproof jacket.

'Put me on your shoulders, Adam,' he commands, tugging at my coat.

'No. Your boots are muddy.'

He stops. Drops his rucksack on the ground. Puts his hands on his hips.

'I'm not walking.'

'You're too big to go on my shoulders.'

'Look.' Alvaro points at a boy perched on the shoulders of a thick-set man in a tracksuit. 'He's on his dad's shoulders.'

'I'm not your . . .' My brain kicks in in mid-sentence, arresting 'dad'. 'I'm not your slave. And this is my work coat, Alvaro. I don't want to get mud all over it.'

'Please, Adam. Please, Adam. Please.' He presses his palms together, assuming the praying stance he deviously uses to get his own way.

'OK. But try and keep your feet off my coat.'

I bend down. He climbs onto my shoulders. My knees crack like dry twigs snapping as I lift up Alvaro and his heavy rucksack. He jiggles while I walk, adjusting his position, turning this way and that to survey the bird's-eye view, waving at passers-by, wanting to be seen. He lifts up his arms and starts waving them from side to side, my neck and torso forced to accompany his rhythm.

He jerks his body to the left. 'Jack! Jack!' he calls to a boy, some distance behind. 'Adam, that's my best buddy. Put me down.'

I creak to a crouch. Pressing down on my head for support, Alvaro swings his legs off my shoulders before banging me affectionately between the shoulder blades. I drop forward onto my hands and knees, wetness soaking through my corduroy trousers and long johns, my knees turning from faded camel to muddy brown. I watch Alvaro sprint off ahead with his friend. They join a group of boys in oversized football shorts, gathered round a young man with rough-hewn features who is wearing a woolly cap.

Alvaro pushes his way to the front of the group. 'Coach, Coach,' he says, 'can I be centre forward?'

'Yes. If you want.'

'Thanks, Coach.'

'Now, boys, remember to wait until the ball comes to you – and think ahead. Be clear about what you want to do when you pass. Concentrate on . . .'

191

'Coach! Coach!' Alvaro raises his arm again.

'Yes, Al?'

'Have you seen my new football boots?'

'They're cool, dude. And I see that medallion hanging from your neck. You can't play football wearing jewellery.'

Alvaro looks down at the wrist of the boy standing beside him. 'Kane's wearing a bracelet.'

'That's a religious bracelet, isn't it, Kane?'

Kane nods his head.

'Well,' Alvaro shuffles his feet while thinking up a reply, 'I'm religious.'

The coach bends down, takes hold of the medallion and smiles. 'Is Elvis your religion, dude?'

The boy is not a natural footballer. He runs around making all the right noises, spitting, jumping on goal-scorers, rarely touching the ball. I notice, with some irritation, that although he is often unmarked, the boy rarely gets a pass. Alvaro is distracted by a red-breasted bird on a nearby tree, by a silver wrapper flapping its way across the pitch, by a terrier standing on the sidelines. I desperately want to shout out encouragement but feel uneasy in this alien landscape of parents and children. Parents glance in my direction, scrutinising me, making wrong assumptions about my identity.

Alvaro is ingested by a shoal of boys. He runs with a group who chase the ball as if it were plankton. Back and forth he rushes with no other purpose than to have fun.

A shambling boy, impossibly tall with uncoordinated feet, floats like a spectral illusion before my eyes. A boy who loved playing but was never desperate to win, who glanced at his mum watching on the sidelines and wished it could have been his dad. Who still remembers with horror the *après*-match experience, who generally skipped the communal shower where those blessed with early puberty strutted proudly, showing off their pubes, swinging their generous appendages. Slapping each other with wet towels, running across to the girls' changing rooms to get a glimpse of bra strap or knickers. I was too thin to be impressive and never entirely at ease with nakedness. I walked home, caked in mud, crusty flakes falling from my trouser legs onto my shoes. My school days were marred like a shadow on the lungs by my own self-consciousness and a whirlwind of confusion at home. It sucked me into its core as I stepped through the door of my home, whirled me around and spat me out, confused and disorientated.

A woman in a skintight jumper approaches and stands beside me. 'I'm Jack's mother, Michelle. And you are?'

'I'm Adam.'

'Nice to meet you,' she says, taking my hand in her manicured claw. Her breasts jut out like miniature traffic cones and look as hard as Mum's scones. She crosses her arms beneath them, accentuating their size, complaining about the cold. I offer her my coat, hoping she'll refuse. She shakes her head and thanks me, unwilling to hide her light beneath a duffel, flashing a practised smile meant to wow. A flirtatious smile that does nothing for me. Michelle's breasts draw

193

gazes like ocular magnets, each glance confirming her mistaken impression that she is beautiful. When men look at Michelle they don't see beauty, they only see sex.

'Come on, Jack! Come on, Jack!' she calls out, as her son dribbles the ball towards the goal and shoots. 'Gooal!' she screams, waving her arms in the air, her breasts wobbling.

'He's a good player, your son.'

'He's football-mad. Best in the team, Coach says.'

'Alvaro's mad about football too.' I fight the boy's corner though I've always hated one-upmanship. Especially when accompanied by a glaring contradiction. Forgetting he is centre forward, Alvaro walks casually towards me, chewing a blade of grass.

'Did you see Jack's goal?' he says. 'It was brilliant.'

'Yes. It was great.'

'Stop talking. Get back in position,' the coach calls from across the pitch.

'Where did you put my medallion?'

'In my pocket. You'd better get back in position, Alvaro.'

'I'm tired. I need a rest.'

'But the ball's coming your way. Turn round, quick! This is your chance to score. Go on.'

The boy turns, stops the ball and dribbles it towards the goal. He is unmarked and has a clear run. If I were a betting man I would stake a fortune on Alvaro scoring. I turn to Michelle with a proud, self-satisfied grin that quickly dissolves into a look of incredulity. Alvaro stops dead in front of the goal mouth and does what can only be described as a Ronaldo shuffle, rotating his shoulders, doing something nifty and unnecessary with his feet.

'It's no time for ball skills,' the coach calls out, 'just shoot!'

The Alvaro Show goes on too long. The ball is quickly tackled from him by a player on the opposing team. 'You idiot!' Jack calls out. Another boy kicks a clod of earth at Alvaro.

'Hey, leave him alone,' I shout, unable to stop myself, surprised by my allegiance to the boy, anger rising inside me.

Coach blows the half-time whistle and the boys run off the pitch. Michelle leans towards me. 'Some kids have got it and some haven't.'

Alvaro stands in goal. He tries to shinny up the post, chats to nearby spectators and judders his legs Elvis-style. The boy is a showman, an entertainer, his natural talents clearly wasted on a pitch. He is so intent on making his audience laugh that a ball rolls slowly across the goal line unnoticed and comes to a standstill at the back of the net. Alvaro more than makes up for his lapse by a dramatic effort after the event. He falls on the ball and clutches it to his chest, rolling around on the floor as if strangling an alligator. The well-built man in the tracksuit spits out a laugh.

'Good effort, Al. Now let's play on,' the coach calls out, smiling.

'Get up goalie,' Michelle shouts irritably. Her son is on the losing side and Alvaro is the team's biggest liability.

'Thank God,' she says, huffing, when the match

finally resumes, grabbing the coach by his arm as he runs past and saying: 'Steven, why don't you put the goalie midfield?'

'He's all right where he is.'

'The goals are going in like water through a sieve.'

The coach gives me an apologetic smile. 'Al's great,' he says, heading off, 'a real character.'

Alvaro fails to save yet another goal. He picks up the ball and kicks it not outwards but vertically. It goes up and comes down with a heavy thud on his head. He totters backwards dramatically, falls onto his back and plays dead. I cover my mouth to conceal a smile.

'Get up,' Michelle screams, shaking her head, 'stop messing around!'

This woman has said more than enough and needs to be muzzled. 'Calm down, Michelle,' I say, mustering my most patronising tone. 'The boys are here to have fun.'

'My son's not here to have fun, he's here to win!'

'Stop being so uptight.'

Michelle's cheeks flush and I am overcome by a warm feeling of satisfaction. I gently elbow her and motion towards Alvaro. 'He's quite funny, don't you think? A real character.'

Jack ambles despondently towards his mother holding the manky gold boot he was awarded for being top goal-scorer. Sullenly, he hands the boot to his mother and zips up his cagoule. Alvaro drapes an arm around his friend's shoulders.

'Hey, Jack,' he says, 'what's wrong?'

'We lost, Dumbo.' He shakes off Alvaro's arm.

I wait for his mother to rebuke him for his surliness but she smiles instead and reinforces his behaviour. 'At least you scored, son.'

'But we lost, Mum. Because Al was rubbish in goal.'

I try to frighten Jack with a glower. He looks up at me with cold, dispassionate eyes that do not bode well for the man he will grow into. Alvaro's eyes glint endearingly with wonder and mischief.

'Perhaps his dad should give him a few football lessons,' Michelle says scowling at me.

Alvaro feels no need to set her straight. I wink at him and reach out for his hand, leading him away, feeling proud to be mistaken for his father.

I ask Alvaro to stand by the car door, intending to take a blanket out of the boot to cover the passenger seat. My request falls on deaf ears. The boy opens the driver's-side door, steps on the seat with his muddy boots, throws his rucksack into the back and collapses into the passenger seat.

'Hey. Why don't you listen?'

My voice is drowned out by the sudden explosion of The Kinks and 'Waterloo Sunset'.

'Turn it down,' I shout, clearing the mud from my seat, climbing into the car and starting the engine. We sing together as I pull away from the kerb. Out of tune but with zeal. I experience what can only be described as a moment of pure joy. Singing with gusto, driving along an uncongested road, sharing my love of a great song with another human being, albeit only an exasperating boy.

'Can we go for a drive?' he says, as the song fades to an end.

'Your mum's picking you up from our place. We need to get back.'

'Just a short drive, Adam. And can I have an ice cream?'

I drive through the back streets of West London, along my favourite tree-lined roads, heading for Chiswick High Road and my old haunts, feeling the sudden need to revisit a place that always triggers fond memories. I stop the car outside Chiswick House and have a fleeting vision of Dad, before the illness, standing tall and proud, wearing his long, camel-coloured raincoat. Together we wandered through the landscaped gardens surrounding the house, Dad naming trees and shrubs, admiring the bushes trimmed into decorative shapes.

'I used to come here with my dad, Alvaro. We used to go for long walks.'

'Can we go for a walk?'

'I'll show you the house but then we have to go.'

I park nearby and we walk hand in hand along the street and through a pair of stone gateposts. Along the curved driveway, towards the Neo-Classical villa, fronted by a portico and six evenly spaced Corinthian columns.

'Wow!' Alvaro says. 'It looks just like Graceland.'

'With a bit of imagination, I suppose it does.'

Alvaro squeezes my hand. 'Do you know, Adam, Elvis died in 1977. He was really ill and he got really fat, but at least he had a girlfriend.'

'Elvis had lots of girlfriends.'

'In my book it says his heart broke when his wife left him. Is that why he got ill and died? Because his heart broke into pieces?'

'His heart didn't actually break. That's just a metaphor.'

'What's a metaphor?'

'It's a figure of speech. A non-literal expression.'

'What's a non-literal ess . . . pression?'

'When you say it's raining cats and dogs, you don't actually mean that cats and dogs are falling from the sky, you mean to say it's raining heavily. And when you say someone's heart is broken, what you really mean is that they are very, very upset.'

'I wish Elvis hadn't got upset and died.'

The boy looks sad. I put a hand on his shoulder and resort to a cliché in an effort to cheer him up. 'Elvis lives on in our hearts, Alvaro.'

'Is that a metaphor?'

'Yes, I suppose it is.'

'Elvis is too big to live in our hearts. And anyway, he's dead, so his body is floating in the sky.' He looks up, as if hoping to catch a glimpse of a spangled cadaver drifting by.

Impressed by my own teaching abilities I make another stab at enriching the boy's vocabulary. 'Perhaps you'd like me to tell you what a simile is?'

'No, thanks,' he says, clipping my wings, 'I want an ice cream.'

A piebald sky slinks by overhead. A noisy wind whooshes through the treetops. I pull away from the kerb, feeling the afternoon to have been a success.

199

Alvaro looks across at me and smiles. 'Adam, can I have my rucksack?'

'It's on the back seat. I can't give it to you now, I'm driving.'

'Please, Adam. Please. Can I have it now, Adam?'

'Not now.'

The boy unfastens his seat belt and stands up to lean through the space between the seats, reaching for his bag. I grab his arm and pull him back round, asking him to sit down and wait. 'Get off,' he cries, yanking his arm out of my grip, trying to climb over the passenger seat. I take hold of his football shirt and pull it, telling him to sit down.

'Ow! You nearly strangled me,' he says, rubbing his neck.

'Just sit down and belt up, will you?' I know as soon as the hostile command has shot from my lips that I have lost control of the situation.

'Don't tell me to shut up!'

'I didn't. I meant, put your seat belt on.' I turn to glare at him, taking my eye off the road, swerving, scraping the pavement with my wheel rims, seeing in my rear-view mirror the flash of headlights warning me to pull over.

'Look what you've done now,' I say, stopping the car. 'We've been stopped by the police.' I wind down my window and wait, my heart pounding, wondering if the six points on my licence will soon become nine.

A policeman walks up to the driver's-side door and looks first at me, then at Alvaro. 'Hello, sir. Can I ask why your son isn't wearing a seat belt?'

The boy looks frightened out of his wits. 'It was my

fault,' he says. 'I wanted my bag. I took my seat belt off. Don't take me to prison. Please.'

'Calm down, son,' the officer says. 'You don't go to prison for not wearing a seat belt.'

'Mum says you do.'

'No, you don't. But your dad should have made sure you were wearing a seat belt before he started the car.'

'I'm not his dad, I'm a friend, giving him a lift home from football practice.'

'Why were you pulling at the child, sir?'

'I was trying to get him to sit down.'

Alvaro starts crying.

The officer pokes his head through the car window. 'Are you all right, son?'

'Adam nearly strangled me,' he replies, rubbing his neck, putting on an inspired performance of an abused child.

The policeman opens my door. 'Can you step out of the car, please, sir? I'd like a word.'

Adam

I sound the horn and wait for Mum. Five minutes pass before the front door opens and she comes out of the flat, swinging her legs determinedly along the front path. Electra follows close behind, her arms outstretched as if pursuing a toddler taking its first shaky steps. She rushes ahead to open the passenger door and help Mum into her seat before hurrying around to my window to plant a quick kiss on my cheek.

'You're all sweaty,' she says, wiping her mouth.

'It's these leather seats, they get really hot.'

'Eh! That's the price you pay for luxury, Adam!'

'This vehicle is a classic, Electra. A gentleman's car. The poor man's Roller.'

Mum is not convinced. She scans the tired interior of my Rover 350 with a look of haughty dissatisfaction.

'Give me electric windows and air conditioning any day,' Electra says.

Mum glances at her watch. 'I'm going to be late for my hospital appointment. With any luck this plaster will come off today.'

'Good luck, Margaret,' Electra calls out, waving us off.

I leave my mooring and sail along the road, past dinghies and motorboats. Proud to be at the helm of a timeless vessel, one that draws the nostalgic gaze of middle-aged men. 'Look at that tank of a car,' they say, 'not one bit of plastic on it . . . they don't make them like they used to.' Plastic pigs, I call these modern hatchbacks. Runts of the litter. If the sun shone too brightly they would melt into the tarmac on which they are driven. True, I have broken down more times than I care to remember but my boot is large enough to house the tools needed for roadside repairs. Heavy-duty jack, spare oil, fan belt, spanners, a selection of light bulbs. My car, with its Viking insignia, has the heart of a warrior. Though its carcass may be pock-marked with rust, the engine is solid, a beast.

I look across at Mum. She wears the superior expression of a woman used to finery stoically enduring reduced circumstances. An aged princess being driven to hospital in a dustbin on wheels.

'Sorry I was late, Mum. I got stuck in traffic. I would have called but I left my mobile at work.'

'That's all right, Adam.' Her tone is stiff and unforgiving. She rubs her arthritic knee and winces.

'Is your knee playing up?'

She puckers her mouth and replies defensively, 'No. I'm fine.'

I delve no further. The state of her health is a sore point. I talk about the weather instead, before falling silent and switching on the radio for company. Mum has never been easy to talk to. At times she is mono-syllabic. Emotions when touched upon are swept like dust beneath a rug, out of sight and out of mind. I generally steer clear of moral and political debates, which only serve to reinforce our differences and end in one or both parties taking offence. Occasionally, she relaxes and talks about her life as a girl. Engrossed in the distant past, she truly comes to life. Her eyes sparkle and her laughter is light, jingly, girlish. A lovely smile lights up her face and wrinkles the narrow bridge of her nose. Her crop of good memories depletes as she talks, assailed by the present and its rank weeds. We inch our way forward along the High Road, the heat as oppressive as Mum's silence. I hum along to a silly tune and tap out the rhythm on the steering wheel.

Fracture patients with plastered limbs sit on plastic chairs, screwed to the ground. They kill time by flicking through old magazines, chatting to one another, staring into space. An obese woman with both legs in plaster is manoeuvred into the waiting room in a bulky hospital wheelchair. She scans the room miserably, hoping her fellow outpatients have registered the enormity of her plight. Her sense of frustration is palpable. Mum sits beside me, looking haughty and unapproachable.

The speakerphone crackles: 'Mrs Parker to X-ray.' A woman sitting opposite heaves herself up. Around her right ankle is a metal frame. Fine rods, like the spokes of a bicycle wheel, circle the frame and puncture her skin. She inches her way across the room on crutches and disappears through a set of swing doors.

A bearded man wearing a filthy overcoat limps into

the waiting room and sits on the vacant chair opposite. He has sunken eyes and bushy eyebrows. He yawns, baring a set of coffee-coloured teeth. Mottled toes poke from under a dirty bandage. A roll-up is wedged behind his ear. The man has drunk or smoked or sniffed himself into an oblivion that is infinitely better than his reality. His head sways back and forth as if his neck were made of jelly.

A gaunt woman in a blue shell suit sits beside him and sucks on a strand of her matted blonde hair. A limp fringe falls across cheeks scarred with red welts. The woman could be twenty-two or forty-two, the man's daughter or his partner. The couple reek of must and tobacco and stale alcohol. The woman pulls an old-fashioned games console from her pocket and begins to play, her head lowered, her thumbs manically working the black buttons. She stops, to claw frenziedly at the red sores on the backs of her hands. I sit wondering how this poor woman went from cradle to gutter, what unfortunate series of events led to her degradation. As if reading my mind, she looks up at me and says: 'What the fuck are you looking at?'

I smile apologetically and look away. I had no right to stare, to make this woman feel like a leper. Mum eyes her up with the same disapproving expression she wore when inspecting the inside of my car.

She leans across to whisper in my ear, 'How can people let themselves get into such a state?'

'They probably live on the street, Mum.'

'Why don't they find a job and clean themselves up?'

'You make it sound so easy. Do you think anybody would choose to live like that?'

In the world according to Mum there is only black and white, good and bad, intelligence and stupidity, perfection and imperfection. In Mum's world practicality overrides sentiment and appearances are paramount. I want to take her by the shoulders and shake her, in the hope that her negativity will float to the surface and dissipate like carbon dioxide bubbles in an aerated drink. If I shook her too hard I fear she might snap in half like a rye wafer. And still she would fail to see the error of her ways. She would look down at her bottom half, stiffen her upper lip and say to herself, 'Margaret, pull yourself together.'

Perhaps it is my need to shake her, to spark a human reaction, which makes me blurt out: 'I have to tell Electra the truth about Dad. About how he died.'

'She knows what happened to your father.'

'She only knows half the story. I can't go on living a lie, Mum. I have to tell her that I can't risk having children.' For months now, guilt has been wringing my stomach like a wet cloth. Twisting and compressing my insides, forcing me along a route I was bound one day to travel. It is time to face my demons head on, to tell the truth and face the consequences.

Mum looks at me with a puzzled expression. 'Are you sure it's not too late for a discussion of that nature with your wife?'

'What do you mean?'

She turns her face away. 'Nothing.'

The bearded man's head slumps backwards abruptly as if his throat has been cut. He comes back to life a few seconds later and looks around the room with bloodshot eyes. Resting his head on the woman's shoulder, he settles down to sleep, his throaty snore sounding like the engine of my Rover.

'I want to tell her everything. About Dad and his family, about your argument with Gran . . .'

'Why do you insist on dredging up the past?'

'I don't like keeping secrets from my wife.'

'But you don't mind keeping them from your mother?'

I feel as if I have acquired a second wife. An older, meaner, less agreeable one. Mum and I desperately need several miles of healthy distance between us. Where is my selfish brother when he's needed? Why hasn't he found a spare moment in his busy schedule to visit Mum? But never mind hey! He sent a man-sized bunch of lilies in his place that could just about fit through the front door. From the look on Mum's face one might have thought he had sent her the world, wrapped in cellophane and tied with a ribbon. Flowers won't help Mum into the shower when she needs to wash. They won't cook her meals and make her tea and tolerate her moods. They are a poor substitute for a son. Mum is a low priority on John's list. She comes below work, below golf, below friends, somewhere between networking and the beamer.

Mum rubs her knee. 'Do you think your wife tells you everything?'

'Yes, of course.'

Her thin eyebrows arch.

'Is there something you want to tell me, Mum?'

'And be accused of interfering!'

'Mum, do you have something to tell me?'

'Don't blame me if you don't like what you're about to hear, Adam. Don't shoot the messenger,' she says irritably. 'Did you know that any minute now the bailiffs could turn up at your house and take your belongings?'

'What on earth are you talking about?'

'I saw a letter from them on your wife's desk.'

'Why were you looking through the papers on Electra's desk?'

'I wasn't. The letter was right there, in front of me. I went into the room to see what she was working on.'

'I'm sure there's a perfectly good explanation. Electra always pays her bills at the very last minute. Perhaps she's a little behind with her payments.'

'If your wife can't afford to pay her bills, why does she send money to her family?'

'I don't want to be having this conversation with you. Justifying our financial arrangements. If you really want to know, her sister's having problems at the moment and needs help.'

'And that's not the only thing I saw.'

'Go on, Mum, though I doubt I could stop you if I tried.'

'Your wife left the house, saying she was going out to buy a pint of milk. When I looked out of her work-room window, I saw her talking to a man in a first-floor flat in that building opposite yours. Do you have a friend in that building, Adam?'

'No. And neither does Electra. Perhaps it was some-one else you saw in the flat.'

She leans closer to whisper in my ear, 'It was her. I'm certain. She was touching his face in a very intimate way. If you think I'm lying, why don't you ask her?'

'What are you insinuating? That my wife's having an affair?' I look up. The woman in the blue shell suit stops playing her game and watches me with interest.

'I'm just telling you what I saw. I saw her in that flat. I saw her touching a man's face. I swear to you.'

I want to cover Mum's mouth with my hand to stop her stream of lies. 'Please, Mum. Stop. I don't want to hear any more.'

'You have to confront her, Adam, and tell her you know.'

'Know what? I don't know anything. I don't believe you. I know my wife, I trust her completely.'

'Then you're a fool.'

'My wife's *not* having an affair.'

'Keep your voice down, Adam. You don't want everyone to know.'

The speakerphone crackles and hisses. 'Mrs Reynolds to X-ray, please.' Mum gets up, not a second too soon, pulling a pained expression, and heads for the swing doors. I stare at the bony hands that lie trembling in my lap and sense people staring, whispering, feeling sorry for me. I sit in a stupor, angry with myself for letting her get under my skin.

And then my thoughts turn to Electra and I realise with alarm that our relationship has changed, that Electra has been distant lately and prone to angry outbursts, that Mum has forced a wedge between us, that

I have nothing to offer my wife. My head starts throbbing, the walls of the waiting room close in on me. I get up and hurry towards the exit, desperate to escape the suffocating atmosphere and a roomful of prying eyes.

Lydia

Lydia stared at the unopened letter lying in her lap, fighting the compulsion to set it alight as if it were an effigy of him. She sat on a wooden bench unable to take the giant emotional leap required to open the letter and read its contents. A dead weight of incendiary feelings sat like an unexploded bomb in the pit of her stomach. The sight of the blue airmail envelope on Consuelo's Welcome to Paradise mat had stopped her in her tracks on her way out of the house. She had recognised his slanted handwriting immediately. Driven Alvaro to school in a trance. Waved him off with a forced smile, the letter burning a hole in her jacket pocket. Whatever the contents, she knew it would be too little, too late. She could never forgive the husband who'd turned his back on the life he'd played a part in creating.

Lydia had called in sick and sought out a patch of open space where she could sit and bolster her courage. A row of elegant Edwardian houses faced her, dwarfed by an imposing white tower block rising up behind them. It drew the eye like a luxury yacht floating in a sea of rowing boats. Sitting alone on a grassy circle Lydia felt like a passenger left behind on a small island. Her vessel too far away to be hailed back. She knew how it felt to be abandoned, to feel helpless, exposed and forced to learn the art of survival. Ian had left when Alvaro was only six months old. Disappeared like a boat in the Bermuda Triangle, as if he had never existed.

She had heard about people going missing of their own volition but had never paid the phenomenon much heed. Now, every time she heard about a disappearance, the news struck her with the intensity of cymbals being bashed together an inch from her ear. She empathised with the families whose lives were blighted like her own. Who sat in limbo beside the telephone, waiting. Who were poised to welcome back the deserter with open arms. Who either blamed themselves or never stopped asking 'why' even when in their hearts they knew the answer. For many months Lydia had imagined an emotional reunion when all ill-feeling would be flushed out with tears of relief. As time passed, sentimentality turned to bitterness. She was not a mother praying for the return of an itinerant teenager, she was a woman jilted in her hour of need. Ian had packed a holdall while his wife and the baby slept, and walked out of their lives. He left no letter of explanation, no forwarding address, no trail of clues that led to his whereabouts. He emptied the joint bank account and vanished.

The police shrugged their shoulders. No crime had been committed. Ian had left of his own accord, his life was not at risk, he had taken money he was entitled to withdraw. They took a statement and filed it away. Thousands of people went missing each year, they said. Teenagers hooked on drugs and alcohol. Elderly people suffering from dementia. Children escaping abuse. What was Ian escaping from? Domesticity? His marriage? An unrewarding job? The demands of a newborn? He had not been happy for a while, this much she knew. His state of mind had been the focus of their lives for some time. Until Alvaro was born, a month premature, and all Lydia's attentions were redirected.

For many months she had blamed herself for her husband's flight. It takes two to make a marriage and two to break it, she told herself. Had she not ignored his needs, his angst, his physical presence? A fragile baby who flopped on her shoulder like a rag doll, his fingers like matchsticks, had become the centre of her universe. Ian skirted the outer edges of her world, like a resentful child usurped by a new sibling. Lydia thought at first he was only making a point, that he would come back after making her suffer for neglecting him.

After six months without word, as Alvaro began to take his first hesitant footsteps, she contacted the Missing Persons Helpline. She added her husband's name to a computerised register, placed an advert in the *Big Issue*, stopped short of pasting his picture on local lampposts as if he were a lost cat.

Recurrent visions haunted her. Opening the door to him. Picking up the telephone receiver and hearing his voice. Bumping into him on the street. When the mortgage fell into arrears and her house was re-possessed she stopped wondering, stopped searching, stopped looking back with unwarranted nostalgia. She moved in with her mother and began rebuilding her life. She suppressed the anger that clawed at her insides. Chased away the questions that hung in the air and had no answers. How could any man forsake his own family in such cruel fashion? Throw off his identity as if it were a coat and start a new life else-where without ties or responsibilities? He was not the victim. She and Alvaro were the victims. The people left behind were the ones who suffered.

Lydia picked up the letter and inspected the New Zealand postmark. Ian, it seemed, had followed his dream of living abroad. She tore open the envelope and pulled out a single blue sheet of paper on which a short note was written.

Dear Lydia,

I have wanted to write to you for a very long time. To let you know my whereabouts, to apologise for the way I left, for leaving you alone to raise our son.

He had said in the first two sentences everything she had waited six years to hear. Words that served no purpose now. How casually he used the words 'son' as if he knew what it meant to be a father, as if assuming a role he had no right to.

I hope you will one day find it in your heart to forgive me. I never meant to hurt you. I was messed up. I had to get away for your sake and mine. Believe me, you were better off without me.

There it was. His explanation condensed into one short sentence. 'I was messed up.' She reread it and wondered if she were meant to feel sorry for him. So he was sick, was he, his flight a gut reaction, a benevolent act? She could never forgive him for leaving her penniless and crippling her confidence, for letting her believe she was defunct in some way, worthy of abandonment, unable to satisfy and hold on to a husband. Every time she looked into the eyes of a child who hankered after a father to play football with, anger coagulated in her throat and choked her. Surely there were other ways to leave a wife? Men left their wives every day. Packed a suitcase. Moved out. Kept in touch with their children. Paid maintenance.

I contacted an old friend who said you were staying with your mother. I am writing in the hope that you will let me see my son. Please, Lydia. I think it would be good for both of us. Your life has no doubt moved on. I hope you have met someone new. Someone who makes you happy. Please write, as soon as you can, at the address above. I wait to hear from you.

How easy he made it sound. Moving on. Meeting someone new. He had no idea what he had done. What emotional scars he had left in his wake. Her life had not moved on. She had dug herself a deep rut and become entrenched. She felt incapable of moving forward when the past was unresolved. If she had only had herself to think about, she might have raised her head above the battlements. But there was a life more precious than her own to consider. Lydia decided she could not risk her son being rejected a second time, by the same man. Her mind was made up. She would not reply to Ian's letter. She would respond to his six-year silence with a silence of her own. He deserved no more.

The comforting sound of Consuelo swearing in Spanish welcomed Lydia home. Here, reassuringly, life was just as she had left it. What new offence had Juan-Carlos committed against the poor, unfortunate Maria? Lydia slipped off her shoes and sank her toes into soft shag pile, glad to be home. Consuelo's blasphemous outbursts were coming from the kitchen and accompanied by another sound. Strangely familiar but somehow out of context. Was her mother liquidising vegetables to make soup? Was Alvaro playing with a new electronic toy? On her way to the kitchen Lydia recognised the sound and dreaded the spectacle that awaited her.

Consuelo stood in the doorway of the laundry room with her arms in the air. Alvaro, wearing a cowboy hat and holster, was pretending to shoot his grandmother not with a conventional toy gun but with a shocking-pink vibrator. Holding the handle designed for coital stimulation, Alvaro jabbed the apron-clad Consuelo in the ribs while the vibrator writhed like a worm.

'I thought you did not approve of gons,' Consuelo said. 'Why did you buy him that thing? He's bin chasing me around the house with it, eva since he gor home from school.'

216

Lydia grabbed the vibrator out of Alvaro's hand. 'Go and wash your hands.'

'Why?' He crossed his arms defiantly. 'I've already washed them.'

'Because . . . because . . . I use that thing to massage my feet.'

'Ughh!' Alvaro ran screaming from the room.

'Is it good?' Consuelo asked, her interest sparked.

'Marvellous.' Lydia was astounded by the naivety of a woman who had been a hospital orderly for twenty years.

Lydia sought out an Alvaro-proof hiding place in her bedroom. The top shelf of her wardrobe, behind a pile of chunky jumpers, had not been safe enough. Her handbag would have to do for the moment. Lydia feared the repercussions of Alvaro's find. Would he now tell his teacher that his mother kept a pink gun in the back of her wardrobe? Alvaro liked to share the intimate details of his home life with school friends, teachers and the local newsagent. He was as chatty and gregarious as his grandmother, and like Consuelo he embellished the facts.

Alvaro sniffed the sausages on his plate and screwed up his face. 'I don't like these sausages,' he said, 'I want the other ones. The ones I normally eat.'

'Littol bogger,' Consuelo muttered under her breath, 'why you don taste them ferst?'

'I don't like the smell. I'll be sick if I eat them.'

Lydia swallowed a mouthful of lentil salad. 'Just try them, Alvaro. Grandma picked up the wrong brand of sausages when she went to the supermarket.'

Consuelo chortled. 'Silly ol woman. I should have been wearing my glasses.'

This was not the first time the optically challenged Consuelo had picked up the wrong groceries. Without her glasses she could not tell an apple from a pear, an orange from a grapefruit, her daughter from the postman. Without her glasses Consuelo could only see roughly defined shapes.

Alvaro pushed his plate away. 'I'm not eating them.'

Lydia pushed Alvaro's plate back towards him. 'At least eat your potato and sweetcorn.'

'But I want sausages. I'm starving hungry.'

'How abour I make you som pasta with cheese sauce?' Consuelo stood up, leaving her own meal untouched.

'Sit down, Mum.'

'Why you don go to the supermarket and buy the sausages he likes, Lythia?'

'Mum. Sit down and let me handle Alvaro.' This was an annoyingly typical scenario. Lydia saying one thing, Consuelo another. Alvaro being bombarbed with mixed messages.

'Is no troble to make som pasta.'

'I want sausages.' Alvaro crossed his arms, preparing for battle.

'The poor boy hiss hongry, Lythia.'

'Mum, please sit down.' Consuelo was exasperating. Undermining a mother's authority without hesitation, yielding to her grandson's whims, however unreasonable.

Alvaro stood up. 'I want sausages.'

'Alvaro, sit down.'

'My name's Al,' he shouted.

This was a new development. Snubbing his name. Lydia looked into her son's eyes and knew instinctively that something was wrong, something was troubling him. Was he rejecting his name because it made him stand out? Had he been teased about it at school? He had always been so proud of his Spanish heritage, prouder than Lydia had ever been. To impress his friends, Alvaro insisted Consuelo spoke to him in Spanish when she picked him up from school while he nodded his head knowingly, saying '*si, si,*' as if he knew what she was talking about.

'Why you don go the supermarket, Lythia?' Consuelo's needle had stuck.

'Because there are plenty of other things in the house to eat.'

Alvaro banged his small fist on the table, unsettling his plate.

'Hey! Don't do that.' Lydia felt like piggy in the middle.

Alvaro ran from the kitchen, slamming the door on his way out. Lydia chased after him, along the hall, up the stairs and into his bedroom. Consuelo followed close behind, reluctant to be excluded from the imminent fracas. Alvaro slumped in a corner of the room, shoulders hunched and generous lips twisted into a scowl. 'Leave me alone,' he shouted, 'get out of my room!'

'Don worry, Grandson. Your mother, she's gonna go to the supermarket.'

'No, I'm not, Mum. I've come to tell my son to stop slamming doors.'

219

Lydia felt she had two disobedient children to discipline.

'You gonna let him go to bed on an empty stomach? I don have the heart myself.'

'MUM! Be quiet. Let me handle this. Stop interfering.'

'Leave Grandma alone,' Alvaro shouted, springing up, running into Consuelo's outstretched arms, making Lydia the enemy, the evil, disciplinarian mother. Consuelo and her grandson often teamed up, pooling their might, overpowering her. In undermining Lydia's authority, Consuelo reinforced Alvaro's difficult behaviour and turned him against his mother. Alvaro and his grandmother were the best and worst of friends. Sometimes Lydia would arrive home from work and find them screaming at one another. Both had a generous lung capacity and a fiery temperament. They seemed to thrive on confrontation. Their arguments were always a prelude to an emotional reconciliation. Consuelo rewarded her grandson for screaming with a generous portion of ice cream. In return she got a hug and a kiss, an affirmation of his love. Lydia fought a lone battle to right Consuelo's behavioural wrongs.

She was grateful to her mother for so many things. For taking her in when she had nowhere else to go. For looking after her son. For cooking her meals, night after night. But the luxury of living in her mother's house and eating at her mother's table came at a price. Consuelo assumed parental rights over her grandchild and pulled rank over her daughter. Her well-meaning comments did more harm than good. By contradicting

Lydia and siding with her grandson she turned disagreements into fierce quarrels. Why should Alvaro take seriously his mother's 'no' when he knew his grandmother would say 'yes' to the same request? Ideally, Lydia would have liked to live in a place of her own, to raise her son without interference. But she was scared of making a move that might jeopardise his emotional security and standard of living. She was afraid of taking a risk and failing, again.

'Please, Alvaro. Let go of Grandma.'

'My name's Al!' he screamed.

'Let go of Grandma.' Lydia bent down. She tried to pull Alvaro towards her, fighting the urge to tug him roughly.

'Let go. You're hurting me.'

'You're hurting him, Lythia.' Her mother's stupid accusation was infuriating. Lydia struggled to remain calm while anger raged inside her. Shouting will not defuse the situation, she told herself. If Lydia raised her voice she knew Alvaro would only raise his and Consuelo would then add hers to the mêlée.

'Let him calm down. Go and finish eating. Leave him to me.' Did Consuelo really think she could eat at a time like this? Lydia's anger was suffocating. She would not allow her mother to take control. She needed to talk to her son, alone, to reason with him, without Consuelo butting in.

'Let go of your grandmother. NOW!' Lydia's anger had got the better of her. She squeezed Alvaro's arm and yanked him towards her.

'Leave me alone. Don't pull me!' he screamed, wrenching his arm back, pushing her away. She fell backwards on to a Lego castle and lay among the ruins, defeated. Alvaro shrank away from her, burying his head in the skirt of his grandmother's apron. Consuelo lifted him off the ground.

'Is no good to push your mother,' she said, before kissing him on the head and carrying him out of the room to further reinforce his behaviour with a plate of cheesy pasta or anything else his heart desired. Consuelo had won the battle of wills and proved, once again, that Lydia had no support. No one to back her up when she tried to discipline her son.

Lydia's thoughts turned to Ian. She felt angry and resentful. Where had he been when she needed him? Sunning himself on a stretch of sandy beach? Drowning his sorrows with an ice-cold beer? Lydia had travelled an exhausting emotional journey with her son. She had put her own needs aside to concentrate on Alvaro's. He was and would always be her priority. What right did Ian have to claim a child he'd played no hand in raising? He knew nothing about sleepless nights, tantrums, childhood fevers, or even how much a new pair of new trainers cost. He had forfeited his paternal rights the night he packed his bag and disappeared.

Lydia sat up and distractedly began rebuilding the castle, wondering what more the day could throw at her. A day destined to end as badly as it had begun. She closed her eyes and leaned back against the bed, head reeling. Anger slowly supplanted by guilt and self-doubt. She had handled things badly. Lost control. She was a bad mother. Perhaps she should have let Consuelo make pasta after all and not dug her heels in?

She had made the unwitting mistake of marrying the wrong man and now her son was paying the price. When, if ever, would she stop feeling responsible for his angry outbursts, his bouts of unhappiness?

How long had she been lying against the bed with her eyes closed, lost in thought? An hour? Two hours? What did it matter? The whole day had been spent in a state of numb confusion. Something jagged was digging into her leg. A Lego brick? The rifle butt of a plastic soldier? The pain was strangely comforting. Her son's small body suddenly slumped into her lap. Alvaro curled up like a cat against her. Awkward fingers smoothed down her hair. Wet lips kissed her cheeks and whispered in her ear. 'Sorry, Mum. I'm really sorry. I didn't mean to push you. Do you forgive me? Please forgive me, Mum. I love you.' Alvaro's voice was tender, pleading. Lydia could feel the warmth of his sweet breath but did not have the energy to open her eyes, to move her heavy limbs, to utter a word, to squeeze him in her arms. 'Mum, Mum, Mum.' His voice grew louder, more urgent but Lydia was lost in a world of her own. She did not mean to ignore him. She was simply recuperating. Alvaro sprang out of her lap and left the room, sniffing. She heard his quick footsteps hurrying down the stairs. She wanted to call out 'Come back, I forgive you', but could not move her lips.

A shrill scream made her sit up with a start. She heard two sets of footsteps running up the stairs. Consuelo flew into the room, clutching the cross that hung from her neck. 'Thank God you're alive!' she said, kissing the cross. 'Alvaro told me you were dead.'

'Mum, you're alive!' Alvaro flung himself against her. His arms wound tightly around her neck. 'I thought I'd killed you,' he said, tears streaming down his cheeks. Consuelo left the room and closed the door. Lydia hugged her son, kissed his face, tasted salt. The warmth of his body brought her back from the dead. She had not lost her son. He did not hate her. The eyes that looked up at her were full of repentance and unconditional love.

'How was school today, son?' she asked, smoothing down his quiff, stroking the dark, baby-soft skin on the back of his neck.

'Fine.'

'Any problems?'

'No,' he replied, refusing to look her in the eyes.

'Can I ask you a question?' She wiped her son's wet cheeks with the cuff of her sleeve.

'Yes.'

'Why do you want me to call you Al?'

'Because Jack said Alvaro's a stupid name.'

'Well, it's not. It's a lovely Spanish name and you shouldn't pay so much attention to what Jack says. Perhaps you should stop playing with him altogether. Perhaps you should start playing with Kane again.'

Alvaro grew agitated. Squirming in his mother's lap. 'Kane can't play football.'

'I've seen him play football at the after-school club.'

'Jack says Pakis can't play football.'

Lydia could not believe what she was hearing. She stifled the urge to grab her son by his slender arms and shake him. She had not raised her child on such

224

xenophobic terminology. Alvaro had always been encouraged to embrace other cultures, not to vilify and name-call. If she let this comment pass, where might it lead? Alvaro had to be set straight before he grew warped.

'What does Paki mean, Alvaro?'

'Is it someone with brown skin?'

'It's a nasty way of referring to someone with brown skin. Would you like someone to call your grandma rude names?'

'No. I'd kill them.'

'Then don't use that word to refer to anyone else. If I hear you use it again I will get very angry, Alvaro. And I will have to come into school and speak to your teacher. Do you understand?'

He shook his head. Looked solemnly at his mother. 'I didn't know. Honestly, I didn't.'

'And Jack isn't welcome in this house anymore. So don't invite him. Do you hear me?'

'But he's my best buddy, Mum. Please, Mum.' His eyes began filling up, his bottom lip quivered. For now, the subject had to be dropped. Lydia could take no more upset.

Lydia was wrapped up in her duvet, safe from the world. Glad the day had finally come to an ond. Tomorrow she would start afresh. Hide the letter. Pretend it never arrived. Her eyelids grew heavy. She felt her body growing light. On the cusp of sleep she heard a loud knock at the bedroom door. Alvaro was not in the habit of knocking. 'Come in, Mum,' she said.

Consuelo walked into the room. Sat on the edge of the bed. Hitched up her skirt and thrust out her bare feet.

'What's wrong, Mum?'

'My feet are killing me, Lythia.'

'Do you want me to rub them for you?'

'No. I don want you toching an ol woman's feet. Can I borrow tha pink thing?'

When would the torture end? 'Alvaro used up the batteries.'

'Don worry. I've got batteries in the kitchen. Loads of 'em.'

Lydia conceded defeat once more. There was no point arguing with her mother. If she said 'the thing' was lost, Consuelo would search the whole house trying to find it. If she told her it was broken, Consuelo would take it apart with a screwdriver and put it back together again. Sore feet were just an excuse for her to get her hands on a new and exciting gadget. She had a kitchen full of them. Revolutionary yoghurt-makers. Futuristic bottle-openers. State-of-the-art cheese graters. Devices that lasted a couple of months before ending up in the back of cupboards, replaced by tried and tested, hand-operated classics. Lydia unzipped the handbag on her bedside table, pulled out her vibrator and handed it to her mother.

'Can you show me how to use it?'

Life had come to resemble a bad sitcom, Lydia thought as she sat up and showed Consuelo how to massage her swollen feet with a vibrator. Her mother clutched the device as if it were a rolling pin and moaned contentedly as the vibrator writhed against the soles of her feet. Lydia realised with regret that her playmate was lost for ever, to another woman. Visions of Consuelo's calloused feet would, from now on, smother any possibility of erotic pleasure.

The sky dribbled like a teething baby. Lydia's heels sank into moist earth. Her fingertips were numbed by the cold. She stood on the sidelines, her hair plumping up like a soufflé, watching her son drag his feet across the pitch. Alvaro reached the ball and kicked it swiftly to a team-mate. Lydia had to admit that his football skills had vastly improved since she had last watched him play. Today, though, Lydia had not come to watch football. She had left work early in order to confront Michelle. She did not intend to use inflammatory language and vilify her son's friend but hoped to keep the exchange amicable. Alvaro had warned her against interfering and made her promise not to speak to Jack's mother. This was one promise she did not feel guilty about breaking.

The final whistle blew. Lydia looked across at Michelle, standing a short distance away, and her stomach clenched. Her adversary was tall and intimidating, a dolled-up Amazonian with lethal-looking nails. Alvaro ran up to his mother, his face glinting with sweat, his cheeks bright red, the Elvis quiff held aloft by a glutinous mixture of mud and sweat. 'Let's go home, Mum,' he said. 'I'm starving.'

'Why don't you go and play with Kane for a couple of minutes? I have something to do.'

Alvaro ran off. Lydia sheepishly approached

Michelle and gently tapped her on the arm. 'Can I have a quick word?'

'Sure.' Michelle waved goodbye to the football coach who headed for the changing block. Jack stood beside his mother, looking sulky and exasperated. He did not respond to Lydia's 'hello' or even acknowledge her presence. To Lydia's relief other parents and their children were drifting away towards the school car park. She took a deep breath and began. 'Jack's been saying unkind things to Alvaro and I thought you should know.'

'Kids say all sorts of silly things. I don't take them to heart.'

'I wouldn't call them silly. I would call them offensive.'

Michelle reached out to take her son's hand but he snatched it away and glared at her. 'What have you been saying, my angel?'

Jack shrugged moodily.

'He told Alvaro that his father hated him, and he said, to use your son's exact words, that "Pakis can't play football".'

Michelle drew close to Lydia with a wry smile. 'Can you name a decent Paki footballer?'

Lydia burned with rage and indignation. 'I'm not the least bit interested in football but I am very interested in the terminology my son uses.' She imagined grabbing a fistful of Michelle's highlighted hair and ramming her face in the mud.

'Calm down.' Michelle looked bemused. 'What's your problem?'

'My problem is people like you, with attitudes like

yours, who raise mirror images of your ugly selves.'
Lydia could feel herself going red in the face and knew
her mouth was running ahead of her brain. She was
only half aware of Alvaro standing beside her and
pulling on her jacket, telling her to stop. 'My problem
is that horrible kids like yours infect the minds of nice
kids like Alvaro.'

'Fuck off, you bitch,' Jack said, glowering.

Alvaro lunged at his friend, pushed him to the
ground. 'Don't call my mum a bitch!' he screamed,
sitting astride Jack, pinning his arms to the
ground.

Michelle flapped her arms around, screeching, 'Get
your little bastard off my son!'

Lydia pulled her son free of Jack, dropped to her
knees and wrapped Alvaro in her arms. Jack
scrambled to his feet and burst into tears, looking like
a small, frightened boy. Lydia knew that he was not to
blame for his spiteful ways. He was simply following
the example set by his parents and repeating phrases
used in the home. Michelle tried to hug her own son
but he pulled away from her and ran off across the
field, covering his face with his hands.

'Is that what you call good behaviour?' Michelle
called out as she hurried away, her sharp heels sinking
into the mud. 'Physical assault?'

Alvaro nuzzled Lydia's neck. Her skin felt moist.
'Don't cry, son,' she said, rubbing his back. 'I'm so
sorry I broke my promise. This is all my fault. I'm
so sorry.'

Alvaro lifted up his head and looked at his mother
with a mischievous grin, his eyes glinting with

delight. 'Did you see how I jumped on him, Mum? Did you hear him crying like a girl?'

'You shouldn't have done that, Alvaro.' Lydia failed in her effort to sound stern. 'Fighting doesn't solve anything.'

'But Jack's always starting fights at school. Everyone's scared of him.'

'You never told me that. Why on earth do you hang about with him?' Lydia stood up and rubbed at the mud caking her trousers.

'Because I didn't want him to pick on me.'

'He's probably going to pick on you now, thanks to me and my big mouth. I'll have to come into school and speak to your teacher.'

'He won't pick on me, Mum. Don't worry.'

'How can you be so sure?'

Alvaro zipped up his rainproof coat and remodelled his quiff. 'Because if he does, I'll tell the whole school that I saw his mum kissing the football coach.'

'You mustn't tell lies, Alvaro.'

'It's not a lie, Mum. I saw her and Jack saw her too, before the match, in the changing rooms. That's why he was so angry.'

Lydia was pleased that her son had the upper hand and would not be bullied at school but she could not help feeling sorry for the confused boy who sprinted across the field ahead of his mother. There were worse things than being brought up by a lone parent, Lydia thought. A child could grow up in a nuclear family that was nothing but a sham.

Electra

The café is thick with cigarette smoke and stinks of stale fat. An elderly woman, bony and wrinkled, hunches over a muddy cup of tea, served in sickly green ceramic. Anaglypta, patterned lino, darkwood tables, candle wall lights, an eclectic mix of tasteless relics, surround us. The extraction system, as old as the fixtures and fittings and suffering from an identity crisis, whirs above us like a lawn mower. The elderly woman drags on the stub of her cigarette and exhales a violent, phlegmy cough. She wheezes, bangs several times on her concave chest, regains her composure and inhales once more on the stub.

'I'm climbing the walls, Lydia. I want to run and scream, to strangle my husband and his mother. I need a cigarette to calm my nerves.' I bite into an over-buttered teacake.

'Is that why we're here? So you can breathe in secondary smoke?'

'No, we're here for the teacakes, the crumpets and the Earl Grey.'

'What happened to almond croissants, espresso and minimalist chic?'

'Pregnancy happened. I have developed a craving for all things English. Well, everything apart from my husband.'

'I can't believe you still haven't told him about the baby. You've got to tell him some time.'

'How can I when he says he's not ready to be a father? I'm praying he will have a change of heart before I go into labour.'

'He'll be thrilled when he finds out, I'm sure of it. Why shouldn't he be?'

'Because he's selfish and immature and doesn't want to share me with a baby.'

'He's not selfish. He's not like Ian. There must be more to it than that. You have to talk to him. I'm surprised he hasn't noticed the changes in your body. Any woman would kill for those breasts, Electra.'

'Adam hasn't looked at my breasts since his mother moved in and sex is a distant memory. Perhaps the penny will finally drop when my abdomen is as round as a football.'

Bubbles fizzle on the surface of my Earl Grey as three sugar cubes plumb its depths. I order two more teacakes from a girl with limp hair who shuffles to the counter, trailing ragged trouser hems.

'Are things still bad at home with Margaret?'

'As bad as they can get. Yesterday I saw her cleaning the sink with my toothbrush.'

'Why don't you tell Adam what's going on?'

'Because we're not communicating at the moment.

He's in a world of his own and I am on the brink of exploding.'

'Electra, I can't bear to think of you and Adam being unhappy.'

The old woman, lodged in the corner of my eye, clears her throat and lights another long, slim cigarette. She inhales deeply, chalky smoke seeping through her nasal passages and out through her wide nostrils.

'Forget about Adam. Tell me about my godson?'

'He's playing up at the moment. Testing my patience. Being an absolute bugger actually. I don't know what's wrong with him. He flew into a rage on Sunday because his Elvis costume was in the washing machine, soaking wet, and he wanted to wear it. Mum tried to dry it with a hairdryer and set fire to the tassels. I spent the whole of Sunday afternoon trawling the shops for a replacement. Elvis, rest his soul, has become the bane of my life.'

'If he weren't obsessing about Elvis, he'd be obsessing about something else. At least Elvis is a positive role model. I obsess about him myself sometimes, dressed in that black leather jumpsuit.'

'Positive role model? Heavy drinker, pill-popper, philanderer?'

'We all have our foibles, Lydia. If Elvis drank stinky green tea and went to bed at eleven-thirty, do you think he would have been a rock 'n' roll legend?'

'I'd rather be married to Adam than Elvis any day. You're lucky you didn't marry a bastard like Ian.'

'Are you going to reply to his letter?'

'Not a chance. I never want to see him again as long as I live.'

I lean back in my chair and rub my bloated belly. 'Ach! My stomach hurts.'

'I'm not surprised, the way you wolfed down those teacakes. You've probably got indigestion.'

'The pain has nothing at all to do with teacakes. I'm constipated.'

'Wait till you give birth. Then you'll know what real pain is.'

'You only gave birth once. I'm constipated every day.'

The coffee-shop door swings open. A gust of wind blows in pavement litter and a dishevelled-looking Sean, on time, as planned, a scab glinting on the side of his injured nose.

'Look who it is, Lydia. My neighbour. The composer.'

'Who? I've never seen him before in my life.'

I raise my arm and call out to Sean.

'Don't call him over,' Lydia whispers. 'I'm not in the mood for small talk.'

Sean comes over to the table. I pull out a chair and ask him to join us. Lydia mumbles a greeting without making eye contact before turning away to scratch at a brown mark on the table with a toothpick. Sean takes off his jacket, orders coffee and settles back in his chair.

'How's work?' I ask, for want of something better to ask a virtual stranger.

'Fine, I'm very busy at the moment.'

I turn to Lydia. 'Sean writes advertising music . . . And the children, are they well?'

'They're fine too.'

'Sean has two children, Lydia. He's separated.'

My friend looks up at me suspiciously, then scratches more frantically at the stain.

'Lydia has a son. He's marvellous.'

She stops scratching to scowl at me. 'Yes, he's marvellous but he's also quite a handful.' Lydia's tone is prickly, her comment an attempt to frighten off the man scrutinising her over the rim of his broken glasses.

Sean appears undaunted. 'I've got a son as well. And a daughter.'

'And do you see your children?' Lydia asks, accusingly.

'Whenever I can. They stay with me most weekends.'

'Where do they live?'

'Not far away. In North London.'

Sean has been well briefed. I warned him Lydia would be defensive and unfriendly at first. Why did he come? Because I also told him my friend was generous and kind and wonderfully pretty.

'Your children are lucky. My ex hasn't seen his son since he was six months old. I blame myself for marrying that man in the first place. We make bad choices, marry the wrong people, screw up our lives, and our children end up suffering.'

'It's that time of the month,' I say, smiling, surprised by Lydia's outburst.

'Lydia's right. I feel the same way. I expect I'll feel guilty for the rest of my life for not being a full-time dad. Men have feelings too, you know. We're not all bastards.'

'I know that,' Lydia says, 'I have a wonderful friend

called Mark. We work together. He's handsome, funny, stylish, the perfect man, actually.'

Sean looks confused, wondering why I have invited him here when my friend evidently has her eye on someone else.

'Mark wears lip-gloss and likes soft furnishings,' I point out, helpfully.

'Mark's wonderful.'

'Mark's not a threat or a challenge. He's safe.'

'He makes me laugh and he'll never break my heart.'

Sean props his elbow on the table and cups his chin in his hand. 'Don't you want to fall in love again? To share your life with someone. Personally, I liked being married. Feeling secure. I just got married too young. Unfortunately my wife and I grew apart.'

'Marriage left a sour taste in my mouth. I'm perfectly happy on my own. Alvaro is the only man I'm concerned about, at the moment. Anyone else would come a very mediocre second to him.'

'Don't you miss having a man in your life. For companionship, if nothing else?'

Lydia's cheeks flush, suggesting Sean has hit a raw nerve. 'No. Not at all. I have friends for companionship.'

'And a very stimulating battery operated gadget,' I add.

Sean smiles. To my surprise, so does Lydia.

'I have no complaints about my life. I have a happy, healthy boy and a roof over my head. It happens to be mother's roof, which is a little stifling at times, but a person can't have everything.'

'My mum calls me three times a day. I might as well be living with her.'

'So you're a mother's boy.'

'No. An only son.'

'Like Alvaro.'

'And mum's on her own. Dad left when I was very young and she never remarried.'

Lydia looks thoughtful as she compares her situation to that of Sean's mother.

'How old were you when your father left?'

Suddenly, Sean and Lydia are talking to each other, without my help, about their children and their lives. I marvel at how quickly they have cut through the crap of first encounters to share the intimate details of their lives. I stand up and head for the loo to give them time alone. My absence is noted but does not halt the flow of conversation.

Five minutes later Lydia is hammering on the toilet cubicle door. 'Are you all right, Electra? You've been in here a very long time,' Lydia calls out, knocking on the toilet door.

'I'm fine. Why don't you go back to the table?'

'I'll wait for you.'

'What do you think of Sean?'

'He looks like he's been in a fight.'

'Perhaps he's had an accident.' I open the door and find Lydia nervously biting her fingernails. 'I think he likes you.'

She screws up her face. 'Don't be ridiculous. He's only just met me. And I've hardly been warm and likeable.'

'You've never heard of animal magnetism? Love at first sight? He's very handsome, don't you think?'

She shrugs and we walk back to the table, Lydia looking nervous.

237

Sean gulps down the last mouthful of his coffee and gets up. 'Lydia, I don't mean to be rude but I have to rush off. I'm picking the children up this evening. I'll leave you my telephone number. If you want to go out for a drink or a meal or anything, just give me a call.' He scribbles his number on a napkin and pushes it across the table, impressing me with his no-nonsense approach. Lydia stares at him, open-mouthed.

'Nice to meet you,' he says, putting on his jacket and turning to leave.

'Did you just fix me up, Electra?' Lydia asks, glaring at me, her lips puckering.

'No. Of course not. But you certainly seem to have made an impression.'

'There's not a chance in hell of me calling him.'

'Then I'll take that.' I fold up the napkin and put it in my handbag, determined to arrange a dinner date for Sean and my friend at the earliest opportunity.

Adam

My head has been spinning all night. Whirling like the bars of a fruit machine, stopping on a succession of distressing images. Was I half-asleep or wide awake when the future flashed before my eyes? When I visualised my wife in bed with another man and imagined beating this man to a pulp. As I watched a tearful Electra pack her bags and walk out of my life. When I imagined Mum empty the workroom of its contents and mark her territory with embroidered cushions and chintz curtains.

The harder I struggle to sleep, the more awake I feel. My head throbs to the rhythm of a distant car alarm. Dull thumping resonates in my blocked ears. I get up. Pace the hallway. Stop outside Mum's room, exasperated suddenly by her meddling and the length of her stay. I return to the lounge and sit on the edge of the sofa bed looking down at Electra, my pent up anger redirecting itself, focusing on my wife. For sleeping peacefully while I suffer pangs of jealousy.

I lie down with my back to her. Not close enough to

touch but near enough to feel her body heat. These days I can't touch my wife without asking myself painful questions. What if Mum's right? What if the woman beside me is not to be trusted? What do I really have to offer a woman like Electra? A woman full of life, who married into a family of anal retentives. She has never received any warmth from Mum or John. We have given her no reason to love us or even to like us as a clan. I am ashamed of my family, of Mum's snobbery and John's aloofness. Things would have been so different for Electra if Dad were still around. He would have welcomed her with open arms. Known exactly why I married her. Looked into my eyes and said, 'She's marvellous, son,' in his thick northern accent. He would have kept Mum in check with a few well-chosen words. He was the balance in her life, the fire that thawed her frostiness. Without him, her less endearing traits have reared their disagreeable heads.

Thinking about Dad is the catalyst for so many feelings of regret and guilt. My past, like the death of the sleeping youth, is nipping at my heels. Saying, 'Turn around and face me, look me in the eye and say you were blameless.' But why do I feel guilty so long after the event? Because I should have made more effort to visit my grandmother? Because I should have voiced dissent as I watched Mum clearing every last vestige of Dad from the house? Packing his cricketing glove, his work suits, his green wellies, his books, into a box and dropping them off at the nearest charity shop. 'I used to love your father dearly,' she'd said, storing her wedding photos in the loft. 'Why don't you love him now?' I wanted to shout. 'Now that he needs you more than ever.' I kept my mouth shut, knowing she had stopped loving him long before he got sick. Instead I locked the door of my bedroom, curled up on my bed like a foetus and wished I had never been born.

I lean across Electra to grab my headphones. My hand brushes against her smooth skin and the hairs on my forearm stand on end. I stroke her hair and a feeling of deep love overwhelms me. I have neglected my wife since Mum came to stay, denied her the physical affection she is used to. Mum's presence renders me emotionally cold and sexually numb. Electra and I have stopped kissing, stopped hugging and stopped having sex. Our conversations are stilted and hurried and snatched. Communication, the key to a healthy marriage, has rusted in its lock. I have held my wife at arm's length, pushed her away when she has tried to get near.

I put down the headphones, knowing music won't calm me but just add to the noise in my head. It won't drown out the questioning voice but only make it shout louder. I get up and leave the room, sidetracked on my way to the kitchen by the sight of Electra's suede bag on the hallway table. As if compelled I pick it up, unzip it, thrust my hand inside, telling myself I must disprove Mum and find peace. I pull out receipts, a purse bulging with coins, loose sweets, a brown pill bottle and a crumpled napkin with a telephone number and the name 'Sean' written on it. What does this mean? Who is this man? I want to throw down the bag and sink my fist into the wall, to shake my wife awake and confront her with the evidence. As I turn to go back to the lounge I see Mum standing in the bedroom doorway. How long has she been spying on me? Long enough, I'm sure, to know that I am snooping. I feel angry and guilty and deeply embarrassed. I have undone five years of good work in seconds and proved to Mum that my wife cannot be trusted.

'Good morning, Adam.' Her tone is upbeat. 'Shall I make some tea?'

I repack Electra's bag and put it back on the table.

'Have you had a chance to speak to your wife?' Mum peers at me over the rim of her teacup. I have given her an inch of satisfaction already today but it seems she wants more.

'About what?'

'About the bailiff's letter. I wake up every morning worrying about that.'

'Please, drop the subject. I'm not in the mood to talk about it right now.'

'I'm only trying to help.'

'You're interfering.'

'I'm protecting my son and his property.'

We drink our tea in silence. Not the comfortable silence one feels in the presence of a partner or a good friend but an awkward, bitter silence. Sitting opposite Mum, feeling tense and tongue-tied, takes me back to a period in my life I have tried in vain to forget. Time does not seem to have healed but picked like a vulture at my childhood wounds. I vividly remember eating breakfast with Mum while Dad sat in a nearby arm-chair, hugging his sides, talking gibberish. I remember chewing mechanically and keeping my mouth full to stop myself from asking questions about Dad's illness, his worsening condition, his eventual fate. Mum ate while Dad rocked and I sat dumbstruck between them, feeling confused and alone, wanting to weep, cursing the maternal voice in my head telling me not to. I feel the same need to escape right now as I felt back then. I gulp down tea, push back my chair and head for the living room to dress.

Electra lies on her side, uncovered, hugging my pillow to her chest, a contented smile on her face. Who is she is dreaming about? The man whose telephone number she carries in her handbag? These days I don't seem to make her smile, let alone laugh. These days we speak in whispers and exchange disgruntled looks. I dress hurriedly and search the cluttered room for my keys. I open drawers, empty pockets, lift up the rug and the quilt cover, feeling inordinately anxious. Calm down, I tell myself, losing a set of keys is not the end of the world. Or is it? Dad's end began harmlessly enough with the losing of keys and the daily search for reading glasses, with the onset of forgetfulness. Could the same be happening to me? Am I losing my mind? Dad wasn't that much older than me when his headaches started and he began to wander the neighbourhood, confused, disorientated, frightened. When his personality changed and his moods became extreme.

Could I subject a child of my own to the torment of watching their father disappear? Do I want my children to know me only from pictures and anecdotes? 'Daddy was a good man,' Electra will tell our offspring. 'Kind, uncoordinated, clean-living, a music lover.' In my absence I will be parodied. When Dad left us a gaping hole took his place. Strangely enough, a trace of him, his physical presence, was better than an empty armchair. I fell apart when he left us, while appearing to hold it together. I played man of the house, for Mum's sake, since I was her only support. John was away at university, living his life, too busy a boy to come home for the holidays. The thought of my self-centred brother strengthens my resolve to be selfless. To tell my wife that I am not the man she thinks I am. That I am damaged goods and can never be a father. I find my keys and hurry out of the house.

Electra

This morning my husband left the house without kissing me. His kiss was not forgotten but withheld. Now that I need Adam's affection more than ever, I am lucky to feel his lips on mine at all. I hope to God he will recover his senses when his mother leaves. I cannot live with the cold, undemonstrative man he has become. I need a drink. My mouth tastes of metal. I hear Margaret's footsteps outside and cower behind the living-room door. I have come to dread our morning encounters, when I am made to feel, by her censorious looks, like something monstrous risen from the deep. The Electra-monster. Nessie's Greek cousin. A fuzzy haired, puffy-eyed, garlic-breathing creature.

This flat is no longer my home. Margaret has rearranged the ornaments and soft furnishings, taken control of our shopping list, stepped up her Post It pad campaign. Composed a laundry, washing up and cooking rota. Adam has allowed his mother to take control and her confidence has snowballed. In her son's hive

Margaret is now Queen Bee, ordering her workers to fetch and carry. When Adam is out at work she barely talks to me and has taken to eating her lunch alone, in the bedroom. A hostile act that is both a blessing and a curse. These days my very existence seems to offend her. When Adam gets home from work, Margaret wakes up, pokes a smiling head out of her shell and shares a bowl of lettuce with her son.

I hear the bedroom door close and put on my slippers to tiptoe along the hallway. The kitchen is a mess, as usual, strewn with breakfast plates, littered with breadcrumbs and vegetable peel. With her leg now in a plastic splint, Margaret is well enough to make a mess but not fit enough to clean it up. My mother-in-law, the goddess of forward planning, has been busy this morning, preparing lunch. Something cabbagey, a stew perhaps, bubbles on the gas hob. The smell of it fills my nostrils and makes me want to vomit. I head for the bathroom and lock the door, breathing hard to try and ease the churning in my stomach. The harder I breathe, the sicker I feel. I stoop over the toilet bowl, stick a finger down my throat and throw up. My throat burns. My eyes stream. The nausea does not pass. I hear footsteps outside the door but no concerned voice asking whether I am dead or alive. I throw up again and feel as limp as a rag, the churning in my stomach finally subsiding.

I wash my face and sit on the floor, biting back tears, wondering how Margaret can be so cold. If I were back home Mama would sit me down, prop up my swollen feet, make a simple vermicelli soup and serve it to me on a tray. 'Home' and 'Cyprus' are becoming increasingly synonymous in my mind. I want to go back and raise my child in the bosom of a loving family. I miss the warm weather, the bright sky and the gaggle of lovely children who call me 'Aunt'. Adam has never ruled out the prospect of leaving England. 'Going back' looms tantalisingly on the horizon. 'Going back' is no longer a question of 'if' but 'when'.

I unlock the bathroom door and head for my desk. The workroom is my only sanctuary, a space with no visible trace of Margaret. Yet even in this room she makes her frigid presence felt. The room is cold. Margaret has taken it upon herself to reduce our fuel bills by switching off the heating during the day. When Adam gets home from work and starts shivering the boiler mysteriously reignites. I stare at the bills stacked up on my desk. Bills that should and would have been paid months ago if my last client had not declared bankruptcy. I am one of a long list of creditors who will never see a penny of their hard-earned cash. Who will ride the storm or cease to exist. I have prioritised my payments. Called my debtors and asked for more time to pay. The bailiffs, baying for my blood, have accepted post-dated cheques. I have negotiated a deal with a long-standing customer and in thirty days cash will flow into my business.

The telephone rings. Margaret answers it before I have had a chance to reach out across my desk. A few moments later she pushes open the workroom door and tells me Miroulla is on the phone. She moves away but leaves the door ajar, so she can listen in on my conversation.

'How are you, my love?' Miroulla asks.

247

'Eh. Not bad,' I reply in a language my mother-in-law cannot understand.

'But not good? What's the matter?'

'I'm not feeling a hundred per cent.'

'What exactly are you feeling?'

'A little queasy. Tired. Lethargic.'

'I'm coming straight over.'

'No. Please. I have work to do. I threw up this morning and I feel much better now.'

The line goes silent. Aunty puts two and two together. 'Are you pregnant, Electra? Are you pregnant, my love?' The question is asked calmly, cautiously. When Miroulla hears a hesitant 'yes' she screams and drops the receiver. It clatters against something hard and Miroulla's footsteps recede across a tiled floor. 'Nikoli, Nikoli,' she calls out in a high-pitched voice. 'We're having a baby. Nikoli . . . Where the hell are you? Close your Goddamn' books, old man. We're having a baby!'

'My dear, sit down,' Nikoli replies anxiously. 'You're not well. You can't possibly be pregnant.'

'Not me, you crazy man. Electra! Our Electra is having a baby.' I hear their squeals of joy and feel momentarily elated. 'Now I'm definitely coming over,' Miroulla says, picking up the abandoned receiver. 'Work or no work. Today we are going to celebrate, Electra. I'll make you some soup, or would you prefer something sweet? Some *yalatoboureko* perhaps? You need to look after yourself, my girl.'

'Why don't you come over tomorrow, Aunty?'

She tuts. 'Why do I hear unhappiness in your voice? What in God's name is going on?'

'I haven't told Adam about the baby.'

'Why ever not? Surely he should have been the first to know?'

'I'm waiting for the right moment. It's difficult with Margaret here. We don't get much time to ourselves.'

'Find the time. Promise me you'll tell Adam?'

'I will, I promise. But please, keep the news to yourself. I haven't even told my parents yet.'

Miroulla breathes heavily into the receiver. 'Whatever you say, my love.'

I stare out of the window, killing time, feeling morose. I curse the hormones coursing through my body, confusing my mind, playing havoc with my emotions. Why do I feel like crying? Because the kitchen was a mess? Because my mother-in-law will never love me? Because my husband is not the man he used to be? A ripple of self-pity swells into a wave that submerges me. I burst into tears and start sobbing like a child. Margaret pokes her head round the door and asks if she can come in. I nod and wipe my eyes, trying to compose myself, not wanting her to see me in this heightened emotional state. She walks up to the desk, lays a hand on my shoulder and asks me why I'm crying.

'I'm just feeling a bit low, Margaret.'

'Why are you feeling low, dear? Why don't you tell me? I'm a good listener, you know. Why don't you get things off your chest?' She looks down at me, not as an enemy but with compassion, and I find myself opening my heart to her.

'The fact is I'm pregnant.'

'I thought you might be.' She gently squeezes my

shoulder and smiles. There is no whoop of joy, no Miroulla-like shout of elation. 'And why is that a problem? I thought you wanted a child.'

'I do. It's just that I haven't told Adam. I'm worried about his reaction. I don't think he's ready to be a father.' I glance out of the window and see Sean standing at his window. He waves and I force a smile. He sticks up his thumb and I know from this coded message that Lydia has agreed to a dinner date.

Margaret takes her hand from my shoulder and turns her back to me. 'Adam has never wanted children. He won't change his mind. You know how stubborn he can be.' Her tone is cold, the formality between us suddenly reinstated.

'I hadn't realised his mind was made up.'

'He told me quite clearly on the day of my check-up that he doesn't want children. Not everyone does, you know.'

'Then what do you suggest I do, Margaret?'

'If you want to keep your husband, you could always abort, dear.'

She walks out of the room, having injected her poison, leaving me stunned, reeling, severing the connection between herself and the baby growing inside me. Margaret's blow is fatal, her remark a sin. It leaves me feeling dead inside. Numb with shock, I start to shiver and pull my cardigan tighter around my shoulders. I sit in a stupor for what seems like hours until a key turns in the front door lock making me start. Adam calls out my name. The sound of his voice lifts my sunken spirit. When he bursts into the room I want to run into his arms and be consoled, to tell him

250

everything that's happened. But the desperate sadness in his eyes is unsettling and roots me to the chair.

'I called in sick. We need to talk. I have something to tell you.' The sombreness of his tone scares me. I wonder if this is going to be the kind of talk that can break a marriage. Is he going to tell me that he's having an affair?

Margaret knocks at the door. 'Adam darling, are you in there?' The sound of her voice and her continual interference is infuriating. 'Is everything all right? Why have you come home?'

'We need some privacy. Please leave us alone,' Adam says, his attention suddenly distracted by the view from the window. 'Who's that man?'

'What man?'

'That man. Your friend.' He points towards Sean, sitting on the first-floor window ledge, flicking through a wad of papers.

'My friend? What kind of friend are you suggesting he is?'

'Mum saw you in his flat. What were you doing there?'

Self-pity quickly gives way to anger. My need to cry is usurped by a powerful urge to punch my husband in the face. 'Is that what you came to talk about?'

'No. But it's a good place to start. Who's that man? Were you in his flat or not?'

If he expects an answer like a child to a teacher, he will not get one. Adam is the sinner, not me. He has blemished his unbroken record, allowed his mother to get between us. 'What's happened to us, Adam?'

'You tell me?'

What do I say to a man no longer in control of his faculties? A man poisoned by his mother and suffering from temporary insanity. 'What do you think? That I popped over there for a quickie while you were out at work? Because who could blame me? You haven't touched me in weeks. That man is simply an acquaintance, nothing more. Are you happy now? Do you trust me again? Or do you prefer to believe your mother's nasty-minded conclusions?'

'Leave Mum out of this.' When did such a phrase enter my husband's vocabulary? When did I become the outsider?

'Is there anything else you want to talk about, Adam? Anything else you want to get off your chest?'

'When are you going to pay those bills, Electra?' He motions towards my desk.

'How do you know I have bills to pay, Adam? I didn't tell you. Have you been going through the papers on my desk?'

'I wouldn't do that!'

'No. But your mother would. I've seen her searching through my things.' My accusation is hissed, my anger choking. 'And how dare you accuse me of having an affair! I've never even looked at another man. How dare you side with your mother against me! How dare you!'

'I'm not. Electra, calm down. I didn't come home to talk about any of this. Please, stop shouting.'

'Don't tell me to stop shouting! I'll shout the bloody house down if I want to.'

'Please. I need to talk to you about something else. Something very important.' He walks towards my desk. Gets down on his knees and takes hold of my hand. I pull it sharply out of his grip, refusing to be touched by this man who questions my loyalty. This is not the Adam I know and love. The wounded look in his eyes intensifies my contempt for the stranger kneeling before me. 'You know how we've been talking about starting a family . . .' He hesitates.

'Hurry up. Spit it out.'

'Electra, I'm sorry but I don't want children. Not now. Not ever.'

'Bastard!' I scream, slapping his cheek, pushing him away, struggling to breathe. He takes his punishment silently as if expecting it, a fan of red lines welling up on his cheek, branding him a fool.

'Electra, please hear me out.'

'There's nothing more to say. You've said it all. And don't worry, your revelation comes as no surprise to me. Your mother took great pleasure in telling me you don't want children. Now, leave me alone. Get away from me. You're an imbecile and I wish I'd never met you.'

'Please, Electra. Don't say things like that.' His eyes water. He reaches out for my hand.

'Don't touch me! Don't come anywhere near me.'

'What's going on in there? Adam, let me in.' Margaret knocks loudly on the door.

'Go away, Mum. Go away.'

'I'm the one who's going away. As far away from you and your mother as I can get.'

'Sit down. Please.' Adam's tears don't tug at my heartstrings, only intensify my desperation to escape. 'There are reasons for my decision. Please let me explain. Perhaps you'll understand then. Electra, I don't want to lose you . . .'

'You've already lost me.' I hurry out of the room, enraged, intent on packing my case and leaving as quickly as possible. Adam follows me on my erratic journey through the flat, picking up my belongings and tossing them into a suitcase.

I sense Margaret lurking in the shadows and hear her conversation with Adam as if it were conducted a long way away and has nothing whatever to do with me.

'What's wrong with your face, son?'

'Nothing, Mum, go away.'

'Has she hit you, Adam? She's hit you, hasn't she?'

'Leave me alone, Mum.'

Adam

The door frame vibrates as Electra slams the door behind her. I stand and watch, paralysed by shock, while Mum's voice buzzes annoyingly in my ear. 'Let her go, son. Let her go.' I had my confession speech all planned. I'd rehearsed it over and over again in the car. When I saw that man standing at his window I got all worked up and forgot my script. I ad libbed, went off track, ended up here. Standing in front of a slammed door, minus a wife. My cheek stings. I touch it. The pain is a cherished reminder of Electra.

'Does it hurt, son? Shall I get some ice?' Mum reaches up to touch my cheek but I don't want her anywhere near me. I want my wife. 'Sit down, darling. You've had quite a shock.'

Mum gazes at me with loving eyes. That love has enslaved and repressed me and lost me a wife. I must break free from it before it destroys me completely. I grab my coat and open the door. Mum follows me along the front path, pleading with me to stay. I climb into the car, start the engine and drive like a madman through the neighbourhood, searching for Electra.

My wife has vanished into thin air. I stop the car and bury my pounding head in my hands, realising my life is a complete mess. The flat no longer feels like home. I can't go back or return to work or drive around for ever. There is only one place left where I have a chance of finding peace and my sanity. I double back and head for the north circular, driving past grotty semis with blackened brickwork and cracked windows. Alongside a multi-storey car park and a huge, yellow furniture store that looms up like a spaceship. A mist of sickly-smelling grease pours from the extractor fan of a drive-in McDonald's and filters into the car, making me feel nauseous.

Memories convey me along the M1 motorway on my journey north. I remember sitting in the passenger seat of the Citroën beside Dad, excited about spending the weekend away from home, away from Mum and John. We both looked forward to our weekend breaks, to staying in the small cottage where there were no rules. No fixed bedtime for me. No early starts for Dad. A place where we could slouch on the sofa, watch telly and eat until we burst. Where just outside the door was an endless playground where Dad and I practised our cricketing skills and kicked a ball to one another. 'Why can't we live up here?' I used to ask, always reluctant to leave. 'Wild horses couldn't drag your mother out of London,' Dad replied.

Even if I find the cottage, there is no guarantee that my grandmother will still be there. That a small woman with strong hands and an infectious smile will answer the door. Sturdy and red-faced, Gran was mistress of her old-fashioned kitchen. She could gauge the heat of the oven by placing her hand inside it. She knew how hot her frying pan was by the density of heat that rose from its surface. She skinned rabbits without flinching and made the most delicious cooked breakfasts. Gran's house opened my eyes to a different style of living and exposed me to dishes I had never tasted. Goose stuffed with apples. Lamb dumplings. Chestnut soufflé. Mum never liked cooking. She hated the clammy feel of meat, the smell of onions and garlic. Her cakes always sagged in the middle. Frying eggs and bacon dirtied the cooker so breakfast at home was invariably buttered toast and cereal. Mum bought puddings and ham in tins. Fruit in cans. Vegetables frozen and sauces in packets. Dad was an undemanding man who ate his supper without complaint, knowing that once a month he would escape to his mother's house and have his taste buds reawakened.

Undulating hills. A patchwork of lush green fields. Miles and miles of walls constructed by hand from grey stone slabs. Mighty oaks and thickets of fern. Pubs from a distant era. Very little has changed. The landscape is as enduring as my memory. I drive instinctively past familiar landmarks, following the road signs, wanting to kick myself for not coming sooner, for not bringing my wife. How quickly time has passed and swallowed up my life. How stupid I have been to let Mum's argument with Gran keep me from this place and its people. Tragically, a sick husband lay at the heart of their dispute, a beloved father who was diagnosed with Alzheimer's on the eve of his fiftieth birthday.

Dad left hospital with his diagnosis, feeling remarkably upbeat. 'I'll get better, son, don't worry,' he said, blissfully ignorant of the facts. He had heard of senile dementia but that, he comforted himself, only occurred in later life. He was convinced his symptoms were due to overwork and believed a well-earned rest would cure him. When he started reading up on the illness, accessing articles from the library, he realised the disease was merciless and incurable. I will never forget the day he sat me down on his bed and explained what would happen to him. He held me in his arms then and began to cry, fearful of the disease that would inevitably destroy his mind. Six months later his sister, Mary, was diagnosed with Alzheimer's and a year after that his brother, Arthur, followed suit. The disease was not hereditary, the doctors reassured us, but Dad's brother Jim was not convinced and began to delve into his family's medical history.

He already knew Granddad had died at an early age from an illness that rendered him childlike. Everyone assumed he had lost his mind in the German POW camp where he was held captive. Granddad's mother had spent most of her life in an institution and died in her fifties, her death certificate citing 'dementia' as the cause of her demise. Jim wondered if his father and his grandmother were also victims of Alzheimer's. He read about a team of professors at a London hospital researching families with the disease and sent them a copy of his family tree. Blood samples were taken from Dad and his siblings and we heard no more.

Eventually, several years later, the researchers came back with their results. The strain of Alzheimer's affecting Dad's family was caused by a genetic mutation and the children of sufferers had a fifty-fifty chance of inheriting the disease. The illness could not skip generations but only be passed from parent to child. By the time my uncle's suspicions were confirmed Dad was too far-gone mentally to realise the significance of these findings.

The kind, articulate, fun-loving man I knew began to lose his powers of reason, his speech, his sense of humour. The man who once took pride in dressing well wore creased clothes and scuffed shoes. The man who had never raised his voice in anger would slam his fist on the table and swear in frustration. He left work eighteen months after the diagnosis and took root in his armchair. Mum did her best to look after him but the strain on her was immense and she was not cut out to be a carer. She often accused him of getting things wrong on purpose and making no effort to get better. Dad begged his wife to let him go home, back to Yorkshire. 'How can your father choose his mother over me?' she complained without realising that Dad was living his life in reverse, that each phase he lived through was swiftly being deleted from his memory. His marital life was slowly being wiped out by the disease. Home to him became the place where he was born and grew up.

He began making hopeless attempts to get back there. One day he boarded a train without a ticket and was brought home by the police. Mum snapped then. She'd had enough, her nerves could take no more. She rang Gran and said she was putting Dad into a care home. Gran pleaded with her not to, offering to look after Dad herself for as long as she could. They argued; hurtful things were said by both parties. That night Uncle Jim arrived to pick up Dad and take him back to Yorkshire. I never saw him or any member of his family again. Mum emptied the house of Dad's belongings and washed her hands of them all. The loss of her mother-in-law was no great injury. I suspect Mum was glad of an excuse to sever all ties with a woman with whom she had nothing in common. Gran lacked Mum's social graces and was a painful reminder of Dad's working-class background. A year later Mum announced with detachment that Dad had died and that his spiteful family had not invited us to the funeral.

Mum should have been grateful there was someone willing to take over Dad's care. He was in the most capable of hands. Gran was strong and patient and a practised caregiver who had looked after her own sick husband. As a boy I traced my finger along the branches of a family tree that led from Great-grandmother to me, believing the connection between us was remote. Later, I realised this branch was as important as the cord connecting foetus to placenta. I have a fifty-fifty chance of inheriting the disease that consigned Great-grandmother to an institution and my father to an early death. If I have the disease, there is a fifty-fifty chance that my children will develop Alzheimer's too. It cripples me to think that I could subject my wife and children to such pain and suffering for years and years. My only consolation is that I have the power to nip this demon in the bud, by not having children. John decided to ignore the risks when he started a family and to keep the ugly truth from his wife.

Bright sunlight breaks through the pebble-grey clouds, catching the top of the rolling hills in the distance. I drive through a pretty hamlet, past a weathered stone church. Just beyond it, set back from the road, is a barn conversion with high windows and a gravelled courtyard. I remember this barn when it was the old and rickety home to two ageing Shire horses. Further along the road is the oak tree my father used to climb as a boy, thick with lobed leaves. I wonder how many climbing boys this aged tree has outlived? And how many more it will outlive.

My destination is only minutes away. The navigation system in my head tells me to take the next turning left. I turn into a narrow lane, drive under an arch of overhanging branches and come upon a row of small stone cottages, bounded front and back by open countryside. Number six is identical to its neighbours and seems frozen in time. Blue-grey slate tiles glint on the roof. Pale stone bricks absorb the wetness of a summer shower. Well-tended baskets, with overhanging foliage and pink flowers, hang either side of the front door. The brass doorknocker gleams. Its freshly polished glare gives me hope that my grandmother might still be alive. She never strayed far from her duster and her can of polish. But how old would she be now? Eighty? Ninety? She seemed old to me when Dad was alive.

I climb out of the car. Walk along a stone path,

shimmering with wetness, breathing hard to calm my nerves. Stooping, I take hold of the knocker and bang it twice, wanting and not wanting to be heard. No one answers. I feel a sense of profound relief. I can scuttle back to my London life and pretend I never came. As I turn to leave, I hear the lifting of a latch and feel the contents of my stomach rise up into my mouth. A short, frail woman with thinning hair opens the door. She wipes her tiny hands on the skirt of her flowered apron and looks up at me through cloudy, blue eyes. She reaches into the front pocket of her apron, pulls out a pair of gold-rimmed glasses and squints at me through flour-dusted lenses.

'Yes. How can I help you, young man?'

I catch my breath. A smaller, frailer version of the woman I remember stands before me, with pale, gauzy skin and pure white hair. I want to scoop her up and hold her like a child in my arms.

'You look lost. Are you lost, lad?'

'No, I'm not lost. It's me Gran. Adam.'

She looks me up and down, pulling a confused expression. 'Speak up. What did you say?'

'It's Adam. Your grandson.'

She reaches up. Touches my shoulders with trembling hands and works her way down to my wrists, needing physical proof of my existence. 'Adam. Is it really you?'

'Yes, Gran.'

'Oh, my Lord.' She takes hold of my hands, kissing and nuzzling them. I feel the wetness of her tears on my skin and bend down to hug her.

'Don't cry, Gran.' Her translucent skin is baby-soft.

She feels so small and fragile in my clumsy arms that I am afraid to squeeze her too hard. 'Don't cry, please.'

Her body begins to spasm as she sobs, the gasping sounds breaking my heart, turning my insides to mush. I gulp down a sob of my own, my eyes brimming with wetness. Gran looks up at me with swollen, loving eyes and I melt into her arms, crying like a baby, until the black cloud inside me lessens its load. I feel like a small boy again, powerless and mixed up and I remember with a sting of pain that I never cried the day I heard Dad had died. Instead I felt angry and confused. Angry that other boys had fathers whilst mine was taken from me, angry that I never got the chance to say goodbye. Now I stroke Gran's soft, white hair, wipe away her tears and tell her with heartfelt remorse that I've missed her and wish I'd come back sooner.

She smiles, throws her arms around my waist. 'You're here now. That's all that matters. Come inside. Come inside, my precious boy.'

The lounge is smaller and more cluttered than I remember it. Ornaments line every shelf, decades of accumulated paraphernalia. We sit side by side on her old, floral sofa, Gran stroking my hand, wave after wave of deep emotion washing over me. Gran fires questions at me. Her mind is still sharp and her curiosity as insatiable as ever. How's John? And your mother? Are you married? Do you have children? I talk about my marriage as if today had never happened, as if Electra were at home warming my slippers. Two decades dissolve into nothing. I feel as if Gran and I were separated only yesterday. She talks about her sons and their children, her great-grandchildren, dizzying me with names I struggle to remember. She sidles up beside me and glances into my face. 'You look just like your father.'

I wonder how much she can actually see. A true representation or a shape filled in by her imagination? She takes hold of my hand. 'I used to sit with your father like this. Whenever he got distressed, I would rub his hands and he would calm down. Brian loved being stroked and patted, he loved physical contact. You know, Adam, a person needs the same loving care at the end of their life as they do at the beginning.'

I bite back tears and ask her to tell me more.

'He was well cared for. I looked after him for you. I looked after my gentle son for as long as I could and made sure he died with some dignity. His brothers helped too. The ones who could. They often came to visit. He may not have recognised them exactly, but he could feel instinctively, from deep within, if his visitor was someone he loved or who loved him.'

I am too choked to speak but desperate to hear more about Dad.

'Your father was a wonderful man. He kept a picture of you in his pocket. He spent hours looking at that picture, knowing it was special in some way but not why. That picture kept him company. It was under his pillow when he died.'

I bury my face in my hands and cry, feeling weak and pathetic, an emotional wreck.

'Let it out, lad. Let it out.' Gran doesn't tell me to pull myself together, to be a man. She runs her hand up and down my back and allows me to grieve, knowing I must suffer this pain before I am healed. 'He couldn't have been in better hands. You know that, don't you?' she says. I shake my head, Dad's smiling face floating like a spectre before me. Gran pulls a crumpled handkerchief from her sleeve and hands it to me. 'Dry your eyes, Adam.'

I blow my nose and wipe my burning eyes.

She smiles. 'Do you know, your father once picked up a slice of white bread and used it to blow his nose. And the cheeky bugger liked to pee in the sink.' She chuckles. 'Let me make you a cup of tea and then I'll tell you about the last few years of your father's life.'

'Last few years? I thought he died a year after he came to live with you?'

'No. He was a stubborn blighter. Or else he liked my cooking too much. Your father lived in this house for five years. He spent the last six months of his life in hospital. I wrote to you every few months, to let you know what was happening. I was surprised you never wrote back.'

'What! I don't believe it. I never got your letters, Gran. Mum must have kept them from me as she did the truth. She said Dad died a year after he came here and I believed her but then I had no reason not to. Why did she lie to me?' I can hardly believe what I'm hearing. Righteous anger overwhelms me. I wonder how many other terrible lies my mother has told me.

'Forget what your mother said. It's all water under the bridge now. You've come back to me, Adam, that's what's important. I'd love to see John too before I go to my grave but I don't hold out much hope of that. He never really liked it up here did he? Perhaps I should just be grateful I have you.'

I nod my head, not wanting to talk about John, knowing he will never come, that my brother is a chip off the old maternal block. 'Tell me about Dad. Tell me all about the years I missed out on.'

'I was lucky with Brian. He wasn't violent like your grandfather. My husband was a good and kind man all his life, but when the illness took hold he became violent and aggressive. Brian got angry too. He shouted and swore, but he never lashed out.'

'How did you cope?'

'I'm no saint, Adam. I coped because I had no other choice. I coped because I began to understand the disease and how a sufferer behaves. Three of my children were struck down with the same illness. I knew not to argue with your father when he was being unreasonable but to talk to him softly and kindly. To divert his attention with a biscuit when a situation became difficult. I told lots of white lies and used bribery, that's how I coped. And I had help. From the family. From Brian's old school friends. From the local authority.'

'I wish I'd helped.'

'You were too young to help and you lived too far away. There's nothing you could have done. You mustn't feel guilty. Your father needed twenty-four-hour care. He couldn't feed himself or change his clothes. He stopped recognising his own brothers pretty early on. I knew it would happen. I had lived through it before and was expecting it.' She turns to look at me. 'Now, I want to hear more about your life, about your wife and your job.'

266

'Things aren't too good at the moment.'

'Is that why you're here, lad? Is there something I can do to help?'

'It's the illness. I'm afraid I might get it and end up like Dad.'

Gran struggles out of her seat. 'I think I'll give your cousin Robert a call.'

A tall man walks into the room in paint-spattered overalls. I look into the blue eyes of my mirror image, a younger version of me. Gran introduces me to my cousin Robert and I vaguely remember him, as a blonde, curly-haired boy with plump red cheeks. I offer him my hand but he throws his arms around me, instead.

'Jesus!' he exclaims. 'I thought I was the only lanky blighter in this family. It's good to meet you again.'

His smile is infectious. I find myself beaming, taking instantly to this warm-hearted man.

'I'll go and make some tea. You boys sit down and talk,' Gran says.

And we do talk. Like old friends, reunited after a long separation. And Gran serves tea and sits in her armchair, watching us. Robert takes a wallet out of his overall pocket and flips it open, showing me a picture of a woman sitting on a park bench, with a child either side of her.

'This is my family,' he says, proudly. 'My wife Laura and our two boys.'

I smile, feeling bereft.

'You don't have children?' he asks.

'No.'

'Because of Alzheimer's?'

The astuteness of his question takes me by surprise. I nod.

'My mother, Mary, died of Alzheimer's.'

I look at Gran, realising now why she invited Robert over.

'And do you know what her illness taught me? Not to waste my life worrying. To live life to the full.'

'But what about your children? What if they get it?' I ask, finally able to vocalise the fears I have kept bottled up for years.

'My children have fifty years of happy, healthy life ahead of them. And during that time half a century's worth of medical research will be carried out. There are new drugs coming out all the time. Treatments are bound to improve. And who knows? One day soon, they might even find a cure. There is a dim light at the end of the tunnel.'

'You do know about the genetic test you can have don't you, Adam?' Gran asks. 'The one that tells you whether or not you will develop the disease.'

I nod my head, reminded of the predictive test I find impossible to contemplate. 'Have you been tested, Robert?'

'No. And I'm not going to be either. I'd rather live in blissful ignorance, thank you very much. A definite answer doesn't suit everyone. Personally, I don't want to know. My brother and sister both decided to have the test. Louise was given the all clear but Mark was told he would develop Alzheimer's at some point in his life.'

'And how has he come to terms with that?'

'He hasn't, completely. He's scared and angry. But he's the kind of person who would rather know than not know. He's given us clear instructions about how and where he wants to be cared for at the end of his life.'

'That's awful.'

'Having some control over the future is a comfort to Mark. He refuses to live his life in denial.'

'My brother John and I have been in denial for years. We've never even discussed the illness.'

'I want to talk about it. I need to communicate my feelings and I try to focus on the positives.'

'There are positives?'

'Living under the threat of the disease really makes you value life. Don't you think?'

'I wish I could see it that way.'

'Talking has helped me, Adam. Talking to my wife and the family. Talking to sufferers of Alzheimer's and to children whose parents have the disease. I've started counselling carers and sufferers. My wife Laura helps raise funds for the Alzheimer's Society. Helping others really stops you focusing on yourself.'

'I'm ashamed to say that I've been wallowing in self-pity for quite some time. I felt as if I was the only person in the world going through this.'

'Well, now you know you're not. There are lots of us in exactly the same boat.'

Robert's simple words are a balm. I feel totally at ease with my cousin, though I hardly know him. Robert and I have suffered the same pain, shared the same bitter experiences and both face an uncertain future.

'Whenever you need to talk,' he continues, 'just pick up the phone and dial my number. I love talking, don't I, Gran?'

'Just a bit,' Grans says, chuckling. 'Why don't you tell Adam about Arthur's son?'

'Do you remember Michael?' Robert asks. 'He's about your age.'

'Yes. I do.'

'Well, he's a professor of medicine at a hospital in London, part of a research team working on a cure for Alzheimer's. He watched his father die and he's passionate about finding a cure to help the rest of us. You should get in touch with him. I'm sure he'd love to meet you.'

'Michael's marvellous,' Gran says. 'Arthur would be so proud of him and Mary would be proud of you too, Robert.'

'I'm a painter and decorator, Gran. There are no letters after my name.'

'What difference does it make? You're a wonderful person.'

I nod my head, acknowledging a remarkable, altruistic man. In a perverse way, the scourge of Alzheimer's has made Robert stronger and given him a voice. I feel angry with Mum for cutting me off from the very people who could have helped me.

Robert leans forward in his chair. 'Remember. If there's anything at all I can do for you, just let me know.'

It is incredibly comforting to know that I have back-up and no longer need suffer in silence. My thoughts turn to John and I realise that he too, might need help.

'You and Gran have already done more than you can ever imagine. And I definitely want to keep in touch. I'll be coming to see Gran as often as I can. I wish I'd not left it so long to come back. I could kick myself.'

'We have a big family get-together once or twice a year. You'll have to come along and meet the rest of the clan,' Robert says.

'I'd love to. Just let me know when and I'll be up here like a shot.'

Lydia

Drizzle plumped up Lydia's hair and dampened her spirits. She stood outside the dimly lit restaurant waiting for Sean, feeling dowdy and unattractive. Other women caught her eye in their shiny belts, glossy lipsticks and sparkly earrings. They carried bags in gold and silver and shone like beacons in the dark while Lydia felt as luminous as a shadow. Like an unused muscle, her ability to dress for an evening out had wasted away. These days Lydia dressed to blend in, not to stand out. She preferred to spend her money on clothes for Alvaro and took more pride in her son's appearance than her own.

She fought the compulsion to hurry back home to her comfort zone and spend Friday night in front of the telly with her mother, dipping *biscotti* into black coffee. It was cold, dark, a miserable night. Going out, Lydia thought, required too much effort. She wore a pair of jeans, flat shoes and a padded jacket. By dressing casually she hoped to give the impression that a date with Sean was no big deal. That she could take him or leave him. These were the lies she told herself to drown out the voice in the back of her head that said ... he's very attractive, he has potential, he loves children. A man is as changeable as a chameleon and will say whatever he thinks a woman wants to hear to get her into bed, came Lydia's retort.

Her heart raced when she saw him approaching. She liked the way he walked, the flecks of grey in his tousled hair, his loosely tied black scarf, the bony hands that reached out to take her by the shoulders. He kissed her on both cheeks. She liked the feel of his lips on her face. They took a table by the window. A flickering candle sat between them, lighting up Sean's face, brightening his hazel eyes. Lydia felt too self-conscious to take off her jacket. Beneath it she wore a V-necked sweater that clung to her breasts.

The place was packed. Lydia was grateful for the din of voices and the clink of glasses, for the informality of the setting and the dim lighting. He had chosen his venue well. She wondered how many other women he had wined and dined at this table by the window. While he complained about the traffic on his journey to the restaurant, Lydia wondered what to do with her hands. Normally they were occupied wiping ketchup from Alvaro's chin or cutting up his meat or grabbing the knife he brandished like a light sabre. She took a packet of cigarettes out of her bag and offered one to Sean.

'No, thanks. I gave up when my son was born.' The comment sounded like a judgement and made Lydia feel guilty.

'Well, we're all going to die of something one day,'

she said, lighting up, wishing she hadn't sounded so glib, sucking on the cigarette to ease her tension.

They ordered drinks from a waitress dressed in black, a white apron tied around her waist. Lydia studied the menu, happy to have something to hide behind. Sean leaned back in the leather-covered chair. 'Electra told me you write songs.'

Lydia felt her cheeks burn. 'It's just . . . a silly hobby. I hum tunes into a Dictaphone because I have nothing better to do when my son goes to bed.' Her tone was more defensive than she'd intended it to be.

'Perhaps you'll let me hear them one day?'

'No way!' she hissed when actually she was flattered by his interest and had always yearned for a soul-mate with whom she could discuss her love of composition without feeling foolish. The waitress arrived with two glasses of wine. Lydia took a gulp of hers for courage and felt her cheeks prickle.

'And what is it you do?' she asked, though she knew exactly what he did.

'I write advertising jingles.'

'Advertising is the bane of my life.'

'In what way?'

'Alvaro is very impressionable. He sees a toy advertised on television and bends my ear about buying it. And then there's my mother who can't see a new product advertised without rushing out to the shops and filling the house with rubbish. How do you feel about making people buy things they don't need?' Again, she heard herself sounding aggressive. She gulped down half a glass of wine, wishing she could rewind and start again, or at least erase her last sentence.

'A man has to make a living somehow.'

'Who am I to talk! I work in a bloody department store. I'd love to do what you do. I hope I didn't offend you.'

'Don't worry. You didn't.'

Lydia wished she had stayed at home. She felt awkward and lost for words. Conversation did not flow as it had on the first day they met, when Electra had been present to gee things along. Lydia felt annoyed with herself for agreeing to a date and angry at Electra for fixing her up with a man she considered perfect. And why was he perfect? Because he had children and an estranged partner because he had baggage too. Lydia had enough baggage of her own to deal with and did not want to be lumbered with anyone else's. Two wrongs, she thought resentfully, did not make a right.

She wanted to ask Sean about his children but stopped herself. She could quite happily have chatted about Alvaro and his latest escapades but she held back. She did not want to appear dull, as if she had nothing to talk about but her son. Children were not a sexy topic of conversation though perhaps they were better than no topic at all. She glanced up at Sean wanting to find fault, a reason not to like him. His hair was not as thick as she had first thought. His front teeth were ever so slightly crooked. She nit-picked to no avail. He was undeniably handsome, exactly her sort of man.

The waitress returned to take down their order. Lydia chose grilled fish and salad. Sean a steak with fries.

'Are you sure you want chips, not boiled potatoes?' Lydia said without thinking.

Sean looked amused. 'OK. If you insist. I'll have boiled potatoes instead.' The waitress scribbled down the order and walked away.

'Sorry. I didn't mean to say that. I'm used to ordering for Alvaro and my mother. I think my mouth just ran away with me.'

'I don't mind. It's nice to know you care.'

Lydia felt herself smile genuinely for the first time that evening. She reached out for the cocktail menu and her hand brushed against Sean's. He looked into her eyes and held her gaze, making her cheeks burn. It was stiflingly hot inside her padded jacket. She could hardly breathe. She hadn't felt so powerfully attracted to anyone in years. She'd thought she was immune to such intense emotions. That she was too old, too cynical, too damaged. Lydia took off her jacket, finished off her wine and sat fanning her face with the menu.

He leaned across the table. 'Your eyelashes are really long. Are they real?'

'Yes. But they're a pain. They're always falling out. By the time I'm forty I probably won't have any lashes left. Or hair for that matter. That falls out too, when I'm stressed. It seems I inherited all my parents' worst characteristics, Mum's nervous disposition and Dad's baldness.'

Sean laughed. 'Well, I think you look lovely.'

'That's the wonder of candlelight,' she said, her skin tingling.

'How's your son?'

She was heartened by his question. Children, it seemed, were not a taboo subject.

'He said he had stomach ache before I left. I didn't want to leave him but Mum forced me out of the door. She said Alvaro was playing up because he didn't want me to go out.'

'Why don't you ring home to make sure he's all right?'

'Mum has promised to call if I'm needed.'

Lydia suddenly felt at ease. She knew Sean was a person she could talk to, be herself with, a potential friend if nothing else, though she wanted far more than friendship.

'This place is nice,' she said.

'It's the first time I've been here. I tend to eat at home. Packet meals for one.'

'Electra told me you had some interesting ingredients in your fridge.'

Sean raised his eyebrows. Lydia cringed realising her mouth had sped ahead of her brain.

'Is that why she knocked me down in the street? So she could entrap me and nose around the kitchen?'

'She knocked you down in the street?'

'Yes. And insisted on coming home with me, allegedly to treat my wounds. Now, I know better.'

'Is that why your glasses are broken and your nose is scratched?'

Sean nodded his head.

'I didn't realise Electra was quite so desperate to find me a man.'

'She nearly knocked me unconscious.'

'Christ! I'm really sorry.'

277

'Thank goodness for Electra and her strong arm tactics,' he said, drawing closer.

Lydia wanted to lean slightly forward and kiss him. Instead, she slumped back in her chair to escape his intoxicating aura.

'And did Electra find anything else of interest?'

'She said your bathroom wasn't quite up to scratch and your duvet cover smelt a little musty.'

'You're joking?'

'No. I'm not. She carried out a thorough inspection.'

'She obviously didn't find anything too off-putting or else I wouldn't be here.'

Lydia's mobile phone rang. She was enjoying herself and answered it, reluctantly. It was Consuelo, calling to say that Alvaro had a temperature and his stomach ache had worsened.

'I have to go. Alvaro's not well.'

'I'll take you home.'

'My car's parked nearby.'

'Then I'll walk you to your car.'

'What about your steak?'

'Sod the steak. I came here for the company, not the food. I'll rustle up a snack when I get home. I'm sure I'll find something interesting in the fridge.'

Saturday morning was the week's sartorial low point. Lydia wore a bleach-stained T-shirt and moth-eaten sweat pants. She thought about her date the previous evening and flushed with excitement. She hoped Sean would call. The thought of him made her feel warm inside as if she had just eaten a steaming bowl of her mother's chicken soup. Consuelo sat at the kitchen table, dabbing her eyes, mourning the death of Prince Rainier of Monaco, several months after the event. Lydia poured herself a cup of coffee and sat down opposite her mother. She had grown accustomed to Consuelo's lapses into mawkishness. Where other people had forty winks to refresh their batteries, her mother had forty weeps.

'Tha poor man he died of a broken heart,' she said, sniffing.

'Mum! He was eighty-one.'

'Hiss never got ova the death of his wife. I'm tellin you.'

Lydia wondered whether Consuelo empathised with Rainier because she too had lost a beloved spouse. As far as Lydia could tell the marriage of Grace Kelly and her prince was not entirely the fairytale romance it was made out to be. Hadn't he negotiated a substantial dowry from her family? And made his fiancée sign a prenuptial agreement in which she agreed to relinquish all rights to their children in the event of divorce? Faced with the same proposition, Lydia would have told her prince to stick his two-hundred-roomed palace up his royal posterior.

'Did you see that poor dog, followin the coffin at the funeral? He was heartbroken too. That Prince Raindeer he was jass like the Pope. Taken before his time.'

'The pope was eighty-five!'

'He was only nine years old than me.'

Lydia handed her mother a tissue. Consuelo blew her nose. Lydia would never understand why her mother and millions of people like her spent the day bawling on the day of the Pope's funeral. Sadness she could understand. Calm reflection – yes. But not acute distress at the death of a stranger (albeit a revered man) loved from afar. The only term she could apply to the crying-fest was mass hysteria.

'And poor Telly Savalas, he died in his prime.'

When would it end? When would she exhaust her list of dead people? Lydia decided it was time to change the subject. 'How's Maxi?'

Consuelo blew her nose. Her tears dried up as quickly as they had flowed. Her lips twisted into a snarl. The mention of Maxi's name never failed to divert her attention, to fire up her sense of marital injustice. Maxi was her nephew who lived in Spain with his wife Carla. Every Sunday his mother would call Consuelo to complain about her daughter-in-law.

'I feel so sorry for tha boy. Hiss wife she espects him to wait on her hand and foot. She even makes him serve her coffee in bed before he goes to work. My sisters says tha girl, she dosen even know how to cook.'

'He looked happy enough to me when I saw him last year.'

'Hiss not as happy as his sister. Now *she* is married to a wonderfol man. He is everythin a woman she could ask for. He even serves your cousin breakfass in bed. He helps around the house and does all the cookin.'

'He sounds a lot like Maxi, don't you think?'

What was right for the goose was not right for the gander. Consuelo's sister was happy for her daughter to be waited on but aggrieved that her own son played the role of waiter. In fact, both daughter and daughter-in-law were blessed with dutiful husbands and had no complaints of their own.

'My sister, she says Maxi hiss lost ten kilos since he left home.'

'Good for him. He was terribly overweight.'

'What do you mean, good for him? Tha boy, hiss lost weight 'cause hiss not eatin.'

The doorbell rang.

'I'm no gonna answer the door in my robe,' Consuelo said.

Lydia got up reluctantly and walked out of the kitchen. She had not combed her hair or put on makeup and opened the door feeling grumpy. Her eyes were puffy from lack of sleepsince Alvaro had kept her up all night complaining of stomach ache. A man stood on the doorstep. Suntanned. Attractive. A smiling man with faintly nicotine-stained teeth. Lydia's stomach clenched, she fought the urge to slam the door in his face and run back indoors. Ian was back and stood brazenly before her, his brown hair cropped short, his bony face radiating good health. His new lifestyle obviously suited him. She felt no compulsion to lunge at him and shower him with abuse but thought only of how terrible she looked. How much at a disadvantage she was. This was definitoly not how she had imagined their first encounter after so long.

'Hello, Lydia.' She was disconcerted by Ian's smile because it reminded her of Alvaro's.

'What do you want?'

'I want to see my son.'

Lydia stepped out of the house and closed the door

behind her. Alvaro was watching cartoons in the living room. The thought of him coming to the door and chancing across his father horrified her. 'Sure. No problem. You can see your son, Ian. By applying through the courts.' The edict was issued casually, unemotionally. She felt proud of herself for keeping it together, for standing calmly before the man who had abandoned her so cruelly. Her messy appearance no longer mattered. She felt nothing for Ian and had nothing to prove. Legally they were no longer man and wife. Her divorce had come through some time ago on the grounds of his desertion.

'Do we need to go down that route?'

'I think it would be wise, in the circumstances. Alvaro needs time to get accustomed to the idea of meeting you. Don't forget you're a stranger to him.'

He looked down at his feet and thought for a while before finally answering. 'You're right. The last thing I want to do is upset him.' The placatory smile vanished from his face. 'I'd better go before he sees me. But promise me you'll ring so we can talk and sort all this out?' He thrust a piece of paper into Lydia's hand with a mobile number scribbled on it and turned to leave. Before she could breathe a sigh of relief the door flew open and Consuelo was standing behind her.

'Who is at the door, Lythia?'

'No one, Mum. Go back inside.'

'Hello, yong man,' Consuelo said cheerily, before recognising Ian and stumbling down the front step in surprise.

'Hello, Mother,' he replied, bowing his head.

'Who the hell are you callin Motha, you son-of-e-bitch!' Consuelo lunged at Ian and grabbed his neck in a vice-like grip, clenching so hard his face began to turn red.

'Mum!' Lydia pulled her mother off and held her tightly around the waist.

'Gerraro here, you bastad, before I kill you ...' Passers-by were stopping to gawp.

'Mum, please calm down.'

The front door swung open a second time. 'Mum, why is Granny swearing?' Alvaro nonchalantly took in the scene, his mouth stretching into a wide yawn.

'Granny's always swearing. Please, go back inside.'

'Who are you? Why does my granny want to kill you?' Alvaro asked looking Ian up and down. Lydia's hands began to tremble. This was the meeting she had always dreaded. Alvaro was too old to be lied to, too canny to be bundled inside and distracted with ice cream. She knew that in a matter of seconds her son would recognise the man whose photo he'd cherished and studied for hours on end. Alvaro's eyes narrowed as he stood thinking. He took a step forward, looked up at Ian and asked in a casual tone: 'Are you my dad?'

Consuelo buried her head in her hands. Lydia invited Ian into the hallway and banished her mother to the living room.

'It's good to meet you,' Ian said, looking tearfully at his son. Lydia was unmoved by the spectacle. For the sin he had committed Ian should have been down on his knees, begging Alvaro's forgiveness.

'You're not as tall as I thought you were,' her son said, making Lydia smile. Her heart swelled with pride. Her little man was handling the situation better than she could ever have imagined, as if meeting a father for the first time was no big deal.

'And you're much bigger than I imagined you.'

'Do you like sport?' Alvaro asked.

Ian nodded.

'Can we go and play football in the park?'

'No, Alvaro. Your dad can't stay long. He'll come back another day.'

'Please, Mum. Please. Dad, will you take me to the park?'

How easily Alvaro had uttered the word 'dad' as if it had been teetering on the tip of his tongue, waiting for Ian's return.

The situation was spiralling out of Lydia's control, moving too fast. She looked at Ian, willing him to say no.

'If your mum doesn't mind, then of course I'll play football with you.'

'I do mind. Alvaro wasn't well last night. I don't want him going out.'

'Please, Mum. I feel fine now. Please say yes?'

Before she had a chance to answer Alvaro had run off to his bedroom and returned with a ball under his arm and a pair of football boots slung over his shoulder. 'Come on,' he said, taking Ian by the hand.

Ian looked at Lydia. 'Don't worry, I'll take good care of him. We'll be back in a couple of hours, I promise.'

When they had turned left, out of the front gate, Lydia began to panic. What if Ian intended to snatch Alvaro? Why had she let her son go at all? What if Alvaro preferred his father to his mother and left her for a new life in New Zealand? Lydia crept out of the house, her heart pounding, unwilling to let Alvaro out of her sight. She trailed them down the hill that led to the park, praying she would not meet anyone she knew. Alvaro and Ian chatted as they walked. Lydia thought she heard Alvaro laugh. Did he laugh like that when he was with her? Would he be won over by a game of football and refuse to come home? When she finally reached the park, Lydia crouched down behind a tree to watch Alvaro putting on his football boots. Ian picked up sticks and used them to mark out a goal and then father and son stood side by side, stretching, bending and rotating their heads.

Alvaro stood in goal and stretched out his arms. Ian kicked the ball. It hurtled past Alvaro's head. He scored goal after easy goal while Alvaro shouted: 'Good kick, Dad. Good kick.' Next, Ian bounced the ball up and down on his head, reminding Lydia of a performing seal. He monopolised the ball, wowing Alvaro with his skills. Lydia's knees ached. She sat down on a mound of sodden earth feeling miserable. A jogger stopped beside her. From the corner of her eye Lydia saw him bend forward to stretch his hamstrings.

'Hello,' he called out.

She turned her head away, feeling insulted. Was this some kind of sick come on?

'Lydia, what are you doing here?'

She took a closer look at the jogger and felt her cheeks burn. 'Sean. Hello.'

This was the man she had spent the morning obsessing about, the man she found wildly attractive and was now staring at with eyes as wide as a marmoset's.

'I was going to call you later. Do you fancy going to see a film tomorrow night?'

Was the man blind? Could he not see the sad scruffy creature hiding behind a tree? 'If you like.'

'No. If *you* like.'

'Sorry. Yes, I'd really love to.'

'Good. Now perhaps you'll tell me why you're hiding under that tree, looking like a vagrant.'

Lydia motioned towards Alvaro and Ian. 'I'm spying on my son. He's just met his father for the first time.'

Sean slumped down beside her. 'Wow! You must be feeling pretty anxious. I'll stay and keep you company.'

'Thanks.' Lydia tried to fathom his motives. Could he really be interested in her when there were so many other single women available, with far less complicated lives?

'Your son's a very handsome boy.'

'Yes, he is.' Lydia smiled as she watched Alvaro running after the football. She loved the look of him. The golden hue of his skin. His rosy cheeks and thick black tousled hair. His bright, inquisitive eyes and the half-grown front teeth that gave him an impish smile.

'My son likes football too. Perhaps Alvaro could come and play with us sometime?'

'He'd love that, I'm sure.' Sean's arm brushed against Lydia's, making her feel hot and flustered. In spite of the bad hair and the wetness soaking through her clothes she suddenly felt desirable. If she were a braver woman she might have leaned over and kissed him then. Instead, she inched herself away and peered round the tree. Alvaro was chasing after his father, trying to get the ball. Ian was laughing as he ran, so intent on showing off his fancy footwork that he failed to notice the boy was getting upset. 'I want the ball,' Alvaro shouted. 'Pass me the ball, Dad.'

'Try and get it,' Ian shouted back, running off across the park too fast to be caught, then doubling back, running his son ragged.

'Why doesn't he pass it to him?' Sean whispered.

Every time Alvaro tried to kick the ball, Ian would whip it out of his reach and sprint away. Lydia could tell from the angry look on her son's face that it was only a matter of time before he blew. Ian was more intent on proving himself a sports star than on getting to know his son and having fun with him. It wasn't long before Alvaro kicked out his foot and caught Ian's shin. He dropped to the ground as if his legs had been cut from under him, clutching his shin.

'You did that on purpose, you little buggor!' he screamed.

Furious, Lydia tried to stand up but Sean pulled her back down. 'You want him to get to know his dad, don't you?'

Alvaro looked down at his father, hands on hips, lower lip sticking out. 'It was an accident. I was trying to kick the ball.'

'You're lying. That was no accident.'

'Get lost!' Alvaro screamed, walking away.

'Don't you dare talk to me like that!' Ian got up and grabbed him by the arm.

'Get off me. I don't want you, I want my mum.'

Ian let go of his arm abruptly and stomped away, out of the park and up the road. Alvaro picked up his shoes and the ball and hurried along behind him, staying a few paces behind. Ian never once looked over his shoulder to check on his son, to make sure he had not run into the road or sloped away. Lydia knew instinctively that her ex had no real experience of children, that he didn't have a family of his own.

'I'm going to get my son,' Lydia said, charging up the hill, anger coursing through her veins.

Sean chased after her.

'Leave him. He's quite safe.'

'I should never have let that selfish bastard take him.'

'It's the best thing you could have done. Alvaro won't be under any illusions about his father, now. He needs to go through this. It'll make him stronger. Believe me.'

'How can you be so sure?'

'Because I went through the very same thing myself. Idolising a man I hardly knew. Thinking Dad was a hero and Mum had somehow chased him away. I blamed her, until I got to know him and realised he wasn't very likeable. Now, I just accept him for what he is and thank my lucky stars that he left when he did.'

Lydia reached out for Sean's hand, feeling calmed and hopeful. They walked back up the hill together in contented silence, keeping a close eye on Alvaro. When they neared the house, Lydia watched Ian ring the doorbell. She smiled when Consuelo opened up, pulled Alvaro inside and closed the glass-fronted door in Ian's face.

'I'll call you later,' Sean said, kissing her on the lips, walking back down the hill.

Ian waited for her at the front gate. 'Is that your

boyfriend?' he asked and Lydia thought she saw resentment in his eyes. She nodded, feeling self-satisfied, her lips still burning from the unexpected kiss. 'Alvaro's quite a handful,' Ian said, his confidence crushed.

'He's a child.'

'I don't think he likes me.'

'Have you given him any reason to?' Lydia hoped he was finally waking up to the reality of having a child. 'When will you come back?'

'I'm leaving England next week. I don't know when I'll be back.'

She had never felt more relieved in her life. She knew then that the man she had married had not changed, that the world would always revolve around him. He was made that way, a selfish man who shied away from any responsibility. For him, the idea of a son would always be better in theory than in practice. Lydia watched him walk away, feeling a weight lift from her shoulders. She had faced her fears and conquered them. Ian's unexpected return had been a necessary evil. A long and unhappy chapter in her life had finally come to an end. She felt energised and ready to begin anew.

Electra

The air smells unmistakably of home: salty, humid, spiced with tarmac from the runway. A stunning blue sky promises a scorching day. I am ferried by bus to the arrivals terminal to have my passport checked and collect my luggage. One suitcase, hurriedly packed, clothes and toiletries as tangled as a hairball inside. As soon as the aircraft took off from Heathrow I shut my eyes, willing myself to sleep, fearing a panic attack. I felt increasingly anxious the further I travelled from Adam, knowing I was breaking my own first rule of marital conduct. On the day I took my vows, I promised myself never to go to bed on an argument. Had I acted too hastily by leaving? Should I have given Adam a chance to explain? Did my anger get the better of me? Turbulence soon took my mind off my husband and his mother. Every time the aircraft lurched I felt like reaching for the sick bag.

I stand nervously at the front door, waiting for Mama to answer. I hear the shuffle of her footsteps and a key turn in the lock. She wearily opens the door and looks at me incredulously. 'Electra!' Her face lights up. She grabs my face and kisses my cheeks, her leathery palms smelling of jasmine-scented disinfectant. 'I knew you would come. Who told you? Was it Miroulla? I told her not to say anything.' She leans closer to whisper, 'She's inside. She's very upset. Don't ask her too many questions. God knows I've tried. She won't answer them. And don't look shocked.'

I follow Mama into the flat, across the hallway, into the air-conditioned lounge. 'Look,' she announces. 'Look who's here!'

Papa darts across the room. 'Electra, my child. What a wonderful surprise!' He envelops me in his arms, kissing me reverently on the forehead as if I were an icon. I scan the room for the 'she' I am not supposed to question. I hear the toilet flush and watch the bright glow on Papa's face fade. Martha walks into the lounge, wearing a headscarf. She sees me and stops dead. In an instant, I register the bruises and scratches on my sister's face and reach my own unhappy conclusions about her scoundrel of a husband. I approach her with outstretched arms, pulling her towards me. Her body is stiff at first before surrendering to my touch. Papa throws his arms around both of us as if trying to protect us from the world. I rest my head on Martha's shoulder and feel the sudden movement of a fourth body within the tangle of our limbs.

I turn down Mama's offer of a pastry, too angry and agitated to think about food. Martha sits opposite me, head bowed, unable to look me in the eye, unwilling to talk. No man has the right to hit his wife. 'You can't let Sotiris get away with this,' I blurt out, breaking the oppressive silence.

'I don't want to talk about it.'

Mama moves closer to Martha on the sofa and drapes an arm across her shoulders. 'You have to leave him now, my child.'

'You mean, you haven't thrown him out yet? When do you intend to do that? When he kills you?'

'Electra, please,' Mama says, 'calm down.'

'And why don't you take that ridiculous headscarf off? It makes you look like an old woman.'

Martha shakes her head.

Mama looks at me and shrugs. 'Your sister's right. Take it off, Martha. Please.'

'I'm too ashamed. I don't want you to see what's underneath.'

I stretch out my hand. 'I'll yank it off your head myself if you don't take it off, right away.'

'You have nothing to be ashamed of,' Mama says, stroking her daughter's face.

With trembling fingers, Martha unties the knot below her chin and slowly takes off the silk scarf. She leans her head forward to reveal an area of bare scalp, the size of a fifty-pence piece. 'My hair has been pulled out by the roots,' she cries. 'It will never grow back.'

Papa slams his fist down on the coffee table. 'I'm going to kill him!'

'Please, Papa. I don't want any more trouble.'

'Your mother has been holding me back all these

years because she didn't want any trouble. And look what's happened. I have stood by and watched for long enough. I have respected your wishes and allowed your husband to mistreat you. I'm ashamed of myself for failing in my duty as a father to protect you.'

Martha stands up and reties her headscarf. 'I'm leaving. I can't take any more of this. Papa, please promise me you won't do anything until you know all the facts?' He nods. Martha hurries out of the house, retying her headscarf. I follow her down the stairwell and out onto a scorching street. Mid-morning sun beats down on the pavement, irradiating a line of parked cars and the windows of the neighbouring apartment block.

I grab Martha's arm as she tries to climb into her car. 'Hey! Perhaps you'd like to know why I'm here?'

She stops. Turns to look at me. 'I thought you'd come for . . .'

'For you? No. You're not the only one in this world with marital problems.'

She closes the car door. 'Let's walk.'

We link arms and walk along the potholed pavement, past a row of shops. A grocery, patisserie, two bakeries and a hairdressing salon. Martha opens her handbag, takes out a pair of sunglasses and puts them on. In profile, with the glare of the sun blurring her injuries, she looks as beautiful as ever. As a child I was always incredibly proud of my sister's faultless complexion and bee-stung lips. What I came to resent over time was the way she squandered her good looks and hid her perfect body under shapeless clothes.

'Shall we go for a coffee along the seafront?' I suggest.

'No, I don't want to see anyone I know. I don't want anyone to see me like this.'

'Let's go in here then. There's no one inside.'

Martha nods. We enter a small café with a metallic shop front. The walls and furnishings are white, ultra-modern, and somewhat at odds with the ramshackle shops to either side. Wedged between a hardware store with flaky window frames and a dusty stationer's, the café is like a hunk of Brie served between two slices of mouldy bread. We take a small table at the back and order two cappuccinos. The coffee machine hisses and bubbles and our drinks arrive, frothy and perfectly made, served with two cocoa-dusted chocolates. Martha bites into one, I take the other. For a moment I forget my problems, enjoying the taste of chocolate and my sister's company, delaying the inevitable heart-to-heart.

'So, why did you come?' Martha asks, sipping froth.

All my pent-up frustration floods out then. I talk about my life over the last three months, about Margaret's coldness and cruelty, about my own mount-ing unhappiness and Adam's stark declaration. 'The problem is, Martha, I'm pregnant,' I finish.

'Pregnant!'

'Yes.'

She squeezes my hands, her face glowing with delight. 'That's the best kind of problem to have. Our prayers have been answered at last. Mama thought you had a fertility problem and was keeping it a secret from us. She's been praying to Saint Irene Chrisovalantou

294

for a miracle and lighting a candle for you every Sunday in church.'

'There's nothing wrong with me. It's my husband who's sick in the head. He's the one who doesn't want children.'

'Adam's a good man.'

'Adam has let me down. I'm not going back to him, Martha.'

'What do you mean, you're not going back?'

'I'm here to stay. I have nothing to go back to. I'm going to have the baby here.'

We order lunch and Martha talks animatedly about her children. Andreas, my nephew, will soon be doing his National Service. My nieces are all doing well at school and Martha expresses the hope that they will one day follow in my footsteps and study abroad. 'I've found a job in the local doctor's surgery but don't know how to break the news to Sotiris. He's never liked the idea of me going out to work. He thinks I have enough to do at home.'

I listen to Martha in disbelief as she weaves her fairytale, paints a picture of a caring husband who has nothing but his wife's best interests at heart.

'You mean, he doesn't want other men looking at you. Well, there's no fear of that now, is there? Not after what he's done to your face.'

'Please, Electra!'

'Please, nothing. Your husband is killing you, both physically and spiritually. You have to leave him, Martha. No man has a right to hit his wife.'

'But . . .'

'No more buts.'

'But *he* didn't do this to me.'

'Then who did?'

'His girlfriend.'

'What! I don't believe it! Let's go to the police right now.'

Martha lowers her head, guilty eyes swivelling up to meet mine. 'I went to find her, Electra, to tell her to stay away from my husband. *I* attacked her.'

'She deserved it!'

'Did she? She wasn't much older than my Andreas. She was a child. I beat up a child, Electra. You should see her face . . . When I had calmed down, given vent to all my hatred, a terrible sense of guilt overcame me. I made the girl a coffee and we sat and talked for hours. It turns out Sotiris has been lying to both of us. He told me the girl wouldn't leave him alone, that she bombarded him with calls. In reality he was paying her rent and popping in regularly for sex, promising to leave me as soon as he could to marry her. He told her I was crazy, that I had threatened to kill myself if he left me.'

'And you believe her?'

'More than I believe my husband.'

'And what does Sotiris say about all of this?'

'He doesn't know. This all happened yesterday and he's been away on a shooting expedition with his friends. He comes back today.'

'What do you want to do, Martha?'

'I want to be happily married, Electra. I want my children to have a father.'

'Would you like your own daughters to be married to a man like their father?'

'Not for a minute.'

'Then what example are you setting them? What message are you giving them? That a woman has no choice but to stay with a cheating husband?'

'I'm not strong like you, Electra. I have never lived alone. I need someone to help me through all this. Someone I can rely upon one hundred per cent. If you hadn't left Cyprus, I might have thrown Sotiris out a long time ago.'

'I'm here now, and I will be beside you every step of the way.'

'Where do we start?'

'By telephoning Mama and asking her to look after the children this afternoon.'

'And then?'

'Taking you to the hairdresser's.'

After Giorgio's salon, where clever styling covers Martha's bald patch, our next stop is the office of an old school friend, Lenia, a lawyer. A gold engagement ring, my handiwork, glints on her finger. I realise from Martha's humble demeanour that she would never have come here alone. She is shy and withdrawn, visibly intimidated by the confident, articulate woman sitting across from her behind a glass-topped desk. Lenia tells my sister she has sufficient grounds to file for divorce and promises to handle her case. We go on, past the point of no return, to Pavlos the locksmith where we order front and back door locks to be delivered and fitted by early-evening. Then Martha makes a call to the local doctor's surgery, accepting the vacant position.

My sister's house is a raised single-storey, charmless rectangular box in need of whitewashing. The house and Martha have deteriorated concurrently, grown old and timeworn together. Both have failed to fulfil their early promise. As I climb the front steps I remember the beautiful eighteen-year-old bride who sat on the veranda of her new house, wowing her guests. They handed over their gifts and walked through the place to admire the new three-piece suite and ornate dining table. The gilt-edged mirrors and the four-poster bed. The 1980s state-of-the-art wood-veneered kitchen and the en-suite toilet, a luxury enjoyed by few. Martha's furnishings, once the envy of every woman in the neighbourhood, are now old-fashioned, tatty and drab. When Sotiris built a house for his wife and furnished it, his job of nest-building was done. For twenty years he has refused to spend a penny more on updating, repairing or redecorating.

We finish packing his clothes and personal belongings into boxes. 'What now?' Martha asks, waiting for her next instruction.

'Let's put the boxes in the car and go.'

'Where to?'

'His mother's house.'

'What for?'

'To drop his things off. His life with you is over.'

'His mother is a good woman. I don't want to upset her.'

'You're not leaving her, you're leaving her son.'

'Isn't that the same thing?'

'Not if the woman has any sense about her.'

* * *

Martha drives slowly down a stretch of craggy road, the ancient Toyota jerking and bumping past a small stone church with a domed roof. We travel along a series of narrow back streets where old colonial-style houses sit alongside apartment blocks, new homes and ramshackle properties. We turn on to a main road where there are brightly lit cake shops, rotisseries and a kebab stall. The smell of barbecuing meat wafts through the open car window. Further down the road an eighteenth-century aqueduct dominates the landscape. The imposing series of stone arches or *kamares* once carried water across a shallow valley into the town of Larnaca. Martha indicates, turns right and pulls up outside a small house with steel girders rising up from the flat roof in readiness for an additional storey that might never be added. A squat fig tree grows in the small front yard and jasmine in flower climbs the front door.

Martha stands nervously behind me. I ring the doorbell, readying myself for battle. A colossal woman answers the door, wearing a shapeless dress and dusty sandals too small for her feet. A coarse hair sprouts from the epicentre of a plump mole just above her lip. A visitor might expect this mountain of a woman to greet them with a headlock, a fireman's lift or a bone-crushing handshake. Instead, she smiles warmly and throws open her arms.

'Ah, In-law,' she says, the customary greeting to a member of her extended family, 'what a pleasant surprise. When did you arrive? And Martha, my sweet, it's good to see you. Come in, both of you.' We follow her into a sparsely furnished 1960-style lounge. She is too excited by our visit to notice Martha's face. 'I'll fetch some coffee and *glyko*.'

My sister perches on the edge of the sofa, looking distressed. I sit in a musty armchair, wondering what in God's name I am going to say. Martha's mother-in-law chatters animatedly from the adjacent kitchen, asking if I have managed to fatten up my spindly English husband. She returns to the living room with a loaded tray offering us coffee, water and cherries preserved in syrup. She sits down on the sofa beside Martha, crossing her cumbersome legs and says, 'Tell me your news, Electra.'

'My news is not good, I'm afraid.'

She crosses herself. 'Heavens! What's happened? Is your father all right?'

'It's Martha who has the problem.'

She puts a hand on her daughter-in-law's shoulder and turns to look at her. 'My Martha? This Martha? My God! What's happened to your face?'

Martha shrugs her shoulders and looks down at her feet.

Her mother-in-law pulls a sour expression and shakes her head. 'My son did this, didn't he? I'm going to kill him. I won't let him get away with this.'

Martha looks up at me, waiting for me to correct the wrong assumption. My eyes implore her to keep quiet.

'That donkey I call a son has gone too far this time. Hasn't he tortured you enough all these years, with one girlfriend after another? I know all about his indiscretions, my sweet. With a wife like honey, why did he need to chase after other women? What must your poor parents think of us? I feel so ashamed.'

'What can we say?' My comment is suitably non-committal. I quiver with excitement inside, knowing that Sotiris will soon be facing his worst foe, the only woman he will ever be scared of.

'He's just like his father. Do you know, he tried to hit me once but I hit him back twice as hard, gave him a black eye, made him the laughing stock of this neighbourhood. He never tried it again. His womanising on the other hand I have learned to accept. You can't straighten a dog's tail. Especially an old dog. My husband is the fool, not me. He thinks these foreign women, all perfume and thongs, find him appealing. It's your wallet they're attracted to, old man, I tell him.'

'Why have you stayed with him?' I ask.

'I should have left him years ago. Now, it's too late. There's no point. He's company. He looks after the garden. I'm used to his ways. Women of my generation stay with their husbands through good times and bad. Things are different for yours, of course. Thank God.' She turns to Martha. 'Things are different for you, my sweet. What do you intend to do?'

'She's not going to the police,' I say, fearing Martha might blurt out the truth.

'I'm very grateful to you for that. Thank you.'

'But she can't live with your son any longer. I'm sure you understand. His belongings are in the car.'

'I do understand. And I'm not the kind of mother

who will side with her son when she knows he is in the wrong. But I do have one request.'

'Anything,' Martha says, taking hold of her hands.

'Please let me visit my grandchildren?'

'My door is always open to you,' Martha replies, taking Sotiris' long-suffering mother in her arms.

Adam

I push open the door of the flat and hear Mum running water in the kitchen, humming along to a tune on the radio. I wonder, resentfully, why she lied to me about Dad. Reluctant to face her, I head for the living room, intending to change and leave for somewhere quiet where I can plan my next move. I pull on a pair of loose corduroys and a jumper. Electra's things have gone but the sweet smell of her still hangs in the air. The sofa bed is unmade. Long strands of black hair, curled up on the sheets, are her only tangible remains. This flat, my first home, a place I professed to love, feels as homely as an empty shoebox. There is no way I could live here without Electra. Memories of her would lurk in every corner and haunt me.

Mum bangs at the base of the living-room door with her walking stick. 'Are you in there, Adam?' She pushes open the door. 'Thank goodness you're back. I was worried sick. Where have you been?'

'Has Electra called?'

'No. No one has.'

'I'm going out.'

'You're leaving me on my own again, Adam?' Her eyes grow misty. 'I've cooked lunch. I hoped we might eat together.'

'I'm not hungry.'

'You look terrible. Did you get any sleep last night?'

'Not much. What do you expect after everything that's happened?'

'You have to put it all behind you, son. Start afresh. I'm sure, in time, you will meet someone new, someone more suitable.'

So in her eyes Electra and her kin have been expunged from our lives like a bad stain and history is on the brink of repeating itself. 'More suitable? Mum, think about what you're saying. Electra drew the short straw, not me. I'm the one with problems. I'm the one with Dad's genes ... or had you forgotten? Do you know where I was last night?'

'Where?'

'Yorkshire.'

'Why did you go all the way up there?'

'Why do you think? To see Gran and the rest of Dad's family. The people you stopped me seeing.' I want to hurt her as much as she has hurt me.

Her face turns pale.

'How could you, Adam? After everything that's happened.'

'What did happen? What *really* happened?'

'What has that woman been telling you?' Mum's mouth twists into an ugly line.

'The truth! She told me Dad lived for five years, not

one. You lied to me, Mum. How could you do that to me?'

'Your father wsn't alive in the true sense of the word. He wasn't the man you knew and loved. He didn't even recognise you. I said what I said to protect you. To stop you getting upset.'

'Upset! That's an understatement. I was devastated when Dad left. I felt even worse because you wouldn't let me see him. I don't know if I can ever forgive you for that or for keeping Gran's letters from me. Why the hell did you do that?'

'What letters?'

'You know perfectly well what letters.'

'Your grandmother's letters were addressed to all of us. I had every right to open them. To read them. To decide whether or not I should pass them on. The contents of those letters was distressing, Adam. I kept them from you for your own sake. You have to believe me.'

I shake my head, knowing this is yet another lie but one I will not swallow.

'Do you want to know why I stayed away from Yorkshire for so long, even though I yearned to see Dad's family? Shall I tell you? Because I didn't want to hurt you. Because I put your feelings first. Because I didn't want to be disloyal.'

'And now it seems you don't care if you hurt me or not?'

'Now, I have to put my own feelings first, to think about myself. And by the way, you're wrong about Dad forgetting me. Gran said he kept my picture by his bedside. He talked about me sometimes as if I were a close friend.'

'And did he talk about me? Did your grandmother mention my name while you were there, other than to criticise and tell tales? That woman never liked me. She lured your father away from me. You and I were better off without her in our lives.'

'And are we better off without Electra in our lives?'

'Without a doubt.'

There is no cure for Mum's disease. Her mind is warped beyond repair. I have nothing more to say. My patience with her fragments as irreparably as a shattered mirror. The telephone rings. I hurry into the hallway to answer it, hoping to hear Electra's voice. Mum follows me, intent on playing her role in the drama my life has become. I pick up the receiver and say hello.

'Adam, something terrible's happened.' Lydia's urgent tone alarms me.

'What's wrong?' I convince myself, in the split-second pause that follows, that my wife is dead and I will never see her again.

'Alvaro's gone missing. He's disappeared, Adam.'

'What!'

'I went to wake him up this morning and he wasn't in bed. I'm worried Ian might have taken him. I've called the police. They're out searching for him now. I'm calling everyone I know who can help me . . .'

'I'll leave right away. Don't worry, we'll find him.' My own problems recede. I put down the receiver, at the forefront of my mind an image of a boy's face.

'What's happened?' Mum follows me to the front door.

'Alvaro's gone missing.'

'That's not really your problem, is it?'

'Yes, Mum. It bloody well is.'

I rush out of the house and jump into the car, beginning my arbitrary search in the streets around the flat. Driving slowly, peering into alleyways and over hedges, crawling the kerb to peer out at pedestrians. Fat raindrops spatter like water bombs on the pavement. This is not the kind of weather a child should be out in. Panic creeps in. Child abduction headlines float before my eyes. Ones I have written, others I have read. About children snatched from their mothers and taken to countries from where they cannot be retrieved. But why would Ian take a son in whom he has never shown any interest? Is it feasible that he broke into Lydia's house and took the boy from his bed? Other alternatives are too dire to contemplate. Alvaro in the hands of a child molester, suffering unthinkable torments . . . Alvaro crushed beneath the wheels of a car or lying face down in a river . . . I can barely breathe for worrying. My mobile rings. I pull up sharply to answer it.

'Adam, it's me.' Lydia sounds breathless. I hear the patter of her feet running. 'Mum found a letter.'

'From Ian?'

'No. From Alvaro. It was under his pillow.'

'What does it say?'

'It says he's run away.'

'Run away? Why?'

'*Where* is what you should be asking!'

'Where then?'

'Graceland.'

An involuntary smile crosses my lips. 'At least we know that no one's taken him.'

'Do we? He's out on the streets alone, anything could happen to him. He's so trusting. He'd go off with anyone. We have to find him quickly, before it's too late. Is Electra with you?'

'No. I don't know where she is.'

'I've been trying her mobile all morning but it's switched off.' I hear a man call out Lydia's name then and the sound of a car engine starting. 'I have to go. Ring me straight away if you find him.'

What was going through Alvaro's head when he wrote that note? I remember writing a similar letter myself as a child but being too cowardly to run away. I marvel at the boy's courage and wonder where he might be headed. I have a sudden hunch, a stab of intuition, and pull the car out sharply, pressing down on the accelerator, adrenaline coursing through my veins. I jump red lights and discern a flash in my rear-view mirror as a speed camera snaps my number plate. Dense traffic holds me up. I bang impatiently on the steering wheel before shooting off like a pinball through a maze of back streets. There is no time to stop for the man halfway across a zebra crossing who shakes his fist at me and swears. 'Sorry, mate,' I call from the open window, surging forward, passing Turnham Green tube, turning left on to Chiswick High Road.

I park the car in a no-parking zone and hurry between the stone gate posts, tramping through shallow puddles. Heading for the portico with its Corinthian columns that reminded Alvaro so much of

Graceland. I circle the house and the rain-soaked grounds looking for him, barely registering the replica Roman temple and the topiary, the eclectic mix of Greek urns and Roman statues. My optimism fades as I walk, my hunch clearly nothing more than wishful thinking. I head back to the car feeling a heavy sense of disappointment.

As I open the car door, wondering where to go next, I spot a shapeless figure, wearing an oversized rain-coat, shuffling through the gates, weighed down by a heavy rucksack. The hooded extraterrestrial heads for the portico, struggling with its load up the flight of stone steps. Letting the khaki rucksack fall, the figure slowly disrobes and rearranges a dome of flattened hair. I want to shout out the boy's name, to jump for joy, to run up to him and take him in my arms. As I watch Alvaro unpack his sandwiches and bite into a hunk of white bread, I realise how deeply I love him. The boy spots me and waves, wonderfully innocent of the pandemonium he has caused. I telephone his mother before climbing the steps and sitting beside him on the cold stone.

'What are you doing here, Adam?' he asks, offering me a sandwich. 'Shouldn't you be at work?'

I take his offering, though the bread is mangled and printed with fingermarks. 'Shouldn't you be at school?'

He shrugs. I bite into the sandwich and chew a mouthful of sweet bread. 'What's in this?'

'Nutella and marshmallows.' Alvaro licks his lips and starts unpacking his bag, lining up beside him a row of action heroes, small plastic people, farm animals, motor vehicles and a dinosaur. He and his entourage sit in a line surveying the view. The boy looks up at me and rests one hand on my leg. 'I like you, Adam.'

I drape my arm around his shoulders and pull him towards me. 'I like you, too.'

'I like you more than I like my dad.'

'Thank you.'

'I wish you were my dad.'

'And I wish . . .' I kiss the top of his head, my eyes filling up '. . . that you were my son. You know I love you, don't you?'

'Yeah,' he says, 'and I love you too.' The boy looks pleased. I am the one aghast, bowled over by the strength of my feelings. I never thought myself capable of loving any child, let alone this child in particular. Alvaro pats my knee. 'Perhaps the baby in Electra's tummy is a boy like me?'

'You mean, maybe one day there might be a baby boy in Electra's tummy.'

'No.' He pulls a face, his tone suggesting I'm the one being stupid. 'Mum told me Electra's pregnant. But it's a secret. So don't tell anyone, will you?'

Suddenly, everything makes sense. My wife's over-reaction, her refusal to hear me out, her weight gain. Mixed emotions overwhelm me. Fear, guilt, euphoria. Then Lydia comes bounding up the path, followed by a man who looks vaguely familiar. She races up the steps and scoops Alvaro off the ground, squeezing him to her chest, hungrily kissing the base of his neck, his cheeks, his mouth.

'Please, Alvaro, don't *ever* run away again.'

310

'I was coming back, Mum. Stop kissing me.' Alvaro wipes his cheeks with the back of his hand and looks across at the man. 'Who's that?'

'Sean. My friend.'

'Is he your boyfriend, Mum?'

'Only if you approve,' the man replies. 'Pleased to meet you, Alvaro.'

He shakes the boy's hand, then mine.

'Don't I know you from somewhere?' I ask.

'I live opposite. Your wife introduced me to Lydia.'

A wave of self-hatred overcomes me. I want to kick myself for ever giving credence to Mum's narrow-minded suspicions. How could I doubt my wife on her say-so? I have abused Electra, pushed her away, and must do whatever I can to win her back.

'Your wife's quite a character,' Sean says, smiling.

'I'm a very lucky man and soon to be a father.'

'So she told you?' Lydia asks, looking surprised.

'No. My godson did just a few moments ago.'

'Alvaro, I *told* you not to say anything.'

'Sorry, Mum.'

'I'm glad he did, Lydia. I turn forty in a week and I couldn't wish for a better birthday present.'

I realize in that moment, as I utter those words, that my desire to be a father is stronger than my fear of the disease and its consequences.

I walk to the car as if through a tunnel, towards a distant shaft of light, feeling calm setting in after the emotional storm. All my questions have been answered, my fears assuaged. Months of mental agony have given way to clear resolution. I know what I want. I know what I must do. The confusion of roads before me, as tangled and twisted as Spaghetti Junction, has miraculously become one. I will not lie down and let life defeat me. I will take it by the horns and ride it like a bucking bronco. I dial my brother's mobile number.

'Adam, how are you?' he answers.

'I've been better.'

'What's wrong?'

'You have to come and pick up Mum, right away. I'm leaving.' I feel no inclination to explain further. It's well past time my brother paid his dues.

'Impossible. I'm at work. I can't come for at least a couple of days.' His authoritative tone doesn't faze me.

'John, I'm not asking you, I'm telling you. Mum can't be left alone for too long and I'm leaving, right now. I'm going abroad.'

'What the hell for?'

'To save my marriage'

I hear his grudging sigh of resignation. 'I'll pick her up this evening then.'

'And when I get back we need to talk. About Dad. There are things you need to know. Things we both need to face up to.'

'I know that. I'll be waiting. And Adam . . . good luck.'

'Thank you.'

Margaret

My younger son has let me down. Forsaken me in my hour of need. He came home merely to pack a bag and rush out again. I expect he's running back to *her*. Adam is obviously intent on ruining his life.

'John will pick you up,' he told me, 'and take you back with him.'

'Do I get a say in what happens to me?' I asked.

'Goodbye, Mum, and take care,' he replied, as if he planned to be away a long time.

He seemed angry with me. Hostile, edgy, cold. What did I do to deserve such treatment? I suppose his wife has finally managed to turn him against me. I have never had anything but my son's best interests at heart. One day he will realise that. He will come back to me, with his tail between his legs, saying, 'Mother, you were right all along.' Thank goodness I can look after myself again. There is nothing worse than relying on others.

I stare out of the kitchen window, anxiously awaiting John's arrival. At least one good thing will come of this awful day – I will get to see my elder son. I have no intention of going to stay with him, however. I will insist he takes me home. A car pulls up outside. It is wide, flat and metallic-blue. Its driver struggles to reverse into a parking space, revving the engine, hitting the kerb, causing a hold-up. Eventually the driver's door opens. A robust woman struggles out, looks towards the kitchen window and waves. The overweight aunt with the unpronounceable name heads for the front door. She rings the doorbell. Raps her thick knuckles on the frosted glass. I open the door with no intention of inviting her in.

'Mar-ga-ret.' She walks straight into the hall and plants an unwelcome kiss on my cheeks.

'Where's Electra?' she asks, glancing around suspiciously as if I might be hiding her. 'She's no answering her mobile. I was worried.'

'She's gone.'

'Gone where?' She crosses herself and rolls her large eyes.

'I don't have a clue. She just took off. And then my son took off after her. They've left me here alone. I'm waiting for John to come and pick me up.'

'Your san? The one who has no cam to see you for ages?'

'He lives a long way away.'

'Thas no escuse!' She shakes her head and screws up her eyes.

'John's a very busy man.'

'Too busy for his poor mather! He should be ashamed. You're lucky Adam he's no like that.'

'I have no complaints about my elder son.'

'Only about your daughter-in-law.' She chuckles. Her rudeness infuriates me but I refuse to be drawn into a catfight.

'What does your busy san do?' she asks.

'He owns a design company. Does everything on computer. He's a very clever man.'

'Ach! Everyone can use a computer nowadays. Even my nephew's six-year-old daughter.'

'John has just negotiated a very prestigious contract. It will make him a very wealthy man.'

'Maney! It dasn't make the man, Mar-ga-ret. Your san, it seems to me, he put maney before his mammy. When did Electra leave?'

'Yesterday.'

She moves a step closer to me, resting her plump hands on her wide hips, her intimidating mass looming over me. 'If you did anything to make Electra leave,' she says, her voice a low growl, 'I will take that walking stick and wrap it round your skinny neck.'

'How dare you!'

'You think you can take me on, Mar-ga-ret?' She points her fat finger in my face. 'Jast try.'

'Please, leave. Get out. Before I call the police.'

'You are the criminal. No me. You made tha poor girl's life a misery.'

'I did no such thing!'

She shakes her head and tuts. 'I feel sorry for you, Mar-ga-ret. Really, I do. You don know a good thing when is staring you in the face. You're a lacky woman and you don know it. You have your son close by and a wanderful daughter-in-law and another grandchild on the way. And what do you do? You chase them all

315

away. There is nathin worse than being alone in this world, Mar-ga-ret.'

'I am not alone. I have John. My son will be here any minute.'

'You think a tiger he can change his spots?'

She utters her final, nonsensical remark and turns to leave. I close the door behind her, hoping I will never have the misfortune of seeing her again.

John glances around the living room. 'I see my brother hasn't got round to redecorating.'

'Your brother can't afford to redecorate.'

'Why is that?'

'Because his wife spends all his money.'

'Mother, you don't know that for sure.'

'Oh, yes, I do. I've seen the evidence with my own eyes.'

John leans back in an armchair and crosses one long leg over the other. He props his elbow on the armrest and cups his chin in the crook between thumb and forefinger. An infinitesimal leap of the imagination takes me back to my childhood, to a vision of my long-limbed father, posed identically, wearing polished brogues, a whisky-filled tumbler at his side. Father, a high-ranking civil servant, was a distant figure who inhabited an adult cosmos of meetings, cocktail parties and foreign travel. A social sphere in which children were neither seen nor heard. I spied on this world from a distance, through keyholes and windows and doors left ajar.

My brother Geoffrey was swallowed up by this world. Introduced to fine wines and important people, groomed for life as a career diplomat. I thought adulthood would secure me automatic right to this enviable lifestyle, that my birthright lay just over the horizon, waiting to be claimed when I came of age. By the time I grew up I found the world had changed for ever, the role of parents redefined, the lion's share of my father's fortune bequeathed to his son and heir. Only an expedient marriage could secure my future. Mother introduced me to a string of eligible bachelors. I was invited to dances and parties attended by the 'right sort of boys', as Mother called them. She was furious when I rejected a marriage proposal from a young man with considerable inherited wealth. A man who later became an MP, whose wife today travels in a chauffeur-driven car and enjoys the best of everything.

Geoffrey was twelve years older than me. We did not grow up together. When he was packed off to boarding school, I was taking my first steps. When I was evacuated from London, he was called up for National Service. When I returned to London, he was sitting entrance exams for the diplomatic corps. By the time I married he was in a posting in some far-flung region of the world, looking after British interests. Fifteen years passed before I saw my brother again. In that time he had squandered our father's fortune on fine wines and a succession of expensive wives. We were reunited at Mother's funeral and spent several days together, not catching up exactly but rather getting to know one another for the first time. And then he took off again, back to the successful life he had carved out for himself among ambassadors, envoys and Government officials. I envied his freedom, especially when my own life began to fall apart.

I was conceived by accident. Mother never wanted a second child. She was too busy travelling with Father and being a dedicated philanthropist to raise her own daughter. I was delivered by a midwife and thrust straight into the hands of hired help. (Mother would never have dreamed of dirtying her own rose-scented hands with amniotic fluid.) I was weaned by a wet nurse, bathed and bundled into clothes by a nanny's rough hands, and presented to my parents when I was quiet and fresh-smelling. Mother only ever took part in the pleasanter side of parenthood.

I was looked after by a succession of nannies. The only one I remember well is Sarah, the bane of my formative years. She was twenty-two when Mother hired her, detached, rigorous, unaffectionate, sometimes cruel. She tugged mercilessly at the knots in my hair with a comb, pressing its jagged teeth into my scalp. Forced me to sit on the toilet for hours until my bowels opened, slapped my legs if I misbehaved.

When war broke out I was sent to live with Sarah's family in Yorkshire, in a small, overcrowded cottage surrounded by muddy fields. For four years I slept in a single bed with my guardian in the cold room she shared with her two younger sisters. If I were still awake when Sarah came to bed she would pinch my arm and make me cry. In sole charge, with no mistress to answer to, Sarah's cruelty intensified. In a house where there were barely enough chairs for the adults to sit on, I ate standing up. When food was in short supply, I was served leftovers. Whenever Sarah felt

frustrated she would take her anger out on me, shouting at me and slapping my legs, making me suffer for
my privileged position in life. All the young men of
her generation had gone to war and she saw no hope
of ever getting married and escaping life in service.

I detested Sarah and often wished her dead. Four
years later, when we had returned to London, my wish
was realised. Father found her slumped at the top of
the stairs, dead of a stroke. As I watched him hold a
mirror to Sarah's mouth and announce she had
stopped breathing I felt a terrible sense of guilt that
stayed with me for many years, as if I had somehow
killed her. Mother was more upset by the inconvenience of having to find another nanny.
Suddenly, she was forced to be my full-time carer. I
remember the time we spent together then with great
fondness. Mother combed my hair and tucked me into
bed. She took me shopping for clothes and we lunched
with her friends in expensive restaurants. A month
later another nanny was hired and mother washed her
hands of any maternal responsibility.

It was during my stay in Yorkshire that I met Brian. He
was Sarah's next-door neighbour, the son of a carpenter,
a tall, demonstrative boy who took me gently under his
wing and protected me from the taunts of the local
children. We would walk for miles together, through the
landscape he loved. I could never see beyond the grey
sky and the dirty stone cottages. I longed for streets lined
with elegant houses, bustling with people. I trudged
through acres of mud with him because he made my
young heart race. As a child I loved him dearly, and
cried bitterly when we had to say goodbye.

We wrote to each other as often as we could after that. Over the years our friendship deepened. Brian wrote about his hopes and ambitions. He wanted to go to university, to study engineering, to leave his small community and live in the capital. One by one he achieved his dreams, and when he secured his first job in London he asked me to marry him. I accepted without hesitation, carried away by the stirrings of my teenage heart.

My parents were outraged and tried to talk me out of my decision. 'He's not right for you,' Mother objected, 'he comes from a different world from ours. How will he support you?' I married Brian in spite of Mother's reservations, perhaps even to spite her, only to discover a decade later that our differences were irreconcilable. I resented Brian's lack of ambition, his upbringing, the crudeness of his manners. Characteristics I had once found charming in him began to irritate me. His inappropriate jokes, his heavy accent, the sound of his laughter. He avoided my friends, calling them shallow snobs, and shunned dinner invitations. We argued fiercely and often, until we realised that we would never agree on whom we should mix with and how the boys should be educated and where we should live. Brian found London a struggle and wanted to go back to Yorkshire. Eventually we simply stopped communicating and led our separate lives. Brian was a good man but he lacked drive and backbone. For most of my married life I hankered after a strong, successful man like my father.

The older he grew, the more Brian was drawn back to the landscape and the people he had left behind. At

320

weekends he would take Adam to visit his family home, returning rejuvenated and stuffed full of his mother's pies. Our inherent differences grew more pronounced over time and destroyed our marriage. We hailed, as mother had said, from different worlds and stayed together only for the sake of the children. It breaks my heart now to think that Adam may be following the same road as his mother, acting according to the dictates of his heart not his head.

'So, what's been going on here?' John asks keenly, leaning forward in his chair.

'Adam and his wife had an argument.'

'About what?'

'I don't know exactly. But I do know that she hit him. Can you believe it!'

John smiles. 'What on earth did he do to her?'

'Your poor brother's face was red raw but that didn't stop him chasing after her, begging her to stay. She packed a suitcase and left, thank goodness. And then Adam left me all alone for a day and a night. He went to visit your father's mother, of all people!'

'You're joking! And he found her? After all this time? I'm surprised she's still alive.'

'Oh yes! She's still alive and she filled your brother's head with all sorts of lies about me. He came back in a very hostile mood, accusing me of all kinds of things. He really upset me, John. Your brother seems to have forgotten what I went through when your father was ill. The sacrifices I made to raise and educate him.'

'Don't worry, Mother.' John gets up to sit beside me on the sofa. I breathe in the clean scent of his cashmere sweater, a smell that reassures me he is well cared for by his wife.

'I was forced to take lodgers into my own home to make ends meet.'

'I know.'

'And looking after your father was the hardest thing I have ever experienced.'

I still live in dread of the flashbacks, the painful and vivid memories of my last days with Brian. Memories of him sitting on a public bench, his shirt undone, no shoes on his feet. Refusing like a petulant child to come home. Pushing me away while people stopped to stare and point fingers but not to help. I blamed Brian for the illness at first, for not getting better, for making me suffer. My friends disappeared one by one at a time when I needed friendship more than ever. I was a victim of the disease as much as Brian. I resented caring for a man I had fallen out of love with, a man who never once thanked me for helping him dress or cutting up his food or putting up with his angry outbursts. A man who begged me incessantly to let him go home. I lost count of the number of times I found him sitting on the station platform, waiting for a train to take him back to Yorkshire.

The strain of caring for a six-foot child was immense. I lost weight and took pills for depression. I could hardly care for myself, let alone Brian, and I had Adam to think about too. At least John was safely out of the way at university. I rang my mother-in-law and told her of my intention to put Brian in a home. She begged me not to, offering to care for him herself. I said no and had every right to. As Brian's next-of-kin I would not give his mother the satisfaction of taking over and questioning my abilities as a carer. She threatened to fight me through the courts. Resentfully, I gave in. I could not face the prospect of a protracted legal battle with my in-laws. That night I packed my husband's bags and his brother came to collect him.

Memories of Brian plagued me for quite some time after that. The events of my life played over and over again in my mind. How did it all go so wrong? At what point exactly did I start to fall out of love? Should I have tried harder to make my marriage work? I tried to stop looking back, to get on with the business of raising Adam and supporting John. But Adam wouldn't let me forget. He kept asking me to take him to Yorkshire, to let him see his father. He was a constant reminder of the husband I felt I had abandoned. I told a lie so I could find peace. So I could function without regret. Yes, I told him his father had died, because in essence he had. And from that day on he stopped hounding me and I could put the past and my husband's family firmly behind me.

The seatbelt glides out of its holder. I pull it across my chest and sink back into the soft black leather. Beneath my feet are pristine velour mats.

'I'm not staying with you, John, I'm going home,' I say, turning to admire my handsome son.

'You can't go home. You're not well enough.'

'I am quite capable of looking after myself. In a couple of weeks I won't even need the walking stick.'

John switches on the headlights and manoeuvres the

car out of a tight space. 'In a couple of weeks I promise to take you home.'

'Please, son.'

'No, Mother. I promised Adam I would look after you, and that's what I intend to do.'

John works the leather-clad steering wheel through his hands. The car engine hums as we drive along dimly lit back streets. I feel as if we're hovering above ground in a Space Age vehicle. He reaches out to turn a knob. 'Climate control,' he says, 'keeps the car at a constant temperature.' Adam's Rover spews out dusty air in summer and burning heat in winter. I should be grateful that at least one of my sons has made a success of his life.

'If you won't take me home, could we at least pass by? I need to pick up a few things. Adam hasn't been to the house for at least a month.'

'It's getting late.'

'Please, John.'

'OK. But we can't stay long.'

He doubles back. The brightly lit main road heaves with traffic. The rusty Vauxhall in front coughs out choking black smoke, filling John's car with exhaust fumes. He sighs impatiently, running his hand through his thick hair. He presses down on the accelerator and overtakes the Vauxhall, glancing angrily across at the driver, an elderly man, sitting close to the steering wheel, staring intently ahead.

John shakes his head. 'Silly old man shouldn't be allowed on the road.'

The traffic thins. My spirits lift as we near the house where I have lived for more than forty years. I look forward to reclaiming it soon, to cleaning it from top to bottom and taming the garden wilderness, to inviting my friends over for afternoon tea and a game of bridge. When John pulls up outside I get the shock of my life. An estate agent's sign at the front gate informs me that my beautiful house has been sold.

'What on earth is going on, John?'

He slams his fist into the steering wheel. 'Damn them!' he shouts.

I assume his anger is directed at his brother, that this betrayal is Adam's doing. 'How could your brother do something like this to me?'

'Adam?'

'I bet *she* put him up to this.'

'Who?'

'His wife, of course. She desperately needs money, John, to pay off her debts. Those two are in dire financial straits.'

John takes off his seatbelt and turns to face me. 'Adam and Electra don't know anything about this.'

'Who else would have sold my house from right under my nose?'

'*I* put your house up for sale. But I told those damned estate agents not to put a sign up. We don't want people snooping round the property when it's empty.'

'But . . . I don't understand. Where are my lodgers?'

'I gave them a month's notice. They've found alternative accommodation.'

'And the cat? Have you found him another home too?'

'Your neighbour has kindly offered to look after the

cat until you are settled somewhere else.' My son betrays no hint of a guilty conscience.

'John. How could you do this? You know how much the house means to me. I won't let you sell it. You have no right. The house belongs to me.' I struggle to take in the enormity of my predicament, to connect with my son's cold and calculating expression.

'Calm down, Mum.'

'You'll have to take it off the market. I insist. I won't leave my house under any circumstances. You can't force me.'

'Do you really think I'm going to let you go on living in that big, impractical house, after injuring yourself so badly?'

'You have no choice. You can't sell my house without my permission.'

'You must remember that talk we had on your birthday. Or have you forgotten already? You agreed that I should act on your behalf.' He talks to me slowly, as if I am a deaf old woman with a fading memory. 'We'll sell the house and get you something smaller. You'll be able to live like a queen on the proceeds, and what you don't need we can invest. There's no point in having all that money tied up in one crumbling old house. It's a good time to sell, Mother, and we've been offered a very good price by a developer.'

'I will *not* sell my home to a developer. I will not have my home destroyed. My grandmother left me this house. It was her pride and joy and I promised to look after it.'

'What does it matter who we sell to, as long as we get our price?'

So the house is no longer mine, but ours, I realise. 'But I love this house and I don't want to move away from here,' Perhaps I can convince him if I try hard enough. 'I've lived here most of my life, John. My friends are here. My life is here. Adam lives nearby . . .'

But he is implacable.

'Adam might not live nearby for ever, and you can't go on living on your own. I've already made enquiries about suitable housing for someone of your age.'

'I'd rather die than live in an old people's home.' And it might come to that. My heart is pounding so loudly in my chest I can barely hear my own faltering voice.

'Not a home, Mother. Sheltered housing where there will be a warden and people of your own age for company.'

'But I like my own company,' I tell him, envisaging with dread the countless tiny infringements on my personal space that will come from communal living.

'Won't you be sad to see this place go, John?'

'Not in the slightest. Why should I? I didn't really grow up here, did I? I grew up in that vile boarding school you sent me to.'

My son looks at me dispassionately, unmoved by the weak tears that trickle down my cheeks. This is your punishment, his expression tells me, rough justice for sending me away.

'You got the best education money could buy,' I say in self-defence.

'Why didn't you send Adam away then? Why did he get to stay at home and go to the local state school?'

'Because of your father and his stupid liberal values! If I'd had my way you would both have been sent away to school. Look how well your life has turned out, John, how successful you are now.'

Surely he's not going to hold against me a choice I made for his own good?

'Do you know how many nights I cried myself to sleep? Do you know how lonely I was? How much I missed you and Father and Adam? Do you know how many times I was beaten by the older boys?' he says remorselessly.

'Boarding school made you strong and independent. It made you into the man you are today.'

He shakes his head impatiently and starts the engine. 'Perhaps it's best you don't go into the house. You may get too upset. And at this rate we won't be back until well after midnight.'

I stifle my objections, wanting to avoid any further dispute in public. When we're back at John's house and my daughter-in-law is looking on sympathetically, I'll convince John that he's acted too hastily.

'Let's go then. There's no point in going inside, not now. And poor Caroline might be waiting up.' For now I'm content to be a pawn at my son's disposal.

'We won't be going to the house,' he tells me then.

'Why not?'

'Because I no longer live there. Caroline and I have separated. I've been meaning to tell you for a while. I've met someone else. Someone really wonderful.'

'But . . . your wife is wonderful.'

I can't believe what I'm hearing, the flat unemotional tones in which he describes the breaking-up of his perfect family. His voice seems to be coming from a long way away.

'She doesn't make me happy, Mother. She never has. Do you want me to stay in an unhappy marriage? To follow in your footsteps?'

John's hostile tone implies that my unhappy marriage has damaged him in some way. For a moment I am shocked speechless by his ingratitude. By his failure to recognise the sacrifices I made to hold my family together.

'I was hoping,' he says in a sweeter tone, 'that when you sell the house you might help me out with a deposit. So I can buy a place of my own and Karen can come and live with me. She's staying with her parents at the moment.'

So now we've reached the truth. The real reason my house has been surrendered to the barbarians.

'Karen! Your secretary? That young blonde girl who can't even string a sentence together?'

John glances at me, not troubling to conceal an expression of pure dislike.

'Do you know your trouble, Mother?' he says. 'You've always been the most terrible snob.'

He turns away then and switches on the radio to drown out any protest I might make. But there is nothing more to say. Studying that cold, dispassionate profile I realise I have lost everything in the world I once held dear.

Electra

The first group of passengers walks through the automatic doors into the arrivals lounge. An elderly man, bald head glinting like a bowling ball beneath the bright artificial light, awkwardly pushes a trolley overloaded with luggage. One case bulges to either side of the blue nylon rope straining around it, like a belt pulled too tight around a fleshy waist. Adam left a message on my mobile phone last night, saying he would be arriving on this Cyprus Airways flight. The sound of his voice angered me, our argument playing over and over again in my head. I am poised to lunge at him.

The trickle of passengers turns into a flood, the rising tide bringing with it a long, thin, frazzled-looking individual who seems to have dressed for a blizzard. The sight of my husband, looking so tired and troubled, unexpectedly disarms me. I hide behind a leaflet rack, feeling weepy and upset, willing myself to be hard and unforgiving. Adam walks through the exit doors and stands outside glancing at his wristwatch, shuffling his feet, looking lost and forlorn. He takes off his padded jacket and slings it across his arm before wheeling his suitcase across the car park, towards the taxi rank. I leave my hiding place to follow him, ducking down behind a Mazda when he turns to glance over his shoulder. Adam walks up to a taxi driver standing beside a gleaming black Mercedes and tries out his broken Greek, pale neck burning lollipop red as he struggles to formulate a coherent sentence.

'I speak English, mate,' the taxi driver says, putting him out of his misery, 'I spent twenty years of my life in North London.'

Adam takes one last hopeful glance over his shoulder and spots me lurking. He comes bounding towards me, calling out my name. I hurry away, through the maze of parked cars, hopelessly trying to outrun him, anger boiling up inside me, Margaret's words still ringing in my ears. He grabs me by the arm. I pull away, tell him to 'Fuck off!' and run as fast as I can back the way I came, my heart pounding, my legs starting to hurt. 'Slow down . . . be careful . . . stop, Electra!' Adam shouts, refusing to give up the chase. My side aches. I stop to rest, doubled over with a stitch, breathing hard, feeling sick and dizzy. Adam pounces on me, grabs my shoulders. I manage to yank myself free but he throws his arms around me, holding me tight, while I scream and kick his shins and bite his hand and burst into tears, and the bewildered taxi driver looks on, scratching his head.

'Electra, I'm so sorry. Please, forgive me.' He turns me round. I bury my face in his soft jumper. The sound of his heartbeat fills my ears. 'I'm so sorry. I let Mum get to me. I've been an idiot.'

I look up into his desperate, pleading eyes and my anger slowly melts away. He squeezes me for some time against his chest before abruptly letting go and standing back to look me up and down.

'I'm not hurting the baby, am I?'

'You know about the baby?'

'Yes, Alvaro told me. And I promise you I couldn't be happier.'

'Then why did you say what you said?'

'Come on.' He takes my hand. 'I have a lot to tell you.'

Papa's ugly old Nissan, blessed with immortality, runs as well today as it did two decades ago. It serves its purpose, taking Papa to work and Mama to the supermarket and both of them to church on a Sunday. I wind down the window, hoping for a blast of cool air, and start the engine. Adam breathes a heavy sigh as we drive out of the airport car park on to the main road, past the salt lake shimmering with blue-grey water. Beyond it, nestled in a grove of palms and cypresses, is the Tekke of Umm Haram, a Muslim shrine.

I glance at my husband. 'What do you want to talk about?'

'Where do I start?'

'At the beginning.'

'No. I'll start at the end.'

Adam tells me about Alvaro's disappearance, about his own trip to Yorkshire and the emotional reunion

332

with his grandmother. He talks about the disease that claimed the life of his father, his grandfather, uncle and aunt. And then he drops his bombshell about familial Alzheimer's and I press my foot down hard on the brake.

'What exactly are you saying? That there might be something wrong with the baby?'

'What I'm saying is that I have a fifty-fifty chance of developing Alzheimer's, and if I do our child will also be at risk. If I don't have it then our child is no more at risk than anyone else.'

'Why didn't you tell me about all this before?'

He buries his face in his hands. 'I'm sorry. I should have done. I think I've been in denial all these years.'

I lean my forehead against the steering wheel, trying to come to terms with this frightening revelation and what it means for our child. Why didn't he tell me? I think resentfully. Because he feared he might lose you, comes the answer. Would I have wanted a child with Adam if I'd known all the facts? Without a doubt. Do I love my husband any less for knowing? I can only love completely, not in half-measures. I turn to look at him. His eyes are red, his face pale and anguished.

'Would you have married me if I had told you?' he asks hesitantly. And there lies the crux of my poor husband's fears.

'Yes,' I reply, taking his hand. 'I've never been a sensible woman.'

'And what if I do have Alzheimer's and in fifty years our child develops the disease?'

'My grandmother thought she saw the Virgin Mary. Who's to say that mental instability isn't lurking in my genes? Should that stop me from having children?'

'That's not quite the same thing.'

'I'm not prepared to sit around waiting for the *shebarni* to drop.'

'What's that?'

'The blacksmith's hammer.'

'There's a genetic test I can have. It will tell me whether or not I will develop the disease, but not when.'

'Do you really want to know? I don't think I do.'

'I'm glad you said that. I prefer to live in hope rather than wake up every morning thinking, Will it be today?'

'What about John? Has he had the test?'

'No. He refuses to talk about the illness. He thinks cutting himself off from Dad's family eliminates the risk in some way, as if that side of the family is contaminated. And Caroline's completely in the dark about the genetic link. John never told her, not even when the children were born.'

'She has every right to know.'

'Of course she has. I'm going to talk to him when I get back. And threaten to tell her myself if he doesn't come clean.'

'I hate to be the bearer of bad news Adam, but it seems Caroline has thrown your brother out. He's been having an affair for quite some time.'

'I knew it! And I can guess whom he's been having an affair with. You don't need to tell me. Poor old Caroline.'

'She's glad to see the back of him. Caroline and the children have been bullied for long enough. According

334

to Caroline your brother was an ogre when he drank too much.'

'We both saw the evidence of that. The sad thing is, I think he drinks to forget. I think Alzheimer's preys on his mind as much as it does on mine. He thinks he's buried his fears but one day soon he'll have to face up to them, just like me.'

Adam falls silent as I drive past my parents' flat deciding on the spur of the moment to head for the capital. This is a day for confessions and confrontations, for telling the truth and facing up to the past.

'Where are we going?' he asks.

'You'll have to wait and see,' I tell him, heading for the motorway.

We enter a suburb of concrete apartment blocks, office buildings and car showrooms. Drive along a bustling High Street lined with designer clothes shops and glass-fronted coffee houses. Women toting tiny handbags totter by in their pointy high-heeled boots, flicking freshly ironed hair. Young men with well-toned bodies and golden skins wear T-shirts moulded to their pectoral muscles. Squeezed among the new and plush and ultra-modern are remnants of the island's eventful history. A Venetian column here, a Gothic arch there, ornate balconies protruding from weathered sandstone walls.

We arrive at the checkpoint giving access to the north of the island. Like Adam I must retrace my childhood steps, exorcise old ghosts, return to the house I was forced to leave thirty years ago. We hand our passports over to a Turkish Cypriot policeman, sign the relevant documents and wait. Sweat beads on my forehead. The sun beats down on the roof of the car. A Turkish policeman cradles his gun a metre away from the Nissan. A barrier lifts and he waves us unceremoniously across the green line. 'Green' might suggest a natural barrier, a strip of wild grass or prickly broom, not the harsh division before us constructed of barbed wire and cement-filled drums. 'Green' in fact relates only to the colour of the felt-tip pen used by a British officer to scrawl across a map of Cyprus and split the island into two. 'How happy to say I'm a Turk' reads a sign that greets us in this place purporting to be a separate country. And in case one should forget, for the buildings and landscape suggest otherwise, everywhere there are fresh reminders. 'Atatürk' etched in giant letters across the hillside; red half-moons blowing in the breeze; place names reinvented in Turkish. Our GMS mobiles are sending us the salutation 'Welcome to Tukcell'. Within the space of one hundred metres there are seven roadside signs advertising casinos, in a half-country where poverty is rife and gambling legal.

'How are you feeling?' Adam asks.

'A little depressed.'

'Do you want me to drive?'

'No.'

We head east towards the Karpas peninsula across a Messaoria Plain which today seems eerily barren. Stretching from the Troodos mountain range in the south to Pentadaktylos – five-fingered mountain – in the north, this plain was once the island's breadbasket, thickly planted with citrus trees, cereals and potatoes.

I vividly remember this fertile landscape in springtime and its patchwork of brilliant yellow cornfields.

A seaside road leads to the village. Along its length are tall real-estate signs offering land and luxury properties for sale. Half-finished villas and holiday villages dominate the landscape. As I struggle to get my bearings we chance upon a sight that both disturbs and excites me, a mantle of rock jutting out of the sea, a short distance from the shoreline. I pull into a dusty lay-by.

'Look, Adam! Over there . . . I used to sit on that rock with my brothers and fish.' On that rock Minos tied lengths of string to bamboo canes and Thomas rolled bread and *halloumi* brine into bait.

'How old were you?'

'Five? Six? I used to roam the village at that age. I had a wonderful childhood, Adam. Free as a bird.'

To our left is a vast swathe of land owned by my uncle. Thirty years ago it was a barley field, now holiday villas line its periphery. The war robbed my uncle of his social standing and his financial security. It broke his spirit where it made others into fighters and turned him into a depressive, dependent on pills. It is sickening to see that others now reap the benefit of his rightful inheritance.

'I don't want to go on, Adam. This is too painful. I'm turning back.'

'You must go on. You have to see this through, Electra.'

I start the engine and pull out of the lay-by, the towers of Kantara Castle, built by the Byzantines, rising in the distance. That stone ruin, two thousand feet above sea level, perched on a peak of the Kyrenia range, was visible from my bedroom window. Elpida used to tell me stories about the legendary queen who'd lived in the castle and the treasure believed to be hidden somewhere amid the ruins, buried underground or contained in secret vaults.

I take a left turn and enter the village. Drive along a familiar road as if in a dream, transported back three decades, looking out of the windscreen on to my past. Large villas, grey and neglected, stand in unkempt gardens. These properties were newly built when we fled, the pride and joy of their prosperous owners. My stomach clenches up like a fist when I see my old home.

'Look, there it is, Adam. Our house.' I stop the car outside a whitewashed house with a sweeping marble veranda and Corinthian columns, the house in which I spent the most carefree years of my life. Images of the past race through my mind at dizzying speed. Adam climbs out of the car, opens my door and offers me his hand. 'Come on.'

I allow him to lead me. Every step I take is accompanied by a vivid memory. I pass the white-painted metal fence from which Minos fell and gashed his forehead. Climb the concrete steps where I sat with Oya, watching the world go by. Walk across the marble veranda where Martha cradled her dolls and played housewives with her friends. Squeezing Adam's hand, I ring the doorbell and steel myself for an unseemly exchange in the front porch. A petite, middle-aged woman answers. Her resemblance to my mother disarms me. Though her clothes are dowdy and old-fashioned, she wears a pair of pretty gold earrings.

'Hello. Can I help you?' she says, glancing up at Adam.

'My name is Electra. I used to live here. My mother and father came a few years ago.'

'Ah, welcome.' She throws open the door and beckons us into the parlour where our guests used to sit, where a handsome sofa once took pride of place and clean lace curtains hung at the window. The room is now shabby and grey and decorated with plastic ornaments. 'Please, feel free to look around,' the woman says in Greek, bowing her head.

'Thank you.' I surprise myself by feeling no animosity towards this meek woman who lives in a house of ghosts.

Adam follows me up the stairs and into the master bedroom where my mind instantly recreates the room that existed thirty years ago with its four-poster bed and glossy wooden armoire. In reality this room is as gloomy as the parlour, filled with melamine and chipboard furniture on its last legs. Further along the hallway is my old bedroom, evidently still occupied by a child. Toys are strewn on the floor and colourful curtains printed with air balloons hang from a lopsided rail. I glance from the window, across at Kantara Castle and then out on to a village which looks far smaller than I remember it.

There is no excitement in our journey round the house, only profound sadness for an idyllic childhood cut short. We climb down the back stairs into an oasis turned desert. The shrubs and vines and citrus trees have been razed to the ground. The yard has become a utilitarian space of concrete and earth where greying

339

clothes hang from a length of fraying string. In a corner stands a large terracotta pot. Thirty years ago a young fig tree grew in that pot and Mama looked forward to its first yield of fruit.

'That's ours,' I tell Adam, enthusing over the cracked relic, an unimpressive, yet poignant reminder that my family once lived here.

Yiayia's outhouse is a shell with smashed windows, warped frames and a door hanging off its hinges. Rubble and pigeon droppings litter the floor of her kitchen home, seemingly emptied by a whirlwind. My mind's eye recreates the space as it once was with Elpida standing at the sink running water through the carcass of a chicken or rinsing rice. Grinding cherry stones in a mortar to make bittersweet *mehlebi*. Colouring eggs for Easter in a pan of boiled onion-skins. And glad as I am to revisit these hallowed memories and paint a picture of my former life for Adam, I reach a point where I can take no more.

'We have to go. I've had enough.'

He takes me by the shoulders. 'Why don't you ask about the olive-oil can? The one your grandmother buried.'

'You don't think I believe that story, do you?'

'Yes.'

'Well, I don't.'

'If you won't ask then I will.' He walks out of the concrete shell and approaches the Turkish Cypriot woman. 'Excuse me. My wife's grandmother said she buried some family jewellery underneath a lemon tree in this yard.'

'There was a lemon tree there,' the woman replies,

340

pointing to a withered stump. 'It was dead when we moved in, along with all the other trees. No one had watered them for years. My husband cut it down.'

'Don't worry,' I say. 'Come on, Adam. Let's go.'

The woman holds up a hand. 'Wait. Just a minute.' She disappears into the house, returning several minutes later with a spade which she hands to Adam. 'Please. Try.'

He takes the spade and struggles to break the hard earth around the trunk, painfully digging up the soil, creating a crumbly heap. Stopping at intervals to rest, wipe his brow and sip the orange juice offered to him by our host. The woman brings me a chair and I sit watching a rare sight – my husband working up a sweat. When eventually the spade hits something metallic Adam leaps into the air.

'We've found it!' he cries, getting down on his hands and knees to scrape at the soil with his fingertips. Sure enough he uncovers the lid of an oblong can. I stand over him as he lifts the heavy tin out of the ground, unscrews a small round cap and peers inside. 'I can't see anything. I need to take the whole top off.'

The woman rushes back indoors and returns with a tin opener. Adam works his way around the lid of the can and gently lifts it off. I wait, holding my breath, expecting to see gleaming gold and tarnished silver. What I see instead is the greenish sheen of thick virgin olive oil.

'Perhaps she dropped the jewellery into the oil,' Adam says, grabbing a stick from beside him and plunging it into the can, finally concluding that the tin contains nothing more than good-quality salad dressing.

'You're not disappointed?' he asks.

I shake my head. 'At least we tried.'

We drive through the village square. It seems shockingly smaller than I remember it. Elderly men with leathery skins sit beneath coffee-house trellises, dragging on cigarettes, sipping coffee, whiling away their time. A woman wearing a headscarf hurries across the paving hauling her shopping bags. A grocer stands at the door of his dusty shop surveying the quiet quadrangle. This was once the busiest village in the region, with its own secondary school and a renowned weekly market. Today the beautiful Venetian houses surrounding the square stand neglected. Plaster has fallen away revealing patches of mud brick. Ornate iron balconies have buckled and rusted. Sun-bleached shutters lurch on broken hinges. At least these places are still standing, I tell myself, when on our side we have bulldozed too many to make way for soulless apartment blocks. Perhaps one day these Neo-Classical buildings will be restored, pieced together like shattered archaeological treasures.

There is one last place I want to visit before I leave. I find it down a narrow street without too much effort. My memory of this place is almost photographic. I stop the car outside Oya's house and recall a friendship nipped in the bud. Two curly-haired boys kick a football, back and forth in the front yard. A woman walks out as if sensing our presence. She is wearing a long colourful shirt and loose trousers, a headscarf tied tightly around her head. She stares into the car and then into my eyes. We recognise each other instantly though we have changed almost beyond recognition. Oya's features have hardened and darkened but her large eyes, framed by thick lashes, are as mesmerising as ever.

'That's Oya,' I say, feeling a rush of exhilaration.

'Are you sure?'

'I'm certain.'

I climb out of the car and walk towards my old friend, smiling irrepressibly, taking hold of her hands.

'I was hoping you would come,' she says. 'I have been waiting for you.'

'I didn't think you would still be here.'

'I have been here all my life.' Oya is a woman resigned to her fate who has given up her old dreams of travelling the world.

We follow her into the house where a cluster of children with olive-shaped eyes gather round to stare at their mother's old friend. And I realise as we talk about our respective lives and sip lemonade that some of those who fled the village were luckier than the people left behind. My life has moved on, taken unexpected twists and turns. Being a refugee left me rootless but gave me my freedom. Oya was born here and will die here. Her future is a foregone conclusion.

'I don't suppose I'll see you again for a long time,' she sighs. 'When are you going back to England?'

'I'm not,' I reply, suddenly sparking the interest of my husband who is crouched on the floor playing with the children.

'You're not what?' he asks, looking alarmed.

'I'm not going back for the moment.'

'You mean, for a week or two?'

'No. I mean for the foreseeable future. I want to have the baby here, Adam.'

'What about me?'

'I was hoping you would stay too.'

He looks thoughtful, then shrugs his shoulders. 'Why not? There's nothing I desperately want to go back to. Apart from my grandmother. I don't want to lose contact with her again or my cousin Robert. Perhaps we could go back for a visit so that you can meet them and we can put the flat up for sale, as well.'

'What about your mother?'

'What about her! Lydia rang me on my way to the airport. Told me exactly what's been going on, about all the terrible things Mum has been saying to you. You should have told me, Electra. I doubt you ever want to see her again.'

'We can't just abandon her. Margaret needs us more than she thinks. Perhaps she's done us a favour, Adam. Made our marriage stronger. If we can survive living with your mother, we can survive anything.'

'Mum's got another son, remember. He can look after her for a change.'

'Your brother's far too selfish to take proper care of your mother. Margaret should spend the winter months out here with us. The mild weather would do wonders for her arthritis. Needless to say, though, the three of us will not be spending a single night under the same roof.'

'You're incredible. After everything she's done to you, you're willing to forgive her?'

'I can't pretend I'm not angry and hurt. And I don't want to see her for a very long time. But Margaret will never stop being your mother, whatever she's done. When I chose to marry you, I knew she would be part of the package.'

'So,' Oya says, 'it seems I will be seeing you again soon, my old friend.'

'It looks that way. But for now we must say goodbye.'

'I almost forgot! Wait here.' She disappears into the kitchen. I hear a cupboard door clattering open. Oya returns to the room carrying a dusty olive-oil tin. 'This is yours,' she says. 'My mother found it in your grandmother's kitchen and brought it home for safe-keeping.'

Adam takes the heavy tin from Oya's arms and puts it down on the coffee table. He pulls off a strip of yellowing tape and lifts off a blackened lid. Beneath it glint our family treasures. Solid gold jewellery from Papa's shop. Mama's heirlooms – the crosses and bracelets she dreamed of passing on to her children. Oya's daughters plunge their small hands into the can and pull out a tangle of chains and bracelets. I take my friend in my arms, thanking her, astounded that this mother of four, who has probably struggled to feed her children, has never been tempted to make life easier for herself.

'You'd better go before my husband gets back,' she says. 'He knows nothing about this.'

I grab a handful of jewellery and share it out among the children. As I walk back to the car my thoughts turn to my parents and how delighted they will be to have their property returned to them. I feel as if Elpida's restless spirit, seeking vindication, has led me to this place. I look at Adam and feel a profound sense of optimism for our future, in spite of the question marks that hang like daggers over our heads. We climb into the car. I start the engine. Adam gently squeezes my hand and leans across the gear stick to kiss me. I pull away from the kerb ready to begin a new life with my husband. We will face whatever fate has in store for us, together.

THE END

Acknowledgements

Thanks to my support network – Nick and Judith, my sister Des, Antonia Marcou, Eva de Marcos, the Makis family, Gill Culpin and my parents. The following children were my muses – my daughter Emily, Theano, Georgie and the King's number one fan Yiannakis. I am very grateful to Judith Murdoch, Diana Beaumont and Kate Marshall for shaping this book, and everyone working behind the scenes at Transworld. Special thanks to TM for making life interesting.

I would also like to thank Chris and Paul, Giorgos Charalambous (Pakoulas) the goldsmith and especially Carol Jennings, adviser for younger people with dementia (who can be contacted for help and advice on 0845 4583208). I drew inspiration from the following publications: *Will I Be Next? Bea Gorman's Life Story* by Lois Bristow and *The Line: Women, Partition and the Gender Order in Cyprus* by Cynthia Cockburn.

EAT, DRINK AND BE MARRIED
Eve Makis

Anna's head reels with plans to escape life behind the counter of the family chip shop on a run-down Nottingham council estate. Her mother Tina wants nothing but the best for her daughter: a lavish wedding and a furnished four-bedroom house with a BMW parked in the driveway. She thinks Anna should forget the silly notion of going to college and focus on finding a suitable husband. Mother and daughter are at loggerheads and neither will give way.

Anna's ally and mentor is her Grandmother Yiayia Annoulla. She tells Anna stories about the fanily's turbulent past in Cyprus, the island home they were forced to abandon. Yiayia practises kitchen magic, predicts the future from coffee grains and fills the house with an abundance of Greek-Cypriot delicacies.

Anna longs for the freedom enjoyed by her brother Andy but spends time appeasing her parents, dodging insults from drunken customers or going on ill-fated forays with her petulant cousin – the beautiful Athena. It is only when family fortunes begin to sour that Anna starts to take control of her own destiny . . .

'HEART-WARMING, FUNNY, TRAGIC AND UPLIFTING
. . . THE STORY HAS A FEELGOOD FACTOR TO EQUAL
MY BIG FAT GREEK WEDDING'
Narinder Dhami

0 552 77216X

BLACK SWAN

THE FAMILY TREE
Carole Cadwalladr

'HALF DELICIOUS ROMP, HALF CALAMITOUS CHRONICLE
OF FAMILY BREAKDOWN . . . EVERY TWIG ON THIS
FAMILY TREE QUIVERS WITH LIFE'
Sunday Times

'A SUBLIMELY FUNNY AND CLEVER FIRST NOVEL, I PREDICT
THAT IT WON'T BE LONG BEFORE THE EXTREMELY
TALENTED CAROLE CADWALLADR IS REQUIRED READING'
Daily Mail

On the day of Charles and Diana's wedding, Rebecca Monroe's
mother locked herself in the bathroom and never came out.
Was it because her squidgy chocolate log collapsed? Because
Rebecca's grandmother married her first cousin? Or can
we never know why we do what we do?

'HOW MUCH ARE OUR LIVES DICTATED BY OUR GENES? IF
WE COME FROM A DYSFUNCTIONAL FAMILY, ARE WE
DOOMED TO FOLLOW THE PATTERN LAID DOWN BY OUR
ANCESTORS? FOR REBECCA MONROE, THESE QUESTIONS
HAVE PARTICULAR IMPORTANCE AS SHE STRUGGLES TO
UNDERSTAND THE LIVES AND CHOICES OF HER RELATIONS
AND ATTEMPTS TO FIND ANSWERS TO HER DILEMMA.
CAROLE CADWALLADR'S CLEVER AND MOVING DEBUT
EXAMINES THREE GENERATIONS OF THE MONROE FAMILY
AND EXPLORES NATURE VERSUS NURTURE . . .
THOUGHTFUL AND IMMENSELY ENTERTAINING'
Observer

'SUCH A PLEASURE TO READ. UNPRETENTIOUS AND
SERIOUS, FUNNY AND MOVING. A RARE FIND'
Monica Ali

'OSTENSIBLY, *THE FAMILY TREE* IS ABOUT THE MONROE
FAMILY: THEY BICKER, GO ON CARAVANNING HOLIDAYS
AND THROW PARTIES TO CELEBRATE THE WEDDING OF
CHARLES AND DI. BUT DEMONS ARE LURKING BENEATH
THE CHINTZ . . . IT'S READING-ON-THE-ESCALATOR STUFF'
Time Out

0 552 77269 0

BLACK SWAN

THE SUMMER PSYCHIC
Jessica Adams

'GIVES NICK HORNBY AND HELEN FIELDING A DAMN
GOOD RUN FOR THEIR MONEY'
Daily Telegraph

No-one can predict the future, can they?

When Katie Pickard is sent by her newspaper to interview
Brighton psychic Jim Gabriel about his predictions for the
year ahead she is shocked and sceptical, especially when
he predicts that he's going to marry her.

Then Jim's other predictions start coming true and Katie is
forced to take him seriously – although as she's just fallen
in love with someone else, the bit about the wedding
doesn't sound too likely.

Will she and Jim really be married by the end of the
summer? And can a famous psychic ever be wrong?

0552772577
9780552772570

BLACK SWAN

COMING APART AT THE SEAMS
Lucy Sweet

Do you believe that your life has a pattern?

Evie does. She's going to Glasgow to be a seamstress,
creating stunning dresses like Audrey Hepburn used to
wear. She's also escaping from her ridiculous, crazed
bohemian parents. They think she takes life far too
seriously – but surely someone in the family has to be a
grown-up?

Glasgow isn't quite what Evie expected: snotty fashionista
people, a volatile landlady and a gorgeous moody boy
who's proving to be a complete distraction – none of this is
part of the tailor-made plan. It's not long before Evie
realises that she hasn't exactly got things sewn up . . . will
it unravel before her eyes?

0552773026
9780552773027

BLACK SWAN

A SELECTED LIST OF FINE NOVELS
AVAILABLE FROM BLACK SWAN

77186 4	ALL INCLUSIVE	Judy Astley	£6.99
77257 7	THE SUMMER PSYCHIC	Jessica Adams	£6.99
77115 5	BRICK LANE	Monica Ali	£7.99
77304 2	PLAYING WITH FIRE	Diana Appleyard	£6.99
77211 9	A ROPE OF SAND	Elsie Burch Donald	£6.99
77269 0	THE FAMILY TREE	Carole Cadwalladr	£7.99
77358 1	THE PRINCE OF TIDES	Pat Conroy	£7.99
77123 6	PAST MORTEM	Ben Elton	£6.99
77285 2	RAKING THE ASHES	Anne Fine	£6.99
77002 7	GENTLEMEN & PLAYERS	Joanne Harris	£6.99
77312 3	UNTIL I FIND YOU	John Irving	£7.99
77154 6	SWIMMING UNDERWATER	Sheena Joughin	£6.99
77274 7	THE UNDOMESTIC GODDESS	Sophie Kinsella	£6.99
77139 2	THE GOOD NEIGHBOUR	William Kowalski	£6.99
77165 1	THE STARTER WIFE	Gigi Levangie	£6.99
77294 1	EATING WITH THE ANGELS	Sarah-Kate Lynch	£6.99
77216 X	EAT, DRINK AND BE MARRIED	Eve Makis	£6.99
77313 1	ONLY STRANGE PEOPLE GO TO CHURCH	Laura Marney	£6.99
77190 2	A GIRL COULD STAND UP	Leslie Marshall	£6.99
77162 7	MAY CONTAIN NUTS	John O'Farrell	£6.99
77250 X	Q & A	Vikas Swarup	£6.99
77302 6	COMING APART AT THE SEAMS	Lucy Sweet	£6.99
77187 2	LIFE ISN'T ALL HA HA HEE HEE tie-in	Meera Syal	£6.99
77309 3	A SAUCERFUL OF SECRETS	Jane Yardley	£6.99